SHEILA ROBERTS

Sand Dollar Lane

mira

mira™

Recycling programs for this product may not exist in your area.

ISBN-13: 978-0-7783-8635-3

Sand Dollar Lane

Copyright © 2022 by Roberts Ink LLC

For questions and comments about the quality of this book, please contact us at CustomerService@Harlequin.com.

Mira
22 Adelaide St. West, 41st Floor
Toronto, Ontario M5H 4E3, Canada
www.Harlequin.com

Printed in Lithuania

MIX
Paper from responsible sources
FSC® C021394

For Linda, KJ and Elizabeth, the beach babes

Sand Dollar Lane

One

To be or not to be? That was *not* the question when your perfect woman decided she was perfect for someone else. The question was, how the @!*!!! did this happen? How had Brody Green gone from being engaged to Jenna Jones to getting dumped by her? How had he gone from saving the Driftwood Inn for her to seeing her honeymoon there with his archrival, Seth Waters? The rival Brody had beaten.

Or so he'd thought. One minute he was engaged to the prettiest, smartest, pluckiest woman in all of Moonlight Harbor and the next he was at her wedding, pretending to be a good sport. Something had gone very, very wrong.

Unlike his first marriage he hadn't seen the great dumping coming. Yes, he'd looked like a villain for a short time, but he'd known that once Jenna learned the truth and he'd proved himself to be a hero, all would be well once more.

By all rights they should have gotten married, then walked off into the sunset together, hand in hand—her, barefoot in a flowing wedding gown, him all duded up in a tux. They'd have sipped champagne on the beach, maybe even made love on a blanket. He'd have whisked her off to Tahiti for a honeymoon to remember.

Instead, she'd chosen that glorified handyman, who hadn't been able to take her any farther than the Driftwood Inn for their honeymoon. Some honeymoon. Some marriage.

Except Jenna was ecstatically happy.

Okay, Brody wanted her to be happy. He was happy for her. He just wasn't so happy for himself. What they'd had was the perfect relationship. What they had now was all whacked out and wrong.

As far as Jenna was concerned, they were still best buds. He didn't want to be best buds. He wanted to go back in time to when they were in love.

Except maybe only one of them had really been in love. Not hard to figure out which one that had been.

Friends. Meh. But that was all he had now, all he was ever going to get. And he had to be good with it. If Jenna was happy, then he should be happy. Right?

Still, it was hard not to feel the sting of unrequited love, to act like all was well when they met at chamber of commerce meetings. Kind of like asking a zombie not to walk funny, look vacant and dopey and drool blood. If they were characters in a book, he'd climb right off the page and slap the idiot writer who hadn't kept them together.

Once he'd been Moonlight Harbor's most eligible bachelor. Now he felt like Moonlight Harbor's biggest loser. He had no interest in dating and he hated the feeling of sadness that settled over him every time he saw Jenna. So, of course, he tried to see her as little as possible.

But then he'd wonder where she was and what she was doing. (Except at night. He didn't want to think about where she was and what she was doing then because he knew exactly where she was, what she was doing and who she was doing it with.)

He couldn't completely avoid her. When he wasn't running into her at Beachside Grocery, he had to see her at the chamber of commerce luncheons. They'd both worked together on the last Seaside with Santa festival and that had left him with a real bah-humbug attitude toward Christmas that he found hard to shake, even when his kids came down to celebrate New Year's at the beach.

After the kids left he'd stuffed himself with chips and binged on *Bourne* movies. He'd found it temporarily consoling that even Jason Bourne couldn't hang on to a woman. That proved it. Heroes walked alone.

He was no hero though, and walking alone sucked. Nobody cared if you stubbed your toe or ate too much crap. Or that your life was crap. The only thing good about the New Year was that the old one was over.

With such happy thoughts he made his way to the chamber of commerce's January meeting. New year, new beginnings, better attitude. Who cared about Jenna Jones?

He did. There she came, entering the banquet room of Sandy's restaurant in a black jacket over a long red sweater and skin-hugging black tights. Jenna Jones had great legs.

Jenna Jones had great everything. He frowned at the sight of her.

She saw him and smiled, and he forced the corners of his lips up. "Happy New Year," he greeted her.

"Happy New Year to you, too," she said. "Did your kids come down?"

"Yeah. We had a good time." He'd have had a better

time if Jenna had been with him. "So, did you make any New Year's resolutions?"

"Yes, to find you the perfect woman."

I already did. He didn't say it. What would be the point?

"You're still the catch of the day around here, you know," she said.

"Yeah?"

Did he sound bitter? It was so hard to be a good sport when you should have won the game. Except it hadn't been a game.

She shook her head at him, making the silvery earrings dangling from her ears dance. He didn't remember seeing those before. Had Waters given them to her for Christmas?

"You know you are," she said.

"Yes, I am," he agreed. Which showed remarkably poor taste on Jenna's part.

It seemed like every conversation they had started off in this vein—her trying to put what they once had together in a completely different way, him trying to pretend it was okay and eventually failing.

They would never get back to where they were before they'd dated. He didn't think they'd even get near it. She felt guilty. He felt…a lot of things. Let down. Resentful. Jealous. Yeah, all of the above. And he still loved her, which complicated things even more. At least it did for him.

He spent a lot of time after every encounter trying to shake off his ignoble feelings. Jenna Jones deserved the best, and if she was content with second best (hey, it was true), then that was okay by him. Waters still didn't like him and he didn't like Waters, but he could rise above all that for Jenna's sake. He could be civil when they met at various functions. He could refrain from kidnapping the guy, tying him up, rowing him out to sea on a dark night and dumping him overboard. He had ethics.

"I see you're selling the Dinglers' house," she said.

"Yeah, they want to move to Palm Desert."

She gave a mock shudder. "Ugh. All that heat."

"My thoughts exactly. Why would you want to live anywhere but here?"

Where you could be miserable. He'd thought more than a few times about moving after they broke up. He still loved Moonlight Harbor, but after losing Jenna he was finding it hard to see the magic in the waves crashing onto the beach or moonlight dancing on the water or a beautiful sunset.

You need to snap out of it, he told himself for the millionth time. So things hadn't worked out? So what? There were other fish in the sea. Other sand dollars on the shore. Other pebbles on the beach. Moonlight Harbor still had plenty of women who'd like to date him.

None of them measured up to Jenna.

He could feel his facade of easy charm crumbling. Time to get away.

"There's Ellis. I need to talk to him," he said, and made his escape. There had to be something he needed to talk to Ellis West about.

Checking in on how things were going with Ellis and his bride only resurrected Brody's frown. Melody West should have been his mother-in-law.

Ellis and Mel were still happy as a couple of Moonlight Harbor clams. Good for them. Good for everyone. Meh. Every man in Moonlight Harbor was getting happily hitched except him. Every man would be getting lucky on Valentine's Day. He'd be getting drunk.

He could get lucky if he wanted. He didn't have to keep

roaming around town all by himself like the ancient mariner. He could have friends. With benefits.

That was as close as he was ever going to come to getting involved with anyone from now on. Never again was he plunging heart-deep into a relationship. Jenna was his second love disaster and he wasn't a big believer in that old saying that the third time was the charm. He lived at the beach. He knew what happened when you were drowning. The third time you went down, you never came up.

Rian LaShell sauntered up to him. Rian was cool. He liked her a lot. They'd dated for a while but, although there'd been some sparks, it hadn't been enough to light a fire under him and get him to commit. Rian was svelte and sexy, and this day she looked hip in tight jeans and a black sweater. But she wasn't Jenna.

"Hey there," she said in that throaty voice of hers. "Happy New Year."

"To you, too," he said. "Did you do anything exciting to ring in the New Year?"

She shrugged. "I managed to ring it in."

A mysterious answer, meant to pique his curiosity over whom she'd rung it in with and make him jealous.

He didn't take the bait. "Well, good. How are things going at Sandy Claws?"

"Doing a fifty-percent-off sale next week. Too bad you don't have a pet."

He should get a pet. Not a cat; cats were too independent. A dog. Dogs were loyal. They stuck with you. Yeah, maybe a dog. Why was it he didn't have an animal, anyway?

Oh, yeah. Animals required time and commitment.

Well, it wasn't like his days were full now.

They could be. They should be. Jenna was the past. He needed to be looking toward the future. But really, who did he think he was going to have a future with?

People were starting to find seats at the two tables in Sandy's meeting room and their waitress had appeared and was taking orders. He and Rian sat down next to each other and he cast around in his mind for something to say to her. His brain locked up.

Good grief. They'd dated for six months. He ought to be able to come up with something. The exotic eyeliner that accented her eyes inspired him.

Ah. The cat. "How's Pyewacket?"

"He misses you."

Brody gave a snort. "Cats never miss anyone."

"Sure they do," said Rian. "You should come by and visit."

"So he can scratch me?" Brody and Pyewacket had never really bonded.

"He'll be good. So will I," she added, her voice as smooth as whiskey.

A hot woman inviting him to her place. Any man in his right mind would be all over that. Obviously Brody was no longer in his right mind.

Their waitress came up, getting him temporarily off the hook.

But it was only temporary. Once they'd placed their lunch orders, Rian was still there smiling at him, waiting for an answer.

"You know, I think I need to stay on my own for a while."

"I'm sorry things didn't work out with Jenna," she said in a low voice, "but that's a closed chapter. Maybe it's time to turn the page."

"Or close the book," he quipped.

But he wasn't kidding. Lightning didn't strike twice. What were the odds he'd ever meet anyone again whom he wanted as much as he'd wanted Jenna?

And actually, he wasn't sure he wanted lightning to strike again. Lightning was destructive.

Two

Lucy Holmes-Anderson was smiling as she made her way to the condo she was showing in downtown Bellevue. She and her husband, Evan, had seen it during a realtors' open house the day before and been sure that it would sell in a moment. And she was going to be the one to jump on that moment. She had a couple she knew the place would be perfect for and she'd arranged to meet them there on their lunch hour.

She'd tried to let Evan know that she had a fish on the line but her call had gone straight to voice mail. It seemed like that happened a lot lately. Hardly surprising, though. Like her, he was busy showing houses, getting listings, writing up offers, and when he was with someone, he never took calls. He had said something about having a noon appointment so he was probably already with his clients.

Sometimes it seemed he spent more time showing houses to other people than hanging out in his own house with her. For a couple who worked together, it sure seemed that they didn't see much of each other.

But that was the nature of the real estate business. No set hours, and evenings and weekends were usually busy. For both of them. They were often either in their separate offices in Anderson-Holmes Realty or meeting with people.

Even when they were together, it felt more like they were simply sharing space. He'd spent most of the evening the night before convincing a hesitant couple to lay out a king's ransom on a dog of a house in a Seattle neighborhood that was supposed to be the next big thing. By the time he'd gotten off the phone, he'd been ready to do nothing more than crash in front of the TV.

There wasn't even such a thing as a cozy breakfast together. Nothing new there though. Breakfast had always been a rush to get out the door. This particular morning it had involved a phone conversation with their daughter, Hannah, about the "little" accident she'd had with the new car they'd given her the summer before for her high school graduation. At least she'd only crunched into a post in a parking garage and the only thing that got hurt was the car, but it was a costly hurt. Not good for the insurance premiums.

"It's not that new anymore," she'd said in between tears and apologies. "I've had it almost a year."

"And we've paid the insurance for the first year. Remember, come June it's going to be time for you to take that over," Lucy had said. "And accidents only make your insurance go up." Which it was going to do to theirs.

Lucy hadn't wanted to be the baddie, but they'd flipped a coin over who was going to have a chat with their baby and she'd lost.

"Remind her that she's got to get a job as soon as spring quarter is over. It's time she started taking some financial responsibility," Evan had insisted.

They were paying for her tuition at the University of Washington, plus housing (which wasn't cheap when you lived in a sorority). Car insurance was something they'd decided Hannah could cover in the future.

So Lucy had done the reminding thing.

This had not been welcome news, and while Hannah could often wheedle one or the other parent into caving when she wanted something (or to get out of something), the parents had stayed united on the issue of a summer job.

"You're not doing summer quarter," Lucy had said. (More reminding.) "You'll have time for a job. I'm sure you can find something fun. Maybe helping Daddy and me in the office."

"Inputting boring stuff into the computer," Hannah had said in disgust.

"And posting listings online. Looking at all those cool pictures of houses."

"Stuck inside like a mushroom."

Lucy hadn't bothered to remind her daughter that mushrooms grew outside in the woods.

"You guys are so unfair," Hannah had concluded.

Of course, that accusation had been enough to make Lucy want to cave. She had always struggled with dishing out discipline, even when their daughter was little, although she'd certainly tried her best. And really, Hannah wasn't a bad kid. Just a little spoiled, maybe.

"We need to do this, don't we?" she'd said as Evan grabbed the keys to his Maserati and started for the door.

"We do. Everybody has to face reality sooner or later, Luc."

And reality included hard work. Lucy knew that firsthand. She'd come from a hardworking middle-class family and put herself through college. So had Evan.

They'd both worked their way through school at the same pizza parlor and slowly fallen in love in between orders. With his degree in business and hers in interior design, they'd partnered up in both business and life. They'd put in long hours to establish their real estate agency, and when the market in the Seattle area turned hot, they'd been more than ready to take advantage of it.

They were now the epitome of success, with three brokers in their office—two hunky millennials who could charm anyone into listing their house with Anderson-Holmes and a beautiful, bright young thing named Pandora who reminded Lucy a lot of herself twenty-two years earlier when she and Evan first opened their doors.

As far as Lucy could see, the girl's only flaw was that she lacked confidence. It seemed she couldn't submit a single offer without consulting Evan. Only the other day she'd called with a silly question about a house inspection that left Lucy shaking her head.

"She just needs some hand-holding," Evan had said.

"I could use some hand-holding," Lucy had replied in a playful tone of voice.

There'd been a time when he would have taken the hint, taken her to bed and gotten a hold of more than her hand. This time, he'd merely chuckled and returned to surfing the internet on his laptop.

She hadn't pushed. They were both going pretty hard and it seemed he was tired a lot.

Still, this wasn't what she'd envisioned their love life looking like now that they were empty nesters. She'd joked to her older sister, Darla, that with Hannah out of the house, she and Evan would probably have sex in every room. That was what you did when you had the place to yourselves, right? She and Evan were only forty-four. He was still in his prime and she was at her sexual peak.

So far, she'd been lucky if she got him stirred up in

the bedroom let alone anywhere else. Where was all that empty-nester-second-honeymoon fun they were supposed to be having? Somewhere in the future—at the rate they were working, the distant future.

But all work and no play... If she closed this deal, she was going to make sure they went on a nice long vacation. They needed to put the romance back in their relationship. She'd been eyeing resorts in both Hawaii and Fiji. She'd also been looking into cruises. One of those European river cruises would be so nice.

Yes, a river cruise. Evan had his boat and his fancy midlife sports car. She should get a cruise.

Her smile grew bigger. The Jorgensons were going to love this slick two-bedroom condo in downtown Bellevue. In addition to a bonus room, it had all the bells and whistles—a generous kitchen with quartz countertops and an eating bar; spacious living and dining rooms; windows with electric blackout blinds; unobstructed views of downtown Bellevue, Seattle, Lake Washington and the Olympic Mountains. The facility offered a spa, fitness center and theater room. What was not to like? For some, the price. But the Jorgensons could afford this.

Actually, so could Lucy and Evan. It might be nice to downsize from their four-bedroom three-thousand-square-foot house. It wasn't like they'd filled the place up with kids. Or ever would.

Okay, maybe not this condo. Their house was on Lake Washington and it was important to Evan to be on the water. She liked the water, too. There was something so calming about it. So someplace smaller. Cozier.

That appealed to her. Yes, it was worth considering.

Meanwhile, here were the Jorgensons. In their late thirties, dressed in trendy clothes, driving a Tesla compact, this couple was more than ready to go from being renters to becoming homeowners. Lucy had convinced them that a condo was a good way to start. Plenty of freedom and no maintenance worries.

"I know you're going to fall in love when you see this condo," she told them as she let them into the lobby.

"I looked at the pictures online," said Emma Jorgenson. "It looks gorgeous." She smiled at her husband, Aaron, who smiled back at her.

"We're excited to see it," he said.

"I'm excited to show it to you. If you like it, we'll want to move quickly. This one won't last."

They rode the elevator up to the twenty-seventh floor. "The view is amazing. You won't believe your eyes," Lucy said.

She let them into the unit. It was gorgeous. Hardwood floors, windows showcasing a million-dollar view (no, make that two million).

But what did she hear? Were those voices?

"Is someone else looking at this place?" asked Aaron.

"No one should be."

Lucy followed the sound down the hallway and into the master bedroom, her clients trailing her.

"This bedroom is fabulous," Emma breathed. Then her eyes fell on the trail of his and hers clothes leading into the bathroom. "Umm."

"Sounds like someone's in the shower," said Aaron.

"That's not possible. The owners are in Cabo." But Lucy had seen the clothes also, and someone was definitely in the bathroom. She could hear water running, and a high-pitched giggle. What on earth was going on?

"Maybe you should wait here," she said to her clients, and moved toward the bathroom.

"Ooh," said a familiar female voice as Lucy stepped through the door and onto the azure porcelain floor.

Oh, no. She had to be hallucinating. Behind frosted sea green glass, etched with marsh grass, under the luxury rainfall showerhead, two bodies were silhouetted.

"Baby," said another voice.

It was a voice Lucy knew well, a voice that had called her baby, too. Dread urged her not to look around that glass wall but anger won out and she did.

There stood Evan with Pandora, the bright young thing. Both naked and sudsy. And Evan wasn't holding her hand. This didn't happen in real life. This happened in books or movies.

Lucy blinked, hoping the image before her would disappear. It didn't. Evan and Pandora Welk were still right where she'd seen them.

"Evan?" Lucy squeaked. He was too busy to hear her. She raised her voice. "Evan!"

Pandora was the first to turn. Those faux-innocent hazel eyes of hers got so big they looked like golf balls. She let out a screech and the soap in her hands shot across the shower.

Evan turned, too, and looked over his shoulder. If eyeballs could bounce, his would have bounced right out of his head and onto the shower floor.

"Luc!" he cried, and stepped in front of Pandora in an effort to shield her.

Caption the moment *What's Wrong With This Picture?*

Plenty. Evan was old enough to be this girl's father. There she was, all slender and perky, and there he was, a forty-four-year-old fool with love handles. It was so inappropriate and unprofessional and...wrong! And furthermore, if he was going to go wild like this, he should have been doing it with Lucy.

The Jorgensons joined the party, apparently too curious to stay behind. "Eeep," said Emma Jorgenson.

"Whoa," said Aaron Jorgenson, half laughing.

"Ack!" said Evan, still trying to shield the home-wrecker from the audience that was gathering to gawk at them.

Red-faced, Pandora hurried out of the shower, grabbed a towel and her clothes, and beat it as if the hounds of hell were after her.

Lucy hoped they were and she hoped they took a great big bite out of that perky, bouncy bottom.

Evan almost got out, but his foot made contact with the soap and down he went with a yelp. Good. Maybe he broke something.

Lucy managed a smile for her clients. "Would you excuse us for just a moment? Feel free to check out the view. From the living room," she added in case they weren't sure to which one she was referring.

They nodded and left, and Lucy stepped into the shower and turned off the water. Evan was still on the floor, trying to get up.

"I think I broke my back," he groaned.

"You're lucky I don't break your head," she snarled and bent to help him up.

Helping him up? Really? After what he'd just done to her?

She told herself it was so she could get him out of there, get him dressed and on his way. But it was more. Helping her husband was ingrained behavior. It was what she did, what she'd always done because, fool that she was, she thought they were a team.

When they were first married, she'd worked so he could

get his Master's degree in business. After she got her real estate license she'd been both secretary and real estate broker when they first started the agency. She was faithful, loyal, always the cheerleader and, when needed, the peacemaker.

And this was her reward.

"Luc, I'm sorry," he said, leaning on her as they left the shower.

She picked up his underwear from the floor and held them out, glaring at him.

He took them, tried to climb into them and groaned.

"Oh, sit down," she said irritably, shoving him out of the bathroom and toward the beautifully made bed.

He fell onto it and she got him into his underwear and pants, helped him stand. "You'd better hope this doesn't get out," she said, biting off every word as she shoved his shirt against his chest. "If it does, we'll probably be barred from the brokers association. Or sued. Or…something. It's so unethical."

There was an understatement larger than Lumen Field. He'd just committed adultery, violated his marriage vows, humiliated her and opened them up to a lawsuit by sleeping with their employee in someone else's home.

But right now it was the rejection that hurt the most. Tears were collecting at the corners of her eyes.

He touched a hand to her shoulder. "I'm sorry you found out this way."

She pulled away. "How did you mean for me to find out, Evan? Were you going to take me out for dinner? Bring home champagne?" The tears spilled out.

He said nothing.

She wiped her damp cheeks and stood. "I need you

to leave. The Jorgensons would like to see the rest of the condo."

He bit his lip, nodded, took his jacket and tie and shoes and socks, and left.

After he departed she took several deep breaths, wiped at her eyes one more time, pasted the world's phoniest smile on her face and walked briskly into the living room area, every inch the professional.

"Well, I guess now you've seen everything," she said, trying for a light tone. Boy, had they ever.

"It looks like you knew him," ventured Emma Jorgenson.

"I'm sorry to say he works in my office."

"Bet somebody's head's going to roll," murmured her husband.

"Yes, indeed. I'm as shocked as you. At Anderson-Holmes, we pride ourselves on our professionalism." And once upon a time, she'd prided herself on her happy marriage. She swallowed down the wail trying to crawl up her throat. "Have you seen the second bedroom?"

"Hopefully, there's nobody using it," cracked Aaron Jorgenson.

Haha.

The Jorgensons loved the condo and decided to make an offer fifty-thousand over the asking price to be sure they got it. Lucy was relieved when she returned to her office with them to write it up to see Evan's office door shut and no sign of the home-wrecker. She wrote up the deal and got things going, then sent the Jorgensons on their way.

Then she marched to her husband's office. She didn't bother to knock.

She found him at his desk, staring out the window at the

Bellevue skyline. He turned at the sound, and she noted that he looked sad. But not distressed.

"Why, Evan?"

He sighed, shrugged. "I was bored."

"Bored!"

He had a beautiful house on Lake Washington, a boat, an expensive sports car, a wife who was, if Lucy did say so herself, pretty darn good-looking and a daughter who could have her own reality show. He had a business that kept him busy six days a week. How could he possibly be bored?

"And this was the only thing you could think to do to relieve that boredom—an affair?"

Of course, because it wasn't his life that was boring, it was her. *She* wasn't exciting enough. Fresh tears spilled from her eyes.

He had the grace to look ashamed. "I don't know what to say, Luc. I felt stalled out, like my life was going nowhere. Maybe I'm having a midlife crisis."

"You're pathetic," she said in disgust, swiping at her wet cheeks.

"I'm sorry. I never meant to hurt you."

In other words he never meant for her to find out. "How long have you…?" She couldn't finish the sentence.

"This was the first time we…" Another unfinished sentence. "It was spontaneous."

Spontaneous combustion. She shook her head. This was the man to whom she'd given the best years of her life.

The best years of her life? What a cliché. The whole stupid mess was a cliché. *She* was a cliché.

Well, she refused to be one. She hadn't given Evan Anderson the best years of her life. Those were still ahead of her. She was going to make sure of it.

"What are you going to do?" he asked.

"What do you think?" she retorted and pulled open the door.

"Luc, wait!" He jumped up and ran across the room.

She didn't wait. Instead, she stalked off toward her own office, trying to ignore their secretary's curious stare and the puzzled look of one of their brokers.

Evan followed in hot pursuit. "Luc!"

Once in her office he closed the door on them. "Now, don't do anything crazy."

"Me! You took a shower with one of our brokers in a condo that's up for sale and you're worried about me doing something crazy?"

"It didn't mean anything."

Why did men always say that? "Yes, it did, Evan. It meant something to me. And it means that we're through."

"Luc, don't be hasty," he protested, reaching for her.

She jerked away, grabbed her purse and pushed past him, yanked open the door.

"Where are you going?" he demanded.

"Someplace where you aren't," she retorted. *I'm going to go find the best years of my life.*

Three

Lucy stopped at the bank before going to the house. There, she took half the money from both their joint checking and savings accounts. Then she went to a different bank and set up accounts in her name only. Her phone pinged with messages from Evan every ten minutes, alternating between saying he was sorry and wanting to know where she was, but she ignored them.

At the house she went to their home office and pulled up the files for their various assets and made copies. She wasn't being vindictive, just making sure she was protected. She loaded her clothes and jewelry into her Range Rover, along with her favorite pots and pans and her Dutch oven, as well as some of her other kitchen toys. Evan didn't need them. The only things he knew how to cook were eggs and toaster waffles.

Lastly, she took down the painting he had given her for her birthday the year before.

Done by an Australian artist, it had caught her eye at a gallery downtown, reminding her of the thrill of childhood ballet recitals. (That had been a short-lived thrill due to lack of talent on her part and lack of funds on her parents'.

With three kids to raise on a limited income, money was only spent where true potential appeared and Lucy had always been a bit of a klutz.) The painting was a charcoal and acrylic portrait of a ballerina, on her toes, arms extended, hair flying. Her skirt was a mass of colorful dots and many of them shot out in all directions like sparks, flying from the woman.

"Because you always keep me on my toes," Evan had said.

Yes, but who had kept Lucy on her toes? Why hadn't she seen this coming?

Her cell phone began to ring. Of course, it was Evan. Yet again.

She took the call, greeting him with, "Stop already. I need to think."

"Luc, we need to work this out."

"Yes, we do," she said fiercely. And if he thought she was going to forget what she'd seen, then it wasn't going to work out the way he wanted. "Meanwhile, I'm sure Pandora is anxious to see you."

"Don't go crazy."

"Don't go crazy?" she repeated, her voice rising. "Why do you keep saying that? I'm not the one who decided to break my marriage vows in a condo that doesn't belong to me. Anyone could have walked in on you, you know." They all had access to the lockbox with the key.

"Nobody was supposed to be showing it then," he argued.

"Nobody but your wife, who actually left a message on your cell. But you were too busy to take my call, weren't you?"

"Look, let's talk this out."

"Let's not. I don't want to talk to you right now. In fact, I don't think I want to talk to you ever again."

"Oh, come on. One mistake."

Mistake. Was that what you called it these days?

"It was more than a mistake, Evan. A mistake is miscalculating on the budget or taking a wrong turn on your way somewhere. This was selfish and wrong."

"You're at the house now, aren't you? I'll come home."

Home. What a joke. Their house was no longer a home. She couldn't bear to be there. It was nothing but a sick carnival fun house, every memory of their life as a couple in it was now distorted and mocking.

"We'll talk this out. Don't do anything rash."

He was the one who had done something rash, not her. "I'm leaving. You won't find me when you get here."

"Where are you going?"

"Do you really care?" she demanded, and ended the call. Then she shut off her phone, stuffed it in her purse and drove off.

She got two blocks away before she stomped on the brakes. What had she been thinking? She made a U-turn and drove back to the house. Inside, she grabbed the sheer black baby doll nightgown with the high slit that she'd bought and squirreled away for Valentine's Day the following month. No way was she leaving that behind for him to find and give to Pandora. The girl didn't have big enough boobs to fill it, anyway.

She marched back to the Range Rover, got in and drove off, resisting the temptation to look in the rearview mirror. Looking back and wishing for what she'd had or thought she had was useless. Lot's wife looked back and she turned into a pillar of salt!

But how could she move forward without towing a truckload of hurt along with her? Evan had been her one and only. She'd never so much as looked at another man.

She'd been loyal and faithful, and he'd rewarded her faithfulness by getting naked with another woman. Her lower lip began to tremble and the tear faucet turned on again. She'd never get the image of him and Pandora in the shower out of her mind. She'd probably never be able to take a shower again as long as she lived.

What had happened to them? She'd thought they were happy. She'd thought she was enough for him. Obviously, she wasn't. While she'd been thinking they were doing fine, he'd been feeling stalled out. Stuck. Stuck with her.

Half an hour later she was sitting at the table in the kitchen of her older sister's house on Queen Anne Hill.

"Unbelievable," Darla said in disgust.

"I can't believe it, either, and I saw it," Lucy said.

"He's always been selfish, but this. He's out of his mind. You're the best thing that ever happened to him and to do this to you." She shook her head.

"I guess he found someone better," Lucy said. The words tasted bitter.

She'd been a good wife, always supportive, always cooperative, never bugging Evan to help around the house when their daughter was little. She'd juggled it all—work, child-rearing, volunteering at Hannah's school. She'd kept her hair the same honey blond it had been since they'd met and she was still a size ten, thanks to regular visits to the gym and weekly tennis games at the tennis club. (Yep, the good life they'd worked so hard for. How quickly that good life had soured!) She had a mouth that Evan used to say drove him wild. Plus, she was stacked. Every man's dream, right?

Okay, so Lucy's boobs weren't as perky as they'd once been, but they still looked pretty darn good. And although she hadn't opted for Botox, she used Retin-A on a regular basis. She didn't have that many wrinkles. She was smart and good-natured and creative and...

Not thirty.

Neither was he, for crying out loud. Why did he get to be bored?

Hadn't she been interesting enough? She read, she watched CNN. And when she could find time, she cooked. Cooked!

Really, Evan was a fool, she reminded herself, steering her mind away from the image of Pandora and her perfect dewy skin, face still free of crow's-feet, and her dopey doe eyes, always so filled with admiration for him.

Darla refilled both Lucy's coffee mug and the bowl of peanut M&M's sitting on the table between them, then helped herself to another handful.

Unlike Lucy, she was not the size she'd been when she got married. She'd packed on several pounds over the years. Her hair, a little darker than Lucy's, was starting to sport some silver threads and she had deep laugh lines around her eyes. She dressed for comfort rather than style and considered diets the work of the devil.

Also unlike Lucy, Darla had a husband who thought she was still beautiful. Orren was a teacher and Darla had opted to be a stay-at-home mom with their three kids. Her oldest was married and would be making her a grandmother in a few months. They didn't even make half what Lucy and Evan did, had no boat, no expensive sports car—only an old Tudor house that was a money pit with troublesome plumbing. Their vacations had always been simple—usually camping, sometimes renting beachside cottages or mountain cabins.

Her sister's life was perfect.

"You need a good lawyer," Darla said, getting to the heart of the matter.

The tears started flowing again. "How did I get here?" Lucy said miserably.

"By marrying a self-centered bastard," Darla said, and nudged the candy bowl toward her.

Lucy dug in. "I thought we were fine."

They'd been busy building a business, raising a daughter. Barbecues in the summer, expensive camps for Hannah, trips to Florida so Evan could play golf at Pebble Beach and to Las Vegas so they could enjoy some shows and fine dining (and so Evan could play golf at Shadow Creek). All right, he tended to be a little self-centered, but he'd still been a good husband.

Right on cue, the image of him in the shower with Pandora popped back into Lucy's mind. Obviously, not as good of a husband as she'd thought. Somewhere along the way, he'd traded good for rotten. *Stalled out.*

"People grow apart, marriages go stale. You have to work at it," Darla said.

"Are you saying I didn't work at mine?" Lucy demanded.

"No. You did. He didn't. Lucy, he's been taking you for granted for years, so I'm not surprised this happened. I'm only surprised it didn't happen sooner."

"Thanks," Lucy said miserably, and dug out another handful of candy.

"You deserve better. You're beautiful and creative and hardworking and kindhearted. Evan should be castrated. I bet Jeremy would be happy to help," Darla added, referring to their younger brother who had just set up his practice as a GP. "But since that's not an option, your best bet is to cut the man out of your life and move on."

Move on. To where and to what?

"I can't even think how to do that," Lucy said. "I've been married since I was twenty-one. I've built a life and a business with Evan. We're a team." Correction. They *were* a team.

"Not anymore. You've been traded." Darla picked up her cell phone. "I'm calling Bridget and getting the name of her lawyer. Bridget said she's a barracuda and that's what you need right now."

Only a few hours earlier Lucy had been dreaming of taking a cruise. Now she was looking for a barracuda. She pushed aside the candy dish, laid her head down on the table and sobbed.

In a matter of minutes, Darla had the lawyer's phone number but Lucy couldn't bring herself to make the call. "I'll do it tomorrow." *After all, tomorrow is another day.*

So said Scarlett O'Hara, who had been so sure she could get Rhett Butler back. But she hadn't. Not in the original book, anyway. Someone wrote a sequel to Margaret Mitchell's classic *Gone with the Wind* and reunited Scarlett and Rhett, but Lucy had never bought into it. If Ms. Mitchell had wanted her characters to be together, she'd have taken care of that. What Scarlett had broken couldn't be put back together.

It was the same with Evan and Lucy, only Evan had been the one doing the breaking. So come the next day, she would go fishing for barracuda. For the moment, she was too numb to think about it.

Darla made their favorite comfort food for dinner, Mom's chicken potpie, along with the broccoli-cheese casserole that normally only made an appearance at Thanksgiving. Lucy managed three bites of the casserole and gave up.

"Good dinner, Dar," Orren said, and then made himself scarce.

Who could blame him? He'd had to spend the last forty minutes listening to his wife ranting and his sister-in-law sniveling. His ears were probably on overload.

After dinner, Lucy put away the food and loaded the dishes in the dishwasher while Darla took on the task of notifying the family of the death of her sister's marriage.

"Jeremy says let him know if you need help moving, plus he knows a dermatologist who's single," she reported. "It's a little early to be talking about replacements," she said into the phone as Lucy rolled her eyes and shook her head.

Next on the list was their cousin Gail. "Yeah, I'll tell her," Darla said. "Gail says to let her know if you need money," Darla reported.

"I'm good," Lucy said. She had her new bank account and a credit card in her name, and she'd just made a sale. On the condo where her husband and his *it didn't mean anything* had been trying out the shower. She was going to barf up that broccoli casserole.

"Everybody has to face reality sooner or later," Evan had said only that morning. She hadn't thought one of those bodies would be her.

Next to be notified came the parents. Donna and Albert were still enjoying the sun in Palm Desert in the condo Lucy and Evan had bought for them. Donna loved Evan. As far as she was concerned, he was practically perfect.

Lucy had felt the same way, happily overlooking his selfish tendencies. But practically perfect and truly perfect were two different things. Now she thought of the many times he'd insisted on getting his way, on everything from where to vacation to what to spend money on. That sports car sure hadn't been her idea.

Her sister was right. Evan was a self-centered bastard.

"I've got some bad news, Mom," Darla was saying. "No, nobody's died."

There you had it. Things could be worse.

"But it's looking like Lucy and Evan are splitting up."

Lucy could hear her mother's outraged, "What?" clear across the room as Darla held the phone away from her ear to prevent deafness. She'd been so successful in her career, raised a sweet daughter. Never made waves, never caused her parents a moment of worry. Until now.

"There's a reason. She caught him with another woman."

So tawdry, so pathetic. So not what Lucy had ever imagined happening to her.

Darla held out her phone and looked apologetically at her. "She wants to talk to you."

To have to tell it all to her mother…

Of course, she told everything to her mother, had always consulted her when she wasn't sure how to deal with childhood illnesses or Hannah's naughty behavior. But to talk to her about this kind of naughty behavior. Lucy was ashamed.

She shook her head violently.

"Get it over with," Darla said, giving the phone an insistent shake.

The minute Lucy took the phone, the tears began streaming down her face once more. She felt like she were twelve again, fessing up to drawing funny faces in Darla's journal.

"Mommy, I'm sorry."

"You have nothing to be sorry about," her mother said firmly. "I know what a good wife you've been. This is all on him."

Was it? Supposedly there were two sides to every story.

"Come down and stay with your father and me," her

mother urged. "We have that spare bedroom just going to waste."

Running home to mom and dad sounded tempting, but Lucy resisted. "No, I need to stay here and sort things out."

"Don't you take him back," her mother cautioned. "If a man will do it once, he'll do it twice."

I was bored. Evan's words came back and slapped her again.

"I know," she whispered.

"Anything you need, we're there for you," her mother said.

"Thanks," Lucy said, and handed the phone back to her sister.

"What about Hannah?" Darla asked after she'd said goodbye to their mother.

That would be even worse than telling her parents. "I don't know," Lucy said. "I need to think about how to handle that. She adores her father."

"I know. It's the old don't-bad-mouth-the-ex-to-the-kids thing. But she's a big girl now. She needs to know the truth. Don't cover for him."

Lucy sighed. Did her daughter need to know this truth?

"I'll think about it," she said.

Except she couldn't think. She could only feel. The raw emotional wound kept her tossing and turning all night.

When she awoke the next morning, it took her a moment to realize she wasn't in her own bed and why. She pulled a pillow over her head and squeezed her eyes shut, letting fresh tears leak out.

What had happened to that woman who, only the day before, had been so determined to find the best years of her life? Who knew? Who cared? She was an idiot.

She stayed in the bedroom, hiding, until she heard

voices downstairs and the front door shutting. Orren was off to work. That meant Darla would soon be knocking at the bedroom door with coffee.

Sure enough, ten minutes later her sister appeared with a steaming mug, the aroma wafting over to Lucy. Coffee. At least that was something in her life that was still good.

Her sister handed her the mug and perched on the foot of the bed. "How are you feeling?"

"Miserable, abandoned, cheated. Take your pick," Lucy said, and took a sip.

"How about angry? You forgot that. Murderous? Ready to hire a hit man?"

"That, too," Lucy said, and downed more coffee.

"You need a plan."

"I know."

"Call the lawyer."

"I will."

"But first get a shower and come down and have breakfast. I just put banana muffins in the oven. Carbs don't really make things better, but they make you feel better."

"Only temporarily," Lucy muttered. And she'd be taking a bath, thank you.

"I know," said Darla. "You aren't going to feel better for a long time. But taking control of your life will help."

The banana muffins were, indeed, delicious. For about one minute.

Meanwhile, there were texts from Evan. I know how this looks.

Did he now?

In a later text, his tone was decidedly different. I stopped by the bank. What the hell, Luc?

Hmm, her thoughts exactly when she'd found him in the shower with Pandora.

In between trying to reply to him without threatening to cut off his favorite body part, there were shrink sessions with her sister and, finally that afternoon, a counseling session with her daughter, who was still clueless about what was happening with her parents.

Hannah was in the middle of her own love crisis. One of her sorority sisters had stolen her boyfriend.

"He was cheating on me, Mom," Hannah said tearfully. "I can't believe it. I thought he was the one."

That's what I thought about your father.

"Should I give him another chance?"

"No!" The one word came out like an explosion. Lucy cleared her throat, aware of her sister perched on the other end of the sofa. "He wasn't honest with you. That's a serious character flaw."

"He was so perfect. I just don't understand."

"Tell her," mouthed Darla.

Lucy ignored her. "Guard your heart carefully, sweetie, because it's easy to be deceived. A man who really loves you won't go off with another woman."

When had Evan stopped loving her?

"Maybe, if we just talk," Hannah began.

"He'll still be a selfish man with no sense of loyalty. If he didn't want to be together anymore, he should have been upfront and said so. He wanted you and another woman on the side. Dump him now. You can do better." *And so can I.*

"I hope you were listening to yourself," Darla said after Lucy finished the call.

"There's no point staying with someone who doesn't appreciate me," Lucy said. "How sad that he doesn't."

There came the tears again. When was she going to stop crying?

"Just shows what a fool he is because there's so much to appreciate."

"Is there? Really?"

"Don't you dare go there," Darla commanded. "Any man with a brain would want you."

"I thought Evan had wanted me," Lucy said in a small voice. Funny how quickly you could go from feeling good about your life, confident and happy with who you were, to feeling like nothing.

"This is about him, not you."

"Is it? Really?" Lucy bit her lip.

It had only taken one moment to destroy her self-esteem. She was still the same woman she'd been before she discovered Evan and Pandora. It was so sad and wrong that she suddenly felt like...less.

Darla jumped off the living room sofa, where they'd been sitting, marched across the living room and up the stairs. She was back a moment later with a hand mirror.

She stuck it in front of Lucy's face. "What do you see?"

A woman with a red nose and bloodshot eyes with dark circles under them. "A mess."

"Wrong answer. You see a beautiful woman. A smart businesswoman with a flair for making things pretty. You could have had your own show on HGTV. Only a fool leaves a woman like you. Remember that."

"Every story has two sides," Lucy said. What had she done wrong?

"That's a myth. Nothing excuses what he did, Lucy," Darla said firmly. "Nothing. You remember that. Stay strong and don't take him back. I don't care how sorry he says he is. He only wants to go back to his comfortable life and doesn't want you walking away with half of the assets you two have. That's what he wants."

Lucy blinked. "Well, that's cold."

"Yeah, it is," Darla agreed. "Remember that. And here's something else to think of while he's busy blowing up your phone. How would you feel about an encore performance of what happened yesterday?"

Lucy called the lawyer.

Four

The Moonlight Harbor Chamber of Commerce Valentine's party took place every year, the first Saturday in February. Brody had often hosted it in the past. Not this year.

This year the party was to be held at the home of Jenna's mother, Melody, and her new husband, Ellis West. Brody wasn't going.

He'd been full of excuses for why he couldn't, all of them lame, when Jenna had run into him at Beachside Grocery. Before she'd cornered him, he'd been trying to pretend he hadn't seen her, which would have given him a perfect excuse not to talk to her at all.

But Jenna was determined that they were going to get past this awkward phase. "I still want to be your friend," she'd said once. The *F* word. No man liked the *F* word.

It was hard to go your separate ways when you lived in the same small town and your ways were constantly intersecting. But he didn't have to go about deliberately intersecting.

"You have to come," Courtney Greer insisted when she dropped by Beach Dreams Realty. "You're our president."

If only he'd been out doing something. Anything. But

he'd been at his desk, inputting a listing into the MLS database. Trapped.

He'd known what Courtney was up to the minute she'd entered the office. She and Jenna appeared to have decided he needed help sorting out the rest of his life and had teamed up. He was sure Jenna was acting out of guilt. As for Courtney, who knew? Maybe because she wanted to repay him in kindness for him helping her buy Beach Babes Boutique. Or maybe it was simply because, like so many women he'd known, including his own daughter, she couldn't stand to see a man remain single.

"I'm sure you guys will manage to party without me," he said to her.

"But it won't be as much fun. And since when do you like to miss a party?"

Since I got dumped.

But he wouldn't say that out loud. That was loser talk.

"I'll think about it," Brody said, which they both knew meant no.

"You should go," put in Taylor Marsh, his broker, who had finished with a call and was sitting behind her desk, happily eavesdropping.

"Come on, Brody. At least put in an appearance," Courtney urged. "What kind of president doesn't care about his people?"

That did it. Next year Brody was stepping down as president of the Moonlight Harbor Chamber of Commerce. There should be term limits, anyway.

"So?" Courtney prompted.

It was hard to say no to Courtney. She was a force of nature.

"I'll try."

"You'd better. Or I'll send Victor King out looking for you and make him deliver you in handcuffs."

He held up a hand in surrender. "Okay, I'll stop by for a while."

"For longer than five minutes."

"For longer than five minutes." *Ten, max.*

True to his word, he did go over to Ellis and Melody West's place. The pair had opted to keep Mel's house and rent it out but move into Ellis's so they'd have more room to entertain their families.

The house was perfect for entertaining. It had the same great never-ending view of the beach from its second story that Brody's had, as well as an open-concept living and dining room and a big kitchen Mel had updated to be worthy of any cooking channel chef.

Most of the members were there—the MacDowell sisters, who owned Crafty Just Cuz (K.J. was single and hot, but he wasn't interested); the Redmonds, who kept all the chocoholics and sugar addicts in town supplied with goodies from Cindy's Candies; the Bells, who owned both Doggy's Hot Dogs and Beachside Burgers; Kiki Strom, the proud owner of the popular tourist shop Something Fishy; and there, over by the dining table laden with goodies, stood Jenna, chatting with Rita Rutledge, who owned Beans and Books.

As if she knew he'd come in and exactly where he was standing, Jenna turned to look at him. Then she smiled and waved him over. This was the new normal—forgetting all the kisses they'd shared, the fun times hanging out, the plans for a future together. Now he had to act as if her rejection meant nothing, as if he was one happy camper. With an inward sigh, he made his way to where she and Rita were standing.

"Hey there," she greeted him. "You're looking like Mr. February tonight."

He was casually dressed in jeans and a slim-fit untucked shirt. Pale pink. Real men weren't afraid to wear pink. And yes, he did look pretty damn good. Brody liked to dress well.

But what was he supposed to say to that casual compliment? Probably not, *You're lookin' pretty tasty yourself.*

Although she was, in a classic little black dress and a short red sweater, along with red heels that were designed to make any red-blooded male think sex. She'd had her hair done. It looked good.

But so what? He wouldn't be running his fingers through it anymore.

He settled for a teasing, "Hey, don't objectify me."

Both women giggled and Jenna said, "I wouldn't dream of it."

No, she wouldn't. Not anymore.

"I would," joked Rita.

He liked Rita, enjoyed talking with her when he went into Beans and Books for his morning coffee. She was smart, well-read and always up for talking books or debating politics with logic and politeness. That alone made her a unique person.

But he wasn't interested in anything more than coffee and conversation.

"We were just trying to decide what the best Valentine's gift is," Jenna said. "I vote chocolate, but Rita says flowers."

"That's for me," Rita clarified. "If it's for the other person, I like to bake."

"Who doesn't love a woman who likes to bake?" Jenna quipped.

Who doesn't love a woman who likes to bake? Was that some kind of subtle signpost, pointing him to Rita as a Jenna replacement? If so, it wasn't working. Moonlight Harbor had a perfectly good bakery where he could get whatever he wanted with no strings attached. And the cookies Annie Albright sold in her food truck were gastronomic gold.

"What do you say?" Rita prompted him. "What's the best Valentine's gift?"

Sex. It was what every man wanted for Valentine's Day. But saying that would be tacky.

"I think the best gift is whatever the other person wants," he said diplomatically.

"And we know what you guys want," Rita joked.

There. He didn't even have to say what everyone knew. He smiled at her. Rita really was cool. Just not someone he was inclined to get romantically involved with.

Brody saw Seth approaching and decided it was time to move away. He turned and went into the kitchen to say hi to Annie, who was catering the event.

"Thanks for putting crab cakes on the menu," he said, pilfering one from the pan before she could get it on a serving plate. "My favorite."

"We have to keep our president happy," she said, smiling up at him.

"Crab cakes will do it," he assured her, and popped it in his mouth. Then he gave her a thumbs-up. "Fantastic," he said after he'd swallowed.

"You're sure easy to please," she said.

Yeah, except for when it came to women, it seemed. He liked Annie as much as he liked Rita, but not enough to get involved with her.

Just as well, he told himself. He wasn't getting seriously involved with anyone ever again, so who cared if there was no available woman in Moonlight Harbor who tempted him?

Staying single wasn't so bad, anyway. You could come and go as you pleased, eat whatever and whenever you liked, and watch anything you wanted on TV. Yeah. He was fine on his own. It was probably for the best that Jenna had dumped him. He was perfectly happy being with no one.

How soon 'til he could leave?

Jenna knew Brody would move away the moment Seth reached her side. In her perfect world, the man she'd married and the man she'd almost married and still cared about would become friends. But that was probably a little warped and a lot unrealistic. Seth would always feel somewhat threatened, even though there was no reason to, and Brody would always feel a little resentful. Although he shouldn't. Much as she had cared for him and valued his friendship—still did—they hadn't had the same soul-deep connection she had with Seth. If Brody were honest with himself, he'd see that.

Brody's soul mate had to be waiting in the wings. She obviously wasn't Rita. Jenna had been observing them for the last few weeks, hoping to see a chemical reaction between those two, some kind of pheromone explosion. Tonight's interaction had been about as exciting as water sitting in a glass.

But watching him flirt with Annie, seeing the way Annie smiled at him, made her wonder if they might possibly be a match. After all, what was there not to like about Annie? She was kind and sweet and pretty. And if the way to a man's heart really was through his stomach, then her cooking would put her on the freeway. Besides her food truck, Annie's catering specialties were legendary.

It would be a good match for both of them. Brody needed to find a woman who would appreciate his humor and generosity. He loved helping people and he needed someone to champion. So why not Annie with her darling little girl? Her loser ex was never going to get his act together, and having someone she could depend on to encourage her would be frosting on the cupcake of all the business success Annie had achieved.

"What do you think about Annie?" she whispered to Courtney, her partner in matchmaking, as their two husbands discussed home-improvement projects.

"They'd be great together," Courtney whispered back. "Except they both work a lot."

"Yeah, but his hours are flexible," Jenna pointed out.

"And she should have someone in her life who's stable," Courtney added. "Although she claims she's happy on her own."

Annie seemed happy enough. But Jenna knew how tough it was being a single mom. And lonely. "Maybe she's just saying that."

"Maybe they need a little push," Courtney whispered. "I've got the perfect game tonight for that."

"Better start the games fast." Jenna nodded to where Brody stood, talking with Ellis, probably saying goodbye before slipping out the door.

Maybe he wouldn't make it to the door. Rian LaShell was zeroing in on him.

Rian was slender and always moved with catlike grace. Jenna had never warmed to her. Partly because Rian had never warmed to Jenna. Brody had been the reason for that, and now there she was, stalking him.

Rian and Brody had been an item for a while, once upon a time. It hadn't gelled, which had to mean they weren't right for each other. Brody didn't need to take a third hit to the heart.

"What are you looking at?"

Seth's words yanked Jenna back into the moment. "Nothing," she lied, and took a sip of her punch. "Wow, this really is good." Happily, one of the white-coated servers Annie had hired stopped next to them, offering a plate of dates wrapped in bacon. "Oooh, I love these." Jenna took one and stuffed it in her mouth. You couldn't answer awkward questions if your mouth was full.

Seth's eyes narrowed slightly. It was what she thought of as his dangerous pirate expression. She pretended not to see.

She also pretended not to be monitoring Brody and Rian. He was talking with her, smiling even, but he was also glancing around the room, always a sure sign that a man wasn't interested in a woman. He was looking to escape.

After some more chitchat, he called for everyone's attention, as he usually did at their gatherings, to acknowledge their hosts. He gave a big thank-you to the host and hostess, which was followed by enthusiastic applause from everyone and made Mel blush and Ellis, who was standing with his arm around her, beam.

"And thanks to our own food queen, Annie Albright, for catering this for us," he continued. "Who needs the Food Network when we've got her, right?"

Ah, yes, Brody did have a silver tongue. He smiled his killer smile at Annie while everybody applauded once more.

"Crab cakes forever," called Nora Singleton's husband, Bill, who'd been enjoying the beer. Bill also enjoyed the ice cream that his wife served up at their popular family-owned ice cream parlor and had the paunch to testify to it.

"And now, I believe Courtney, our mistress of mayhem, has some Valentine festivities lined up for us," Brody said.

"Oh, yeah," Courtney said. As he was edging away, she caught him by the arm. "You may as well stay put. I have plans for you."

"Uh-oh, look out," joked Cindy Redmond's husband.

Good plan, thought Jenna. Making sure Brody stayed involved in the fun and games was a sure way to keep him there.

Still holding onto Brody, Courtney picked K.J.'s sister, Elizabeth MacDowell, along with her husband and Ellis for the first game. K.J. was instructed to escort Elizabeth to a bedroom down the hall and blindfold her.

"Bring her out when we call you," Courtney finished as she and Tyrella Lamb set up three folding chairs in the center of the room.

Then she seated Elizabeth's husband in one of the three chairs. Next to him, Courtney put Ellis and Brody.

"This is called Find Your Man's Knee," she informed everyone. "Okay, men, roll up your pants and show us your legs."

This produced much laughter and hooting.

"Can you even get your pants up over that tree trunk of a leg," Cindy's husband teased Ellis.

Of course, everyone found it hilarious watching as a blindfolded Elizabeth knelt before the various men, feeling their legs and trying to figure out which one belonged to her husband. It was even more entertaining when she picked Brody.

"Seriously?" her husband said, holding out his hands in protest once her blindfold was off.

"That's enough singling people out for public humiliation," Courtney said. "Now I'm going to humiliate you all. Everybody form two lines, alternating men and women. We are going to play Pass the Orange." This produced groans and giggles.

Jenna and Seth moved into a line, him muttering a sarcastic, "Oh, boy."

"Don't be a poor sport," she teased. Then she grabbed Brody's arm. "Come on, Brody."

"You are not going to play pass the orange with him," Seth hissed.

"I know," she hissed back. "Come on, Annie, be on our team," she said, and caught Annie by the arm as well, positioning her right next to Brody.

Annie's face turned Valentine pink, and she frowned at Jenna.

"Come on, Annie, it'll be fun," Brody said, trying to put her at ease.

She nodded and got in line next to him while Rian managed to slip in on his other side.

Kiki's husband, who was still spry at seventy-nine, edged in next to Jenna. At least Seth would have no cause to get jealous of her going neck to neck with Oscar.

"Okay, now, I bet you all know how to play this, but for those of you who don't…" Courtney held up two oranges, then gave one to each person at the head of the two lines. "Put these under your chins and then all you have to do is pass it from person to person. No hands allowed. Wherever the orange goes, your chin goes. And if you drop it, you have to start all over, so stick together," she added with a smirk. "First line to finish wins." She held up a small red gift bag. "I have Godiva chocolate bars for the winning team, and if that doesn't motivate you, I don't know what will."

And so the orange passing began with people giggling as they got into clinches, lining their chins up and trying to get the orange from one person to the other. Many of the husbands were perfectly happy to let that orange slide down their wives' chests.

Jenna watched as Brody bent to pass the fruit to Annie. It was so cute, seeing them standing there, neck to neck. She would have been very pleased with herself if she hadn't felt those irritated man vibes coming from her husband behind her. She got her orange from Oscar and turned to pass it to Seth.

"I know what you're doing," he whispered in her ear.

She put her arms around his waist and pulled in close. "Playing with you."

"Brody does not need your help."

"I know," she said after she'd transferred the orange. "Love will find a way."

But there was nothing wrong with putting up a few signs to nudge it in the right direction.

Brody figured out what Jenna was up to the moment she drafted Annie to stand in line next to him. Guilt-matching. As a sop to her conscience, she was looking for a Jenna substitute. Well, there was no substitute.

A woman had a right to choose whom she wanted to marry. If Jenna wanted to make the wrong choice, that was her prerogative. But she didn't need to be putting herself in charge of his love life, her and her accomplice, Courtney.

Did Jenna honestly think he couldn't find a woman to be with on his own? He could. If he wanted one. But he didn't. Right now, he just wanted to be left in peace.

And poor Annie was still blushing over their orange exchange. He'd gotten a firm grip on it to make sure it didn't go sliding places it shouldn't, making the embarrassing process as quick and painless as he possibly could.

"Hurry up back there," he called to the couple at the end of the line, a ploy to assure Annie that he wasn't thinking of their moment of close proximity.

It had been a nice moment. Annie was a pretty woman with delicate features and small soft curves. But she wasn't his type. She was too quiet. He liked a woman with more spark, a woman like...

It was time to go home.

The game ended and the members of the winning team—his—were each given a small chocolate bar. He gave his to Annie and thanked her for being a good sport.

Okay, he'd done his duty as chamber president and showed up. Now he was going to un-show himself.

Courtney was about to lead everyone into another goofy game, involving tying people together with string. It was the perfect time to leave.

He quickly went over to where Ellis and Melody stood. "Hey, you two, thanks for hosting."

"Out of here already?" Ellis asked, surprised. There was a time when Brody would have been the last to leave.

"Yeah, I've got a date," Brody lied. He got his coat and made for the door. "Gotta go, guys," he said with a casual wave.

"Already?" protested Courtney.

"It's past my bedtime," he joked, and several people laughed.

"Party pooper," called Kiki.

Yeah, that was him. The party had ended the day Jenna got married.

* * *

The Valentine party continued until the wee hours, and once Jenna and Seth got back home, they kept the party going. She was sure they'd left the subject of her matchmaking far behind until he'd turned off the bedside light and they'd settled in for sleep.

"No more matchmaking, okay?" he said.

It was too dark for him to see her fakey, wide-eyed innocent look, so she didn't bother. "I just want everyone to be as happy as us," she said.

"No one can ever be as happy as us," he murmured, and nuzzled her hair. "Anyway, he's a big boy. He can find himself a woman without any help from you."

"Yeah, just like you did?" she teased. "I seem to remember you needing some help."

"That was different. Go to sleep, Jenna."

"Good night," she said, glad he didn't extract any promises from her to stop with the matchmaking. "Pleasant dreams."

"Always, thanks to you," he said, and gave her a final kiss.

A few minutes later his breathing had settled into the regular rhythm that signified he was asleep. She curled up against him, enjoying the feel of that hard muscled body next to hers. Seth Waters was as close to perfect as a man came. Strong, sexy, caring. He didn't even snore, for heaven's sake. He was her fantasy man come to life, her pot of gold at the end of the rainbow.

Really, the only thing marring the perfection of her life was knowing that she'd hurt Brody when she went for that perfect life. It somehow didn't seem right that her happiness had cost him his. So who could blame her for wanting to help him find his own pot of gold?

The next week she and Courtney and Annie met for lunch at Sandy's restaurant.

"It seems like another life that I worked here," Annie said after they'd been served.

"In a way it was," Jenna said, and dug into her shrimp Cobb salad.

"And look at you now," said Courtney.

"Look at us all," Annie said. "Jenna owns the Driftwood, you've got Beach Babes and I've got my food truck and the catering business."

"Clothing, hospitality and food empires. We are amazing," Courtney said, raising her glass of strawberry lemonade in salute to both of them. Then she slipped in, "And two of us have found our perfect men."

The smile on Annie's face ran away and she stabbed a chunk of crab in her Crab Louie.

Jenna could feel the steel walls going up. She and Courtney exchanged looks.

Your turn, Courtney's said.

"I'm sure yours is right around the corner."

Annie just shrugged.

"There are still good men left in Moonlight Harbor," Courtney added.

"Like who?" Annie scoffed.

"How about Vince at Beachside Grocery?" Jenna said, opting to ease into the Brody option.

Annie rolled her eyes. "Yes, I need another child in my life."

"Just because he likes to play softball," Jenna said.

"And beach volleyball and video games and fantasy football, whatever that is. Are you guys forgetting that one date we had in September?"

Jenna had been way too preoccupied with her new husband to remember much of anything that had happened outside the bedroom the last fall.

It looked like Courtney had, too. "Oh, yeah. I forgot."

"If I ever get married again, I want more than burgers and fries and football games on TV," Annie said.

"But think of the great Super Bowl parties you could host," Courtney teased.

Annie didn't laugh.

"He's not the only one," Jenna said.

"He's the only one I can think of," Annie told her.

"What about Brody?" Jenna threw it out there, sounding as casual as possible.

Annie gasped. "Brody?"

"Well, why not? He's a great guy," said Courtney.

"And he's still in love with Jenna. Anybody with eyes can see that."

"He just thinks he is," Jenna insisted. "Much as I cared about him, we were never a total match. He just can't bring himself to admit it."

Annie shook her head. "No, I knew Brody before you came to town. Heaven knows I served him enough food when I was working as a waitress. If something was going to happen between us, it would have."

"But before I came to town, you were still married. He could hardly be chasing around a married woman," Jenna pointed out.

Annie nodded, admitting the point. She speared an avocado and studied it. "But ever since you came to town, he hasn't been able to see anyone but you."

What was behind that remark? Was Annie interested in Brody?

"What if he was?" Jenna asked.

"I don't see that happening anytime soon, if ever," Annie said.

"You never know. He only needs a little push," Courtney said.

Annie looked at her in horror. "Don't you dare try to push him my direction."

"Why not?" demanded Courtney. "Sometimes men need motivating."

"Oh, no." Now Annie was shaking her head violently. "I've seen you in action trying to motivate a man and I've seen how that can blow up."

Courtney scowled and fell silent.

"Look, you two, I appreciate your concern, I really do. But if I'm ever to find someone again, it will happen organically. And maybe I haven't found someone because I'm supposed to get back with Greg," Annie finished softly.

Both her friends groaned.

"It could happen," she insisted. "He hasn't had a drink in almost a year."

"What's the longest he's gone in the past?" Jenna asked.

"A year," Annie said, staring at her salad.

"He's still immature and selfish," Courtney insisted. "You don't need his crap back in your life."

"Maybe I don't need anyone," Annie said.

Jenna didn't believe her. Everyone needed someone.

"I don't know," her sister said dubiously when they were talking on the phone later. "I think for Brody to forget you, it's going to have to feel more like a gift from Heaven. Lightning striking."

"Annie would be a great gift for any man," Jenna insisted.

"Yes, she would. But probably not for Brody," said Celeste. "You know how love works. It sneaks up from around the corner and grabs you."

"Or it can be right there in front of you and you don't even see it."

"I don't think it's Brody whose eyesight needs adjusting."

"What's that supposed to mean?" Jenna demanded.

"That you need to stop feeling guilty because you didn't marry him."

"I don't feel guilty." She felt…sorry. Sorry that she'd hurt him. "I want him to be happy, that's all."

"He will be. He's too great a guy for somebody not to snag him."

"So why not Annie?"

"'Cause she's not right for him?"

"Maybe she's not," Jenna conceded.

She heard a faint, "Mama, mama," in the background.

"Guess who's had enough of her nap," Celeste said. "I gotta go. Love you."

"Love you, too," Jenna said, but she was already talking to air. She set aside her phone and returned to checking out the new reservations that had come in through the Driftwood Inn website.

She supposed her sister and her husband were right. Brody was more than capable of finding his own woman and she didn't need to designate herself as his personal Cupid.

But if she happened to meet someone he might like…? All kinds of people came to stay at the Driftwood Inn. Her own sister had met her perfect match there. You never knew. Someone could blow in like a gift from the sea. Or State Route 3.

Five

Lucy had just gotten off the phone with her lawyer and Darla was consoling her with brownies when a text came in from Hannah.

WHAT'S GOING ON?!!!

Uh-oh.
"Okay, now who's texting you?" Darla asked.
"Hannah." Lucy bit her lip and stared at the text. How to answer this?
"Tell her," Darla said.

Dad says u r staying at Aunt Darla's????

For a while, Lucy texted back, trying to stay vague.
"Are you telling her?" Darla demanded.
"How am I supposed to do that?" Lucy shot back.
"Easy. Say your dad cheated on me and I moved out."
Another text came in from her daughter.

Dad says u 2 had a misunderstanding????

Lucy's eyes narrowed. *A misunderstanding.* Was that what you called it?

"Don't prolong the agony. Tear off the bandage," Darla advised.

The agony would continue long after Lucy had torn off the bandage. But her sister had a point. Hannah would find out about the other woman eventually. Lucy was only postponing the inevitable.

She took a deep breath.

I'm sorry. There's no easy way to say this. Daddy and I are splitting up.

WHAT?!!!!!!!!!!!

Exactly Lucy's reaction when she'd discovered her husband with another woman.

I know this comes as a shock, she texted. But it's for the best.

"Tell her about the other woman," Darla commanded. "Don't you dare let him make you look like the villain here."

"The villain? How could *I* look like the villain?"

"You left him. He's probably telling her all kinds of lies. Your mother left me. I wanted to work out our problems but she wouldn't. Blah, blah blah."

All right. It was bad form to diss your ex (or ex-to-be), but it was also bad form to cheat on your wife. And telling the truth didn't count as dissing.

Your father has found someone else. There was no way to sugarcoat it.

Actually, there was and she just had. She could have

told her daughter all the sordid details of how she'd discovered his infidelity. She half wanted to. *This is how rotten evil your dad is.*

But Evan wasn't rotten evil. He was deluded and selfish. He still loved their daughter though, and their daughter loved him. Sharing all the dirty details of what he'd done would make Lucy the evil one and she wasn't going to go there.

Daddy loves u. U do everything together.

Not everything. He'd found someone else to help him try out the shower in a luxury condo.

Not anymore. Maybe he still did love her, a little. But she had no need for that kind of love.

The texts stopped. Lucy could envision her daughter throwing down her phone and bursting into tears. This was a terrible way for her to find this out.

"We blew it," Lucy said miserably.

"You mean he blew it."

"No, we blew it. We should have sat her down and talked to her like reasonable people. Instead, I went running away and now she's found out like this. Who tells her child she's getting a divorce in a text? I'm an awful mother."

"Are you kidding? You're a great mom. Don't you dare take any blame for this. It's all on Evan."

No new texts appeared on the screen. Lucy set her phone on the kitchen table and started crying.

Darla sat down next to her and put an arm around her. "You have done nothing wrong. Don't lose sight of that."

Her sister was right. Lucy hadn't done anything wrong. But Hannah was going to pay the price, anyway.

* * *

Maybe so was Evan. On learning that Daddy had found someone else, Hannah had quickly chosen sides and stopped speaking to him.

Lucy's conscience wouldn't allow her to detour around the moral high road. "What's going on between your father and me has nothing to do with you," she said to Hannah one afternoon in April as they sat at a Starbucks in the U District, drinking Fraps. "He'll always be your father." He'd turned into a lousy husband but Lucy knew he'd still be a good dad, there for his daughter whenever she needed him.

"He'll always be a douchebag," Hannah retorted.

"Darling, you have to forgive him," Lucy said.

"No I don't, and I don't have to like her. If they get together, I'm never going to their house. Ever."

In spite of trying to be noble and encourage her daughter to do what was right, Lucy couldn't help taking a tiny bit of secret delight in the fact that her daughter was a long way from forgiveness. Let Evan suffer for a while. He'd earned it.

She was determined to move on though. After all, what was the point in being bitter and angry? "Be better, not bitter," she kept telling herself as the days marched on.

Her divorce would be final by May. Mediation had been civil and the assets had been divided. The house had sold immediately and for above the asking price and the money was sitting in escrow, just waiting for The End to be stamped on their marriage. Evan was already in the process of making an offer on a house that was equally expensive. He kept the boat and his stupid sports car. Lucy was keeping the Range Rover and all the contents of the house—most of which she'd already sold, which had been fine with him. Wherever she landed, she was going to start decorating from scratch. Nothing to remind her of her ex.

Except for that painting of the ballerina. Even though Evan had given it to her, she still loved it. Looking at it made her feel hopeful. She'd hang it in her bedroom. When she got a bedroom.

Splitting up their business had been much harder than dividing their possessions. There was more emotion attached. It was something they'd worked so hard to build together and now it was over. Anderson-Holmes Realty would become simply Holmes Realty. They were no longer a team.

Now he was teaming up with someone else.

What was the appeal? Lucy kept asking herself that question over and over. Had Evan simply traded her in on a newer model?

After seeing a counselor and having many conversations over coffee with her sister, she finally realized it hadn't so much been about the fact that the other woman was younger. It had been about the fact that she had kept Evan's ego better fed. Lucy was his equal. Pandora had been his slavish admirer, his sycophant. His ego had swelled to the point of blinding him to what he had.

Soon he wouldn't have what he had at all. He'd have a new shiny toy to play with. And Lucy would have...?

"You need a plan," Darla told her as she sat at the kitchen table, staring into her half-empty coffee mug.

"You're right. You guys have got to be sick of me," Lucy responded.

Heck, she was sick of the sight of herself. She hadn't bothered with makeup in ages and her hair was a mess.

She looked down at her white sweater. It had a stain on it where she'd spilled coffee two days ago. She was pathetic.

"No way. We like having you with us," Darla insisted. "That's what guest rooms are for."

"Yeah, for guests. Not mooches who dig in and become permanent boarders."

"Permanent boarders who buy our groceries and enough gift cards to make us feel like it's Christmas. But don't worry. If you make it permanent, we'll charge you rent," Darla added with a grin. "Seriously though, have you thought about what you're going to do next?"

Lucy shrugged. "I'm having trouble bringing the future into focus. I feel like I'm stuck neck-deep in wet cement. Lethargy, I suppose," she said. *Or depression. Maybe a little of both.*

"Maybe you need to get going before it hardens," Darla suggested.

Lucy sighed. Her sister was right. "I need to find a place to live."

"How about something nearby?"

"No, I don't want to be in Evan's sphere or anywhere near it. I need to get away and start fresh."

Probably the sooner the better. What happened to finding the best years of her life?

"Where would you like to go?"

Good question. If she could go anywhere she wanted? Which she could now. A vision of sand and sea and a beachside cottage came to mind.

"The beach," she said dreamily.

"California?" Darla looked horrified. "That's too far away."

"Well, there is such a thing as air travel," Lucy pointed out. "But no. California real estate is too expensive."

"I guess I could live with the Oregon coast," Darla conceded.

"I think I want to stay in Washington."

"That sounds good. There are lots of beaches to choose from in Washington. Kitsap Peninsula?" Darla grabbed her phone and started searching the internet. "How about an island? Bainbridge? An easy ferry commute to the city."

Lucy shook her head. "You're at the mercy of the ferry schedule. Too pricey for the inconvenience."

"Vashon?"

"No bridge."

"Whidbey Island? They have some really cute towns there."

"Too big."

Good grief. She was like Goldilocks trying to find that one place that was just right.

"How about this?" Darla turned her phone so Lucy could see the website she'd found. *Welcome to Moonlight Harbor* it said.

"Remember this town? You and I took the kids down there once when they were little."

Lucy did remember. It was a funky tourist town that had sprung up in the '60s. It had still been stuck in the '60s when they'd visited.

She brought up the website on her own phone and checked it out. The main drag through town had been somewhat updated. She checked out a cluster of cabana-styled shops, each painted different beachy colors, adding some freshness to the older architecture of the other buildings.

Some of the tourist lures she remembered were still there, like the ice-cream parlor and the souvenir shop with a facade shaped like a shark. You entered through the shark's mouth. Hannah had loved that.

Lucy switched to an online real estate search site. The town offered more than beachfront. In addition to two lakes, it also had a system of canals that the average tourist would never even be aware of. Many of the houses for sale had views to die for and they all had prices that assured you'd die with a smile on your face. Property was still affordable. Hmm.

Next, she checked to see how many real estate offices the town had. Only one. Room for competition. Moonlight Harbor had potential.

"Girls trip?" she suggested to Darla.

"Definitely. But let's stay someplace affordable."

"Don't worry about the cost. This is my treat."

"Someplace affordable, anyway," Darla insisted. "There's no sense wasting money." She typed and scrolled around and, once more, turned her phone so Lucy could see. "How cute is this?"

"The Driftwood Inn," Lucy read. She brought it up on her phone and checked out the pictures. "Looks like it's been totally remodeled."

"'We're proud to be a family-owned business,'" Darla read aloud. "'My great-aunt and uncle built the Driftwood Inn and were one of the first businesses in Moonlight Harbor. We've lovingly restored this vintage motel to its former glory and take pride in welcoming guests with a friendly smile and home-baked cookies...just like Aunt Edie used to do. It's signed Jenna Waters.'"

"That is so sweet," Lucy said.

"And the rooms look cute and kitschy."

"All right, you sold me." Lucy called the Driftwood

Inn and made reservations for the first week in May. By then she would officially be a single woman.

The day presented itself bright and cheery with an azure sky decorated with a few wisps of clouds and a bright sun. It felt like a sign. And a blessing.

With each mile they put between themselves and the city, another coil of unhappiness unwound itself from Lucy's heart. As they drove through the monolithic stone entrance that announced they had arrived in Moonlight Harbor, she felt as if a heavy weight had fallen from her shoulders.

There were no gigantic modern buildings forced to stand shoulder to shoulder here, no million-dollar twenty-story condos, either—just simple structures housing humble restaurants and businesses offering everything from moped rentals and kites to art.

And what was this? A candy store. The large glass windows in front of Cindy's Candies showed the biggest display of saltwater taffy Lucy had ever seen. She made a hard right and squealed into the parking lot.

"Whoa," said Darla, bracing herself. "Do we have a death wish now?"

"No, just a candy wish," said Lucy. "Come on, let's stock up."

"Stock up. More like overdose," her sister said when they walked inside. "Look at that mountain of saltwater taffy."

It was, indeed, a mountain, taking up the center of the shop and sectioned off to display every imaginable flavor, from root beer to huckleberry.

The sisters each grabbed a little straw bucket and got

busy filling them. "Oh, cinnamon," Darla said with a groan. "I am undone."

"And orange, my fav," Lucy added, happily dumping a large handful of wrapped taffies into her shopping bucket.

After the taffy, they splurged on fudge and some chocolate-dipped Oreos.

"This place is amazing," Lucy said to the redhaired woman who was ringing up their sales. "Is it yours?"

"It is," the woman replied with a smile. "I'm Cynthia Redmond, Cindy to my friends."

"I assume you live here in Moonlight Harbor?" Lucy asked as she handed over her credit card.

"I do. It's a great place to live. The people here are here because they want to be, so everyone's pretty much happy all the time."

"How supportive are they of new businesses?" Lucy asked.

"Very. We have a lot of women down here who own their own business and our chamber of commerce is the best." She handed back the credit card and receipt.

"So, nothing bad to say about Moonlight Harbor?" Lucy asked.

Cindy's smile got bigger. "Sure. Give me a few years to think on it."

"You sure make it sound like the place to be," Lucy said as Cindy got busy ringing up Darla's purchase.

"It is if you like living at the beach. Oh, I guess that's one thing. It's not warm all year 'round like beaches in other parts of the country. We get storms and rain and some cold weather in the winter. But I personally like being here when it's stormy. Once in a while you lose power, but normally they get it back on pretty quickly. We had one year when it was really bad but that's not the norm."

Lucy nodded. "I don't mind rain. I'm from Seattle."

"Ah, then you're used to it. So, you thinking about moving here?"

"I'm seriously considering it."

"Well, if you are, check in with Brody Green over at Beach Dreams Realty. He'll get you fixed up."

"Thanks," Lucy said.

"Are you going to go see Brody Green?" Darla asked as they got back in the Rover. "I'm up for being a lookie-loo."

"I think I'd rather drive around and check the town out on my own," Lucy said. "I don't want to rush into anything."

Theoretically, anyway. Although she sure liked Moonlight Harbor's vibe. The place felt like a fit, like home.

They stopped in the kite shop and bought a kite, then grabbed a late lunch at a restaurant called Sandy's that offered a fish and chips lunch special they couldn't turn down.

The waitress looked almost old enough to be their mother, with salt-and-pepper hair and crepey-skinned arms, but she had a youthful vibe and was as smiley as Cindy the candy shop lady had been. There weren't many diners left, so she was more than happy to chat with the sisters.

"Where are you staying?" she asked.

"The Driftwood Inn," Darla told her.

"That's a cute place," the woman said. "Mind you, every place down here is great to stay at. We got fancy ones and family-friendly ones and budget specials—you name it."

"Which kind is the Driftwood?" Lucy asked.

"Everybody-friendly and easy on the budget. They don't have all the modern fancy stuff people like nowadays—no

Jacuzzi or room service, but they're good people. Jenna Waters, who owns it, is on the city council."

"Oh, you're a city?" Darla asked.

"Well, almost," their waitress said with a grin.

So Jenna Waters is a mover and shaker. It might be good to get to know her, Lucy thought.

"Looks like we picked the right place to stay," Darla said as their server went off to get their check ready.

"I think so. She'll be able to tell me a lot about this town."

The Driftwood Inn was as cute as it had looked in the pictures on the website. The building wasn't the latest and greatest—just a single story leftover from the sixties, stretching out at the end of an asphalt parking lot. But it had been painted a cheery blue with white trim and was obviously well-maintained. Beyond it, Lucy glimpsed beach dunes and grass. She could hardly wait to get out there, take in the sight of the ocean and smell the salt air and enjoy the afternoon sunshine.

Jenna Waters herself was working the reception desk, and, as promised on her website, she greeted the sisters with a smile and an offer of chocolate chip cookies from the large blue plate shaped like a shell that sat on the counter.

"We make them every morning," she said. "Tomorrow it will probably be peanut butter."

Darla groaned. "My favorite. At the rate we're going, I'm sure to gain twenty pounds while we're down here."

"We stopped at the candy shop on the way in," Lucy explained.

"Ah, that would explain it," Jenna said knowingly. "Her chocolate-mint fudge is my kryptonite. And you're down here from…?"

"Seattle," Lucy said.

"We get a lot of people from Seattle, especially when it's really hot in the summer," Jenna told her.

"I can imagine. I remember spending some lovely days here many summers ago," Lucy said.

"You'll have to come back for a summer encore."

"I might do that," Lucy said.

"Meanwhile, enjoy your stay," Jenna said, handing over a set of room keys. "I think you'll like this room."

Room keys, not a key card? Lucy looked at them in surprise.

Their host blushed. "We're still updating. But don't worry. You're perfectly safe. We keep a close eye on things here. And really, about the only crime we get in Moonlight Harbor is a few traffic violations and an occasional graffiti attempt."

"So, low crime, everybody happy," Lucy mused as the sister's moved the Rover to the parking lot in front of their room.

"It's Mayberry," said Darla.

"I'll take Mayberry. I'm ready for a calm, happy life."

The room had a beachy flair. The bedspreads on the twin beds featured sand dollars and sea horses, and Lucy loved the bedside lamps with their glass bases filled with shells. A framed photo of a sunrise over the ocean hung on the tan wall.

"Cute, isn't it?" said Darla.

"It is. It's homey."

Certainly not like the slick high-end hotels she and Evan always stayed in. But those were impersonal. Sterile. This place felt welcoming. She could hardly wait to explore the rest of the town.

First though… "Let's take a walk on the beach," she

said to her sister as soon as they'd brought in their clothes and snacks.

"Sounds good to me."

As they walked down the beach, the gulls circling overhead and the waves hitting the sand, the beach seemed to be saying, *Welcome.*

"This place is like medicine," Lucy said.

"It is nice."

"I think it's more than nice. I think I might be able to create a great life for myself here. It is charming. And it's far from Evan."

"A definite plus," said Darla.

"Hannah will definitely come down a lot, I'm sure. She might even want to stay with me and get a summer job."

Lucy could envision her and her daughter enjoying life at the beach. She'd lost her husband but not her girl. They'd always had a good relationship, but they'd become even closer in the aftermath of the divorce, almost like two shipwreck victims helping each other survive on a deserted island.

Of course, there were others on that island with Lucy— her parents, who checked in regularly and kept offering her money she didn't need; Darla, who had taken her in and been her shrink; her brother, who'd prescribed her some handy little pills to help her survive those times when she simply wanted to sink beneath the warm water in the bathtub and stay there. It took a village.

"Think you could sell real estate down here?" Darla asked.

"I know I could sell real estate down here." Lucy was good. She could sell real estate anywhere. "Maybe I'll get into flipping houses. I bet there are some great fixer-uppers just waiting for me."

That evening it was dinner at The Porthole, a local restaurant that offered a view of the beach. This was followed by an evening watching reruns of *Virgin River* on the TV in their room and stuffing themselves with the goodies they'd bought at Cindy's Candies.

"I think I'm going to be sick," Darla said, looking at all the empty taffy wrappers next to her on the bed.

"Me, too," said Lucy. She was sure she'd just added a pound to each hip. But darn, those chocolate-covered Oreos had gone down easy. "You know, it seems grossly unfair that you should be punished with extra pounds when you're self-medicating with chocolate."

"Life's not fair," said Darla.

As if Lucy needed to be reminded.

"But what the heck. Have another cookie. You deserve it," Darla said.

Yes, she did.

Six

The following day the sisters toured the town, checking out the various neighborhoods. They drove across little bridges built over the many canals, which Lucy learned had been built long ago by the army corps of engineers. Lots of cute houses along those. A couple were for sale and they got out of the Rover and walked around them, peering in windows and checking out the yards and the waterfront. Many houses along the canals had kayaks sitting on their docks, or party barges moored and ready for a sunset cruise. Most of the lakefront houses had docks and, again, kayaks and boats abounded. The part of town looking across the bay to Westhaven offered a view of water and mountains, and the homes there were bigger and costlier. Although nowhere near as costly as homes in the city were. The houses along the beach varied in size as well as shape. Most were at least two stories high to get a better view across the sand dunes to the water, and their colors ranged from gray with white trim to bright turquoise. The sisters also passed several lots, many of them with houses under construction or sold signs in front of them.

"This is a boom town in the making," Lucy said as they

settled in at the fast-food restaurant next to the Driftwood to enjoy clam chowder.

"And only one real estate company," put in Darla.

"Which is shocking, actually. The town is a gem."

"City," Darla corrected, and they both smiled.

"It's well on its way. I'm betting the real estate market here is going to continue to heat up."

"Sounds like you've made up your mind."

"I'm close to it," Lucy said.

"So, where would you like to live?" Darla asked.

"Waterfront somewhere."

"That's a lot of somewhere to choose from. There were some cute houses inland as well," Darla pointed out.

"But what's the sense of moving to the beach if you can't be on the beach."

"Good point."

"I think we need some dessert," Lucy said as Darla scraped the last of the chowder out of her bowl.

"Oh, yeah, I need dessert like I need another roll of fat," Darla said, then added, "But it's good to have a spare for in case I get some horrible disease and need that extra poundage to live on."

"There you go," Lucy said, and stood up.

The ice-cream parlor was exactly what an ice-cream parlor should be, with white ironwork tables hugging one wall and more tables, some large enough for four, along the windows. It offered every imaginable flavor, including wild huckleberry and blackberry. Darla limited herself to one scoop of rocky road in a sugar cone. Lucy ordered two scoops of the huckleberry in a waffle cone. After everything she'd been through, she deserved two scoops.

"Good for you," approved the woman who helped them.

She was older with an ample figure and a large smile. She pointed to the sign behind her. Life's Short, Eat Ice Cream.

"Exactly," Lucy said with a smile.

They strolled out of the parlor and down the little boardwalk that ran along it. In addition to the ice-cream parlor and Funplex, which sat on the other side, there was a store that sold handcrafted soaps and a craft store. They didn't get that far. Lucy stalled out in front of an empty storefront right in the middle of it all with a for-rent sign in the window.

"Wow, what a great location," she said, and peered in the window. The space was huge. Plenty of room to grow. She turned to her sister. "It's a sign."

"A sign of what? Somebody's business failing?"

"Of my new business succeeding," said Lucy. "This is the perfect spot for a real estate office, right in the center of everything."

"Everything tourist," Darla said, unconvinced.

"Tourists often turn into residents. People love to stop and look at pictures of houses for sale in a real estate office window when they visit a town."

"I don't."

Lucy frowned at her. "Okay, most people. Lots of people. You couldn't ask for a better location than this."

"With your competition down the street."

"They'd better watch out," Lucy said.

"Maybe so should you. That business is already here and established."

"But it's the only one. Remember? There's room for more and I'm not afraid of a little healthy competition," Lucy said. "Anyway, they're way down there, out of sight and out of mind." She pulled out her cell phone and tapped in the number on the for-rent sign in the window. Then she got right to the point the moment the man on the other end of the call said hello. "I'm looking at your space here on Harbor Boulevard. I assume it's still for rent since the sign's still in the window."

"It is," he said. "You interested?"

"I am. What are you asking for rent?"

He told her. Compared to what office space cost in Seattle, it was a steal.

"I'd love to see it if you've got time," Lucy said.

"I do in about an hour."

"That will work for me. My name is Lucy Holmes."

"Edgar Morgan. I'll see you in an hour," he said, and ended the call before she could even say goodbye.

"Are we going to look inside?" guessed Darla.

"You bet. We've got some time to kill. Let's go look at soap."

Inside the store, Darla picked up a soap shaped like a starfish and examined it. "I'm worried you might be rushing into this."

"I'm not rushing. I'm being decisive. And aren't you the same woman who told me I need a plan?"

"Yeah, a plan. I didn't say jump out of the plane before you even get your parachute on."

Lucy smiled. "I know. But I think I've been forming a plan all along and didn't realize it. That empty space is a sign. I'm not going to give up being in real estate just because things didn't work out with Evan. I'm good at it. I can buy a house down here and have money left to invest and live on. And what's the worst that can happen?"

"You'll hate living here year-round."

"Then I'll pull up stakes and move in with you and set up my office in your basement," Lucy said with a grin.

"Well, there you go. Perfect planning."

"Look, I have a feeling about this town. Now is a good time to invest in property. I can buy a fixer-upper and put my own stamp on it. If I decide I don't want to live here full-time, I can keep it as a summer place. Or I'll sell it at a profit. You can't—"

"Go wrong with real estate," Darla finished with her.

"It's still one of the best investments a person can make. So why not make an investment here?"

"Because you can't walk away from a business lease."

Her sister was right. Leasing office space wasn't the same as staying at a motel. You couldn't simply decide you were done and pick up stakes and leave. Not without consequences.

Yet she had to settle somewhere, do something. And she didn't want to settle near Seattle and do anything there. Moonlight Harbor was a charming community. She could see the town's potential and the idea of living at the beach appealed. How many people dreamed of living on a beach somewhere but never made it happen. She could. Nothing was tying her down.

That last thought was a sad one. She was like a kite, fighting the wind with no one holding the strings to keep her anchored.

Except that wasn't true. She still had her family. She'd make friends, maybe even better ones than the ones she was leaving behind. Because she'd always been so busy working, those friendships had never put down very deep roots. Here she could make time for that.

"I need to look into this," she said. "If opportunity is knocking on the door, I want to be ready to open it."

"I guess you know what you're doing," Darla said.

"I think I do. Anyway, I have to do something. It's stupid to keep moping around over what I've lost."

"Which, if you're talking about Evan, is nothing."

Yes, theoretically. But they'd had a good life before everything imploded. She'd loved her husband and had loved building their business together. Sure, she'd had her moments of frustration, just like any woman, but she'd thought she and Evan had built something solid and she couldn't help mourning the fact that it had crumbled.

But she could multi-task. She'd mourn and plan for the future simultaneously.

She looked in the window again and envisioned how she'd decorate her new office. The reception area would have to have a beachy feel—wicker chairs with colorful cushions. A couple of glass floats placed next to a jardiniere of silk daisies, pictures on the walls of seascapes. She'd pick a desk that was pretty and feminine, maybe something whitewashed and antique-looking. She'd need a receptionist desk at some point also. The thought of how pretty she could make the office look had her smiling.

Her smile got even bigger when Edgar Morgan, an octogenarian dressed in slacks and a Hawaiian print shirt, showed them the space. It was great—plenty large enough for a couple of desks and a comfy reception area, and she loved the gray wood floor. Very beachy. The walls were a neutral cream, perfect for those seascape pictures she was envisioning.

"This will work."

"Five-year lease," he said.

Darla's worried expression practically screamed, *What if you fail?*

Five years was a long time to commit to something so iffy. Lucy bit her lip and considered. Yes, it was a big commitment. But if she got a steal on a house, she'd have plenty of money left over to live on… Not for five years.

Still, even with competition down the street, she was bound to get some business.

No, more than some. She could do this. She nodded. "A five-year lease gives me plenty of time to establish my business."

He studied her a moment. "What's your business?"

"Real estate."

He frowned. "You don't want to rent this space. Brody Green's got the market sewed up. You'll be lucky if you last a year."

Was that so? "I owned a very successful real estate company in Seattle. I think there's enough business here for both of us."

"I don't know," he said, dubious.

Good grief. Did he want to rent this space or not?

"I'm happy to show you my financials. I'm a sound risk."

He hesitated.

She got the underlying message. As far as Edgar Morgan was concerned, she may as well have had a big *L* tattooed on her forehead. She'd prove him wrong. "Let's talk," she urged.

He handed her a business card. "You get together the paperwork and meet me at my house."

"What if you go under?" Darla asked as he hobbled off to his car.

Lucy made a face. "Gee, thanks for the vote of confidence."

"Hey, girl-who-always-figured-she-could-leave-if-things-didn't-work, I'm just trying to look out for your interests. You could start small, you know. I bet that Brody Green we're hearing about would be happy to have you work for him. Then you could start slow, work out of his office."

"No," Lucy said emphatically. "I'm going to be my own boss."

"You get stuck in a lease and you could have problems," Darla pointed out.

Yes, she could. It was almost impossible to break a commercial lease. But this was a prime location, and when you owned a real estate agency, you needed to be both visible and accessible.

"I've got a gut feeling about this place," Lucy said. "I think it's where I'm supposed to be." She loved the town, she had the expertise and experience needed to make a go of this, so why not go for it?

"I just hope it's not where you get punched in the gut," Darla said.

"Old Edgar doesn't look like the gut-punching type. How old do you think he is?" Lucy asked. "I'm guessing eighties."

"At least," Darla said. "Pretty impressive that he's still working."

"I hope I am at that age," Lucy said.

And why not? A person needed to stay busy, and she knew she'd always need to be active, always need to have something to do with her life.

"It's good to have a purpose," Darla agreed.

Now that her sister's children were grown, Lucy wondered if she'd want to find something new to do with her life. "What about you?" she asked once they were back in the Rover.

"What about me what?"

"What do you see yourself doing in your old age?"

Darla shrugged. "Pretty much what I've always done, only with grandkids."

Her sister did have training in interior design, but once the kids came along, she'd concentrated on raising them, only spending her expertise on her own house.

"Do you ever think of going back to work?" Lucy pressed.

"Not really," Darla replied. "Not that I have anything against working, and if we needed the extra income, I would. But we've always gotten along on Orren's salary and we've got a nice chunk in savings for retirement so I don't see the need. I'd rather keep my time free to volunteer."

Which she did. Darla was a natural born caregiver, happiest when she was watching out for others. In addition to caring for her family, she made quilts for homeless shelters and volunteered three days a week at a local food bank.

There had been times when, in spite of her career success, Lucy had compared herself to her sister and found herself lacking. "You're so noble," she said, half-jealously.

"What, because I work at the food bank?"

"It's more than I can say."

"We all do different things. I give time. You give money. Nonprofits need both."

"I guess," Lucy said.

"You still giving to that world hunger relief program? Doctors Without Borders? Literacy?"

"Of course."

"Like I said, we all do different things. Don't feel bad about the fact that you've made a boatload of money. Even though we probably don't say it enough, we're all proud of your success. I hope you know that."

Lucy thought of her failed marriage. "Semi-success," she corrected.

"You are not going there," said Darla the mind reader.

Thanks to the cloud and a copy shop, Lucy was able to pull together the necessary financial information. She left her sister to enjoy the beach and the kite they'd purchased and made her way to Edgar Morgan's house.

Located on one of the canals, it was a rambler with a double car garage. Judging from the size, Lucy guessed it had three bedrooms.

She was barely inside when his wife, a plump white-haired woman dressed in jeans and a sweatshirt that said she'd been Moonstruck in Moonlight Harbor, greeted her.

"May I offer you a cup of coffee?" she asked as her husband hobbled into view.

"Oh, no, but thank you," Lucy said.

"Then how about a brownie? I just took some out of the oven."

"This ain't no tea party, Lorna," Edgar said, sounding a little grumpy.

Hmm. Would he make a grumpy landlord?

"This lady's got things to do," he added.

Like write him a check.

Lucy resisted the urge to give the man a disciplinary frown. Instead, she smiled at his wife and said, "I'd love a brownie."

Lorna went to fetch brownies and Edgar led Lucy to a bumped-out area facing the canal where he'd set up a small office with a desk, chair, computer and filing cabinet, and they settled down to talk business. Once he was convinced she was financially solid, he dug around in the filing cabinet and pulled out a lease form.

Which Lucy proceeded to read carefully.

"It's a standard lease form," he informed her.

"I'm sure it is, but I always read things before I sign them," Lucy said pleasantly.

"That is a good idea," he conceded.

She was relieved to see that his contract included the option to terminate the lease. It did stipulate stiff penalties, but she was okay with that. Fair was fair, and besides, she had no intention of breaking the lease. She'd made up her mind and she would make a go of her business in this beach town.

Once the lease was signed and the check written, Edgar gave her a key to her new office space and, after staying long enough to chitchat and eat that brownie, she left his house feeling like a kid who had just won a trip to Disneyland.

"This is going to be great," she predicted when she met up with her sister.

"I hope you're right," Darla said.

"I am," Lucy assured them both. This was a brilliant stroke of genius.

Or the stupidest thing she'd ever done.

But each walk they took on the beach, each pleasant visit with a shop owner convinced Lucy that this was the perfect setting for crafting a new life.

"I'm a little jealous," Darla said the day they were to check out. "This place is idyllic. Make sure that house you buy has a guest room."

"Of course," Lucy promised.

"I hope it all goes as you plan."

Did anything ever go as you planned? Lucy was living proof that it didn't.

The best years of your life are ahead of you, she told herself. And the sandy soil of Moonlight Harbor was the perfect place to nurture them.

* * *

"I'd like to reserve a room for next week," Lucy Holmes said to Jenna when the sisters checked out.

"Sure, we have a couple of vacancies," Jenna said "For how long would you like to reserve it?"

"Can we leave that open-ended? I have to find a place to live."

"So you've decided to move down here? Congratulations," Jenna said, smiling at her.

Lucy nodded. "I think it's a great place to start again. I just got divorced."

Jenna nodded soberly at that. "Been a member of that club. It's not easy."

Sadness drifted across Lucy Holmes's face, like a dark cloud trying to take over blue sky. She quickly replaced it with a determined smile and said, "Oh, well. We can't all win the love lottery."

Jenna finally had.

"I thought that, too. Then I moved here and met my soul mate."

"That is so romantic," Lucy said wistfully.

"It happens," Jenna said.

"Did you get the last available soul mate?" Lucy's sister joked.

An image of Brody Green with his killer smile flashed into Jenna's mind. "Oh, no. There could be one waiting for you," she told Lucy.

The woman was pretty and friendly. Obviously, she had a good relationship with her sister, which, as far as Jenna was concerned automatically put her in the good-person category. Maybe, just maybe...

Seven

Once back at Darla's house in Seattle, Lucy began her search, hunting for the perfect house at the beach.

"What would that be?" Darla asked, joining her at the kitchen table where Lucy had set up her laptop. "We saw quite a few when we were down there."

"For sale by owner."

"Not going to give the competition any notice you're coming?" Darla guessed.

"That and I'm cutting out the middle man."

"A good idea to save money."

"Usually. People tend to think they can get more for their homes than they really can, but sometimes you can find a great bargain on a house for sale by the owner. Anyway, I certainly don't need a real estate broker."

"Carrying coals to Newcastle," Darla said.

"What on earth does that saying mean?"

"It means you don't need a real estate broker," Darla said, making Lucy chuckle.

"Look at this," Lucy said. "Right on the beach."

Darla made a face. "It looks ready to fall down right on the beach."

"The deck could use replacing."

"The whole house could use replacing."

Lucy clicked on another picture. "Check out this one."

"Not bad," Darla conceded.

"Three bedrooms, which is nice."

"My guest room," Darla said.

"On a canal, and it has a dock. Oh, and don't you love the street name? Sand Dollar Lane."

"Do those kayaks come with it?" Darla cracked, pointing to the picture.

"They might," Lucy said, and started clicking through the pictures of the inside.

"We just traveled back in time," Darla said.

The kitchen cabinets and countertops looked like they'd been around since the '70s and, although it appeared clean, Lucy suspected the carpet had, too. But those things were cosmetic, easily fixed. "I'd knock out that wall between the kitchen and living area for a great room. I doubt it's a load bearing one. I can see shiplap on the entryway wall and that one wall in the living room, white shaker cabinets in the kitchen, gray quartz countertop. Tear up the carpet and put down laminate flooring—a nice maple, I think. Lose that tan exterior and paint the house gray with white trim. Ooh, and a turquoise front door. It will be charming."

"At that price you could practically rebuild the whole house," said Darla.

"I bet they could get more for this place than they're asking," Lucy mused.

"So, you're going to rob them," Darla teased.

"Of course not. I'll offer five thousand over asking. But I still intend to get a bargain. Caveat emptor."

"That means let the buyer beware, not the seller," Darla corrected her.

"Well, whatever the seller version of that is." Lucy picked up her cell phone and called the number.

A man answered on the second ring. His hello sounded downright eager.

"I just saw your charming house online and I'd love to come see it in person," Lucy said. "Is it still for sale?"

"So far, but we got interest."

For that price, it wouldn't surprise her. "If I like the house, I think I can make a cash offer that will make you happy."

"I'm up for hearing what you have to say," said the man. Judging from the tone of his voice, he was more than that. He was salivating.

"My name is Lucy Holmes. Could I come by for a chat tomorrow morning?"

"Okay," he said.

"Would ten o'clock be convenient?"

"Sure."

"All right. I'll see you tomorrow," Lucy said, and ended the call.

Next she called Jenna Waters and told her she was coming right back down that very night and was in need of a room. "I know it's earlier than I said."

"We'll have a room ready for you," Jenna assured her.

As far as Lucy was concerned, it was another sign. Everything was aligning. She was completely on the right track.

"I'll see you this afternoon, then," she said.

"Looking forward to it," Jenna replied.

"All right!" Lucy crowed after she ended the call. She shut her laptop. "Help me load my clothes in the car, sissy. I'm driving to Moonlight Harbor tonight."

"You're moving so fast you're making me dizzy," Darla said.

Lucy took the last gulp of her coffee. "You have to strike

while the iron's hot. I really like the price of that house. If I don't move on it, someone might beat me out."

"If they do, you weren't meant to have it."

Lucy gave a snort. "That's what people say when they hesitate and lose out on a deal. She who hesitates…"

"Doesn't wind up neck-deep in quicksand," Darla supplied.

Lucy chuckled. "Don't worry, real estate is my business. Remember? I know what I'm doing."

"Yeah, buying a house in a town you've only spent a couple of days in. You could rent, you know, make sure the town is really a fit for you."

"Too late. I've already signed a commercial lease. Anyway, renting is just building someone else's equity. I'd rather take my chances buying a bargain in a charming town that's only going to keep growing. If worse comes to worst, I can flip it. Anyway, you should be glad. If all goes well, you'll be getting my boxes out of your garage and my behind out of your guest room."

"Guest rooms were meant for guests," Darla said, sounding almost grumpy.

Lucy sobered. "You've been great, but it's time to hit restart on my life. I refuse to let what Evan did keep me hanging in limbo any longer."

Her sister nodded, managed a reluctant smile. "You're right. I'll help you load some of your stuff."

An hour later, armed with a chicken salad sandwich and apple slices her sister insisted she take to fend off starvation on the drive, Lucy left Seattle behind and headed for the beach. And the rest of her life.

Jenna Waters was still in the Driftwood Inn office when Lucy pulled in, her SUV loaded with boxes of clothes and some paperwork she needed to deal with while waiting for a house deal to close. Her dishes, linens and cleaning supplies she'd left behind, along with her ballerina painting, Darla promising she and Orren would bring them down when Lucy had a house to move them into.

"Welcome back," Jenna greeted her.

"No, it's welcome home," Lucy corrected. "I'm ready to buy a house."

"All right!" Jenna said as she got a key for Lucy. "Brody Green at Beach Dreams Realty is great."

"I'm looking at a place that's for sale by the owner," Lucy said, taking the key.

"Ah." Jenna nodded. "Well, if you need advice or help with the contract..."

"Actually, I'm a real estate broker myself."

"Really? Well, you and Brody have a lot in common. I'm sure he'll want to talk to you. His office handles almost all the real estate deals in town."

Lucy and Evan had had real estate in common. Look how that had turned out. And she very much doubted this Brody Green would be happy to talk to her once he learned she was his new competition. But you couldn't be the only dog in the show forever.

She made no response to Jenna's prediction. Instead, she thanked her, left and moved her things into her room.

After that, she walked across the parking lot to the Seafood Shack where she and Darla had eaten and got an order of fish and chips, which she took to the beach to eat. There was a cold breeze coming off the water but the late afternoon sun was warm on her shoulders and the air was fresh. The water was sparkling, the gulls circling and the fish and chips were the equal of what she'd get at Ivar's, Seattle's gold standard for fish and chips.

She bit into a French fry and smiled, and then realized

she was feeling hopeful. After her misery of the last few months, she almost didn't recognize the feeling. But there it was, a sure and final sign that coming to Moonlight Harbor had been the right decision.

Right before sunset she returned to her room and fetched the box of old photos she'd hauled down, along with some matches and a bit of newspaper. She didn't need old pictures of herself and Evan back when they were dating, and she sure didn't need their wedding album.

She walked back along the path through the sand dunes to the beach where she found some twigs, then dug a small hole in front of the same log she'd been sitting on earlier and assembled her fire makings. There was a strong breeze, and for a moment she wasn't sure she was going to be able to get a fire going, but eventually she was able to shield her paper and twigs and produce some flames. There. Time to burn Evan at the stake. Or rather sticks.

She began with a picture of the two of them at Green Lake, one taken after they'd just started dating, her looking great in a bikini and him looking gorgeous in his swim trunks. They had made a handsome couple. She crumpled it and dropped it into the flame, watched it curl up and turn to a blackened scrap, then blow away on the wind. Next came a picture of them at a friend's party. That, too, burned instantly and floated away. She added on several more, not bothering to look at any of them.

Until she came to a picture of them right after they'd gotten engaged. She was wearing a big smile and a ring with a small diamond.

She looked at that excited smile and shook her head. "Poor fool," she said, "if only you'd known," and threw it onto the fire.

And yet if she hadn't let Evan into her life, she wouldn't

have had Hannah, which was probably proof that good things could always manage to find a way to grow out of the bad.

That one was followed by her wedding pictures and many tears. There was so much happiness on their faces. How sad that it had faded.

She added more—pictures of her and Evan at a resort restaurant, a picture of them toasting each other on their tenth anniversary. Each one she gave a vicious crumple, strangling the very life out of the memory. The wind continued to pick up the blackened scraps and blow them away. Lucy kept her back turned, not looking to see where they went. It didn't matter.

By the time she stood up, there was nothing left in the sand but ash. She thought of the legendary phoenix and smiled. Ashes didn't always mean the end. Sometimes they meant the beginning.

That night there was no fitful tossing and turning. Lucy slept soundly and dreamlessly and awoke refreshed.

The welcoming reception she got from the Cooks, the owners of the house on Sand Dollar Lane, confirmed that this was Lucy's town and this would be her house.

The whole place needed updating. The appliances in the kitchen looked like they'd never been replaced. She'd need to add that to her buy list, right along with furniture.

"Our kids want us to move to Puyallup to be near them," Mrs. Cook told her as the three of them stood on the back deck, checking out the view of the canal and the homes on the other side of it.

The water looked peaceful in the morning light and the neighborhood was quiet. A middle-aged couple in kayaks passed them and gave a friendly wave.

"It's nice to be close to family," Lucy said.

Mr. Cook grunted in disgust and shoved his hands in his pant pockets. "They think we're in our dotage."

The pair looked to be somewhere in their sixties, maybe toward the end, right about the time people often started talking about life changes and downsizing.

His wife sighed. "I guess there does come a time. I'll miss this place though."

"I can see why," Lucy said.

Although the modest rambler needed a facelift, the couple had kept it in excellent repair. The houses across the canal were all well-maintained, some with decks, some with patios. All had yards and docks and a variety of water toys—kayaks, canoes, paddleboards. One two-story house had a party barge docked in front of it. It wasn't a pretentious community, but it was easy to see everyone had enough money to enjoy a good life.

"What brings you to Moonlight Harbor?" Mrs. Cook asked.

"I'm making a new start," Lucy said. "I'm recently divorced."

In spite of her new happiness and her confidence in her future, those words still tasted bitter. She reminded herself of the phoenix and spat out the bitterness.

"I'm sorry," Mrs. Cook said.

"Don't be. Life goes on, and I'd love to live mine in this house," Lucy said. "I promise I'll take as good of care of it as you have."

Mrs. Cook teared up. Mr. Cook asked how much Lucy was offering.

On hearing her offer, he, too, teared up. "Sold," he said, and stuck out his hand.

They went over the Cooks' downloaded contract, talked

details and made arrangements to meet and finalize the deal the next day.

Lucy was standing on the front walk, the Cooks on their porch, saying final goodbyes when Mrs. Cook caught sight of a neighbor out watering her flowers and called her over.

"This is Bonnie Brinks. She's a musician," Mrs. Cook added, almost reverently.

"Not that that's anything to brag about unless you're Adele," Bonnie said. "Hi. Nice to meet you."

A great little house to fix up and a friendly neighbor. It just kept getting better and better. "Hi, I'm Lucy Holmes," Lucy said. "And I think being a musician is pretty impressive."

"She has a band," Mrs. Cook said. "The Mermaids."

"Plays a mean guitar," added Mr. Cook.

"But never late at night," Bonnie promised.

"It's okay. I like music," Lucy said. "That's a great band name."

She was missing the fish tail, but even so, Bonnie looked like what Lucy envisioned a mermaid should look like. She had auburn hair that fell in waves past her shoulders, green eyes, the symmetrical face you saw on models and movie stars, and a smattering of freckles across her nose. The only thing that kept her from being completely perfect was a slightly crooked front tooth that showed when she smiled. That small imperfection made her interesting, which, of course, made her even more perfect. She was maybe forty, and svelte as a twenty-something. The kind of woman Lucy might envy if she were insecure.

Lucy reminded herself that she wasn't insecure. Wounded, maybe, but that was healing.

"I still won't play late at night," Bonnie said with a smile, and Lucy knew she was going to like her.

"I hope you'll play for me once I get settled in," she said. Then, before Bonnie could ask her what she did, she claimed she needed to get going and, with a cheerful wave, hurried down the walk.

Not that she'd have minded telling her neighbor what she did for a living, but she wasn't sure she wanted to tell the Cooks. If she'd told them she was in real estate, they'd be bound to think she was cheating them or lying about wanting to live in the house. Too many people watched HGTV and knew about the profits to be made flipping houses, but Lucy wanted to make this one her home. She could hardly wait to move in.

She got her sister on Bluetooth as she made her way to the town's coffee shop to celebrate. "I got it!"

"Congrats. Let the fun begin," Darla said, her voice a mixture of happiness and sarcasm.

"It will be fun." A new house, a new adventure.

She ended the call with her sister and pulled into the parking lot of Beans and Books, the town's coffee shop. Once inside, she saw that it lived up to its name. In addition to lattes and iced drinks, it offered shelves with a selections of new best sellers as well as gently read paperbacks.

A college-aged girl was stationed at the drive-up window while a thin woman who looked to be somewhere around Lucy's age was busy with the espresso machine. "Be with you in minute," she called to Lucy as she worked the frothing wand.

"No hurry," Lucy said, and used the time to study the board boasting what the coffee shop had to offer.

There were plenty of interesting drinks to choose from, all with clever names such as The Beachcomber, Sunrise Smoothie, and a blended coffee drink called the Chocolate Clamshell.

The woman finished making the order, handing it off to her helper, and smiled at Lucy. "What can I get you?"

"I think I have to try that Chocolate Clamshell," Lucy said.

"Good choice," said the woman and got busy.

The Chocolate Clamshell turned out to be a blended coffee drink offering tiny bits of toffee as well as the requisite chocolate. It had a small chocolate candy embedded in a pile of whipped cream drizzled with caramel and topped with toasted coconut.

"Oh, my, this has to be the best thing I've ever had," Lucy said after taking a sip. "No calories, right?"

"None you can see," the woman said with a smile.

"In that case I'll have to become a regular customer," Lucy quipped.

"Are you new to town?" the woman asked.

"I am. I just bought a house here."

"Congratulations. You'll love it here," the woman said.

How many people had told her that so far? With so many endorsements, surely she would.

She thanked the woman and left, sipping her treat as she went. Yep, she could almost feel those invisible calories climbing onto her butt for a ride. *So worth it,* said her taste buds. *Now, you know what would go really good with this?*

She did, and stopped at the Driftwood Inn office for her daily cookie fix. Sugar cookies. Perfect.

While she was in the office, she told Jenna about her new purchase. "It could use some updating though," she finished.

"We've got lots of good contractors in town. And handymen."

"Maybe you could recommend one," Lucy said.

"Well, my husband does some jobs on the side when

he's not busy with his business. He just installed granite countertops in our kitchen. He also has a friend who does remodels and he's done some projects for people. You're welcome to come over and check out my kitchen if you'd like to see a sample of my husband's work."

"Thanks. I might just do that," Lucy said.

The house was taken care of. Next came the office. Phone in hand, she went to the beach to finish her drink and see what fun beachy furnishings she could order online.

She'd just settled on a log with the last of her drink when her daughter texted. I hate Pandora!!!!

Pandora was the past, right along with Evan as far as Lucy was concerned, but obviously, something had set her daughter off. She decided to call instead of going through the endless texting. Honestly, sometimes it was still better to talk voice to voice.

"Mom, he's moving in with her," Hannah said the minute she picked up the call.

"Well, I suppose we shouldn't be surprised," Lucy said. They were divorced and Evan was free to do whatever he wanted. Still, hearing the news left her feeling like something heavy had landed on her heart.

"It's gross. Hashtag pathetic."

"People do a lot of pathetic things when they're in…" No, she couldn't bring herself to say love. That wasn't what Evan was in. Lust, heat, yes, but not love.

Fortunately, her daughter didn't care if she finished her sentence or not. "He wants me to stay with them this summer. No way."

Okay, that was tacky. "I guess he's trying to make sure you know this isn't about you."

"Well, it is. I'm part of this. He's my father."

"True." Poor Hannah. Unlike Lucy, who could unhitch her trailer and go away, Hannah was still stuck with the man.

Actually, in a way so was Lucy. Their daughter was the link that would keep them forever bound even though they weren't together.

"Anyway, no way am I living with them. I can come stay with you at the beach, right?"

"Of course, you can," Lucy said, and couldn't help smiling at the thought that Hannah was choosing her over him. Maybe that was a little immature, but hey, she was human. "I just bought a house down here and there's plenty of room for you."

"Is it on the beach?"

"No, but it's on a canal. Perfect for kayaking."

"And paddleboarding? Can we get paddleboards?"

"Of course."

"Send pictures. I want to see what it looks like."

"It doesn't look anything like our old house," Lucy warned her. "It needs work."

"Oh, my gosh, is it like in those house-flipping shows? Is it full of bugs?"

"No, it's not full of bugs. But it's an older home. It needs updating."

"Can I help update it?"

Lucy already had a vision for the house, but her daughter had inherited her eye for style. Fixing up the house together could be fun.

Or it could be stressful.

"You can help," Lucy said. "But I get the final say."

"Except for my bedroom. Wait a minute. There is a bedroom for me, right?"

"Of course, there is. It has three."

"Good. So then I can decorate one?"

Why not? "Sure."

"This is going to be so shook."

"It will be awesome," Lucy agreed. "But you still have to get a job like Daddy and I said, even if you're going to be down here for the summer."

"Can I work for you?"

Lucy needed a new website, and she'd need someone to answer phones and help with social media. Hannah's generation grew up with a cell phone in one hand and a tablet in the other. Her daughter would have no problem creating a website for her. Plus, Hannah did have that generous helping of artistic flair.

"All right," Lucy said. "Minimum wage."

"With the chance for a raise?"

"We'll see." Of course, she'd wind up giving her daughter a raise. She was the world's softest touch.

"All right. When is moving day? I want to be there."

Lucy told her and ended the call, then got back to picking out her office furniture. This was going to be a great summer.

A sudden image of Evan in the shower with Pandora invaded her mind. She shoved it away. It *was* going to be a great summer.

Brody had finished his Saturday morning doubles with the group of men he'd been playing with regularly for the last five years. They'd dubbed themselves the Beach Bums but none of them actually were. Whit Gruber was Brody's accountant, Andy Lent owned Beachside Grocery (as well as a seriously cool fishing boat that he often took the guys out on) and Ellis West was the proud owner of the Seafood

Shack. He and Ellis would have been related if Brody and Jenna had gotten married.

Jenna.

Brody was past that now. Okay, working toward being past it.

"What you need is a new woman," his pals kept telling him.

"Yeah, well, I'll get right on that," he'd say.

As soon as he found anyone he wanted to get on it with. Which meant never. He was stuck in the doldrums. But that was better than being blown about on the stormy sea of love.

Anyway, his life was good. He enjoyed summer fishing expeditions, visits from his kids and Saturday morning doubles, which he followed with ice cream at Good Times Ice Cream Parlor. When Nora was working the counter, she always gave him extra-large scoops. After his mid-morning ice-cream fix, he would head to his office.

Another good thing about Saturdays. He loved what he did for a living, loved the negotiating and finessing involved in making deals. Loved helping people find their perfect home, loved picking up the occasional bargain to flip.

And there were still a few bargains left in Moonlight Harbor. Not as many as there once were though. The town was becoming increasingly popular. He had a couple of beachfront lots he was hanging onto. He was confident that in another few years they'd be worth three times what he'd paid for them.

There was no parking to be had in front of Good Times this Saturday, and Brody had to settle for a slot a little ways down. No big deal though. He parked his convertible and strolled past the soap shop and Crafty Just Cuz, on toward Good Times. Next, he'd pass the office space Edgar Morgan had been trying unsuccessfully to rent for the last six months.

Hardly surprising it had continued to stand empty for so long. It was a great location, but Edgar was charging way too much. Brody had tried to tell him but the old coot wouldn't listen.

Except, what was this? A new business moving in.

Brody blinked and came to a sudden halt. The fancy banner in the window of the once-vacant space made him blink. What the…?

COMING SOON. DREAM HOMES REALTY. LET LUCY HOLMES MAKE YOUR DREAMS COME TRUE.

Who the hell was Lucy Holmes and who'd invited her to Moonlight Harbor?

Eight

Competition is good, Brody told himself. Moonlight Harbor was growing. There was room for more than one real estate business.

He frowned. Who was he kidding? He felt like a medieval king whose kingdom had been invaded. This Lucy Holmes person had blown into town and was setting up camp without so much as a courtesy call. Not only that, she'd picked a business name that was a cheap hack of his.

Dream Homes Realty. Could she have gotten any closer to Beach Dreams Realty? People would be bound to confuse the two. Which, of course, would be exactly why she'd done it.

He could envision this invader asking herself, "What name could I use that might piggyback on top of the success of an established business? Use the word *dream*. Yeah, that'll work."

It was a free country. The mysterious Lucy could set up business anywhere she wanted and she could call it whatever she wanted. But she wouldn't be able to compete with Brody. He knew practically everyone in town and his reputation was solid gold.

So, let her go ahead and try to sell the houses listed with Beach Dreams…if she could outwork Brody and his broker, Taylor Marsh. And good luck with beating them to getting listings. Lucy Cheap Imitation Holmes was welcome to whatever crumbs fell from the table. That was all she'd get though, crumbs.

In a way he almost felt sorry for her. She was in for a rude shock. "I hope you've got a backup business plan, lady," he muttered. "You're going to need it."

And that was all the time he could spare to think about Lucy Holmes. He had work to do. He bagged the ice cream and drove to his office.

The office itself said "Welcome to the beach." It was tastefully decorated with prints of seascapes by a popular local artist. The reception desk always sported fresh flowers and was manned by Missy Warren, the organizational wonder who'd been with him since he first opened for business.

Missy looked like everybody's favorite grandma, plump and gray-haired with bifocals hanging from a chain around her neck. She favored pastel blouses and beach-themed jewelry and had a gift for making people feel at home. Half the time Brody would come in and find her oohing over pictures of their kids on their phones. Yep, one big happy family at Beach Dreams Realty. Who better to help you find your perfect home or sell the one you have and trade up to something even better?

Brody and Taylor's desks were right out in plain view—friendly and approachable.

Any client walking in would love to approach Taylor. She was in her thirties and always dressed like the quintessential successful real estate broker, in power suits and sky-high heels, with diamond earrings winking in her ears, a subtle hint that she was successful. When showing land that required walking on sand or through weeds, she switched to sandals and skirts that showed off tanned legs. She kept her nails painted the color of the inside of an oyster shell and her chin-length hair the color of a sandy beach on a summer day. She w,as smart and ambitious and competitive, and she had brought in a lot of business since he hired her a few years earlier.

Brody himself was no slouch. He understood the power of charm and a friendly smile. And patience. Buying and selling property was a big step for most people, and he had no problem hanging in there with his clients until they found the one place that called, "I'm the one."

His mahogany desk sat next to the wall opposite the reception desk. No seascape prints there. Instead, it featured a graceful grouping of framed pictures and letters of thanks from clients he'd helped find their dream home.

To further proclaim his success, he had the requisite collection of real estate sheets in the window, letting one and all see that he had plenty of houses listed for them to choose from. What would Lucy Holmes have to put in her window?

Not that he was bothering to think about her anymore. That would be like a runner with the race already sown up bothering to look back at the pack struggling along behind him.

"Have you seen who's moving into the space by Good Times?" Taylor greeted him as he walked in.

"Yeah, I have," he said.

Taylor frowned. "She's gonna take business from us."

"She's going to try."

"What are you going to do about it?" Missy wanted to know.

"Show her we're the big dogs around here."

Then he'd hire movers to help her when she had to leave town. He could be a gracious winner.

Taylor frowned. "That's a better location," she said, referring to the space Lucy Holmes had taken.

"Only if you can afford it, and I doubt she'll be able to."

Anyway, Brody was perfectly happy with his location. He owned the building that housed Beach Dreams Realty along with several other businesses, including an architect to whom he often referred clients who'd bought land and his accountant and tennis buddy, Whit. He much preferred collecting rent to paying it.

"Don't worry. We'll be fine," he assured Taylor. "There's two of us and one of her."

"We don't know that for sure. She could be bringing down a whole team," Taylor fretted.

"You're not worried about a little healthy competition, are you?" Brody teased.

"No," Taylor said, her voice steely with determination.

"Good. Now, how did things go with the Burwells?"

Taylor beamed. "I got the listing."

"Way to go," Brody said, and gave her a fist bump. "See? We'll be fine."

Yes, they would. Lucy Holmes was paying a fortune to rent that office space and all she was going to do in it was twiddle her thumbs.

He settled at his desk, checked his emails, then pulled out his cell phone and called Jimmy Cook. The guy had been trying to sell his place on his own for the last two months with no luck. Brody had made him an offer that Jimmy had sneered at, sure he could get more for his place. By now he should be coming to his senses and ready to take Brody's offer.

"Jimmy," he said cheerfully when Jimmy answered the phone. "It's Brody. How's it going?"

"Great," Jimmy said. He sounded awfully chipper for a man whose house hadn't sold.

"Good. Hey, I thought I'd check and see if you've reconsidered my offer."

"No need to," Jimmy replied, sounding even more chipper. "We just sold the place."

Huh. Who had Jimmy suckered into buying his place? With the updating it needed, there was no way it could compete with all the new homes on the market. Brody knew this for a fact, since those new homes happened to be listed with Beach Dreams.

"That's great," Brody said. Great for Jimmy, anyway. "Who'd you sell it to?"

"A woman who's new in town."

And didn't know what was available. Probably knew as much about real estate as old Jimmy. Caveat emptor.

"She paid cash," Jimmy added. "Offered us more than we were asking."

Okay, the woman really didn't know what she was doing. But in the process of bumbling around, she was messing things up for people who did, darn it all.

"Well good for you," Brody said. He wasn't so small that he couldn't be happy for people when things worked out for them.

"Yeah, we liked Lucy right away. Cute little number. Divorced. Said she's looking to make a new start."

"Lucy," Brody repeated. "As in Lucy Holmes?" Had to be. There were no other Lucys in Moonlight Harbor that he knew of. The good loser smile slid off his face.

"Yeah, that's it. Have you met her?"

"Not yet," Brody said. They hadn't even met and Lucy Holmes was already a thorn in his side.

He needed coffee.

"I'm making a run to Beans and Books," he announced after ending the call. "You ladies want your usual?" he asked, looking for all the world like a happy man, a man who hadn't just been beaten out of a property he'd been sure would eventually be his.

"If you're buying, sure," said Missy.

"I am."

"Then I'm drinking," she told him.

"Me, too," said Taylor.

"Okay, be back in a few."

Once inside his car and tooling down the street, he dropped his happy mask and stewed over being beaten out by the invader. Of all the towns in all the world, she had to move to his.

It was inevitable that, eventually, another real estate broker would discover the gold mine that was Moonlight Harbor. So, really, what was he getting so stewed up about?

Everything. The name of her company, the fact that she'd beaten him out of the Cook place, the fact that her business had sprung up overnight like a mushroom. The fact that he was feeling...

No way. He was not feeling threatened. He had no reason to. And he refused to. He was the better man, er, person. Broker. He wasn't some loser who didn't know what he was doing.

At least when it came to business. Obviously, when it came to relationships, he hadn't a clue. But that didn't matter much, since he'd decided to steer clear of ever falling for a woman again.

He pulled into Beans and Books as Aaron Baumgarten was pulling out in his hybrid Toyota. Brody gave the town's number one newspaper reporter a wave and Aaron saluted him with his to-go cup.

One other car was in the parking lot—a red Range Rover. He didn't know anyone in town who owned such pricey wheels. Tourist season was almost in full swing so it had to be a weekend visitor.

With lots of money to spend—good for the local economy.

He sauntered into the store and saw the Rover's owner up at the order counter, chatting with Rita. Stylish jeans clung to a great butt, and her honey-colored hair was caught up in the casual wad women called a sloppy bun. It had to be long enough to at least hang to her shoulders. Brody wondered casually what the front of her looked like.

Not that he was interested. He was just curious. Nothing wrong with appreciating God's handiwork, and women were His greatest work of art if you asked Brody.

Rita had said something that made the woman laugh— not some silly giggle, but a genuine happy laugh that made you want to join in.

Rita greeted him as he walked up to the counter. "Hi there, Brody. Here for your usual?" she asked.

"Yeah, and for the team, too."

"Sure," Rita said, and got busy.

The woman she'd been talking to turned, to-go cup in hand, and looked at Brody. The curves in front were as perfect as the ones in back. Her face could have been on the big screen with those lush lips and big blue eyes.

She smiled at him. Oh, wow. That smile was bright enough to power the whole town. He hadn't been so attracted to a woman since Jenna hit town.

Jenna. He quickly shoved all thoughts of her out of his mind.

He needed to shove all thoughts of getting to know this woman out of his mind as well. That would be the smart thing to do. He could tell this would be someone with whom it would be hard to keep a relationship light and easy. And no way did he want to end up on the sea of heartbreak again.

No ring on her left hand. How was it this little doll wasn't taken? He didn't need to know. *Tourist, remember?* he told himself.

It didn't work. Lord help him, he felt like a nail coming near a neodymium magnet. He had to talk to her, had to find out who she was.

"Hi there," he said, flashing a smile of his own.

"Hi," she said right back.

"I see you've found the best place in town to get coffee," he said.

"I have, indeed. I'm discovering there are a lot of best places here."

"That there are. It's a great town," he added, opening the door to offering to show her around. Because…he was an idiot. He couldn't seem to stop himself from asking, "Are you in Moonlight Harbor for a while?"

"I am," she said. "Right now I'm staying at the Driftwood Inn."

It was still hard to hear the Driftwood mentioned. It brought back memories of Jenna's bitterness when he had appeared to be the one who'd inherited the vintage motel and their subsequent breakup.

He ignored the jab to the heart and said, "It's a popular place."

"But that's only temporary," the woman informed him. "I'm moving here."

Brody's smile broadened. For the first time in months, he felt… He wasn't sure what he felt. Hopeful? Like the clouds were finally going to part? Maybe just plain good.

A friendly newcomer with a killer smile and warm laugh could be just what he needed.

Don't go there, warned his gut. *Don't get involved. You'll be sorry.*

"Starting over," she added.

New woman in town. Starting over. His earlier conversation with Jimmy Cook began to flash at the back of his mind like a giant warning sign.

Nah. What were the odds?

"Brody can help you find a house," Rita said. "He owns Beach Dreams Realty." Good old Rita, always helping a fellow Moonlight Harbor business owner.

"Actually, I've already found a house," said the newcomer.

The odds were no longer in his favor. He braced himself.

The beautiful woman with the killer smile and the infectious laugh held out a small hand tipped with pink fingernails. "I'm—"

Don't say it. Please don't say it.

"Lucy Holmes."

Nine

What kind of sick cosmic joke was this? Here was the most interesting woman to hit town since Jenna and she turned out to be Brody's competition.

"Lucy Holmes," he repeated.

"What made you decide to move to Moonlight Harbor?" Rita asked her.

"I wanted to move to a beach somewhere," she answered.

So you had to pick here.

"My sister and I came down a few days ago and checked it out. Everyone was so friendly and the town is so cute. Looks like it's growing," Lucy added. She aimed that super smile at Brody. "You've probably got more business than you can keep up with."

What? Was she taunting him?

"I've been keeping up fine," he informed her, smiling back to show her that her presence in Moonlight Harbor wasn't intimidating.

"Competition is a good thing. In a healthy market people need choices," she pontificated, making him feel like he was back in the classroom. What was she, his professor?

It irritated him but he stayed pleasant. "Oh, I think our market here is already pretty healthy."

Her smile turned teasing. "I hope you're not afraid of a little competition."

She *was* taunting him.

He shrugged to show how completely unaffected he was. "No need to be. I know almost everyone here."

"Did you know the Cooks?"

Yes, serious taunting. He bagged the smile. "You bought their place," he accused. *You little thorn in the foot.*

"News travels fast."

"It's a small town," he said.

"So far," she conceded.

Brody hoped it stayed that way. Once word got out about how great a place was, it seemed the whole world rushed to live there, charging in and changing the vibe. He knew Moonlight Harbor was going to keep growing but he hoped it didn't grow too fast or too big. He hated the thought of it becoming crowded and losing its laid back, friendly atmosphere. A strange attitude for someone who sold houses and benefited from all that growth, but there you had it. He was happy with the market the way it was and he already did plenty of business.

Or he had.

"They didn't list with you?"

Was she asking or pointing that out? Boy, had his first impression of Lucy Holmes been wrong. He did *not* like this woman. And no way was he going to tell her he'd thought about buying the house himself to flip.

"I couldn't convince Jimmy it was in his best interest to go with a professional. By the way, you paid way more than it was worth."

Now she shrugged. "It was way cheaper than anything in Seattle."

"That's part of why people are moving here," Brody told her. "It's still an affordable place to live." *Until people like you come in and drive the prices up to the point that everything inflates and the long-time residents all have to move.*

"Prices are bound to go up," she argued. "This is a good time to invest in real estate here. I can hardly wait to move in and start remodeling."

Okay, rein in the animosity and be magnanimous. "If you need the name of a reliable contractor—" Brody began.

"I'm good," she said airily. "Seth Waters is going to help me and he knows someone."

Seth Waters. Brody forced himself not to grind his teeth.

But so what if Waters was picking up some odd jobs around town? What did it matter? And what did it matter if Lucy Holmes was staying at the Driftwood?

It didn't.

Except for the fact that he felt like he had salt in a wound. First Jenna rejected him, now she'd joined forces with his competition. It didn't seem right.

Shake it off, he told himself. He didn't need to worry about what little competition Lucy Holmes would give him, and he wouldn't let it bother him that Jenna was helping her. And he didn't need to get to know Lucy Holmes any better.

Never mind that friendly smile. The woman was a shark and she would like nothing better than to rip him to shreds. Good luck with that.

Rita had his lattes ready. He took the cardboard carry tray, thanked her, and then said a polite if insincere, "Nice to meet you," To Lucy Holmes. Then couldn't help adding, "Good luck."

She'd need it.

"He's a great guy," Rita said as Brody Green went out the door.

Lucy made no reply to that. She was already forming her own opinion of Brody Green. Yes, he was good-looking—tall, trim, broad-shouldered and blue-eyed, with blond hair that showed off tanned skin, both a sure sign he enjoyed life at the beach. Factor in that wolfish smile and she could see why Rita had looked at him the way she did when he entered the coffee shop. At first sight, Lucy herself had been attracted to the man like a lookie-loo to an open house on a hot property. He was hard to resist.

But she'd seen past that slick facade of his in a hurry when she saw how his smile had changed once he learned who she was. It had been obvious he was threatened by her, a sure sign that he was insecure. And who did that remind her of?

The last thing she needed in her life was another insecure man—or any man!—so fine, let him turn off the charm. And let him feel threatened. He should. Lucy was good at what she did, and she didn't have time for men who were afraid of someone better than them, men who turned into juveniles and acted out. Men were overrated.

She complimented Rita on a great latte, then said goodbye and left. She had a business to launch.

She'd ordered the office furniture she needed online but for the decor she decided to shop local. So latte in hand, she made her way to The Beachcomber, a shop that sold home decor and gift items. There, she found some lovely candles that would make her office smell welcoming, as

well as a seashell-trimmed mirror for the powder room
and a tall vase shaped like a mermaid that she could fill
with silk flowers. At the local art gallery she picked up
a couple of seascape prints by a local artist, along with a
hand-painted sign on weathered wood that said The Beach
is My Happy Place. Perfect.

She'd just loaded her purchases into the back of the
Rover when she got a text from her daughter wanting to
know how things were going with the house.

Great, Lucy texted back. Can hardly wait for you to
see it in person.

Me 2, texted Hannah, ending the text with smiley faces
and hearts.

Hearts and smiles from your daughter. The best. She
sent back some of her own.

G2G. LYSM, Hannah finished.

Love you so much. Lucy smiled and texted back, LYSM2.

Poor Evan. He wasn't getting texts like that from Hannah. She'd stopped speaking to him.

Lucy could almost feel sorry for him. He'd blown it
big time, exchanging the love of his wife and his daughter for an affair with a younger woman who probably only
wanted him for his money. (Of which he only had half as
much now thanks to the divorce.) Yep, a bad bargain, if
you asked Lucy. Not that he had.

And not that she cared.

Okay, maybe a little. You didn't wave goodbye to almost
twenty-five years together and bounce right back. In spite
of those burned pictures and her resolution, she still had
the occasional teary moment when she wished she could
return to when times were good. Or at least to when she
was completely clueless.

But life didn't work that way. There was no rewind. Only forward.

Now she was excited to move forward and fast. Her office was going to be a work of art and her business was going to thrive. She'd have her daughter with her for the summer. She'd make new friends.

She'd probably never have a love life.

Oh, so what!

Hannah was excited about staying at the beach for the summer. Yes! And working for Mom. Probably boring office work but maybe Mom would let her help stage houses or something. And help decorate the new house. At least she was going to get to do her bedroom. She already knew it should be painted light blue, like the sky on a summer day. And there should be some cute sign with a beachy saying on it, like The Beach is My Happy Place.

Her mom in a new house. Sometimes Hannah still couldn't believe her parents really had split. One minute they were all a family and the next, the house Hannah had grown up in was for sale and her dad had a new girlfriend. And her mom was staying with Aunt Darla.

It was all so wrong. Here was Mom, all trusting and happy, while Daddy was out having sex with a woman barely older than his own daughter. Then to move in with her! Hannah wasn't sure she was ever going to speak to her father again. So far he wasn't getting the message. Here was another text, asking her to reconsider staying with him and the homewrecker.

Staying with Mom at the beach 4 sure. Working 4 her. DON'T CALL.

There. That let him know how she felt.

Actually, he already knew how she felt. She'd told him. But he still kept texting and leaving her phone messages, wanting to meet and talk and saying stupid things like, *I'm still your father.*

Yeah, well, he was also a heartless bastard. She should block him.

Her fingers hovered over her cell phone but that was as far as she got. It was always as far as she got.

She tossed aside her phone. She had stuff to do, like study for her last final. And pack her beach clothes.

It wasn't going to be like past summers where she and her friends hung out at the house on Lake Washington and water-skied and lounged around the yard, listening to music and slurping root-beer floats. It could be if she moved in with Daddy. He'd told her he'd bought another lake house, insisted she'd love it. The house, maybe, but not the people in it. Spending the summer with Daddy would be like stabbing Mom in the back. No way was she going to be on his side, not as long as he was with Pandora.

Anyway, the beach would be great. She could hardly wait to see the house Mom bought. And to see Mom. It would be good for Mom to have a shoulder to cry on.

Hannah wouldn't be crying. She was too pissed for tears.

It wasn't going to take long for Lucy's house deal to close. Ah, the beauty of cash offers. Meanwhile, she had a business to organize and an office to set up. She was on hand when her office furniture was delivered—two L-shaped chalked chestnut desks with plenty of room for laptops as well as the requisite storage drawer and a file drawer. They were so pretty! And the furniture she'd picked for the reception area was perfect—white wicker with tan cushions in a seashell print. She'd taken the Keurig from the Anderson-Holmes office—spoils of war—and it would be perfect for making clients coffee and serving it in the mugs she'd ordered. They sported a beach umbrella and the saying Life's Good at the Beach.

It sure was, she thought as the two delivery men assembled the desks and set them where she wanted, flirting as they worked. When they were leaving one of them, a cutie who had to be ten years younger than her, smiled back at her and said, "Any time you need help." Yep, she was getting on with the rest of her life just fine.

The male interest was an ego boost, and it got her thinking about how much she'd both depended on and taken for granted the appreciation of a man, specifically the man who used to be hers. Evan's betrayal had been both a hit to the heart and to her self-esteem. In spite of how much she kept telling herself that what had happened to them was on him and not her, no matter how much she told herself she was still attractive, there were weak moments when she allowed his betrayal to make her feel like less of a woman.

But she wasn't. She was a woman worth wanting. More important, she didn't need to be wanted by anyone to be a woman of worth.

She got to work putting up the sign she'd ordered in her window and hanging her pictures and setting out the rest of the decor. A door at the back of the space led to a small area with a bathroom and a counter and sink and cupboards to use as a break room. An ancient refrigerator hummed away, waiting for her to clean it. That she could do the next day. She also still had to get a table and a couple of chairs but figured she could find those at a thrift shop. She set her coffee maker on the counter and called it good.

Back in the main area, she took pictures of her new office with her cell phone to send to her daughter to put up on the website Hannah was already designing. Then she locked up and drove to the beach for some shots. The dunes, the driftwood, the waves—it was all so picturesque. Who wouldn't want to come live here? And let Lucy Holmes help them find their dream house.

On the way back to the Driftwood, her temporary home away from home, she stopped at Beachside Grocery to pick up some fruit to snack on later. She got sidetracked by a cute collection of beachy dishes and glasses. She was especially attracted to a set of four wine glasses that said Wine in Hand, Toes in Sand. Just what she needed.

There was only the one set left and the fifty-something woman who'd come up next to her reached for it at the same time as she did.

They both drew their hands back, saying, "Sorry."

"I think you were ahead of me," Lucy said.

"Maybe by a second. I don't really need them," the woman told her.

"Me, either, but that shouldn't stop us from getting cute wine glasses, right?"

"It should stop me," the woman said. "It looks like we're going to be moving and I really don't need anything more to pack."

Moving? Music to Lucy's ears.

"Really?" she said. "Where?"

"Icicle Falls."

"That is a fun town," Lucy said.

"My husband's been offered a teaching job there. We love the water but we also love our winter sports."

"If you get a house by the river, you'll still have water," Lucy said.

"It won't be quite the same," the woman said, "but we're ready for a change."

"I might be the very person to help you make that change possible," Lucy told her, and introduced herself. "I just opened an office here. Dream Homes Realty. I specialize in helping people make their dreams come true. And your name is?"

"Glenda Heatherton."

"What a lovely name!" Rule number one of good salesmanship: find something on which to compliment the other person. Not that it was a challenge to compliment this woman on her name. Lucy genuinely liked it.

She also genuinely liked people, so when she paid a compliment she always made sure it was sincere.

"I'd love to meet with both you and your husband," Lucy said.

"Well, Martin was talking to Brody Green."

"Oh." Talking or committed to working with? "Have you signed a listing agreement with him?"

"No. We haven't found a time to get together."

You snooze you lose. "I've got time today. Tell me a little about your house."

"It's a four-bedroom on Duck Lake."

"People love to be on the water," Lucy said. "And lakefront is nice because the houses there don't take the beating the ones right on the beach do. I bet your house is in great condition."

"We do our best to maintain it," Glenda said.

A little dab of humility backed with pride of ownership. Lucy was willing to bet that house was in great condition.

"How about I come by and take a look at it and let's see what we can do to get you to Icicle Falls and that house on the river?"

The woman considered a moment.

"Since Mr. Green isn't able to fit you in," Lucy added.

It was all the nudging Glenda Heatherton needed. She nodded. "Okay."

Lucy checked her phone. "Let's see, it's three thirty now. Why don't I swing by around five with some wine to go with those glasses?"

"That sounds good," Glenda said, and gave Lucy her address.

After learning what kind of wine the Heathertons liked, Lucy said goodbye and then hustled on over to the liquor section to make her selection. She picked a pricey bottle to convey to the Heathertons that she valued their business.

After purchasing the wine, she stopped in at Sunbaked, the bakery she'd discovered recently. In addition to the best bear claws on the planet, it also offered to-die-for oatmeal M&M cookies. Between the bakery and Cindy's Candies plus the cookies Jenna doled out at the Driftwood, Lucy was going to turn into a beach ball with legs.

She got to the bakery in time to snag the last half dozen cookies, which would be enough to leave with the Heathertons. The bakery was obviously a popular destination for locals, and locals always knew the best places to go. Knowing the best place for baked goods was dangerous knowledge when you were trying to watch what you ate. It was a good thing the local community club had a gym.

Promptly at five o'clock she was knocking on the door of the Heatherton place—a rustic two-story house with stone trim, clean lined, yet traditional. It had a front lawn, which would make it great for a family.

Glenda opened the door and Lucy held up the bottle. "Is it wine o'clock?"

"I think it is," Glenda said.

"I thought you might also enjoy some cookies," Lucy said as she handed over the bottle. She'd taken them out of the bag and placed them on a fish-shaped plate she'd picked up at the Beachcomber, which gave the illusion of the treats being home-baked.

"Those look delicious," Glenda said, eyeing them.

"They are," Lucy assured her as she followed her into the living room.

It was spacious and came complete with a stone fireplace. It was open concept and Lucy could see the deck and, beyond it, the lake framed by picture windows.

"You have a lovely view," she said as she followed Glenda to the kitchen.

"We like it," Glenda replied.

Lucy set the plate of cookies on the kitchen island and continued her visual sweep of the first floor. Kitchen with updated appliances, hardwood floor. Nice, nice.

Glenda's husband appeared, a trim man with a head shaved in acceptance of a vanishing hairline.

"This must be your husband, the teacher," Lucy said, moving forward to shake his hand.

"Martin," he said.

As Lucy shook his outstretched hand, she covered it with her other hand to convey friendship in addition to a possible business relationship. "You have a lovely house. I can tell you've worked hard to keep it up."

He smiled at that. "Yep. Been here almost ten years. Love the place."

"I'm sure you'll want whoever buys it to love it as much as you do," Lucy said.

He nodded.

"I can find that person for you."

"I think my wife told you, we have been talking to Brody Green," he said.

"Yes, and it's a shame he hasn't been able to fit you in. I imagine he's a very busy man." Once again, the implication being that he was, obviously, too busy for them. He had to be if he couldn't find the time to move on a property with such potential for a sale. "I love your view," she said, moving to the sliding glass door. "Can you show me your deck? It looks perfect for sitting outside, enjoying the sunset."

They moved onto the deck, which she learned Martin had added on himself, then crossed the lawn to check out the dock. A small boat was moored next to it.

"I bet you can fish in this lake," Lucy said.

"Oh, yeah. Good fishing."

"That's always a nice selling point."

Back inside the house, the Heathertons showed her the bedrooms—three upstairs and one down, as well as the bathrooms. Everything was tastefully decorated and fairly clutter-free.

"This house will show well," Lucy predicted. "I wouldn't be surprised if we got multiple offers."

Now she had Martin's interest. "Really?"

"Oh, yes. I believe in aggressive marketing. And really, right now it's a seller's market so you are in the driver's seat."

The Heathertons exchanged smiles and Lucy beamed at them both. A glass of wine and some chatting, a discussion of how much she was sure they could get for their house and the Heathertons were signing an exclusive listing agreement with her.

"I'll get going on this right away," she promised as they walked her to the door. "Meanwhile, enjoy those cookies."

"Oh, we will," Glenda said.

Her first listing in Moonlight Harbor. It was all Lucy could do not to skip to the Rover. She'd do right by the Heathertons and make sure they got top dollar for their place. She already foresaw a bidding war.

She was driving away when she passed a convertible, cruising up from the opposite direction. The top was down and it was easy to see who the driver was—Brody Green, her competition. He was in for a not-so-pleasant surprise.

But it was one he had coming. Being the only game in town, he'd obviously gotten complacent and lazy. Lazy realtors didn't deserve loyalty.

She smiled, feeling rather smug. Brody Green had no idea how formidable of a competitor she could be. By the time he realized what had hit him, he'd be down for the count.

Brody's brows pulled together at the sight of the Range Rover driving away. The same Range Rover he'd seen in the Beans and Books parking lot. What had Lucy Holmes been doing here? She just got to town. She couldn't know the Heathertons.

He parked his car, got out and walked up the drive to the front door, a feeling of foreboding trotting at his heels.

Ten

Martin Heatherton answered the door and, at the sight of Brody, looked instantly guilty. Brody knew before Martin even said anything. Lucy Holmes had pounced on the Heathertons and stolen the listing for their house. And they'd aided and abetted her.

It was hardly good business to accuse Martin of what they both knew he'd done, so Brody offered a friendly smile and a handshake. "Good to see you, Martin. I should have called before I came, but I was in the neighborhood and thought I'd stop by."

"Uh, sure," Martin said. "Come on in. Glenda," he said to his wife as he ushered Brody into the living room, "Brody Green's here." As if she couldn't see for herself since she was sitting right there on the couch.

She choked on the wine she'd been drinking, set down the glass and managed a nervous, "Hi, Brody."

"I caught you guys trying to relax," Brody said. "Sorry."

"No worries," Martin said. "Would you like a glass of wine?"

"Sure," Brody said, and seated himself in a chair opposite the couch. "How are you doing? Still thinking about moving to Icicle Falls?"

Glenda took a quick swallow of wine. "Yes. Martin's decided to take the job offer." She shot an uneasy glance in her husband's direction, probably hoping he'd rescue her from an awkward moment.

In cases like this, there was no rescuing. You had to wade through it.

Brody kept his smile casual. "I assume you're going to put your place up for sale, then?"

Martin cleared his throat. "About that."

Here it came. Brody willed his facial muscles not to scowl.

"We just now listed the house with Lucy Holmes from Dream Homes Realty."

Et tu, Brute? First the Cooks, now the Heathertons. Where was people's loyalty these days?

"You and I had talked," Brody reminded Martin.

In spite of Brody's easy tone of voice, Martin handed him a glass of wine and stepped back quickly as if Brody might hit him. "I hadn't heard from you."

It was true. Brody had gotten busy with some other clients and pursuing the house he'd wanted to flip and he'd fumbled the ball. He had no one to blame but himself.

And Lucy Holmes, the poacher.

Granted, Brody and Martin had nothing in writing. Only a gentlemen's agreement that once the Heathertons made a definite decision to move that Brody would be the one they called to help them sell their place. Of course, he'd be the one. He'd been the only game in town. Until now.

Glenda picked up a plate of cookies from the coffee table and held it out like a peace offering. "Have a cookie."

Brody had lost his appetite. "No thanks. But they look good."

"Lucy brought them," Glenda said. Her eyes flew wide as she realized what she'd said and her cheeks turned pink.

"And the wine," put in her husband, as if to say, *She made an effort, bro.*

Brody set his glass on the coffee table.

"She said you could still work on selling the place," Glenda added earnestly.

He could and he sure would. No way was he going to let Lucy Holmes get both the listing and the selling commission on this.

"I can. And I'll bring you a qualified buyer," he promised. He'd find one if he had to beat every bush between Moonlight Harbor and Seattle.

"We'll take the best offer," Martin warned, and Brody knew it was game on.

"You should," he said.

Glenda looked gratefully at him. "Thanks for being so understanding."

"No problem," Brody lied.

But, of course, it was a problem. He hated getting beat out and this was the second time it had happened. Granted, he could have offered the Cooks their asking price and their house would have been his.

The Heathertons were another story. Yes, he should have kept closer tabs on them, but he still couldn't help feeling a little betrayed. Even though he and Martin weren't close friends they'd seen each other around the golf club, even played in a couple of tournaments together, so they weren't exactly strangers. And here, when it came time to look for a real estate expert, instead of going with Brody, Martin had turned to Lucy Holmes, the cookie queen.

"You need to find another pond to fish in, lady," he growled as he started his car. Moonlight Harbor wasn't going to be big enough for the two of them and the sooner she figured that out, the better it would be for her.

Sadly, Lucy Holmes didn't seem to be showing any sign of figuring that out. The invader even showed up to the Moonlight Harbor Chamber of Commerce lunch meeting at Sandy's restaurant. She sashayed in, wearing a full-skirted sundress that showed off a fine pair of legs, heels and a coral sweater, and started charming people the minute she walked into the room.

Heck, if he weren't so irritated, he'd have been charmed. She spread that smile of hers like a net and caught everyone she approached in it. He watched as she patted Ellis West's arm with a delicate hand tipped with pink fingernails as she was talking to him. Ellis smiled on her like a doting father.

And good grief, now she talking with Jenna as if they were old friends. That felt all wrong. Brody wasn't sure why, but it did.

She continued to work the crowd, stopping for a word here, a friendly touch to the arm there. Brody watched her in action and forgot to smile. This was his turf. He was president of the chamber, for crying out loud, and here was Lucy Holmes, practically campaigning for votes. He really didn't like this woman.

Don't be a shit, he told himself, and forced a smile when she finally walked up to where he stood, half listening to Kiki Strom, who was raving about her new great grandbaby.

"We meet again," Lucy greeted him. Then, before he could say anything, she turned to Kiki and introduced herself. "I love your hair," she said.

Kiki had been playing with putting all kinds of interesting colors on what had once been white hair thanks to Moira King over at Waves Hair Salon. Lately, she'd been wearing something that looked like a mix of pink and lavender all swirled together. Kiki may have been a senior citizen but she never let that stop her from being trendy. She was a cross between everyone's grandma and Betsy Johnson, that lady designer Brody's first wife had liked so much. Kiki had always been a favorite of Brody's and he of hers. Now, here was Lucy Holmes, horning in.

And he was thinking like a shit again.

"Thanks," Kiki said. "Moira over at Waves does amazing things with color."

"It sure looks like it," Lucy said. "I'll have to get over there and introduce myself."

In case she wants to buy a house, Brody thought in disgust. Lucy Holmes was so easy to see through.

She turned that smile of hers on him, and his heart rate picked up. Why couldn't this woman have been an interior decorator or house-stager, soap-maker, firefighter—anything but what she was? He'd known she was trouble the minute he met her and he'd been right.

"Jenna told me about your chamber of commerce meeting," she informed him. "I'm glad I came. Everyone is so kind and welcoming."

He wasn't feeling kind or welcoming in spite of the fact that the very sight of Lucy Holmes made him salivate like one of Pavlov's dogs. How was it that someone could simultaneously repel and attract you?

"We have a great bunch of business owners here," he said, and put a proprietorial hand on Kiki's shoulder.

"Yes, you do. I'm looking forward to being part of the community."

"What's your business?" Kiki asked politely.

"I own Dream Homes Realty," Lucy said, beaming at her.

"Dream Homes," Kiki repeated and shot a glance at Brody.

"Similar to Beach Dreams," he said, and shrugged as if it didn't matter.

"Maybe a little," Lucy conceded. "But people will be able to tell the difference."

Was she taunting him again? It sure sounded like it. "The difference?"

"I'm sure we both have our own style," she said.

"We probably do," he agreed. "Hard coming in and competing with an established business," he couldn't help adding. Fair warning. "People usually go with a name they know."

"Like the Heathertons?" she shot back, and raised an eyebrow.

Smack talk. His stretched out his fingers, willing his hands not to clench into fists. *Don't let her get to you.*

He knew how to raise an eyebrow, also, and he did. "Interesting how you bribed them to forget they'd even talked to me."

"Easy enough, considering how you seemed to have forgotten you'd talked to them," she retorted.

"If you two will excuse me," Kiki said, and hurried away.

"That was pretty low," Brody said to Lucy, his voice practically a hiss. Yep, not letting her get to him.

"You had nothing on paper."

"A handshake has always been enough," he retorted.

"Did you shake hands?"

There'd been no reason to strong arm the Heathertons.

He hadn't seen the need to rush or pressure them. And when he'd first talked to Martin, there'd been no such thing as Dream Homes Realty.

He frowned at Lucy the Poacher. "We talked."

"Uh-huh," she said with a smirk. "All talk and no action."

Brody considered himself a people person. He liked people, and he got along fine with most people. But he was not going to get along with Lucy Holmes. She was pushy, sneaky and conceited, just the kind of person he couldn't stand.

"Look, let me give you some good advice. Flip that house you just bought and then take the money and move, find a different market. This one's all sewed up."

"I can see that."

Lady, you are in for a rude awakening. "Look, nothing personal, but you're out of your league here."

There went the eyebrow again. "Oh, really?"

"Yes, really."

She gave a little snort. "Do you know where I was selling houses before I moved here? Seattle, Bellevue, Mercer Island. I've made more multi-million-dollar deals than you've ever wished to make."

Okay, now she was really pissing him off. "Yeah? Then why aren't you there, showing those multi-million-dollar houses?"

Her smile turned into a flat line and those big eyes narrowed. "I worked with someone like you—conceited, self-absorbed, cocky."

"Sounds like my kind of guy. What happened to him? Did you eat him for breakfast?"

"I divorced him," she snapped, then turned her back on Brody and moved to the far end of the room.

Whoa, there was an interesting fact. So, Lucy Holmes had a chip on her shoulder. No, more like a two-by-four, probably put there by the ex. He got that. But if she'd been so successful back in Seattle, why hadn't she stayed to make *his* life miserable? What was she doing here? Even more important, what would it take to make her leave?

Brody Green was a conceited, insecure oaf who had obviously been king of the hill for too long. Now he thought he owned the hill. They'd just see how much he owned now that Lucy was here.

She settled in at the table between Cynthia Redmond of Cindy's Candies and Jenna Jones, happy to be as far away as she could get from where Brody was sitting down next to a dark-haired woman wearing glasses. The woman was a svelte Audrey Hepburn–type with plenty of style, probably a model once upon a time. Judging from the way she looked at Brody, Lucy saw it was obvious she wouldn't mind modeling lingerie for him.

She was willing to bet that Brody Green was a player. He'd probably dated every woman in this town. He was good-looking enough to attract every woman in town.

So what if he was good-looking? Who cared? That hot exterior and facade of charm hid the human equivalent of dry rot. Brody Green was the type of man any woman with a brain would steer clear of, and that was exactly what Lucy intended to do.

Not only was she going to steer clear of him, she was going to drive him out of business and out of town. They'd see who was out of whose league.

"It looks like you had a chance to talk to Brody," Jenna said.

"I've had a couple of chances now," Lucy replied lightly.

"He's a great guy," put in Cindy.

"Yes, just ask him," Lucy muttered.

Jenna chuckled. "He is definitely aware of his good looks."

And Lucy knew you couldn't trust a man like that. Heck, you couldn't trust any man.

Their server was starting to take orders, so conversation shifted from Brody Green to what was on the menu.

"The shrimp Louie here is excellent," Cindy told her. "It comes with their garlic cheese bread, and that's to die for."

"Then I'll have to have it," said Lucy. Although her encounter with Brody had left her with a sour stomach.

Oh, no. She wasn't going to let the likes of him ruin her appetite or this luncheon. When the food came, she dug right in.

Cindy was right. The garlic cheese bread was to die for. And the salad was good. And why did she keep sneaking glances down the table at Brody Green? Ugh.

Halfway through lunch, he started the meeting, welcoming everyone.

"Don't forget our visitor," someone reminded him.

There came the fake charm and the smile, but Lucy could tell that smile hadn't made it to his eyes.

"Oh, yes," he said as if neglecting to acknowledge her had been nothing more than a forgetful moment. "Everyone, welcome Lucy Holmes, who's just moved here and is setting up business. I'm sure you've all had a chance to talk to her and learn about it. Now, speaking of business, we should probably get our meeting started. If we could have our secretary read the minutes from the last meeting."

So, no mention of her company's name. The skunk. Yep, Brody Green was the epitome of insecurity. Well, if he was feeling insecure now, just wait 'til she was done with him.

Eleven

The first Friday in June found Hannah on the road, heading for Moonlight Harbor to help her mother move into her new house, after which she'd return to school for finals. She had a Starbucks iced chai in the cupholder and BTS serenading her via Spotify.

Mom and Aunt Darla had taken her and her cousins to the coastal town when they were kids but she didn't remember much about it except for that cool souvenir shop with the entrance shaped like a shark's mouth. She hoped there were things to do there. And people her age.

Especially cute guys. She was still feeling salty over her breakup with the shit boyfriend but her grandma always said everything happens for a reason. So maybe the reason they broke up was because someone better was waiting right around the corner. Right in Moonlight Harbor. You never knew.

The trip down took forever, but at last she drove through the entrance to town with its two white Stonehenge rock walls rising up on both sides. She passed all kinds of shops and stores and restaurants. Oooh and a family of deer grazing on the grass meridian. Sooo cute!

She pulled over and took a picture on her phone to post on Instagram, then drove on. There was the funny store with the shark's mouth. A couple of kids stood in the doorway with their mom, pretending to be devoured while their dad took a picture.

The sweet sight of the happy family turned her sour. That had been her and her parents. Until Daddy cheated on Mom and broke her heart.

Not that Mom ever let on that her heart was broken, but Hannah knew it was. How could it not be?

She'd help her mom heal, keep her distracted with working on the new place. In fact, Hannah had an idea she hadn't yet shared with her mother. Her girlfriends all thought it was a great one.

"You could become so famous," her friend Desirae had told her.

So could Mom. And wouldn't that serve Daddy right if she did!

Hannah could hardly wait to see the place. Mom was moving in the very next day but she'd promised to take Hannah over to check it out beforehand.

Not much farther past the souvenir shop, Hannah found the Driftwood Inn, where her mother was staying. It was no Hilton, but it was cute in a retro sort of way. She spotted the pool as she pulled into the parking lot. It was a far cry from the resort pools she'd played in when her family went on vacations, but what could you expect? This wasn't exactly Hawaii.

She parked and knocked on the door of the room Mom said she was staying in. It opened a minute later and there stood her mother, wearing jeans, sandals and a cold shoulder chain strap black top and a big smile.

To look at her you'd never know she was old, and she

sure didn't look like a woman with a broken heart. In some ways that seemed a little wrong. Shouldn't her eyes be red from crying? Shouldn't she look even a little sad? She and Daddy had been married forever. And Daddy was with a younger woman now, a woman only six years older than Hannah for heaven's sake.

"You made it," Mom said, all chipper and happy, and gave Hannah a hug. "Come on in."

Hannah came in and looked around. The room was cute, decorated all beachy, with a couple of framed beach photos hanging on one wall, lamps with glass bases filled with seashells sitting on the nightstands, but it was small. It had two single beds—where was the king?—a small stand holding a microwave and coffee maker, and a dresser with a TV sitting on it. It was half the size of the room her parents always put her in when they'd vacationed.

"This is where you've been staying?" she couldn't help asking.

Mom and Dad made a butt-load of money and they had to have sold the house for another butt-load. Hannah had seen a fancier place when she first came into town. Why wasn't Mom staying there?

Mom shrugged. "It's fine. This is where I stayed with Aunt Darla."

It looked like the kind of place Aunt Darla would pick. Daddy used to joke that pennies saw Aunt Darla and Uncle Orren coming and ran away before they could get pinched to death.

Not that Hannah cared what Daddy said about anything.

"And the owner is really nice," Mom continued. "They bake cookies for us every day."

"Cookies?" Okay, there was a plus.

"We can grab one on our way out," Mom said. "I thought you'd like to see the house before we get something to eat."

"For sure," Hannah said.

"Let's bring in what you need for tonight and then we can get going."

Mom was so happy she was almost manic. It was like they were getting ready for a party or something. Of course, she was moving into a new house so it would be weird if she weren't excited. And it was good that she was doing well, but this well? How could she be so happy when Daddy had ruined her life?

She was hiding her heartbreak, of course. Putting on a good face for her daughter.

They unloaded Hannah's backpack, then stopped by the motel office where Mom introduced Hannah to the woman who owned it.

"Welcome to Moonlight Harbor," Jenna Waters said to Hannah. "How about a lavender sugar cookie? My daughter made them."

That sounded gross. Hannah took one just to be polite.

"They are amazing. I had one this morning," Mom told her.

Wow! They actually were.

"Feel free to have another," Jenna said to Mom.

"I'd better pass. You're turning me into a sugar addict," Mom said with a smile. You'd have thought she was on vacation.

"Uh, Mom, are you okay?" Hannah ventured once they were in the Rover and on the way to the house.

Her mother looked puzzled. "Yes. Why shouldn't I be?"

Okay, she was in denial. "Because Daddy broke your heart."

"Yes, he did," Mom admitted.

"I thought you'd be more…depressed."

"Darling, a girl can't cry forever. Your father's moving on. I am, too."

"But you were together for so long."

Mom nodded, and her expression turned sober. "Almost half my life."

Now she was alone, left behind. Mom was still a pretty woman, and so sweet. It didn't seem right. How could Daddy have done this to her?

"That's so sad," Hannah said. Just thinking about how her father had turned life upside down for both her mother and her brought up the tears.

"Sad things happen," Mom said. "But so do good things, like us spending the summer together at the beach. Life's too short to waste it thinking about the bad. I'd rather focus on the good. Wouldn't you?"

Hannah shrugged. Yeah, she would. But it seemed wrong that her mother could so easily forget what her father had done, and she said as much.

"You don't forget," Mom said softly, "but you don't dwell on it. The only place you need a rearview mirror is in your car."

They turned off the main road and drove over a little bridge spanning one of the canals her mother had told her about.

"They call this the Grand Canal," Mom said. "Funny, when your aunt and I came down here with you kids, we had no idea any of this existed. We thought all there was to the town was the beach and the town center with the shops and motels."

"That is so lit," Hannah said, looking at the houses lined along the canal. She could see some people sitting on the deck of one nearby, enjoying drinks. Farther down someone was on the water, kayaking.

"We are gonna get paddleboards, right?" she said to her mother.

"Yes," Mom said. "And the owners left behind their kayaks for us." They drove farther on and turned down a couple of streets, and a moment later Mom stopped the car and pointed to her future home. "This is it."

That was it? You could have put that plus the house next door to it inside the one Hannah had grown up in.

"It needs work but when it's finished, it will be a gem," Mom said.

"A tiny gem," Hannah muttered.

"I don't need to rattle around in a big old house," Mom said.

Because she was all by herself. *Poor Mom.*

"Don't you miss our old house?" Hannah asked as they went up the walk.

"I liked that house," Mom said, "but it was for a different time. This is the perfect one for now. I intend to make a lot of happy memories here."

"I'll help you," Hannah said, smiling at her, and Mom reached out and gave her hand a squeeze.

They could have fun in this house. Hannah would make friends and invite them over, paddleboard on the canal. She and Mom could watch movies. Launch the new project. It would be great. What more did they need?

Daddy.

Nope, he was out of the picture now. Maybe Mom would find somebody here at the beach. You never knew.

The inside of the place looked like a grandma house, especially the kitchen. "How old is that stove?" Hannah asked, eyeing the thing. "Does it even work?"

"Of course, it does. And it's not that old. But don't worry. I'm replacing it. And the fridge as well."

"And the cabinets and counters, I hope," Hannah said, wrinkling her nose.

"Yes, it will all get upgraded."

She opened the sliding glass door and led Hannah out onto the deck. The deck had a hot tub. Then there was the dock and the canal. Two kayaks sat on the bank.

No ski boat though. This wasn't Lake Washington, that was for sure.

"I'll have paddleboards here by the time you're done with finals," Mom promised.

"That will be good," Hannah said, deciding it would be best not to mention the big lake, big dock and fast boat they'd once had. That was rearview-mirror stuff and Mom wouldn't appreciate it.

"And you can help me get the office organized," Mom said.

Booooring.

"I'm going to meet with a contractor soon who will help me remodel the house," Mom said as they walked back to the Ranger. "I've got some ideas for the kitchen cabinets and counters and I've narrowed the choices down to two for flooring. If you want, you can help me decide."

"Just like on a HGTV show," Hannah said. She and Mom had watched more than a few of those together. Hannah had no desire to sell real estate like her parents did— very long hours and intense people—but she loved houses, and she could envision herself staging homes, becoming a HGTV house-flipping star, even. Like Christina in *Christina on the Coast.*

Maybe now was the time to present the idea that had dropped into Hannah's brain. She studied her mother as she pulled the Ranger away from the curb. Mom had a great personality, and she knew a ton about houses. Hannah was young and cute. (Not bragging, just sayin'.) She looked a lot like Mom had when she was young except her hair was lighter and she had a fairy tattooed on her shoulder. Together, they could make a pretty good impression on two different generations. Mom was buying a house to renovate. Hannah was down for the summer to help her. Mom and Hannah, together at the beach. A mother–daughter project. Turning a ho-hum house into a dream home and creating a dream life, too. There was a ton of inspiration in that.

And inspiration was what people searched for online. There were already a lot of amazing influencers out there, like René Daniella and Sazan Hendrix, inspiring people with pictures of great products they'd found to make their homes and themselves beautiful. But there was always room for one more if you came up with something fresh. Hannah was sure she could do that.

Influencers were the new celebrities. In addition to having a dedicated website, they set up their own YouTube channels and Instagram accounts. People followed them just to see how they organized a pantry or to enjoy pictures they posted from some exotic trip. Once an influencer got enough followers, she got free products and then sponsors, and actually made money. In some cases, big money. The whole influencer thing was a woman-dominated, growing industry, and Hannah felt sure that she could succeed at becoming an influencer.

She just had to convince Mom that her idea was a good one. And that she was capable of pulling it off. Sometimes Mom still thought of her as a child.

Well, okay, so she'd never worked much, except for

babysitting the neighbor kids when she was younger. But she wasn't lazy. She'd always worked hard in school and got good grades. She was smart. She could do this. She'd already gotten a book that told her how.

"Mom, we should document this."

"Document what?" her mother asked.

"Reno-ing the house."

Mom shot a quick glance her way, eyebrow cocked. "Why would we do that?"

"Because it would be awesome."

Mom said nothing. Okay, not the best argument in her favor.

"We could get a ton of followers on Instagram, have our own YouTube channel and make money. You could be like Joanna Gaines."

Still nothing.

"It would be good for your business, give you more of an online presence."

Mom looked thoughtful.

"Daddy would be so jealous."

The corners of Mom's lips lifted the tiniest bit. *Ha! Success.* Mom might not have been looking back but looking sideways and flipping off Dad was another thing altogether.

"You're just as smart as those house experts on HGTV," Hannah continued. "And you have just as much style."

"Well, I don't know about that," Mom said, but Hannah could tell from the way she said it that she was already picturing herself with her own TV show, probably envisioning Daddy watching it with tears in his eyes.

"It would be fun," Hannah pressed. "And it would be a great learning experience, for both of us."

Mom shook her head. "Those people all have film crews."

"Big deal. I've got a cell phone. That's all you need for an Insta account." Of course, as they got bigger and better... She decided not to mention that just yet.

"Darling, you don't get famous putting pictures up on Instagram."

Little did her mother know. "It's not about getting famous exactly," Hannah said, although in a way it was. "It's about sharing ideas and inspiring people. And you can get a following. You for sure can on YouTube. Visibility is so important, and these days you need a strong online presence. You know that. Anyway, why not try something and see if anything happens?"

"I guess, if you want to take some pictures—"

"And reels."

"And reels. You can."

"Yaas." This was going to be great.

"But remember, that's not what I'm hiring you for. You have to work in the office and do my social media."

What did she think Hannah was talking about? "It'll all go hand in hand," Hannah assured her. "And everything we do is that much more exposure for the business. You'll have so many people wanting you to find them houses, you won't be able to keep up."

Mom gave one of those tolerant mother smiles that Hannah had come to know so well, but Hannah knew she was hooked on the idea. It was a done deal. Now she'd just have to prove that it could be more than an idea.

Mom wanted to take Hannah to a fancy restaurant for dinner, but Hannah was dying to try the funny fast-food fish place next to the Driftwood Inn. Who wouldn't want to eat at a Seafood Shack with a giant wooden razor clam on its roof?

Of course, she took pictures, including a selfie of Mom

and her in front of the place with Mr. Clam in the background. It would be a perfect Insta intro to their adventure.

After they'd eaten most of their fish and chips, they went to the beach and she recorded a reel of Mom feeding the gulls, throwing out bits of fish and fries. Which was great, because once the birds caught on and came for her, she freaked out, threw the carton with the last of her food in the air and ran for it.

"Don't worry, Mom, I'll clean up your mess," Hannah called, getting that recorded as well. Then she turned the phone on herself and added, "I bet I'll have to clean up a lot of Mom's messes this summer." Perfect way to end the reel.

Mom frowned when Hannah showed her. "Wait a minute. You're going to put that up for people to see?"

"Sure. You want people to connect with you."

"As a real estate broker, not a clown."

"You don't look like a clown. You look human. And cute. People will love this. Everyone loves Lucy," she added.

"Ha ha," Mom said, not amused. "That was a TV Lucy who was funny on purpose."

"And you're being funny without even trying," Hannah said.

"Making a fool of myself," Mom said with a frown.

"Trust me, people are going to love you, just like I do," Hannah said, and hooked an arm through her mother's.

Mom shook her head and gave a reluctant smile. "You flatterer, you."

"It's true. Everybody loves you."

Everybody except Daddy.

Mom must have had the same thought because she suddenly didn't look so happy.

But she covered it up quickly, saying, "Come on. Let's

go see if we can find some episodes of *Flip or Flop* to watch on TV."

"Great. It will inspire us."

"Let's get a few things clear," Mom said as they made their way back to the Rover. "We are going to have some serious segments on this YouTube channel you're proposing and some lovely posts on Instagram. If you're hoping to turn this into *The Real Ex-Wives of Moonlight Harbor*, I'm pulling the plug right now."

"Don't worry."

"Nothing of me goes up without my permission. I need to stay professional."

"Of course," Hannah said, and decided not to ask if the deal they'd just made included the reel she'd shot of Mom and the seagulls. Better to ask forgiveness than permission.

The rest of the night passed happily. Mom had bought chocolate-dipped Oreos and saltwater taffy from the town's candy store, and between the sweets and the microwave popcorn she'd gotten as well as pop from the vending machine outside, they had plenty of treats to eat as they did their part to keep the HGTV channel in business. It was a little like having a mother–daughter slumber party, and the small room felt more like a cozy cocoon than a room in a low-budget motel.

After stopping at the motel office for a cookie (chocolate chip) the next morning, Hannah got why Mom had wanted to stay at the Driftwood. Jenna Waters was so friendly it was more like staying with a friend than at a motel. She insisted Hannah take an extra cookie for the road.

"She's really nice," Hannah said as she and her mother crossed the parking lot.

"She is," Mom said. "Her husband's friend is the contractor who's going to take care of my remodel."

"So you'll have your own team, just like in *Flip or Flop*."

"Except I'm not going to flip this place."

"You could and get something bigger."

"Bigger isn't always better," Mom said.

"Neither is smaller," Hannah argued, remembering how awesome their old house had been. They'd even had a media room that sat twelve in super comfy theater seats.

Mom gnawed on her lower lip a moment, a sure sign she was searching for the right words. It took a couple of minutes for her to find them.

"It's funny how many things you think you need that you really don't. I don't need as much as I once thought I did."

"Yeah, but don't you miss the old house at all? It was awesome."

"Was it the house that was awesome or the good times we had in it?" Mom countered.

"Uh. Both?"

"I know you and your friends enjoyed all those fancy trappings, but fancy trappings aren't everything, and without those relationships, those people to share them with, they don't mean much."

"So you don't miss the house."

Mom shook her head. "Not really. I miss the life we lived in it, miss us all being together. That's what a home really is. It's the setting for a family. The people are what make a place special. We made some lovely memories in that house. We'll make new ones in this house. Right?"

"Right," Hannah agreed. Mom really was a wise woman.

But Hannah was still going to miss their house on the lake and that speedboat.

Mom had promised her breakfast on the beach, so she bought them cinnamon rolls at a cute little bakery surrounded by cement seagulls and driftwood and painted bright yellow outside. Then they did a drive through at a coffee shop called Beans and Books.

As they were driving out, a man in a convertible pulled into the parking lot. He was her mother's age and pretty good-looking for an older guy. So, there were men down here. Maybe Mom would find somebody.

Hannah looked her mother's way to see if Mom was checking him out. Too soon after breaking up with Daddy, probably.

She was surprised to see her mother press her lips together like she was trying to digest something sour. "Do you know him?" Hannah asked.

"Not really," Mom said, then quickly moved on to new conversational territory. "We should probably stay in the car to eat. It's not very warm yet."

It suddenly wasn't very warm in the car, either. What the heck? Hannah knew better than to ask. When Mom didn't want to talk about something, the talking didn't happen.

Just the sight of Brody Green was enough to make Lucy lose her appetite.

But not for long. This was going to be a great day and she refused to let the sight of that irritating man put her in a bad mood. She and Hannah finished their breakfast, parking at the edge of the shore, watching the waves come in, then, after getting a text from Darla to say they had hit town, Lucy drove to her new home to meet them.

They arrived there just before Darla and Orren pulled up with a U-Haul loaded with Lucy's things, along with the retro white-and-chrome kitchen set Darla had found for her at a garage sale and Hannah's bedroom set. (Lucy had a new one coming. No way was she sleeping in the bed she'd shared with the cheater.)

Hannah insisted on taking pictures for Instagram, of the house and the whole unloading process, including shooting a reel, which caught Lucy tripping over the front porch step carrying a box of sheets and blankets. She went flying, landing bottom end up.

"You okay?" Orren asked, helping her to her feet.

"I'm fine," she said, brushing off her throbbing knees.

Her deviant daughter giggled and showed her the moment captured on her phone. *Ugh.*

"Delete that," Lucy commanded.

"No way," Hannah said, and predicted that everyone in Insta-Land was going to love it. It made Mom so human and adorable.

"Creative control," Lucy reminded her and Hannah frowned and deleted the embarrassing moment.

A man who looked like he was pushing ninety came over from next door and offered to help bring in the few things they had left, but Lucy assured him they had it under control.

"That's so sweet of you to offer," she said to him.

"Gotta help the ladies," he replied, and introduced himself as Frances Sullivan. "Here, let me get that for you," he said, taking a box of pots from her.

There was nothing to do but thank him and watch as he staggered up the walk with it. Everyone needed a purpose. And, unlike her, he managed not to trip.

Mr. Sullivan, it turned out, was a widower, and Lucy suspected he would probably be over a lot. That would be okay because everyone needed friends and a place to belong.

Lucy's other neighbor, Bonnie, stopped by to welcome her to the neighborhood, bringing chocolates from Cindy's Candies shaped like seashells along with a plate of brownies. "From a mix," she confessed, and Lucy assured her brownies from a mix would be lovely. Nobody made brownies like the ones her sister made from scratch but Bonnie didn't need to know that.

"We've just ordered pizza. Stay and have a slice," Lucy urged.

"No. You're trying to get settled," Bonnie protested.

"There's plenty," Lucy assured her. "If you don't mind a shortage of chairs. I'm going to be doing some renovating, so I don't have much furniture at the moment."

"Another time," Bonnie said. "Meanwhile, if you need a place to sit, you're always welcome to come on over to my place."

"Thanks. I'll remember that," Lucy said. Bonnie seemed like someone she would enjoy hanging out with. Hopefully, they'd get a chance to get to know each other better.

Mr. Sullivan didn't stay for pizza, either. "Acid reflux," he explained. But he was happy to take home a couple of the brownies Bonnie had brought.

Hannah grabbed a slice of pizza from the box, then went out to try one of the kayaks the former owners had left for them.

"She's going to love it here," Darla predicted.

"I hope so," said Lucy.

"And you. Are you going to love it?"

"I'm going to love fixing up this house. And my neighbors are great." Lucy sat down across from her sister at the table and took a slice of pizza and set it on a napkin.

"No regrets?" Darla looked concerned and Lucy wished she hadn't complained earlier to her sister about Brody Green.

"None," Lucy insisted. "I'm already doing great."

"Except for Mr. Fly in the Ointment."

"Flies are a fact of life."

"Things will probably settle down eventually. Brody Green can't be as bad as you've been making him out to be," Darla said.

"Ha! I bet you'll never see him in sandals. He's probably got cloven hooves."

"And he keeps his pitchfork in the garage?"

"Something like that."

Darla shook her head. "It's too bad you two got off on the wrong foot."

"Cloven foot."

"He might actually be a nice man. And you do have what you do for a living in common."

"Yeah, so did Evan and I." Lucy shook her head and clamped her teeth down on her pizza.

"Not every man is an Evan," Darla pointed out. "Look at Orren."

At that moment Orren sauntered into the kitchen from the deck where he'd found a loose board to nail down. "You talking about me?"

"We're talking about what a great husband you are," Darla said, making her husband's cheeks turn pink.

"Can we clone you?" Lucy teased.

Orren made a face and snagged a slice of pizza. "The old guy next door was telling me you can fish that canal. Next time we come down I'm bringing my fishing pole."

"Look at all the nice green lawns those houses across the water have," Darla said to him. "And think of all the chemicals they put on those lawns. I bet every time it rains they trickle right down into the water. Any fish you catch out there is liable to have three heads."

He made another face, turned around and went back outside to inspect the canal further.

"He is a great guy, perfect for you," Lucy said to her sister. "You were lucky to find him."

"You could get lucky down here."

Unbidden, the image of Brody Green came to mind. Why did he have to be such a jerk?

"Not holding my breath," Lucy said. Love was overrated. Sex was overrated. Men were overrated.

Brody Green was especially overrated.

Twelve

Hannah returned to Seattle for finals week but finished on Wednesday and was back that very evening. She was glad to see that Mom had made good on her promise and gotten paddleboards.

"I am so going to try one of those out tomorrow," Hannah said.

"After work," said Mom.

Oh, yeah. That.

The next morning Mom woke her up at eight o'clock, stuffed eggs down her and then insisted Hannah get going so they could get to the office.

Why did they have to get up at the butt crack of dawn?

"The early bird gets the worm," Mom said when Hannah protested.

Such a stupid saying. There were plenty of worms to go around. And how many worms could one bird eat, anyway?

"I didn't think I'd get stuck in the office the second I got here," Hannah grumbled.

"Sorry, but I need someone there to greet walk-ins and answer the phone when I'm out."

"I bet it won't even ring."

"It might. And speaking of phones, no playing games on yours until you get the website finished. That should keep you busy at least for today."

That and working on making them into influencers.

Hannah was surprised when they walked into the Dream Homes office. The one Mom had shared with Daddy had been slick and modern and not all that inviting. Mom's office here looked almost like you were coming into someone's house to hang out. The desks were feminine and pretty and both the decor and the furniture in the reception area screamed beach. People would enjoy sitting in these chairs with the comfy-looking cushions and drinking iced coffee or bubble tea and talking about what kind of house they wanted Mom to find them. Whatever they wanted, she'd find. She was that good.

"It's so cute," Hannah said, looking around.

Mom smiled. "I think so. And it's welcoming."

"For sure," Hannah agreed. She walked over to the desk nearest the door. "Is this one mine?"

"Yes, it is," Mom said, and handed her a cell phone. "You're going to be my receptionist slash secretary slash social media manager. That should give you enough work for the summer."

"You may have to pay me overtime," Hannah said.

"If you put any in. You are at the beach, after all. I'll be lucky if I can keep you working part-time."

Hannah was mildly offended. "I'm adulting now. I'll do my part."

Mom came over and hugged her and kissed her cheek. "I know you will, and I promise I won't keep you chained to your desk all day."

At the moment Hannah didn't have anything else going on, so what the heck.

The rest of that day she was busy setting up a Dream Homes Facebook page and putting the final touches on her mother's new website, posting pictures that both she and Mom had taken of the town as well as of Mom's first listing. The next day Mom got another listing, and come Friday morning she had set up an appointment to show it that afternoon to a client she had coming down from Seattle. She'd barely gotten started and already she had deals going. Mom was amazing.

Too amazing to be alone. Hannah sure hoped somebody in this little town would fall for her mother. Not that she was in a hurry to see Mom hook up with just anyone, of course, but it would be a good ego boost if somebody wanted to hang out with her. Who knew? Once Mom became an internet celeb, all kinds of men were probably going to want to date her.

She hadn't been quite as on board with Hannah's plans to make them the next big thing when Hannah asked to use her credit card for a couple of things she needed, things that neither Hannah's allowance nor her minimum wage would cover (especially since she was paying for things like car insurance, for crying out loud).

"What do you need to get?" Mom had asked suspiciously.

"Just some stuff I can use to film our house project. Don't worry, it won't cost much."

Much, it turned out, was a relative term, and the relative known as Mom wasn't exactly thrilled when she saw the invoices Hannah had printed for the various things she'd ordered online.

"What on earth!" Mom had exclaimed, looking through the pile of printouts Hannah had left for her.

"It's all stuff we need. Trust me."

"This from the girl who told me we'd be good using her cell phone? And why do we need a microphone?"

"A cell phone mic isn't all that good."

"And a lighting kit?" Mom squeaked.

"You want to look good, don't you?"

"Green screen?"

"We might need one."

Mom frowned "Tripod? Digital camera?"

"You can take it out of my salary," Hannah offered.

"You're right, I can," Mom said irritably.

Which meant, after paying for insurance and equipment, Hannah would be standing on the street with a cardboard sign that said Anything Helps. She frowned.

Mom sighed. "I tell you what, we'll split the cost."

"But you can afford to pay for all this," Hannah pointed out. Which, of course, made more sense. Mom was the one making the big bucks. Hannah was only making minimum wage.

"Yes, I can, but you're adulting now. Remember? And this is your project, so you can help. If it works out the way you think it will, maybe you'll get that raise you talked about."

"Fine," Hannah had said, also irritated. When had her mother turned into a hard ass?

"Don't worry. I won't make you split it fifty-fifty," Mom had said with a grin that looked positively evil.

Like that was supposed to make Hannah feel better.

It was four in the afternoon, and they were both in the office, Mom checking out other houses for sale in town and Hannah trying to outline her plan for making her mother a celebrity realtor, when Mom's cell phone dinged a reminder.

"I've got to get going," Mom said. "Time to show the

Heatherton house. I'll be back later, hopefully to write up a deal. If I'm not back by five, you can close up. Meanwhile, you're in charge."

"Yeah, right," Hannah muttered. "In charge of nothing."

Even though Mom was getting busy, they'd only had a couple of walk-ins so the office would be dead.

"Things will pick up," Mom predicted.

She was probably right. But meanwhile, being stuck in the dead zone was a yawn-o with no work to do. The website was up and running and Hannah had finished with her influencer website—*Always Beachin'*—where she'd already posted an intro to who they were along with lots of beach pictures and promises to share ways to make life pretty and perfect. She'd also posted her reel of Mom and the seagulls on their new YouTube Channel, as well as getting the dedicated Instagram account set up. She resigned herself to a boring afternoon.

Oh, well. So what if no one came in? She had friends she could check in with on Facebook and Insta. And she needed to finish reading her how-to book on becoming an influencer. Hannah could fill the rest of the afternoon. Like Mom always said, only boring people got bored.

She sighed. She could fill the time better with a cute guy by her side. Where in this town were the *men*?

She got her answer half an hour later when a pair of board shorts walked past the office plate glass window attached to the cutest guy she'd seen in a long time. He had sandy hair, undercut with the top slicked back, and a squared jaw that would make him perfect for a superhero in a Marvel movie. And then there was the amazing body. Oh, yeah. Beach Man. Was he here visiting? Did he live here?

No, she couldn't be that lucky. But maybe he lived in

Seattle. Oooh, that would actually be even better since she was only in town for the summer.

She ran to the door and poked her head out in time to see him turn into Good Times Ice Cream Parlor. It was a hot day. She suddenly felt an overwhelming need for an ice-cream break.

She locked up and hurried down the walk. Then casually sauntered inside.

Mom had taken her into the ice-cream parlor the day before for a cone and it had been a major tongue treat. The parlor itself was a treat for the eyes with old-fashioned furniture scattered around. The long glass order counter offered so many bins of flavors that it actually turned a corner with another counter sweeping the length of the store. Hannah didn't have to pretend to have a hard time choosing.

The older woman behind the counter greeted her. "Hello again. I remember you from yesterday. Lucy Holmes's daughter, right?"

It was enough to make Beach Man turn and look.

Hannah pretended not to see. "I am. I'm working right next door."

"Well, welcome back," said the woman. Then to Beach Man, "So, Declan, what would you like?"

Declan. What a sexy name.

"How about I have what she's having, and I'll pay for both?" he said, nodding in Hannah's direction.

She turned her head to look at him, letting her hair cascade to the side. "Thanks. That's really nice."

"No problem," he said. "What flavor do you like?"

She still loved bubble gum, but to ask for that sounded... childish. And rocky road? Everyone asked for rocky road. Boring. She scanned the tubs.

"How about huckleberry?" she suggested.

He nodded his approval. "Love that. It tastes like huckleberry pie with ice cream."

She'd never had huckleberry pie. What had she been missing?

"Want another scoop of something?" he asked.

Yes, but she was no pig. "One is great."

"Okay."

The transaction was completed, the cones handed over and the ice cream sampled. And it was good.

"You got some place to go?" he asked.

"I have to get back to the office," she said. "But I can take a break."

He beamed at her like she'd done him a really big favor and they settled at one of the fancy little tables, her fitting in the space just fine, him having to stretch out his legs.

"You new here?" he asked. "I've never seen you before."

"My mom just moved here. I'm down for the summer, working for her."

He nodded. "My dad lives here. I'm working as a lifeguard at the pool."

"Cool."

Lifeguard Man. She wouldn't mind being rescued by him and given some mouth to mouth. But not if she'd actually swallowed water, of course. That could get gross. He had great lips. Talk about a tongue treat. Was she staring?

She quickly took a bite of ice cream and looked around the shop, playing it casual.

"What's your name?" he asked.

"Hannah."

"Cute name. I bet you've got a boyfriend. You have to have a boyfriend."

"I did." The douchebag. "We broke up."

Declan smiled. "Yeah?"

She pointed her ice-cream cone at him. "You're gaming me. You've got a girlfriend."

He shook his head. "Nope. We broke up."

"Right."

"Truth."

"How come?" Had his girlfriend caught him cheating? Like any guy would confess to that. Hers hadn't. She'd had to learn about it from a friend.

He shrugged. "It just didn't work out. She didn't like to do a lot of the stuff I like to do. Not too into sports."

Hannah couldn't help wrinkling her nose. "Like football?" Uh-oh. He was probably a football player. "Not that I don't like Superbowl parties," she hurried to add.

He smiled at that. "No, I mean stuff you can do together. Like tennis and skiing and waterskiing. She was afraid of the bunny slope and she hated waterskiing. Never could get up no matter how much I tried to help her."

"I love snowboarding. And waterskiing. I can slalom."

His eyes popped wide. "Yeah?"

She was awesome on water skis but she shrugged like it was no big deal. "We had a house on a lake. I waterskied a lot. I like to play tennis, too."

And she was just as good at that. She'd been on the tennis team in high school. But hey, she didn't brag.

"You'd probably kick my butt," he said, but she could tell he was teasing. "We should play some time."

"Yeah, we should," she agreed. They should do a lot of things together. He had to be a great kisser. As gorgeous and nice as he was, how could he not be?

"So, what kind of work are you doing for your mom?" Declan asked.

"A bunch of different stuff—designing her website,

helping with social media. She just bought a house and I'm going to help her fix it up. We're going to turn it into a show. I already set up Insta for us and a YouTube channel."

"Wow," he said, impressed.

"I'm excited."

"If she bought a house, I bet my dad helped her."

"She did it on her own. She's a real estate broker."

"Yeah? So's my dad. He owns Beach Dreams Realty."

"Mom just set up Dream Homes Realty. Her office is right next door. That's where I'm working."

He nodded, thoughtful.

"What?" she prompted.

"Just wondering what Dad's gonna think of that. He sort of owns the town."

Not anymore, Hannah thought. "A lot of real estate companies work together and show each other's houses, right? So it shouldn't be a problem."

"It shouldn't be," he agreed. "Hey, wanna get burgers tonight? I can pick you up when you're done working."

"Okay," she said to him. And to herself, *I just struck gold!*

The buyers wanted some time to talk about the house they'd just seen. So far there had been no other offers for the Heathertons to entertain, no bidding war, but this couple had already intimated to Lucy that they'd have no problem paying full price. They were going to grab a drink at one of the local restaurants and discuss, then get back to her. She returned to the office to wait to hear from them.

She came back to find her daughter bubbling over with excitement. "I met the most amazing guy," Hannah informed her. "He is gorgeous and he's so nice. And we have so much in common. I'm sooooo glad I broke up with Peter."

"Things have a way of working out," Lucy said.

She was happy to see them working out for her daughter. This would probably be nothing more than a summer romance that would burn itself out by fall, but it would be nice for Hannah to have someone her own age to hang out with.

"Tell me more about this amazing guy," Lucy said. "Where'd you meet him?"

"At Good Times. I took a quick break," Hannah hurried to say.

Before or after she saw Mr. Soooo Everything Fabulous walk past the window?

"The office was dead," Hannah said defensively. "Anyway, we're gonna get burgers. He's coming by in a little bit to pick me up so you'll get to meet him."

"Well, I can hardly wait," Lucy said. "Is his family vacationing down here?"

"He's here for the summer, staying with his dad and working as a lifeguard at the pool. And get this, his dad's in real estate, just like you."

Real estate. Just like her. Oh, no. Lucy braced herself for what she knew was coming next.

Thirteen

There was no need to ask, but Lucy did. "What's his name?"

"Declan Green," Hannah said as if she were talking about a movie star.

Declan Green, which meant son of Brody Green. If the boy looked anything like his father, he would be an eyeful. But if he was anything like his father...

You're jumping to conclusions, Lucy told herself. And she was scowling. She forced her eyebrows up in pleasant surprise and made her lips lift at the corners.

She'd been too slow. "What?" Hannah demanded.

"Nothing," Lucy said.

"It is, too, something."

"I'm sure he's perfectly nice."

"He is. So what's the problem?"

"I've met his father."

Okay, that had come out bitchy. And biased. Lots of nice people had parents who were stinkers.

Hannah looked at her in surprise. "You've met his dad?"

It was too late to backpedal now. Best to be honest.

"Yes, and let's just say he's not going to go down in my

journal as my favorite person," Lucy said. "I'm afraid I did a little bit of lumping together just now."

Hannah looked disappointed. "That bad, huh?"

She should have kept her mouth shut. "I'm sure his son's nothing like him." Lucy's cell phone rang. It was the people she'd showed the house to. Saved by the ringtone.

"We've decided we want to make an offer," said the woman. "Full price. We don't want it to get away."

Yes! "It's a great house," Lucy said. "Why don't you come on over to the office and we'll write it up."

"We'll be right there."

"I'll see you soon," Lucy said. "I know you're going to enjoy the house."

Her first sale in her new hometown and she'd just opened for business. Oh, yes, she was going to do well in Moonlight Harbor.

She ended the call to find her daughter studying her, looking almost judgmental. "What?" Great. Now she sounded defensive.

"What's so bad about Declan's dad?" Hannah demanded.

"He's just…" *A conceited jerk.* This was probably an opinion best kept to herself. "Never mind."

"No, I want to know."

"His father and I didn't happen to hit it off when we met. That's all."

"Well, Declan and I hit it off great. And I'm gonna go out with him."

"That's fine," Lucy said.

And it was. Her daughter was certainly free to see whomever she wanted.

Brody Green's son. *Ugh.*

* * *

Brody picked up a couple of steaks on his way home from the office. He and Declan could grill them and eat that potato salad he'd gotten at the deli the other day. A couple of beers, a movie on TV—yeah, some father-son chillin' would be good.

The kids came down a lot, but having Declan staying with him for the whole summer was a bonus. He loved his kids, loved that they wanted to be with him.

Which was more than he could say for how his ex had felt after a few years of marriage. It had been hard to see her growing discontent, especially when they'd been so happy at first. At least he'd been happy. He'd liked being a family man, liked playing with the kids, bringing everyone down to the beach for a week in the summer, camping or staying at the Driftwood Inn. The town had felt like home.

Not so much with Camille. She'd wanted trips to Hawaii and Cabo.

She'd also wanted a bigger house, better car, designer shoes and purses. He'd tried to give her everything she'd craved, but in the end he hadn't been able to keep up. Their divorce had bloodied him emotionally and left him angry and feeling like he wasn't enough.

It had taken a long time to get past that. He'd worked hard to build both his business and his confidence and he took a secret pleasure in the fact that he now made enough money to travel to any exotic locale he wanted. Camille could have had her trips and her designer clothes and her designer life if she'd stuck with him.

She hadn't, and at first that had worked in her favor. But then the big shot exec she married lost his job and eventually had to take a position way down the corporate ladder. No more exotic vacations. They struggled to make the payments on their big, fancy house. Meanwhile, Brody had recovered nicely. Poetic justice.

Then Jenna had dumped him and set him back three squares on that giant cosmic game board. Women had no idea the power they had over a man's psyche.

But his psyche had recovered again. He'd been doing okay.

Until Lucy Holmes blew into town. He would never admit it to a living soul, but he felt threatened by the woman, felt deep down that he was going to lose all the ground he'd gained and be made to feel like not enough yet again. That feeling was like a virus that kept coming after him.

He wasn't going to let it take him down, not when it came to real estate. He knew he was good. This was his town. Lucy Holmes and her little business was nothing more than a gnat—small and irritating, but no threat. She'd give up soon enough and buzz off someplace else to irritate someone else.

The classic Chevy Corvair convertible Brody had helped Declan buy and restore a couple of years earlier was still sitting in front of the house, but when Brody walked inside, he found his son ready to leave, all scrubbed and cologned up, wearing a T-shirt and jeans and some flip-flops.

"Where are you headed?" Brody asked.

"Out for burgers."

So much for the steak.

Brody hid his disappointment. "You got a date?"

Declan's face lit up like the Fourth of July on Moonlight Beach. "Oh, yeah."

"Met a girl at the pool?" Brody guessed and wondered who it was. He probably knew her parents.

"Nope. Met her at Good Times."

"Hitting on the tourists," Brody teased.

"Actually, she lives here. Well, sort of."

"Oh, yeah?"

"Yeah. She's staying with her mom."

One of the locals. Who were the parents? Brody started going through his mental Rolodex.

"Her mom just moved down here and she's working for her."

"Just moved down here," Brody repeated.

"Her name's Hannah."

Just moved here... Just moved here. There was only one person who had just moved to Moonlight Harbor and that was Lucy Holmes, the listing thief. Brody felt like he'd gotten hit with a sneaker wave. He could feel it tossing his brain every which way.

Declan had the smarts to look wary as he delivered the bad news. "Her mom owns the new real estate company."

Brody's face was betraying him, he knew it, showing exactly what he thought about his son having anything to do with Lucy Holmes's daughter.

Declan frowned at him. "Shit, Dad. It's just burgers."

"Hey, that's cool," Brody managed, then bolted for the kitchen, swearing under his breath as he went. "I'll see you later," he called over his shoulder. "Use protection." The last thing he wanted was his son hooking up with Lucy Holmes's daughter and getting her pregnant. Related by baby.

He heard Declan do some swearing of his own before he went out the door.

Okay, that had been a dumb thing to say. Talk about overreacting.

"Just burgers," Brody told himself as the door shut. "Just burgers." Declan never got serious about any girl.

If the daughter looked anything like her mother... Shit.

But if the daughter behaved anything like the mother, no worries. Declan was smart. He knew what kind of woman to steer away from, and, after seeing what had happened with his parents and with Brody and Jenna, he was one cautious guy.

So what did it matter if Declan wandered off into the enemy camp? It had nothing to do with Brody. Even if he took up with the girl, it would be no more than a summer romance. Let the kids hang out.

Anyway, Declan was a legal adult now. He could make his own decisions, and if he decided he wanted to be with Lucy Holmes's daughter, so be it. Just because Brody and this girl's mom were business rivals, just because Lucy Holmes was an aggressive little sneak, it didn't mean his son had to take sides. To expect him to would be both stupid and immature, and Brody assured himself that he was neither. Who knew? The girl could be the sweetest thing since powdered sugar.

He stuck the steaks in the fridge and ordered pizza instead. He and Declan could have steak another night. Hopefully, there would be a night when his kid wasn't with Lucy Holmes's daughter.

Hannah and Declan wound up hanging out with Sabrina Jones, whose mom owned the Driftwood Inn, and her boyfriend, Scotty. After eating the world's best burgers and fries along with a milkshake dubbed a Sand Dune, Sabrina invited everyone back to her house to play games.

Sabrina's mom was on hand to offer sodas and popcorn, and she and Sabrina's stepdad even played a game of Hearts with them all. It was almost like being in a family with brothers and sisters—something Hannah had often wished she'd had.

Her parents had always let her have other kids over, and living on Lake Washington in a kick ass house with a dock and a speedboat, she hadn't lacked for friends. But friends weren't the same as brothers and sisters.

And even though her parents had taken her on some pretty awesome vacations, they hadn't necessarily involved being together. Daddy was often golfing, leaving Hannah and Mom to shop or check out the pool. To just hang out and play a game, to eat popcorn, to joke around together, that had not been part of her life growing up. When she was in grade school, she'd watched old sitcoms about families on TV and felt downright jealous.

For the longest time she'd wished for a brother or sister, but by the time she was twelve she'd figured out that wasn't going to happen, and by fifteen she'd figured out why. Her parents were so busy working they probably never had time for sex, let alone another kid.

Was that why Daddy had found another woman? So unfair. Mom probably would have liked to have more sex, too.

It was too bad there wasn't somebody down here for her. But Mom was a grown-up. She'd have to figure that all out for herself.

Hannah had already figured out what she wanted, and what she wanted was Declan Green. He was checking a lot of her perfect-man boxes. He'd insisted on buying dinner. Granted, it was only burgers—but that, coupled with the gift of ice cream earlier, proved to her that he wasn't stingy. He liked to do a lot of what she liked to do and they'd already set a date to hit the courts the next afternoon after they were both off work. So another box checked. He'd even thanked Sabrina's mom for letting them come over, so he was obviously civilized. Then, of course, there was the cute factor. That wasn't at the very top of Hannah's wish list, but hey, if the universe wanted to bring her a cute guy, she wasn't going to object.

Now, how did he kiss? She refused to be with somebody who was a sloppy kisser, no matter how nice he was or how much they had in common. So after Declan had walked her to the door, she dragged his face to hers and gave him a chance to prove himself.

He passed. A+!

"Wow," he said. "I could do that again."

"Me, too," she said, so they did, him pushing her up against the door.

"You kiss great," she told him, which made him smile.

"I do everything great," he informed her.

She just bet he did.

He pointed a finger at her. "Tennis tomorrow."

"Tennis tomorrow," she said. "See you on the courts at five."

"I'm there."

She floated inside the house. Declan Green was amaaaazing.

Mom was in her room, sitting on her new bed (other than the kitchen chairs, their bedrooms were the only places to sit inside the house), reading a book when Hannah came home. She didn't look up from it when Hannah knocked and entered the bedroom.

"How was your date?" she asked, her gaze still glued to the page.

"Great," Hannah said, and plopped onto the foot of the bed. "Do you know where I was just before I came in?"

"On the front porch, going at it?"

Hannah's cheeks heated, even though she was a grown

woman and free to kiss (or do more) with anyone she wanted. There were some things you just didn't want to talk about with your mother.

She brazened it out. "Before that."

"At the beach."

"No. At Jenna Waters's house. Declan's friends with Jenna's daughter, Sabrina. She's going to a community college near here."

"Sounds like you're finding all kinds of people to hang out with," Mom said. "I'm glad."

"Me, too," Hannah said. "It's going to be a great summer."

"Umm-hmm," Mom said vaguely.

Well, it was. At least for Hannah. She was going to keep right on seeing Declan. Mom would have to deal with it.

Fourteen

Brody had invited Declan to join him and the Beach Bums for their Saturday morning tennis gathering. This week they were down by one and he'd thought Declan might like to play before he went to work.

It turned out Declan had plans. With Hannah Holmes. Again. Burgers, tennis, the beach and now the girl had invited him over to her house for breakfast and some morning paddleboarding on the canal.

Breakfast with Lucy Holmes and her daughter at the house she had grabbed right out from under Brody's nose. It had taken extreme effort for him not to grind his teeth. *Okay, let that one go.* He couldn't fault Lucy for getting to the bargain before him.

He really couldn't fault her for happening to be in the same business as he was, either. But he could fault her for that irritating superior attitude of hers, and for being underhanded and manipulative. No wonder she was divorced. She'd probably driven the poor man away.

Still, every story had two sides. What was Lucy's?

You are not interested, he told himself. Lucy Holmes was trouble. She was going to make his life miserable enough as it was simply being in the same town. He didn't need to get any nearer the woman.

The Beach Bums found a fourth and the game was on, but his game was off. He kept double-faulting on his serves, not to mention biffing a lot of backhand shots that were normally no problem. It had nothing to do with Lucy Holmes though. Men could compartmentalize and he had locked her up way at the back of his brain. He was just having an off day, that was all.

"Did you forget to take your vitamins?" Ellis West teased him after their final set.

"I guess so," Brody said. "Enjoy that while it lasts. Come next week you and Whit won't get off so easy."

Come next week he'd be bringing his A game.

He went home and showered, then swung by Beans and Books, where he complimented Rita on the new hairstyle she was sporting and picked up a latte. Then he went to the office.

Missy greeted him with a concerned look. "Did you read the morning paper?"

"Not yet. I was running late. Figured I'd read it later. Why? Did somebody die?"

"No, but you might want to murder somebody when you see the ad your competition has taken out." She held out the copy she'd been reading and Brody took it to his desk and sat down with it.

It didn't take more than a minute for him to find what she'd been talking about. Lucy Holmes had struck again, with a half-page ad. There she was, Photoshopped in front of a McMansion on a sunny beach that he knew was not any of their beaches. She looked lovely and professional in that suit, and her smile promised, "I'll be your new best friend."

You'll Love Lucy, the ad was captioned.

"Yeah, 'til you get to know her," Brody muttered and read on.

Buying or selling—Dream Homes Realty will make it happen for you. Let Lucy Holmes, premier real estate expert, make your dreams come true.

With a growl, he crumpled the page.

"My thoughts exactly," Missy said. "You gonna run an ad?"

"You bet I am," he said. Online and in print. And his would be a full-page ad.

Taylor Marsh walked in, wearing a frown. "I passed the Dream Homes office on my way to the soap shop just now. Do you know how many listing sheets Lucy Holmes has on her window? Four," she continued without waiting for an answer. "She's barely been here and she already has four listings."

"And we've got a dozen," Brody said, going for nonchalance.

"One of those should have been mine," Taylor grumbled. "My daughter's in school with Suzannah's daughter. She was going to list with me. You know why she went with Lucy Holmes?"

"She's a crummy friend?" guessed Missy.

"Because Lucy Holmes told her she was experienced and she could get Suzannah more money for her house," Taylor said hotly.

"She downright dissed you?" Missy asked, shocked.

"Well, not exactly," Taylor admitted. "But she did talk up how much experience she has and how she's sold all these super expensive houses back in Seattle."

"This is not Seattle. I suppose she let your friend think she'd get a million bucks for her place."

"That's the impression I got."

"Look, she's bound to get some business. Let it go," Brody said.

"Let it go? Have you seen the ad she took out in the paper?" Taylor shot back.

"Yes, and don't worry. I'm going to be doing one of my own. You'll sell that house of your friend's that Lucy Holmes listed and get the sales commission and it will all balance out."

Taylor said nothing to that. She plopped down at her desk and took out her cell phone.

Brody smiled as he listened to her conversation. "Angela, what are you doing this weekend?...I have just found you the perfect beach house down here. You have to come see it. Tomorrow? Great. I'll contact the broker and set up a time to show it."

So a little healthy competition was good. It was motivating Taylor.

And it was sure going to motivate him. This was his town and it was about time Lucy Holmes realized that.

Come Monday he was at the *Beach Times* office, arranging for a full-page ad to run all week. Competition was definitely good for the local paper. Late that afternoon he followed a lead he'd gotten from Ellis West and visited a couple who wanted to sell their place. He got the listing.

It was a newer two-bedroom with sleek lines and he was pretty sure he had the perfect buyer for it. He took a perverse pleasure in the knowledge that it was right down the street from where the invader lived. Every day she'd get to drive past the For Sale by Beach Dreams Realty sign in front of their front lawn. Followed by the Sold banner.

The only thing not so perfect was the fact that whenever he showed the house, he'd probably drive by and see his son's car parked at Lucy's place. Dec's car wasn't there that afternoon but Brody noticed the truck that belonged to Seth Waters was.

Doing under-the-table work for Lucy Holmes. Brody's jaw clenched.

It shouldn't have irked him to see Waters's truck parked there but it did. And he shouldn't have felt betrayed, but he did. He and Waters had hardly been buds since they'd both been rivals for Jenna. But Jenna, the woman he'd helped and protected, the woman he'd asked to marry him... Darn it all, here she was loaning out her husband to help Brody's competition. Everyone did, indeed, seem to love Lucy. It was all wrong. She wasn't that loveable.

Let it go, he told himself.

That was easier said than done when he drove past her office the next morning and saw his son standing in the doorway with two to-go cups from Beans and Books. The door opened and a little cutie with honey blond hair like Lucy's and big eyes smiled up at him with the same killer smile her mother wielded. Declan followed her inside the enemy camp.

Brody let out a growl and clawed his fingers through his hair. Lucy Holmes was like a siren, luring people to her right and left. And whoever escaped the mother was sure to be caught by the daughter.

Of all the beach towns in all the world...

"That was so sweet of you to bring us coffee," Lucy said to Declan.

He shrugged off the compliment. "Just thought you might like it."

"Oh, I do," Lucy said, and couldn't help taking perverse

pleasure in the fact that the son of Brody Green the Jerk was bringing her daughter and her coffee.

Unlike his father, Declan was proving to be a nice man, the kind of man a woman would want her daughter to fall in love with. Too bad his father the skunk came with him.

Wednesday morning Lucy settled at her desk with her coffee and the paper and opened it to admire her lovely ad, which was still running. She'd already gotten one call as a result. It looked just as lovely as it had the last time she admired it. She turned the page and nearly choked on her drink.

When You Want the Best, it began. There was Brody Green in all his beautiful, smiling glory, wearing slacks and a sweater, seated on the porch of a charming beach cottage. *A longtime resident of the community, Brody Green knows your needs and will help you make your dreams come true.*

Make your dreams come true. She'd said that!

She read on. *It's your home, your investment, your future. Don't settle for second best.*

She knew exactly whom he was calling second best. What a snake! She hoped he slithered off into the ocean and drowned. No, drowning was too good for him. He deserved to be roasted over a beach fire.

Okay, these were not nice thoughts. But darn, that man brought out the worst in her.

Don't get mad. Get better. Yes, they'd see who was the best. She was already looking ahead to the Fourth of July and had some ideas for making her presence known. Then they'd see who was best and who was second best.

Meanwhile, there were plenty of other people in Moonlight Harbor to enjoy, and come Friday evening she had the opportunity to hang out with several of them. She'd been invited to Jenna Waters's house. The women who gathered in Jenna's living room to drink wine and compare notes on how their businesses had done that week were all welcoming and had plenty to share about both their own lives and the town's history.

And, oh, good grief, about Brody Green.

"If it weren't for him, I'd have never been able to get my shop," said Jenna's friend, Courtney Greer, who owned Beach Babes Boutique.

"If you haven't shopped there yet, you need to," said Tyrella Lamb, owner of the lumberyard and hardware store where Lucy was buying her flooring.

"Of course, when it comes to Brody, the Driftwood has the best story," Jenna said. "Although I don't exactly come off looking like Snow White."

"How could you know? Edie was so tight-lipped," said Patricia White, who owned the Oyster Inn.

"Jenna remodeled the Driftwood and brought it back to life," Tyrella explained. "And her great aunt left it to her when she passed. Well, sort of."

Lucy raised inquisitive eyebrows.

"I was lucky I had Brody watching over it for me," Jenna said.

"Watching over it?" Lucy asked.

"My aunt Edie left it to him with the proviso that, after I was done paying spousal support, Brody would hand it over to me. Which he did. But I didn't know about that. Aunt Edie had left me the house, for which I was grateful. But not the Driftwood. After all the work I'd put into making it a paying business, to be just the manager... I was pretty bitter." She shook her head. "Poor Brody. I thought he'd somehow convinced her to leave it to him and just keep me on as manager. I was so mad at him for so long."

"Broken engagement," put in Courtney.

Engagement? Jenna Waters had been engaged to Brody Green?

Jenna sighed. "Poor Brody. He never said a word to defend himself. Just kept the secret as Aunt Edie had instructed until I was done paying spousal support and he could safely transfer the Driftwood to me."

"He's a pretty amazing man," put in Courtney.

Amazing was not the word Lucy would have used for Brody Green. It was as if these women were talking about a completely different man. Listening to them, he sounded like he should have been made a saint. Lucy was more inclined to think of him as an urban myth.

Never mind Brody Green, she told herself. He was nothing more than the human equivalent of a light sunburn— irritating and quickly forgotten. She intended to treat him exactly like that sunburn. She had a business to run and a house to renovate.

Come Monday Seth's friend Carl Hawthorn, proud owner of Carl's Construction, was knocking on her door promptly at eight thirty as promised. He appeared to be somewhere in his thirties and was big enough to alarm a grizzly bear. He wore jeans and a T-shirt and work boots on feet that could double as water skis. In defiance of approaching hair loss, he'd shaved his head, which could have made him a little scary except for the fact that he had a friendly smile and *I Love Mom* tattooed on one arm.

"Hiya, I'm Carl," he said, just in case Lucy couldn't figure it out from the truck parked out front.

"I'm Lucy. It's nice to meet you, Carl. Seth Waters tells me you are great at house renos."

Just as she was speaking, Hannah rushed up, waving

her cell phone. "Wait! Can we shut the door and start this again?"

Carl blinked in confusion and Lucy frowned at her daughter.

"I want to film this," Hannah explained to him. "For our YouTube channel."

Carl looked impressed. "You got a channel?"

"We do. It's called *Always Beachin'* and we're recording everything we do on the house for it."

"Like Chip and Joanna?" he asked, his papa-bear voice practically quivering with excitement.

"Yep," Hannah replied, all confidence.

"Sure," he said, and stepped back.

Lucy still wasn't sure how she felt about this. Hannah kept assuring her it would be great for business. They could become influencers. They could become famous.

Yes, if her daughter filmed her right at this moment she'd be famous for looking dumpy. That would hardly attract sponsors. The women on those shows were always perfectly made up and dressed to impress. Lucy was wearing no makeup and had on sweats and a pink T-shirt with a half-full wine glass on it that said Gotta Love Women Who Wine—a leftover from a girls' weekend she'd had with a girlfriend and her sister in Icicle Falls two years before.

She shut the door on Carl and said to her daughter in a low voice, "Give me a minute to change. I'm not dressed for this."

"You look perfect," Hannah assured her. "Real."

"No one looks real in those shows, not even the real housewives."

Hannah kept saying how good this would be for her brand. How would this help her brand if she looked like a slob? Oh, yeah, she'd look like a *real* slob. Not happening.

"Come on, Mom, trust me."

Right. As if a nineteen-year-old knew all about marketing.

Hannah aimed her phone and called, "Knock on the door."

"Okay," came Carl's muffled voice.

"Not yet!" called Lucy.

"Uh, okay," Carl replied.

"Give me five minutes to put on makeup or I'm not doing this," Lucy said sternly.

"Okay," Hannah conceded. "Makeup, but keep the shirt. Please? It'll come across great. And if some winery sees you in it, they might sponsor us."

It was a stretch, but Lucy decided she could compromise as long as she had on cute jeans and makeup and her hair looked better. She rushed to her bathroom, applied foundation, eyeliner, mascara and lipstick, then took her hair down and brushed it. Okay, that was better.

She lost the sweats and slippers, then donned jeans and the sandals and hurried back to the front door.

She got there just in time to hear Carl, on the other side of it, asking, "Can I come in yet?"

"Count to three real slow and then knock," Hannah instructed him through the door.

Then she aimed her phone and started talking. "We're about to meet our construction genie. Mom doesn't want you all to see her looking normal, but I think she looks cute. Don't you? Show us your shirt, Mom."

This was embarrassing. Lucy was sure her face was turning red.

But, oh, well. She struck a pose and pointed to the wine glass on her T-shirt. "If you drink enough of these, I'll probably look fine," she quipped.

Carl knocked on the door again, so hard it looked like it might bounce off its hinges. Lucy opened it and said, "Hi there. You must be Carl."

He looked momentarily confused, probably because he'd already introduced himself. Then he blinked and nodded and grinned. "Yeah, that's me. I hear you need help."

"Boy, does she," said Hannah the comic.

Oh, yeah, this was going to be great branding. Not. Lucy pointed a finger at her daughter. "At this rate, you're going to be out of the will," she joked. Ha ha. She could be clever, too.

Carl guffawed and Hannah giggled. "That was great," she said as she stopped recording. She played it back for them to watch.

"I look fat," said Carl.

"No, you look manly," Hannah assured him, and he smiled.

So did Lucy. It was rather cute and, really, her daughter was very clever.

She followed Lucy and Carl around the house, taking reels and pictures, sometimes using her phone, sometimes her camera, making them wait while she set up lights and microphones.

"This is taking a lot of your time," Lucy apologized to him.

He shrugged. "No problemo. I got 'til noon."

Lucy didn't. She had work to do.

They discussed removing a wall, opening up the living and dining areas and redoing the kitchen. She'd settled on flooring during a visit to Tyrella Lamb's hardware store with Hannah and Tyrella had given her a deal. Cabinetry for the kitchen and the quartz countertops would come from another source and Carl assured her he could get a builder's discount. They discussed dollars and cents—off-camera, over Hannah's objections.

"People want to know how much all this costs," she protested.

"They may want to know but they don't need to," Lucy said. "You should have plenty of material for YouTube and Instagram with what you've already shot."

Hannah frowned but respected her mother's wishes on the matter. She also agreed to shoot some pictures and reels at the office with Lucy dressed like a professional.

"I not only love fixing up houses, I also love selling them," Lucy said later as her daughter filmed. "Which is why I'm a real estate broker in beautiful Moonlight Harbor on the Washington coast. Here at Dream Homes Realty, we specialize in helping people find their dream house."

"Let's do it again and add *just like I found mine*," Hannah suggested. "That'll be good for both businesses."

It was a good suggestion and Lucy was impressed. "You are a clever girl," she said to her daughter.

"I take after my mom," Hannah replied with a grin.

That afternoon when Lucy stopped in at Waves to make an appointment for a haircut, she offered to do exactly what she'd promised on the reel. A woman had come in while she was visiting with Moira, the creative genius behind so many of the great hairstyles she'd seen around town. The woman's name was Tamara Gordon and she and her husband were ready to sell their landlocked house and get something on the beach.

"I doubt we'll be able to though," Tamara concluded with a sigh. "Houses are more expensive in the area where we're looking and the one we want is just out of reach. We wouldn't get enough from the sale of our house."

"Are you sure?" Lucy asked.

"It looks that way."

Lucy handed her a business card. "I tell you what, why don't we set up a time for me to come by and take a look? The market down here is heating up, so you never know."

Tamara perked up. "I'll call you."

She did, late that afternoon as Lucy and Hannah and Declan, who Hannah had recruited to be her cameraman, were walking into Builders Best Outlet to choose their cabinetry and countertops for the kitchen.

"How about I stop by this evening," Lucy suggested. She knew after their filming at the building supply store was done that Hannah and Declan would be hanging out together so her daughter certainly wouldn't miss her company.

Lucy smiled as she ended the call. Another potential client. Life was good at the beach.

Inside the store, Declan filmed while she and Hannah checked out cabinets. This time Lucy had dressed for the part, more upscale casual, wearing a filmy gray blouse half tucked into jeans, accented with a necklace sporting a glass starfish and ballet flats on her feet.

"I'm going for a look that's subtly beachy," she explained to her invisible audience. "So I'm picking out this white and pale blue quartz for my kitchen countertops, which will go beautifully with these white shaker cabinets. There's something about white cabinets that says beach house to me. The shaker style is simple and classic, which is good, as you don't want the interior of your house to look dated before it's barely done. Of course, no matter how conservative or classic you go, styles will change, so pick out what you like, but don't go wild. Pink bathroom tile will go out of style really quick. Remember the '80s," she added with a wink.

"What about ones with glass?" Hannah suggested.

"They always look charming in a display setup, but you might want to keep your dishes and cereal boxes hidden. Personally, I like the look of wood, and if there's a mess behind the door, no one has to see it."

"How about this for a backsplash?" Hannah asked as they moved on, pointing to a chalky natural stone in a herringbone pattern.

"I think that will go nicely," Lucy said, pleased with her daughter's selection.

"My mom has the good taste to appreciate my good taste," Hannah said to anyone who would be viewing the post. "But can we settle on paint colors? Stay tuned."

And that was a wrap. They'd purchase the paint from Beach Lumber and Hardware and that would be a choice for another day.

Back in town Lucy bought dinner for Hannah and Declan at The Porthole, then the kids left to play tennis and Lucy went to meet with Tamara Gordon and her husband. For this visit she brought a box of chocolates from Cindy's Candies and Tamara's eyes lit up at the sight of it.

Lucy's eyes had lit up at the sight of the Gordons' house. While it wasn't on the water, it wasn't far from the beach. It was a two-story gable front house with a bay window, painted white with blue shutters and a blue front door. The lawn wasn't huge but it was well-maintained and enclosed with a white picket fence.

The inside, however, needed a facelift. The living room and dining room were separated by an arch and were good-sized, although the overabundance of furniture made them look small. Both rooms were painted hunter green. Added to that, the brass chandelier hanging over the maple dining table with its carved chairs made the place look dated. But those were cosmetic and could be easily fixed.

"You've got a good house here. Lots of potential," Lucy said, starting them off on a positive note.

Tamara and her husband, Steve, exchanged smiles.

"Let's check out the kitchen," Lucy suggested.

The kitchen appliances looked fairly new but the walls needed a paint job. The eating bar only needed some updated lighting to make it more appealing. The bathroom had been updated with a newer shower and had double sinks, always a plus. And the bedrooms weren't bad. Again, they were stuffed with too much furniture—extra dressers and chairs, an antique hope chest loaded with stuffed animals. One bedroom was doubling as an office and, in addition to a bed and nightstands, held a desk and a computer, as well as an electric keyboard.

"I think you'll have no trouble selling this house for top dollar if you're willing to make a few cosmetic fixes," Lucy said once they'd returned to the dining room.

Tamara looked at her eagerly. Her husband suddenly turned wary.

"What do we need to do?" Tamara asked.

"Sounds like a lot of work," her husband said after Lucy had shared her suggestions.

"It would be a little work, but it would be worth it. You'd be amazed at the difference a fresh coat of paint and a few small updates can make. And when you remove some of the furniture, you show buyers how spacious your rooms really are."

"How much do you think we could get?" Steve asked, cutting to the chase.

Lucy threw out a price that she felt sure was realistic.

"I'd have to do some comps to be sure, but I think I'm pretty close."

Tamara was ready to pull the trigger but Lucy could tell her husband wasn't.

Sure enough. "We'll have to think about it," he said.

"It's a lot to think about, I know," she told him. "I'll be happy to help you when you're ready."

They both thanked her and walked her to the door, sent her on her way with a wave and a smile. She waved back, confident she'd be hearing from them.

Brody was in the hardware store, buying stain for his deck when he ran into Steve Gordon, who was buying paint.

"Hi, Steve. Time for some home improvement?" Brody greeted him.

Steve gave a guilty start. "Uh, yeah."

Brody's real estate radar started going off. If the Gordons were doing home improvement, they could very well be ready to move. He and Steve had talked about it a couple of times over beer at The Drunken Sailor while Steve's wife was line dancing. The couple longed for waterfront but they'd been through some hard times financially over the last few years and waterfront hadn't been in the cards. Were they feeling more flush? If so, it was news to Brody. And why was Steve looking like he'd just been caught doing something illicit?

"You thinking of selling your place?" Brody asked.

Steve's cheeks turned ruddy. "Well, uh, Tamara was talking with this, uh, woman."

Oh, no. "Lucy Holmes?"

Steve nodded. "She came over the other night and looked at the house."

The very same house that Brody had found for them ten years earlier.

"She suggested some things we could do to it. Said she could get top dollar. We've been eyeing one over on Ocean View."

Brody knew exactly what house he was talking about. Taylor had the listing. It needed some work but the bones were good and the location was great.

"It's a nice house," he said. But if Lucy had told the Gordons they'd get enough for their house to be able to buy that one, she'd lied. Or else she was delusional. "And so is yours. You guys have kept it in good condition, and fixing up the bathroom was a great idea. But..."

"Here comes the but," Steve said with a frown.

"I don't think you can get enough money from your place that you can buy that one."

"Lucy seemed to think we could."

Lucy was definitely delusional. "She's new to town and doesn't really know the market."

It was shitty to diss the competition, but in this instance Brody wasn't dissing, merely telling the truth. Lucy Holmes would get their hopes up, sell their place for less than they needed and they'd be no better off than they were and would have to give up on their dream house. They'd wind up settling for less because there wasn't anything currently on the market that would give them as much for their money as what they already had.

Now Steve was looking glum, and Brody felt like a giant raincloud that had just found a parade to ruin. But it was the truth, and it didn't do any good to get people's hopes up. Still, that house on Ocean View had been on the market for a couple of months and the owners, who were getting divorced, might have reached the point where they'd be willing to come down in price. Then, if Brody kicked in half of his commission…

It wasn't something he normally did, but he'd known the Gordons a long time. In addition to some financial problems, they'd also endured the agony of losing a child to drugs. They deserved a break.

"I might be able to help you," he said. "If the seller is open to a contingency…" It was a gamble. When the market was good, contingencies rarely flew.

Steve cut him off. "Sounds like we still wouldn't have enough money."

"And if I kicked in part of my commission."

Now Steve looked horrified. "You can't do that."

"Sure I can."

For a minute he thought Steve was going to cry and he braced himself for an uncomfortable moment, but the guy got ahold of himself and instead set down the paint cans and vigorously pumped Brody's hand. "If you could help us get that ocean view we've always wanted, man, that would be awesome."

"I'll give it my best shot," Brody said. "How about I come over tonight and we'll iron out some details?"

"Great," said Steve.

Lucy Holmes probably wouldn't think it was so great when she found out but who cared?

Lucy got the shock of her life when she checked in with Tamara Gordon the next day. "We are going to sell, but we've listed our house with Brody Green," she said.

Lucy had been sitting at her desk, leaning back in her chair, all comfy, knees crossed, swinging a leg. The swinging stopped.

"Brody Green," she repeated, nearly choking on the words.

"I'm sorry, Lucy. I kind of feel like a traitor after all the advice you gave us."

What a coincidence. Lucy was feeling a little bit betrayed.

"But we've known Brody a long time. He got us this house, and he's going to help us get the house on the beach that we want. He's actually going to kick in part of his commission."

So that was how he'd done it. She'd given advice in good faith and he'd…bribed the Gordons!

"That was very generous of him." What else could she say?

"Thanks for being so understanding," Tamara said.

Oh, Lucy understood all right. She ended the call and looked up the number of Beach Dreams Realty. Grinding her teeth, she punched in the numbers so hard it was a wonder she didn't put her finger clear through the phone. She had a thing or two to say to Brody Green.

"Beach Dreams Realty," a woman answered with a pleasant voice.

"I'm looking for Brody Green," Lucy said, equally sweet.

"Uh-oh," muttered Hannah from her desk.

Lucy ignored her.

"This is Brody," said a friendly male voice a moment later.

Lucy dropped the sweetness. "Mr. Green, this is Lucy Holmes."

"Lucy Holmes, fancy hearing from you. Do you have a client interested in showing one of our listings?"

The last thing she wanted to do was show any of the homes he had listed. "You have a very interesting method of getting those listings," she snapped, cutting right to the chase.

"So do you," he fired back. "Nothing like giving people an inflated idea of what their place is worth. And if that doesn't work, you can always bribe them with wine, right?"

"Oh, you're a fine one to talk about bribes. I just spoke with Tamara Gordon."

"Then I guess you know they won't be needing your help getting their place on the market."

"I already gave them plenty of help."

"So did I."

"Kickbacks."

"Hey, what I did is perfectly legal. And, frankly, if I didn't help them, they'd never end up with enough money to get into the house they want. Those people have been through a lot and they deserve a break."

"And you're just the man to give it to them? Aren't you noble?" she sneered.

"Sometimes," he said, unaffected by her scorn. "Look, Lucy Holmes," he sneered back, "you'd never be able to get those people the asking price you told them and you shouldn't have led them on."

"Led them on!" As if she would do such a thing. "Are you accusing me of—"

"Blowing smoke," he provided.

"I would never purposely mislead someone! And if you think I couldn't get them that asking price, then you don't know me very well."

"And I don't want to," he said. Then, before she could come up with a comeback, he said, "Have a nice day," and ended the call.

"Of all the nerve!" she sputtered. "That man is…evil."

Hannah was looking at her as if she'd had a psychotic break. "Jeez, Mom, aren't you overreacting just a little?"

"No, I am not," Lucy said hotly. "He is trying to put me out of business. Well, we'll see who puts who out of business."

"Oh, boy," Hannah said miserably.

"What did *she* want?" Missy asked.

"To play the sore loser card," Brody replied, and left it at that.

He'd have liked nothing more than to vent about Lucy Holmes, the two-legged red tide, but it went against his good-guy code. Lucy Holmes was free to go on a rampage if she needed to but he wasn't going to. And really, he regretted lowering himself to her level and being snotty to her but she'd provoked him to abandon diplomacy. The woman was impossible.

What was really irrational was that little seed of regret at the back of his mind that they hadn't met under different circumstances and that they were competitors because, like it or not, he was drawn to her.

And where was the logic in that? There was none. He wasn't some teenage boy with hormones so out of control they knocked his brains loose. He had no reason to give Lucy Holmes so much as a second look. But the memory of that smile of hers was embedded in his brain—pretty, friendly. Ugh. She was a siren and she'd be more than happy to ruin him.

Ah, well, Odysseus had resisted the sirens. Brody could resist Lucy Holmes.

Hannah and Declan had just snapped a shot of themselves perched on his convertible with the top down for

Twitter's Topless Tuesday, him in his board shorts and
T-shirt and her in her bikini. It was a perfect shot, with the
beach in the background, waves curling in. She captioned
it *Topless and Beachin' in Moonlight Harbor*. They also
shot a reel for TikTok so she could capture the sound of
the gulls crying. Too bad you couldn't capture the smell
of sand and surf.

"I love it here," she said when they were done.

"Me, too," Declan said. "I could see living down here."

So could she. With him.

"How about you?" he asked.

"Oh, yeah," she said.

Being with Declan was so much fun and she was starting to have the feels for him. It was almost like they'd been
destined to meet.

Like an approaching storm cloud, a new thought entered
her mind. What if they got serious? How was that going
to work if their parents hated each other?

She absolutely had to do something to fix that problem.
It was time for a mother-daughter talk.

Fifteen

Lucy was relaxing on her bed, surfing the internet for ideas on carpet and wall colors for the bedroom when her daughter appeared in the doorway, looking troubled.

It was only eight o'clock. Something had gone awry. Declan must have turned out to be not as fabulous as he'd seemed.

Like father like son, just as Lucy had suspected. Still, that had to be disappointing. Lucy started preparing her comforting speech.

"You're back early," she said diplomatically.

Hannah shrugged, came into the room and plopped on the end of the bed. She was not smiling. Yep. The Greens were no longer a part of their lives.

"What's wrong, Hannah Honey Bear?" Lucy asked, falling back on a favored nickname from her daughter's childhood.

"I think I'm falling in love with Declan," Hannah said.

So Declan was turning out to be a cut above his father. Then what was the problem?

And what was the rush? The last thing she wanted was to see her daughter hurry into another heartbreak.

"Darling, it's way too soon to tell," she said.

"How long did it take for you to fall in love with Daddy?" Hannah argued.

"Not nearly long enough and look how that turned out."

"Declan's different. He really is amazing, Mom."

Well, then, he wasn't at all like his father. "So, what's the problem?" There was a problem. Hannah was picking at Lucy's new bedspread, not looking at her.

"You."

Ouch. Lucy was rarely at a loss for words, but suddenly she couldn't find a single one. She blinked in surprise.

"What's going to happen if we get serious? How's that supposed to work at graduations and weddings and... babies if you and his dad hate each other."

"We don't hate each other," Lucy insisted.

We just can't stand each other. Not the same thing.

"Well, it would be nice if you'd stop calling him and yelling at him," Hannah scolded, making Lucy feel ten years old.

Maybe because she'd acted ten years old. She bit her lip.

"You worked with all kinds of other realtors in Seattle. Why can't you work with Declan's dad?"

Because he's a selfish jerk. Lucy gated her mouth before that response could escape. "The man has been undermining me ever since I came to town."

So how was Lucy the villain here? Since when was she Maleficent? Brody Green wasn't exactly Prince Charming.

"Can't you guys work something out?" Hannah pleaded. "I mean, come on, Mom. Don't you want me to be happy?"

"Of course, I want you to be happy," Lucy said, trying not to smother under the truckload of guilt her daughter had just dumped on her.

"Well, then can't you quit feuding with Mr. Green?"

Hannah made it sound like the situation with Brody Green was all Lucy's fault. Well, it wasn't.

"Honey, that's a two-way street," she said.

"Maybe if you start down it one way, he'll come down it the other."

The suggestion sounded so logical, so easy.

So adult and mature.

But they were talking about Brody Green. Lucy wished her daughter would stop looking at her so earnestly.

She also wished she had more faith in building an amicable working relationship with the man. She'd always considered herself a woman who possessed excellent people skills but they went missing when she had to deal with him. Maybe she didn't have as excellent a set of skills as she'd always thought.

Or maybe—here was a dreadful possibility—she'd changed. Before what had happened with Evan, she'd been positive and happy. And trusting. More tolerant of people's faults. Easy to work with. Maybe she wasn't so much so now. It was a terrible reality to consider having to embrace. If it was a reality.

"I'll try," she said.

"Thank you!" Hannah beamed at her and hugged her.

"But remember, I'm only half of the equation."

"The good half," Hannah said, and kissed her cheek.

She bounced out of the room, happy and bubbly once more, bequeathing her misery to Lucy.

The misery continued for the rest of the evening and on into Lucy's dreams. She found herself hurrying to a small wedding chapel on the beach, all dressed up in the black flowing robes and creepy horned hat of Disney's Maleficent. From inside came the strains of Pachelbel's "Canon in D." She picked up her pace and ran to the door.

Once she pulled it open, she could see past the foyer and into the sanctuary, which was packed with guests. Up at the front stood Declan, with his father at his side. Both men were dressed like Prince Charming. And there, waiting to march down the aisle, stood Hannah, beautiful in a wedding gown trimmed with seed pearls, her arm slipped through the crook of her father's arm. Evan was wearing a purple robe and a crown. A crown he didn't deserve!

Hannah turned and glared at Lucy. "What are you doing here?"

"I came for the wedding," she replied. "My invitation must have gotten lost."

"You weren't invited," Hannah said. "Nobody wants you here. You'll only start trouble."

A big man who looked a lot like Carl the builder came lumbering up. He was dressed in a tuxedo and carrying a pail of water. "You need to go," he growled.

"No, it's my daughter's wedding."

Hannah turned her back on Lucy. "Get her out of here."

"Okay," said Carl and tossed the water on Lucy, who immediately began to shrink and cry, "I'm melting."

Wait, that was the witch in *The Wizard of Oz.* "I'm not a witch," she cried. "I'm not a witch!"

She woke up with the words still on her lips. Oh, Lord, had she really turned into a witch?

The thought wasn't a pleasant one and it was hard to shake. She tried to move through her workday as if nothing were bothering her. She showed a house and closed a deal—all in a day's work for Lucy Holmes, real estate broker extraordinaire. She should have been ecstatic. Instead, she felt grumpy and her smiles were forced.

Come Friday she proved to herself that she wasn't a witch by stopping by Sunbaked and buying chocolate chip cookies to take to the gathering at Jenna Waters's house and extra for her neighbors.

Mr. Sullivan was delighted when she knocked on his door that afternoon. "Thank you, Lucy. You're a good neighbor."

Yes, she was, which surely let her off the hook for being an evil witch.

"These look great," Bonnie said when Lucy next delivered a plate to her. "I just made some lemonade. Want to come in for a minute?"

Lucy was all about getting to know her neighbors, and she loved checking out people's houses. "Sure," she said, and followed Bonnie inside.

Her house had a friendly vibe, with comfortable-looking furniture—a light green microfiber couch and matching loveseat. A two-tiered rustic barnwood-finished coffee table held a glass bowl filled with seashells. A framed photo hanging on the wall over a fireplace with an insert immediately drew Lucy's eye. Lucy recognized the beach. It was the one at the end of town down by the pier. The forefront showed a close up of beach grass. Beyond it lay a stretch of sand with one lone log on it. Beyond it was sparkling blue water, and on that water, gently blurred by distance, some sort of giant tanker sat under blue sky and clouds. It could have been for sale in an art gallery.

"Did you take this?" Lucy asked.

"I did. Photography's a hobby of mine."

"It's fabulous."

"Thanks. Make yourself at home. I'll get the lemonade."

The house had an open-concept floor plan, and Lucy settled into the loveseat and watched as Bonnie went to work in the kitchen, pouring their drinks from a glass pitcher. The kitchen had older cabinets and a Formica counter top, but, with the exception of a glass fish on the eating bar, it was free of clutter.

She brought Lucy a glass, saying, "I think we need to sample those cookies right now."

She picked up the paper plate from the coffee table where she'd set it and held it out to Lucy, who shook her head and said, "I already sampled one."

"When it comes to cookies, one is never enough," Bonnie said.

Slender as she was, she could afford more than one.

She picked up a cookie, took a bite, then groaned and looked heavenward. "This is to die for."

"Wish I could take credit for it, but I got them at the bakery. I am looking forward to doing some baking once my kitchen is done."

"I'm not much of a baker," Bonnie confessed.

Lucy pointed to the guitar propped on a stand and leaning against a wall. "You obviously have other talents."

"I think I'd call that more an addiction than a talent." Bonnie shook her head. "If I'd just gotten a normal job back when I was a sweet young thing, I'd have a fat IRA by now."

"But to have a band. That just sounds so cool. Anyway, there's more to life than money," Lucy said. "You can have all the money in the world and not be happy." Money sure hadn't saved her marriage.

"You're right," Bonnie agreed. "There's more to life. But it's nice to be able to pay the bills, and that's always a scramble for a musician. I'm just glad my gram deeded me this place. Between that and what I make with the band and the small royalty checks, it may not always keep the wolf from the door but it at least stops him from blowing it down."

"Royalty checks?"

"I had a couple of cuts on CDs. No huge hits, but I still get a little money."

"So you're a songwriter," Lucy said in awe.

"Starving musician would be more accurate," Bonnie said, then asked how Lucy was settling in to Moonlight Harbor.

Lucy would have loved to know more about the songwriting thing. Had Bonnie lived in Nashville? What were the songs? The subject was obviously closed, so she moved on to chatting about the town and how much she was enjoying settling in.

"I'm having an open house at the office on Sunday. I hope you'll stop by," she finished.

"Even if I'm not planning on moving or buying a house?"

"Even if you're not planning on moving or buying a house," Lucy assured her.

"Sure. That would be fun. And by the way, if you've got nothing to do, our band is playing at The Drunken Sailor on Friday and Saturday nights all summer. Come hear us."

"I'll have to do that. What do you play?"

"A variety. A lot of country and rock—'80s and a few oldies from the '50s and '60s. Mostly stuff people can dance to. They've got a great dance floor there."

"It sounds fun," Lucy said, and wished she had someone to go dancing with.

She stayed a few more minutes, then downed the last of her lemonade and left. She felt less grumpy after her cookie delivery, but grumpiness was replaced with wistfulness. It would be nice to have someone to dance with, to enjoy a meal with, to make love with.

After what she'd gone through with Evan, it would be

hard to trust a man. And here in Moonlight Harbor, she was beginning to suspect it would be hard to find a man. Period. Too bad Frances Sullivan was so old. Other than him, she hadn't met any single men.

Except Brody Green.

Who, if her subconscious was right, brought out the wicked witch in her.

That evening she couldn't help feeling a little jealous as Tyrella Lamb showed off her engagement ring. "He's moving down here. Can you believe it?" she gushed.

"Absolutely," said Nora Singleton. "You're worth it."

"But what about his church?" Jenna asked.

"His son's going to step into his shoes and he'll help out Pastor Paul down here. And he'll help me run the hardware store. Hallelujah! That store is aging me before my time."

"Are you aging?" teased Cindy Redmond. Cindy herself didn't look all that old, with her round baby face and that smattering of freckles.

Tyrella rolled her eyes. "Girlfriend, just 'cause it don't show doesn't mean it's not happening. He says he's always wanted to live at the beach," she finished with a smile.

"I'm so glad for you," Jenna said. "It makes all the difference when you find the right person."

It made a difference when the right person turned out to be the wrong person, too. It was hard for Lucy to keep her own smile in place. Where had she and Evan gone wrong?

"How are you settling in, Lucy?" Jenna asked after the excitement over Tyrella's news had died down.

"Fine," Lucy said. "I'm excited to fix up my house and the business is going well. I hope you'll all come to our Dream Homes Realty open house on Sunday afternoon," she said to the group.

"If you're serving these cookies, I'll be there," Courtney said, holding up one.

"You can't have an open house without goodies," Lucy said. She turned to Annie. "I suppose it's too late to ask you to do up some appetizer platters for me." Annie's food truck was open for the tourist season and she'd been talking earlier about how busy she was.

"I think I could manage something," she said, and gave Lucy her phone number so they could talk.

"I hope you're managing to get some business," said Cindy. "Brody pretty much has the market sewed up here."

He's dropping some stitches now. Hehe.

Okay, she should just give in to her inner Maleficent.

Except how would her daughter feel about that? Not good, of course. Oh, she was bad. She could feel Jenna studying her and tried for an insouciant expression.

But as some of the women drifted back to the refreshment table, she found herself confiding in her new friend. "My daughter's dating his son. It's a little awkward."

"I can imagine," Jenna said.

"Hannah's sure I'm going to ruin her future if I don't..." How to finish this sentence? *Play nice. Get over my irritation with Brody Green.*

"You are business rivals. That can be awkward," Jenna said diplomatically.

"More like mortal enemies." Oh, no. Had she really just said that? Her face burst into flames.

Jenna chuckled.

Lucy shrugged. The truth was out now. "I guess you could say we've got a bit of a turf war going. That makes it hard for the kids. Frankly, I'm not sure how to handle this."

"I guess you'll have to start peace negotiations."

Yuck.

"Brody really is a good guy," Jenna said.

Maybe when he's asleep.

This last thought launched an instant round of word association. *Sleep. Bed. Sex. Sex with Brody Green.*

Do not go there, Lucy instructed herself.

Too late, she'd gone.

Darn the man. He was like ants at a picnic, crawling all over every aspect of her life. He needed to be dealt with.

But how?

"He's done a lot of good things for many of us," Jenna added, and Lucy remembered the testimonials of how he'd helped some of the women in that very group of friends.

Brody Green had a good side. If she could find it, then maybe they could manage to coexist in Moonlight Harbor. There was only one way to find that good side and that was to look for it. She knew what she had to do.

On Saturday morning Lucy went to Beach Dreams Realty bearing banana poppy seed muffins from Sunbaked. The woman manning the reception desk gave her a polite smile. But when she said her name, the smile dissolved, and the other woman in the office seated at a nearby desk looked at her as if she were that Wicked Witch of the West. *Grab your broomstick and scram.*

I'm not the witch. I'm Dorothy. Lucy forced her lips to stay up. "I'm looking for Brody Green. Is he in?"

"He just went on a coffee run," the receptionist said, polite but frosty. "He should be back soon if you'd like to wait." The look in her eyes said, *Do that at your own risk.*

"I assume he went to Beans and Books?" Lucy asked, and the receptionist nodded. "I'll find him, then. Meanwhile, I hope you ladies will enjoy a little something from the bakery."

If they did, they'd obviously both rather choke than admit it. Lucy received a reluctant thank-you, then scrammed before they could throw one of the muffins at her.

She floored it to the coffee shop, preferring to risk a speeding ticket to having to go back into Brody's office. Fortunately, she found his convertible still in the parking lot. She could see him through the plate glass window, leaning on the counter, chatting with Rita Rutledge, the owner, while her barista made coffee drinks. More like flirting, likely. Brody Green probably had every single woman in town besotted with him.

Lucy started for the door, then backed away, deciding she preferred to converse with him without witnesses. Her heart was beginning to play jump rope as she leaned against his car, opting for a casual pose. How was this going to work? How should she start negotiations? As a humble supplicant? Tease? District attorney offering a deal?

Jenna had insisted Brody was a nice man, but so far in their dealings Lucy hadn't seen it. She hadn't been nice herself, either. This was not going to go well, she just knew it. The last thing he would want to see when he walked out of the coffee shop was her in her white skirt and red-checked blouse.

The blouse was V-necked with a ruffle and a flounced sleeve and she'd thought she looked pretty cute in it. Until that moment. Suddenly, she wondered if she didn't look more like a throwback to the '50s—an over-the-hill model trying to sell a new car. This was a bad idea.

She could see him in there, yakking away. He must have said something funny because Rita laughed and shook her head at him. Brody Green was everyone's darling.

Except hers. The man was insecure with strong jerk tendencies. She should leave. This was pointless.

The barista put three to-go cups in a cardboard carrier and he picked it up and left, smiling. Of course, he was smiling. Every woman in Moonlight Harbor thought he was fabulous.

Lucy was the only one who saw that the emperor had no clothes.

No clothes. Sex. Stop it! She needed to scurry on over to her Ranger and leave.

Except she'd waited too long. He'd shouldered his way out the door and was already starting for his car.

He saw her, hesitated and frowned, then approached slowly. Cautiously. Like he was afraid she'd bite.

She still hadn't come up with exactly the right approach now that she had no goodies to give him. She winged it, opting for a smile and a slightly playful tone.

"It's a shame I left my peace offering at your office. They'd have gone well with coffee."

He moved a step closer to her and she caught a whiff of aftershave. The jump-roping got faster.

He cocked an eyebrow. Brody Green had very expressive eyes. "Peace offering?"

"You can't open negotiations without one," she said lightly.

"What are we negotiating?" His answering tone did not match her light one.

"A truce, maybe. Are you free for dinner tonight?"

He looked downright skeptical. "You're asking me to dinner."

"I am."

"No strings attached?"

"None."

"Not planning on slipping poison in my drink?"

"Not so much as a drop."

He still looked wary, but he nodded. "All right."

"The Porthole?" she suggested.

It was the best restaurant in town and the only way to impress him, she was sure. Judging by the way he dressed and the snazzy car he drove, Brody Green was all about appearances and he liked the finer things in life. He wouldn't stoop to eating at the Seafood Shack.

"All right."

"Seven o'clock?"

He nodded. "I'll meet you there." Then without another word, he got in his car and zoomed away.

Dinner with her archenemy—Lucy hoped her daughter appreciated the sacrifice she was making.

What had he been thinking agreeing to dinner with Lucy Holmes? He hadn't been thinking, of course. He was like some dumb fly sucked into a spider web by the electrical charge of its own flapping wings. His maleness was the equivalent of those wings on an insect, flapping away, his hormones buzzing, drawing him ever closer to the sticky web that held his doom. Lucy Holmes was trouble, Brody knew it, not only for him as a businessman but for him as a man. She was pretty and ambitious and, he was sure, a natural born heartbreaker. Nothing good could come out of meeting her for dinner.

So, of course, he showered and shaved a second time and splashed on cologne before donning slacks and a crisp shirt. He was an idiot.

He found her already waiting at a window table. The view was great. Not of the sand dunes and, in the distance, the waves, but of her. She wore a form-fitting black dress with a neck scooped deep enough to offer hope of a peek at her cleavage. A dirty trick, if you asked him, since this was a business meeting as far as he could tell. Flirty silver earrings shaped like seahorses dangled from her ears. An image flashed into his mind at lightning speed of him sweeping the dinnerware off that table and laying her out on top of it.

He needed a drink.

"I wasn't sure you'd come," she said when he slid into the chair across from her.

"I wasn't sure I would, either," he said honestly. "But I was curious." Curiosity killed the cat.

And spiderwebs caught flies. But what a pretty web this woman could weave. Look at that smile. Not since Jenna had a woman's smile gotten to him so easily.

Jenna. Did he want a repeat of that? He steeled himself and told those wings to stop beating.

Their waitress appeared, a woman named Chara, who had been his server many times. "Hi, Brody," she greeted him. "Would you like your usual?"

"Yes," he said. "And something for the lady." *Lady? Ha!* "Put it on my tab."

"This is my treat," Lucy said.

"You said dinner. I'll take care of the drinks."

She shrugged, then smiled up at Chara. "Whiskey sour," she said, surprising him.

"Same as yours," Chara pointed out to Brody.

"What a coincidence," he quipped.

"Most popular drink in the world right now, I read," Lucy said.

As if he was influenced by what was popular? "I've been drinking them for years."

"Me, too."

"No white wine?" he taunted as Chara left to fetch their drinks. "I thought every woman liked white wine."

"I'm not every woman."

That was for sure.

"And I prefer red. A good Cab." She might as well have added, *So there*.

"Me, too," he said.

"Look how much we have in common." Her smile almost seemed genuine.

But he doubted it was. Lucy Holmes knew how to work people. She was working him.

Or maybe she really was holding out the old olive branch. He needed to give her the benefit of the doubt.

"I guess we do at that," he said, and dredged up a smile in return.

"This is a great restaurant," she said as they waited for the drinks. "You can't beat the view."

He was trying hard not to look at the view. "You can't beat the food, either," he said, keeping his gaze from straying below her neck. "This restaurant may not have a Michelin rating but it's still worth the trip to Moonlight Harbor."

"There are so many things that make it worth the trip here," she said. "It's a wonderful place."

"It is," he agreed. Another thing they had in common— they both appreciated the town.

Their drinks arrived and they each took a sip. When, he wondered, was she going to get around to the purpose behind this meeting?

She set her glass down and cleared her throat. Okay, here it came.

"I guess you know my daughter and your son have been hanging out together a lot."

He nodded.

"I don't know if your son has said anything to you..."

Brody wasn't going to share what Declan had said. This was Lucy's idea. She could do the talking. He remained silent, forcing her to continue.

"My daughter seems to think we're making life difficult for them."

Brody studied the contents of his glass. "Really? Interesting."

"I hate to make things awkward for the kids."

Actually, so did he. But when it came to making things awkward, that wasn't all on him. He kept his mouth shut.

"There must be some way we can both do business in Moonlight Harbor without stepping on each other's toes."

Yeah, and who'd stepped first? "You would think so," he said.

She bit down on her lower lip, moved to pick up her glass, then left it on the table. "You're not making this easy, you know."

"What would you have me do?"

"Work with me here. Obviously, we're both competitive."

"Not necessarily. If you want to talk about competitive..." he began.

Those big eyes flashed lightning. "I'd call it more than competitive when you tell someone another broker doesn't know the market."

"It's true if she doesn't. And how about you telling my broker's friend you could get her more money for her house?"

"I never said that," Lucy insisted hotly.

"Oh, that's right. You just talked about how much more experienced you are."

"I said I was experienced. And I am! You were worse."

His head was starting to ache. He held up a hand. "Okay, okay. Water under the bridge. Maybe we both got a little carried away."

"Maybe *you* got carried away," she muttered, and took a big gulp of her drink.

"We'll be showing each other's listings so let's try to remain professional," he said.

She managed to simultaneously lift her chin and look down her nose at him. "An excellent idea."

"We each have our own circle of friends."

Her eyes narrowed. "Oh. So, since I'm new in town, do I need a list of people who are off-limits to become friends with? Maybe you should tell me right now whom I can safely get to know." She held up a hand before he could speak, and continued, "Oh, but you already know everyone here, don't you? So that leaves me a circle...this big." She held her thumb and index finger half a quarter of an inch apart.

Brody did not have high blood pressure, but he could feel his climbing. "You seem to be very good at ingratiating yourself. You'll have no trouble finding friends. Just sneak around with some cookies."

"Sneak!"

"What would you call it?"

Out of the corner of his eye, Brody could see Chara the waitress approaching to take their orders. She took one look at them and made a U-turn.

Meanwhile, Lucy was digging out her wallet. She slapped a twenty and a ten on the table, then rose. "I don't care what Jenna Jones says. You are insufferable." With that parting shot, she marched out of the restaurant.

What *had* Jenna said about him?

What did he care?

And what did he care what Lucy Holmes thought of him? The woman was unreasonable and impossible, sneaky and...

Charming.

Yeah, well, so were snake charmers.

Wait a minute, that would make him a snake. He was no snake. He was the good guy here.

Chara edged up to the table. "Do you still want dinner?" she ventured.

Oh, yeah, that. The dinner Lucy Holmes had invited him to share. "How about bringing me an order of your seafood lasagna to go?"

"Sure thing," she said.

Lucy Holmes was rude enough to waste the restaurant's table space on nothing more than a drink, but he had better manners. He paid for the dish and left another tip, then went home, consoling himself with the sure knowledge that the woman would be gone within the year. She'd already shown her true colors to him. It wouldn't take long for everyone else to see them.

She'd begun their meeting calm and diplomatic and had morphed into a shrew. What had happened?

Brody Green, that was what.

How could she have let him get to her like that?

Lucy sighed as she pulled the Rover into her driveway. Thank heaven her daughter and Declan were nowhere around. Hannah had known Lucy and Brody were meeting for dinner. She'd have been expecting a glowing report of how the evening had gone. Declan probably would have been right by her side, all ears. She could hardly explain to her daughter what a boor Brody Green was with his son standing right there.

And how to explain her behavior? Ugh.

The boor and the bitch—the evening's entertainment at The Porthole. She turned off the engine and dropped her head onto the steering wheel. What was wrong with her?

Disillusionment, that was what. Evan had opened the door to it and she'd invited it on into her heart. Now she was becoming cynical. And rude.

And, yes, she had to admit it, bitter. In spite of the fun of revamping her house and having her daughter with her and making new friends, her fragile happiness was becoming infected. The rose-colored glasses she'd always worn were gone and now she was looking through a darker lens, especially when she looked at men.

Really, could she blame Brody Green for reacting to her the way he had? She'd made no courtesy call when she first moved to town, made no effort to work together.

Until that night. She'd gone to the restaurant with the best of intentions. Surely, that emotional whirlpool they'd wound up in hadn't been all her making.

She sighed. They were going to have to find a way to peacefully coexist in Moonlight Harbor because she wasn't going anywhere. She wasn't sure how she knew, but she did know that this was the place she had to be to heal.

How could she heal if she and Brody Green kept throwing punches at each other? They should have been able to sit down and talk like mature adults.

Darn it all, she'd made the effort. As far as she was concerned, the ball was now in his court.

She only hoped he didn't try to knock off her head with it.

Sixteen

The grand opening open house at Dream Homes Realty was well-attended. Jenna even saw a couple of unfamiliar faces among all the familiar ones. The Friday night gang had all turned out, although a couple, like Courtney and Nora, had confided to her that they felt guilty over coming.

Courtney especially, since Brody had been so instrumental in helping her get Beach Babes Boutique. She stayed long enough to eat one of the bacon-wrapped dates Annie had made for the occasion, then left, claiming a backlog of work at home.

Jenna and Seth didn't stay long, either. They'd put in an appearance, partly because Seth was doing part-time work on Lucy's house and would be painting it, and partly because Jenna was becoming friends with Lucy and trying to stay neutral. It was difficult though, as she owed Brody a debt of gratitude for watching over the Driftwood Inn for her. She still felt guilty over not trusting him. And she didn't want to look like she was choosing sides in the Moonlight Harbor Realty Wars.

She suspected those competing ads in *Beach Times* were just the opening salvos. Ugh. In an ideal world Brody and

Lucy would team up, go into business together and turn themselves into a power couple.

She could see them together, as business and life partners. Both of them were people persons, both of them loved real estate. The perfect match. But what looked like a perfect match on the surface wasn't always. Maybe that was the case with these two. It sure would make things easier for everyone who knew them if it was.

"Who are we going to go with when your mom comes up to look at houses?" she asked Seth as they drove away.

"Lucy," he said. "I'm working for her."

"But I owe Brody a lot."

He scraped a hand through his hair and frowned. "I know."

"I don't want to be an ingrate," Jenna said.

"Me, either."

"Who do we owe the most loyalty to?"

The answer to that was a no-brainer and Seth's frown deepened. "Okay," he said at last. "We use Brody, but I'll be the one going with Mom and him to look at houses when she comes up for the Fourth. Deal?"

"Deal," Jenna agreed.

That was fine with her. Spending a cozy day looking at houses with Brody, even with her new mother-in-law as a buffer, would be awkward. Being around Brody at all still felt awkward.

The only way to pave over that awkwardness, really, was for him to find someone. Darn it all, the man needed to hurry up and get his love life sorted out.

Fourth of July weekend was always a big holiday for Moonlight Harbor. People came from all over to enjoy the miles of fireworks madness that took place on the beach.

In addition to fireworks at night, there was a parade during the day, as well as rides and arts and crafts and food booths down at the pier. The night before, locals and visitors enjoyed a street dance.

Lucy had made sure she'd be a presence, and had set up a bounce house for the kids down at the pier. Her daughter had been manning it during the day, handing out spatulas with Dream Homes Realty printed on the handle and business cards attached. But once five o'clock rolled around, it was Lucy's turn to watch over the bounce house.

Before the changing of the guard, Hannah insisted on getting a reel for Instagram. Once they started filming, she tried to convince Lucy that she wanted to go in the bounce house with the kids. But Lucy turned the tables on her and refused, instead insisting on Hannah doing it.

"But you're a child at heart," Hannah said, winking at the camera.

"Nice try." Lucy gave her a gentle shove. "Mother knows best," she said as Hannah went inside.

Declan turned the camera on Hannah and got the needed footage, and she popped back out, gave two thumbs-up and said, "Beachin'," and that was a wrap.

"Now, go have fun," Lucy told her.

She watched as Hannah strolled off with Declan and joined a cluster of kids their age, who were in front of a food booth, consuming corn dogs.

Kids. She had to stop thinking like that. They weren't really kids anymore. Her daughter was a young woman and Declan, Lucy had learned, would be graduating from college the next spring. Young adults. Old enough to fall in love and mean it.

Still young enough to mess that up. Lucy shoved away

the thought as she greeted a young dad and sent his son inside the noisy bounce house to add to the pandemonium.

"My boy loves this stuff," the dad said to her.

Oh, yes, she knew what people liked. And she knew how to make them happy and work with them. It made her good at what she did. So sue her.

Was there a bit of a bad attitude slipping in here? Probably. She looked over to where Bonnie's band was setting up and again wished she had someone to dance with.

The band consisted of Bonnie and three other women. One of them looked around her age; the other was younger, maybe in her early twenties. She had hair the same color as Bonnie's, cut chin-length, and similar features. A daughter, perhaps? If so, how cool was that? The fourth woman, a very attractive sixty-something, was assembling the drum set. She wore skin-tight jeans and the same jade green spangly top the others were all wearing—a bit of a mermaid look, which was fitting. In addition she had streaks of green in her spiked white hair, another nod to the band name.

Come seven o'clock, the band began to play, a newer up-beat tune that Lucy wasn't familiar with. One or two couples began to dance and several people gathered in front of the bandstand. The Mermaids moved from their opening song to a classic dance favorite, "Footloose," which got the crowd moving. It also got Lucy remembering how she and Evan used to love to go dancing.

She missed that. She missed a lot of things about her old life, sometimes even him. There was a quick cure for that. All she had to do was remember seeing him and Pandora in that shower. No loss. And if she really wanted to dance, she could turn on the music in her own living room and have at it.

Bonnie was rocking both her guitar and a short denim skirt and cowgirl boots, and when she began singing "Eternal Flame," Lucy could see several men stopping to check her out. Lucy chuckled as she watched one man's girlfriend give his arm a yank and tow him away.

Bonnie could have been a star. What had happened? Maybe, at some point, she'd share more of her past.

Meanwhile, Lucy could enjoy the music, and she spent the evening keeping the action going with her bounce house and chatting with parents. And, of course, passing out her spatulas.

The band took a break and Bonnie and her drummer, each enjoying deep-fried Twinkies, sauntered over to say hi.

"You guys are great," Lucy told them.

"Thanks," Bonnie said, and introduced the woman. "This is my mom, Loretta."

"You were amazing on that drum," Lucy told her.

"Thanks. It keeps me fit," said Loretta. "I only started playing in my fifties. I was a singer before that. And I played bass. Back in those days there weren't very many of us doing that."

"Mom was a force to be reckoned with."

"Still am," said the older woman with a wink. "So's my granddaughter."

"That's your daughter in the band?" So Lucy had been right.

"She's just here for the summer. She comes down on the weekends," Bonnie explained.

"Incredibly talented," bragged Grandma. "Just like her mom was."

Bonnie held up a hand, once more pulling a curtain on

her past. "Okay, enough already. Looks like your bounce house is a hit," she said to Lucy. "Great idea."

"I'm full of great ideas," Lucy quipped.

"Good for you," Loretta approved. "A woman's gotta be aggressive, go out there and get what she wants."

From the mild look of irritation on Bonnie's face, Lucy suspected that this was a subtle message from her mother and one she didn't particularly want. "We'd better let you get back to work," she said, and moved them away.

Lucy went back to working the crowd, handing out her spatulas and chatting with parents of hyped-up children, excited to burn off energy. She also kept an eye on the crowd, waving to the few people she knew and…not looking for Brody Green.

She never did catch sight of him, which seemed odd. Surely, he would have been at something like this, schmoozing. Oh, well, she didn't need to see him. She certainly didn't need to talk to him.

Where was he and what was he up to?

She knew he'd had a float in the parade. Declan had told her when she casually asked.

She should have had one as well, but it took time to build floats. Next parade she would have her float, as well as her bounce house, which was proving to be a huge success.

The Fourth brought sun and blue skies—another great day for both residents and visitors alike. Lucy stopped at the office and put up a little sign, inviting people to visit her at her bounce house on the pier. *We're offering fun for the kids and a special gift for you.*

She and Hannah were going to take turns manning the bounce house again, and Bonnie had stopped by that morning and offered to help out.

"It will be a zoo today," she'd told Lucy. "About the only

break you'll get is the during the parade. If you like, I can fill in for you so you can watch it."

Lucy had decided to take her up on her offer. She wanted to see what Brody Green's float looked like.

Not very original, she decided as she stood in the crowd next to Hannah and Declan and watched it rumble past. It was a gingerbread house with a fake grass lawn. He and the women she'd seen in his office were positioned on each side of it, throwing saltwater taffy out to the crowd.

"And here's our competition at Moonlight Harbor," Hannah was saying. "What do you think of that, Mom?" she asked, turning her phone on Lucy.

At least her daughter had warned her about this clip so she was ready, makeup on and hair done, and had the perfect comeback. "I think people are going to enjoy the house we have set up on the pier even more." This little bit would preface what they'd filmed the night before. *Take that, Brody Green.* (Yep, peacefully coexisting … while staying competitive.)

Declan shook his head when they'd finished. "Dad's gonna like that bounce house as much as he'd like stepping in a pile of shit."

Shit for the shit, Lucy thought. Peacefully, of course.

Brody had skipped the street dance. Not because he couldn't dance—if it was the kind where you actually got to hold a woman—but because there was no one with whom he wanted to dance. He was sure to run into Jenna and Waters and that wouldn't exactly put him in a good mood. And if he ran into Rian, she'd want to dance, and that wouldn't be a good idea. He knew she'd like to get back together, but he didn't want to, and he didn't want to lead her on in any way.

The Fourth was a different story. He always had a float in the parade, and he always wandered around the pier after, schmoozing and spending money at the various arts and crafts booths. It was a good way to support local artisans and get in some Christmas shopping for his mom and aunts and his daughter.

He'd just purchased a hammered silver bracelet made by local artisan Homer Smith for his daughter and was wandering toward one of the local church booths for strawberry shortcake when he caught sight of the bounce house.

And the woman in front of it, handing out kitchen spatulas and patting people on the arm like they were old friends. Lucy Holmes the ant at the picnic.

He was irked, both that Lucy had one-upped him and that he hadn't thought of the idea. He couldn't help admiring her creativity. The woman was a force to be reckoned with, for sure.

And he was already getting sick of reckoning with her. He got his strawberry shortcake and turned the other way.

Just in time to run into Jenna and Waters. Damn. Moonlight Harbor was becoming a minefield. Bad enough he'd had to follow two floats behind Jenna in the parade but he had to see her here. Shouldn't she have been back at the house getting ready for her annual Fourth of July beach party?

He forced his lips into the right position. He knew the smile didn't match the lack of enthusiasm in his eyes but that couldn't be helped.

"Hi there," she said as he juggled his shortcake and the bag with his purchase to shake Waters's hand. "I see you're busy supporting our local economy."

"Always," he replied. He turned his attention to the woman with them, an older woman, short with chin-length dark hair shot with silver. Waters's mom. It was easy to see the resemblance.

"I'm glad we ran into you," Jenna said. "Seth meant to call you."

Right. Brody was buying that.

"My mom's hoping to buy a small house here," Waters said. "Mom, this is Brody Green."

"It's nice to meet you," the woman said.

Her smile was warm. Obviously, no one had told her that Brody and her son had a history. Hardly surprising. Waters had always been tight-lipped. One of those brooding types women always fell for.

Brody could feel his polite expression slipping. He shored it up. This was business, after all, and if Jenna wanted to throw some his way, he wasn't too proud to put on his catcher's mitt.

"Got some nice properties right now. I'd be glad to show you a few."

"Nothing too expensive," she said. "One bedroom would do and I'd be fine with a condo. Just so I'm somewhere in town."

"I think I can find something for you," Brody said, and offered to show her some the next day.

"We're having our annual beach party tonight," Jenna told him. "You know you're more than welcome."

"Thanks," he said. "I appreciate the offer." *Sort of. Maybe. No, not really.* "But I've got plans," he lied.

He set up a time to meet with Waters and his mother and then scrammed. A Fourth of July beach party at Jenna's. She might as well have offered to hit him on the head with a hammer.

Anniversaries should be celebrated, but not the anniversary of the day the woman you loved dumped you. No, thanks.

He left the pier, went to the grocery store to stock up on beer, then went home to sit on his deck with a bottle of IPA and watch the waves and, later, the fireworks. Yep, he had plans. Plans to put this day behind him as quickly as possible.

The next morning he woke up with a headache and a strong desire to back out of house hunting with Seth and Mama Waters. But if he did, they'd go to Lucy Holmes and the idea of Team Jenna switching loyalty from him to her was not one he wanted to entertain. He sucked it up, got dressed, went to the office and gathered some listings he thought would appeal.

Waters was borderline friendly as Brody tooled them around town from place to place. In the end, he almost warmed up when Brody was able to negotiate a good price for his mother on a two-bedroom unit in the Dreamscape Condominiums, which would give her a view of fishing boats coming in and out of Westhaven as well as the occasional whale sighting.

"Appreciate it," he said, shaking Brody's hand after their offer was accepted.

"Happy to help," Brody said.

No lie. He always had been and always would be happy to help Jenna's family, for her sake and to honor Edie Patterson, her great aunt, who'd been a good friend.

As he did with all his clients, he took them to dinner to celebrate at The Porthole. It seemed they'd barely been served when Lucy and her daughter took a table on the other side of the room. Declan was with them. These days Lucy was seeing more of his son than he was.

Brody lost his appetite. He summoned the waiter and ordered another whiskey sour.

Jenna had followed his gaze. "She's actually a really a nice woman. And smart. Maybe you two should join forces."

"I'm sure at some point we'll be working together," he said and left it at that. It was a free country and he couldn't stop her from showing houses he had listed. Nor would it be smart to block her even if that were possible. Business was business, and they both needed inventory to sell.

But he was sure glad that the condo he'd sold was one of Taylor's listings.

"You're doing it again," Seth said to Jenna later that night after he'd returned from walking his mom to the room they'd put her in at the Driftwood.

Jenna looked up from the book she'd started reading. "What?" she asked, trying to appear the picture of innocence.

He raised an eyebropw. "Is that how you're going to play it?"

"You're being cryptic."

He came to the couch, sat down and put an arm around her shoulder. "You're playing matchmaker."

Look offended. That will work. "I'm not."

"And I know what you're up to with that look, too," he said.

"I was only making a helpful suggestion."

"Men don't like helpful suggestions about their love lives," he said, and snugged her up against him.

"Well, sometimes you need them."

He half chuckled. "Most times we don't. I told you, Green can sort out his own life."

"He's not doing a very good job of it if you ask me."

"Did I?"

She frowned at him. "You can be a real smart-mouth sometimes. You know that?"

"I do," he said and grinned. "But I can think of better things to do with my mouth," he murmured, and ran it along her neck.

Oooh, yes, he could.

"Give the guy a break," Seth said, and moved his lips to her chin. "Give him time to get over you. It's gonna take a while. It would for me."

She turned to face him. "How long would it take you?"

"'Til the day I died," he whispered, and kissed her.

Jenna sighed and slipped a hand through his hair. Brody was on his own. She had other things to think about.

At least for the moment.

Seventeen

Lucy had plenty to do after the Fourth—another ad to run in the paper, a couple interested in selling their house, which was another waterfront property on the end of town with a view of the bay and Westhaven. This one, she knew, would end up in a bidding war, something that was already the norm back in Seattle.

And she had her own house remodel to supervise. With her daughter in the mix, it involved a lot of filming footage of Lucy talking with Carl and his crew, of her supposedly helping pull up old flooring, which ended with a fall on the bottom.

"This is great," Hannah assured her as they sat on the front porch, watching it.

"I look ridiculous," Lucy said in disgust.

"You really don't, Mom," Hannah said earnestly. "You look cute and adorable and approachable. I know you want to be as polished as those women on the HGTV channel, but don't you think sometimes people want to see someone who looks just like them, managing to do the things they want to do? Don't you think they might actually be more willing to try when they see someone who's not totally perfect making her life good? And you did have on makeup," she finished, giving Lucy a shoulder bump.

It was a well-thought out and convincing—not to mention impressive—argument. "You should go into sales," Lucy said.

"In a way this is sales, right? We're selling inspiration," Hannah said happily. "We've already got eight-hundred followers. Maybe by the end of summer we will be micro-influencers, which means we might be able to get some sponsors."

Lucy hadn't looked properly awed so Hannah went on to explain what a good living they could make becoming influencers. As if Lucy couldn't make a good living selling real estate. But she wasn't doing this for herself. It was for her daughter.

"I might want to make this my career."

Helping her daughter enjoy her first business exposure was one thing. Hannah was working hard, and Lucy didn't want to discourage that. And maybe she could turn what she was doing into a viable business. But...

"After you finish school," she said.

"After I finish school," Hannah repeated, her voice losing some of its earlier enthusiasm. "Meanwhile, remember, you wanted me to work this summer. With this, I can keep working all year long."

Lucy was glad to see how well her daughter was doing the adulting thing, but she knew the importance of an education. "Just make sure your grades don't suffer."

"I know," Hannah said. "I have to run to the beach real quick while it's overcast. The light is perfect right now and I want to get some pictures of my beach must-haves."

"Speaking of must-haves," Lucy said. "We need to start

talking about all the expenses this business venture is racking up."

"Mom, you know you have to spend money to make money," Hannah said.

"Money you've budgeted for," Lucy said. "That book you've been reading does talk about things like budgets and expenses and profits, right?"

Hannah looked a little less enthusiastic. "Yes."

"Well, I think it's time you skipped ahead to that chapter. Let's start talking about how you're going to manage your business in a way that doesn't send you into Chapter Eleven."

"Mom," Hannah said, half laughing.

"I know you're starting small, but right now is the time to learn these important business principles when the cost is small. No business has unlimited funds. Neither do moms."

"Okay, I'll start budgeting...once we give me a budget."

"That is going to the top of our to-do list," Lucy said.

"I'm not sure I'm going to like this."

"I'm not sure you are, either," Lucy joked. At her daughter's crestfallen expression, she said, "Don't worry. We'll make sure you can still keep your influencer doors open, but let's start thinking of some creative posts you can make that will inspire women who don't have a lot of money to spend on home decor and clothes. We do live at the beach, and I bet you can dream up all kinds of great finds to make this house look great."

Hannah accepted the challenge. "I bet I can."

Lucy could hardly wait to see what she came up with.

She left her daughter to her photo shoot and Carl and company to continue doing their thing and headed for the *Beach Times* office, where she was going to talk about getting a bigger ad.

* * *

Hannah had just pulled up in front of one of the paths to Moonlight Beach when she got a text from Declan. U at the beach now?

Yep, she texted.

K. On my way.

He knew exactly where to meet her. It would be the same spot where they'd watched the fireworks the night of the Fourth. They'd produced plenty of fireworks there themselves, and she knew it was going to be their spot.

She'd spread out her beach towel and done a spill that showed off all her favorite beauty products and had taken a couple of really good pictures using her new camera lens when Declan showed up to help her with some other shots.

"Look at you," he said, taking in the shorts and top and sunglasses. He slipped an arm around her and kissed her neck so as not to mess up her lipstick. Such a smart man. "Ready to do this?"

"Yeah," she said, handing over the camera bag. "I want to get some shots of me balancing on that driftwood."

"Good idea," he approved.

He took several shots of her hamming it up on the driftwood, along with a reel of her hopping from one giant log to another. Then they did a selfie of the two of them sitting on a log with the sand dunes in the background.

"These are great," she approved. "You've got a good eye."

He smiled, pleased by the compliment. "Did you get any more followers from the post of the pictures I took on the Fourth."

"Picked up ten more," she said.

He nodded approvingly.

"In another year, who knows? I could be traveling and getting comped all kinds of cool stuff like Alyssa Bossio."

"Traveling with somebody?" he prompted.

"Maybe," she said coyly.

"I'm into traveling. We'd make a great team." He turned serious. "We already do, dontcha think?"

"I do," she said, equally serious.

She could see herself hitting the road with him in a classic Airstream or staying in an Italian villa. She could even see them getting married on the beach in Hawaii someday. Or on Moonlight Beach.

She could also see their parents glaring at each other during the ceremony. Ugh.

"What's wrong?" Declan asked.

"Nothing," she said, not wanting to spoil the moment.

Too late. Thinking about how much her mother hated his father kind of already had.

Declan studied her. "Come on, Hannah, something's wrong."

He was so in tune with her—so much more than any boyfriend she'd ever had. Had they been together long enough for him to be a boyfriend?

She shrugged. "Our parents hate each other."

"Yeah, I don't think they're too into each other. Dad didn't stay at The Porthole very long that night your mom invited him out."

"I don't think it went well," Hannah said, and sighed.

"So what if they don't like each other?" he said with a shrug.

"I guess it doesn't matter if nothing happens between us."

He frowned. "I thought something was happening between us. Is it just me, then?"

"No," she hurried to say. "Not at all. But if there is something…if we really got serious."

"That would be fine with me," he said with a grin. "And they don't have to travel with us."

"But we'd be like the Montagues and the Capulets."

"The who?"

"You know. *Romeo and Juliet.*"

He dropped the happy face. "Oh. Them."

"I mean, not that our parents are gonna start getting into sword fights but…" Would Mom boycott the wedding?

"Look, I'll talk to my dad. Maybe they just got off on the wrong foot. He's really a nice guy."

"And my mom's normally sweet. She never yells. It's just the whole divorce thing. Daddy really messed her up."

Declan nodded. "I get it. That happened with Dad, too. And then he was all serious with someone down here and then that blew up. I don't think he trusts women anymore. Can't say I blame him."

"You don't trust women, either?" Hannah asked. As in her?

"Not all women. Just, uh, well. I don't know. I don't want to end up like my dad someday."

"I don't want to end up like my mom," Hannah said. "I know she doesn't trust men. I don't blame her. But she doesn't have to take that out on your dad. All they have to do is be friends and quit stomping on each other's toes."

"Don't know how they can keep that from happening when they're both in the same business and fighting over the same customers."

Hannah frowned and shook her head. "Mom's worked with tons of other real estate companies. They show each other's houses and make deals all the time. It's ridiculous that she's having such a hard time working with your dad. Honestly, I think Daddy scarred her for life."

She sighed. Declan sighed. They sat in silence on the log, looking at the water.

"They need to talk," Declan said. "Again."

"Good luck with that," Hannah said.

Brody had felt sour ever since seeing Lucy enjoying dinner with his son. She hadn't so much as looked in his direction or come over to say hello.

He hadn't made a move her way, either. Hmm.

He was still in hmm-mode on Thursday morning, down-ing his second donut along with a mug of coffee, when Declan entered the kitchen, poured himself a mug and sat down at the table opposite him.

Brody shoved the box of donuts his way and said, "Help yourself."

Declan did, took a big bite, swallowed and then said, "Dad, we need to talk."

When your son said you needed to talk, it could mean anything. Anything bad.

Brody braced himself and said a cautious, "Okay."

"You got to fix things with Hannah's mom."

"Fix things," Brody repeated. And how, exactly, was he supposed to do that? "I'm not sure that's possible."

"If you don't, it could get awkward. Hannah and me, well, I think it could be serious."

Brody almost choked on his coffee. "How serious?" There was serious and there was *serious*.

"Forever. Maybe."

This inspired more choking. "You barely know the girl."

"I'm getting to know her pretty good."

Brody didn't even want to know what that meant. "You're too young to get serious," he protested.

"Dad, I graduate next spring," Declan reminded him. His tone of voice felt like a spanking. "Anyway, you were young when you married Mom."

"And look how that turned out."

"Hannah's different."

Not if she's anything like her mother. Not that Brody would know since he hadn't met the girl. So far she hadn't set foot in his house but Declan had been to her place more times than Brody could count. Paddleboarding on the canal, eating sandwiches on the back deck—he was becoming a regular member of their family. It was a far cry from how Brody had envisioned summer with his son turning out.

"You're too young to get married," he insisted.

"Maybe. But what if we move in together?"

That probably wasn't a good idea, either.

"What if we get married eventually?" Declan continued. "How's that gonna work if you and her mom hate each other?"

"We don't hate each other." *We just can't stand each other.*

"Dad. You need to do something to fix this. Serious."

"What do you expect me to do, give the woman a lobotomy?"

"Give her a chance."

Brody grabbed another donut, took a bite.

Stalling didn't help. "Come on, Dad. You're good at making deals."

Not with women. His marriage had failed and he'd lost Jenna.

"Look, if things work out with Hannah and me, you two

will be stuck seeing each other a lot. You might as well start getting along now."

Wise advice. Who was the parent here and who was the kid?

Brody heaved a sigh and tossed the rest of the donut back on his plate. "Okay, I'll see what I can do."

He didn't want to do anything.

Well, most of him didn't, and in the end that part won the mental battle. He was too busy that day to make time for Lucy Holmes, anyway.

His son was far from happy with him that evening when he learned Brody had made no effort to contact Lucy and stormed off. His parting words, ringing in Brody's ears. "Jeez, Dad, you're being a shit."

A shit. When did he go from the dad his kids loved to visit to being a shit? Since a certain woman came to town, that was when. *Thank you, Lucy Holmes.*

But he needed to shoulder some blame as well. She'd at least made an effort at a peace accord. Now it was his turn. Hopefully, they could find a way to be in the same room without one or both of them plotting destruction.

At eleven the next morning he drove to her office. If she was there, he'd ask her to lunch. If not, well, he could say he tried.

She was there. He saw her through the plate glass window, sitting at her desk, which looked both feminine and expensive, rather like the woman herself. He could see part of what she was wearing—a simple white blouse and a gold chain necklace. Her hair was pulled back and he caught a glint of small gold hoops at her ears.

She was talking on her phone, smiling that great smile. An old-fashioned yellow legal pad sat on the desk, and she made a note on it. She talked another minute, then ended the conversation, still smiling.

Until she looked up and saw him. There went the smile. Her lips moved. He wasn't the best lip-reader, but he was pretty sure she'd said, "Shit."

Her daughter was seated at the other desk. She looked at her mother, puzzled, then looked to where Brody stood and smiled at him.

Well, at least someone was glad to see him. He lifted a hand in greeting and opened the door, half wishing he had a white flag to wave. No, not a white flag. That meant surrender.

"I come in peace," he said, going for the smart-ass approach.

The daughter was amused, but Lucy remained stone-faced. She stood up but made no move to walk toward him. The pants she wore were leg-hugging in a black-and-white check and she was wearing white heels. She looked both cute and professional at the same time.

"Mr. Green, what brings you here?" she asked in a business-polite voice.

"I'd like to take you to lunch," he said simply. "Are you free?"

"Yes, she is," her daughter answered before Lucy could say anything. The girl joined her mother. "Hi. I'm Hannah."

"Ah, the amazing Hannah," he said. "My son's been singing your praises. It's nice to finally get to meet you."

"Same here," she said.

The girl had inherited her mother's electric smile. It was easy to see why Declan had fallen so hard.

"If you go now, you'll avoid the lunch rush. I can hold things down here," she said to her mother.

Lucy looked anything but happy with her daughter's

eagerness to get her out the door, but she nodded to Brody and said, "All right. It looks like I can do lunch." Then she quickly added, "I'll follow you in my car."

So she'd be able to escape. Maybe that wasn't a bad idea. Maybe he'd want to escape, too.

He led her to The Porthole. Maybe not the best choice, since it was the scene of their last ill-fated meeting. As they pulled into the parking lot, he chided himself for not taking her to dinner. Lunch looked like he was trying to cheap out.

That wasn't the case. He just wanted something with a built in time limit. This felt like the equivalent of going for a prostate exam. He simply wanted to get it over with as quickly as possible. Lunch could be fast because, well, people had to get back to work.

But once they were seated at his favorite window table, he half regretted the decision. Lucy Holmes was smiling at him. A little suspiciously, but smiling nonetheless. Even when it wasn't turned up to high, it was something else. A man could bask in it.

He cleared his throat. "We need to make another stab at a peace accord."

She cocked a perfectly arched eyebrow. "Do we?" Her expression went from suspicious to almost teasing. Almost.

"Look, I know I've been a shit." According to his son.

"A little," she agreed, but not in anger, which he took as a good sign.

He wasn't sure where to go from there and was relieved when their server arrived to take drink orders. Iced tea for her, the same for him. Then it was the two of them again and his mind was a blank.

He'd never had trouble talking to a woman before. Even when he was married and squabbling with his wife, words had come easily. He was known for his charm. Where was that charm now? Why couldn't he think what to say next?

She paved the way. "I'm sorry about the last time we were together. I flew off my broom handle," she cracked. "We do need to find a way to get along. It's a small town."

His gut unclenched. "But growing all the time, which means there should be enough business for both of us. One of us might list a house while the other might sell it. Or vice versa." It was something he should have, could have acknowledged earlier. He *was* a shit.

"Does that mean we're done playing king of the mountain?"

She made it sound like he was an emotional twelve-year-old. He could feel his earlier humility shifting into something not quite so conciliatory.

"Or queen," he said.

She nodded. "Or queen. I think we can fit both of our castles up there."

He softened. "I think so, too. So let's try working together. If one of us has a fish on the line, the other stays out of the pond. Fair enough?"

"Fair enough."

"And no undercutting each other, because we both have our own strengths."

"Let's make that apply to print as well as in person," she added and he nodded.

"Fair enough. Shake hands on it?"

"Shake hands on it," she agreed, and held out that pretty little hand for him to take. It was small and smooth, and holding it gave him an appetite to touch more than her hand.

Taking Brody Green's hand felt like taking hold of a live wire. Lucy felt the zing all the way up her arm and clear down to her toes, and the zing about set her panties on fire on the way through.

It had nothing to do with him. She was sex-starved, that was all. Her reaction was the equivalent of standing at a bakery window, drooling over the goodies inside, when you were on a diet.

So quit standing in front of the bakery. She broke the contact and grabbed for the iced tea their server brought like it was a shield.

"Tell, me, how did you end up here in Moonlight Harbor?" he asked. His tone was conversational rather than adversarial. Could the man really adjust to sharing the mountain that quickly?

She couldn't help comparing him to Evan, whose insecurities had often been present in snide remarks or criticism when she ignored his advice and listened to her own instincts instead. Her instincts had rarely been wrong and that had often resulted in man hurt for him. It had required her best skills in both seduction and diplomacy to keep things on an even keel.

Seduction. Obviously, that skill had faltered.

Brody was waiting for an answer.

My marriage was a disaster, and like all good disasters, I never saw it coming. Way TMI.

"This looked like the perfect place to make a new start," she said.

He nodded in agreement. "That's why I wound up down here."

Their server was back and they placed their orders—Cobb salad for Lucy, wild salmon for him. Then it was time for more conversation.

She decided to start it and take them in a better direction.

"You know, people talk about you behind your back," she teased.

"Yeah? What do they say?"

"It's all good. According to Jenna and Courtney, you're Saint Brody."

"Yeah, that's me," he scoffed, and took a drink of his iced tea.

She couldn't help but keep the teasing going. "You don't think you're wonderful?"

"Maybe a little wonderful," he conceded with a grin.

"And does it get lonely up there on that pedestal?" she persisted.

He sobered. "It can get lonely no matter where you are." It was as if he'd revealed some secret he shouldn't have. He quickly backpedaled. "But I'm okay on my own."

"It's good to be okay with yourself, wherever you are," she agreed.

Their food arrived and conversation switched to lighter topics. Best places to eat in Seattle. They both agreed that Canlis topped the list. Favorite kinds of movies. Action for him. For her, too, but she liked a little romance thrown in for good measure.

"Not very realistic, I'm afraid," she said with a shrug. "I used to love a good action-romance movie…"

Okay, that was wandering a little too close to personal wounds. "Hobbies?" she asked, turning them in a safer direction.

"Well, I don't collect things," he said.

Except for female admirers.

"I like football and basketball. Used to love to go my son's games."

"Oh, yes," Lucy agreed. "I used to love watching Hannah's tennis matches."

"I heard that she plays. How about her mom?"

"When I have time," Lucy said, and then moved the conversation away from the courts.

She and Brody Green were getting way too cozy. The last thing she needed was to start playing tennis with him. Next thing she knew they'd be doubles partners, planning out their strategies against the opposing team. She wasn't about to go partnering with any man ever again, not even on the tennis court, and especially not this man. Brody Green had the potential to be a real heartbreaker and her heart still hadn't healed from the near fatal wound Evan had dealt it.

She needed to keep things business light between Brody and herself. That was the wise thing to do.

And she was determined to be wise. She ate two-thirds of her salad, chatted a little longer, then decided it was time to leave.

"Thanks for lunch. I'm glad you suggested this," she said, and meant it. They'd proved that they could actually behave like civilized adults.

"Me, too," he said.

"Adulting. My daughter would be proud." He lifted a questioning eyebrow and she shrugged. "Never mind. Thanks again. I enjoyed getting to know you."

And now she really did have to scram before she got to know him any better. She was beginning to like this civilized Brody way too much.

Brody watched Lucy Holmes thread her way between the tables and thought of the old joke: hate to see you leave but love to watch you go. The woman was poetry in motion.

She also had a real knack for maneuvering a conversation in whatever direction she chose. She'd made sure to keep things light and had revealed as little of her personal history as possible. The one time they got near the deep end of the conversational pool, she'd paddled back to the safety of the shallows as quickly as she could.

He could hardly blame her. They hadn't exactly built up a close friendship. Just as well, he told himself, because now he was wandering into dangerous territory. He wasn't simply attracted to Lucy Holmes. He was intrigued by her.

She hadn't suggested getting together again for a meal and had adroitly blocked the road to any suggestion to meet on the tennis courts. Too competitive to risk losing to him? Lucy Holmes was definitely a woman who wouldn't take loss easily. What was her story? How had she wound up a single mom?

He didn't need to know. He didn't need to fall for another woman.

Man, that smile. Those lips. Those big eyes.

Nope. Not falling.

Eighteen

Hannah seemed to think that one lunch signaled the beginning of two family togetherness and promptly invited Declan and his father over for dinner the following night. It was a good strategic move that she announced it when she and Lucy got home from the office and there were witnesses. Carl and Seth and one of Carl's employees were all still present, covered in dust.

Like the whole house. Kitchen cabinets had been torn out, floors torn up and the dumpster outside the house was full to the brim. Of course, their present state made the perfect excuse to not entertain.

"Oh, Hannah Honey Bear. The house is chaos," Lucy protested. "Let's do this later in the summer."

"It'll be fine, Mom," Hannah said, undeterred. "The patio table has four chairs and we have paper plates."

"And nothing in the fridge but pop and wine." And right then wine sounded like what the doctor ordered. As soon as the crew was gone, she'd dive into a large glass full.

"I'll pick up some stuff at the deli tomorrow and get some cookies at the bakery," Hannah said easily. "You won't have to do a thing. Anyway, Declan's dad wants to see what progress we're making on the house."

"Let's reschedule for after the kitchen is done."

Hannah frowned at her. "Mom, I already invited them. You can't take back an invite. It's rude."

"You can if you didn't check with your mother first," Lucy said.

The doorbell rang and Hannah rushed off to open it, calling over her shoulder, "That's Declan."

Good. Lucy would explain to him that Hannah had gotten carried away and this wasn't a good time for visitors. It especially wasn't a good time for a tall handsome visitor who could easily shift her hormones into overdrive.

A moment later Declan was walking into the scene of chaos, looking casual in a T-shirt and shorts. "Wow, they got a lot done today."

"Yes, and as you can see, we are in a mess here," Lucy said. "I know Hannah invited you and your father over for dinner but—"

It was as far as she got. "Yeah, Dad wants to see what you've done so far. Thanks for inviting us. He says he'll bring the wine."

Lucy would probably drink the whole bottle single-handedly.

"You ready to paddleboard?" Hannah asked him, putting a period to the topic of dinner.

"Sure," he said, and followed her out the sliding glass door.

"We're done for the day," Carl told Lucy. "Cabinets should be here to install by Tuesday."

"Great," she said, and thanked him.

The next week would have been so much better for company. She'd at least have had half a kitchen. She said adios to Carl and company, then dug a plastic glass from the cardboard box in a corner and poured herself some wine. She slipped out onto the back deck and settled at the patio table, watching as the kids launched their paddleboards.

They got on as fast as otters, stood upright and took off. Youth made everything look so easy.

Why did life have to become so complicated when you got older? Lucy had no answer for that question. At the moment the more pressing question was how to serve a meal in the midst of chaos and keep that chaos from entering her heart.

Saturday she sent Hannah to Beachside Grocery to pick up potato salad, coleslaw and fried chicken from the deli, along with cola and bottled lemonade. While Hannah was picking up the main course, Lucy went to a little bargain store she'd found and picked up paper plates and beach-themed paper napkins sporting seashells. Then she swung by Cindy's Candies and purchased chocolate-covered Oreos and fudge. There. They were set for a perfect picnic meal.

The deck in the back of her house was large enough for both a patio table and chairs and extra seating. She'd kept the patio table as a placeholder until she found something she really loved and had bought a wicker sectional for cozy conversations around a firepit. That was also yet to come as she was still researching what would be best and safest.

Her first entertaining in her new house...way before she was ready, but oh well. She could be flexible. Although she would have preferred inviting Brody into a perfectly remodeled and decorated house. She didn't look too closely into the reasoning behind that, choosing to simply chalk it up to pride.

Even getting herself ready for entertaining became a fashion challenge. Jeans or a skirt? Hair up or down? Jewelry?

"You're being ridiculous," she finally told herself and opted for hair down, no jewelry, a simple top, jeans and flip-flops. This was dinner with the kids, nothing more.

When he and Declan arrived, she was glad to see Brody had opted for casual also. Jeans and a shirt with the sleeves rolled up. Loafers with no socks. The man was a human Venus flytrap, too pretty to resist.

But she would. They were getting along for the sake of the kids, and because they were grown-ups and needed to act like it. That was all there was to this, so her hormones could just settle down and behave.

He handed over a bottle of Cabernet sauvignon that she suspected had cost a pretty penny.

"Thank you," she murmured, stepping aside to let them in. "I assume Declan warned you that you'd be entering a scene of complete chaos."

"I did," Declan said before his father could speak. "Thanks for having us over."

Hannah joined the group at the door. "We love having company," she said, speaking for Lucy.

It was as if neither her daughter nor his son trusted either of them. Parent-handlers. "We're out back on the deck," Lucy said, and led the way.

"No chaos out here," Brody observed, taking in the layout.

"This is a work-in-progress, too. I'm going to update the patio table and install a firepit," Lucy said. "Shall we try some of this wine?"

"Sure," he said, and made himself at home while Lucy went to the kitchen to open the wine.

Hannah and Declan were already in there, helping themselves to lemonade and raiding the cookies.

"Man, these are good," he said around a mouthful.

"Yes, I really slaved over those," Lucy joked, and he grinned at her.

Declan was a nice boy, and hanging with the kids in the kitchen as she uncorked the wine felt relaxed and so very Hallmark. It was what she'd tried for all the years she'd been with Evan but had never quite been able to achieve. Work had kept their lives moving at a hectic pace. They'd been a family, of course, but sometimes it had felt like they were sitting on the edge of something rather than settling in. This moment felt like sinking into a comfy armchair.

Family, it was something people took for granted. How Lucy wished she could have another bite of that apple. When her marriage ended, she'd felt as if she'd been cut into a million little pieces, each one trying to find its way back to being whole. How strange it was that standing in a torn-up kitchen, missing everything from its cabinets to its flooring, with only a stove and fridge that would soon be replaced, she felt more whole than she had in months.

She poured wine into plastic glasses and followed the kids out to the deck. "Only the best glassware for our company," she quipped, handing one to Brody. Hard to believe he was here on her deck and they were actually being cordial.

"*Invaders* would probably be a better word," he said.

"Mrs. H is cool with company," Declan said, smiling appreciatively at Lucy.

"I'll be more cool when the house is finished," Lucy said as she lit the citronella candles on the table.

"It's going to be great when it's done," Hannah put in.

"Meanwhile, we keep getting more followers on Insta and subscribers to our YouTube channel."

"You've got a YouTube channel?" Brody looked at Lucy in surprise. What else did she see there? Maybe a little grudging respect?

"We're going to become influencers," Hannah concluded.

Lucy shook her head. "We're going to become something."

"Hey, I think it's great," Declan chimed in.

"You wouldn't believe how many views we're up to now of that reel of Mom falling over pulling up flooring," Hannah said to him.

Lucy could feel the heat of embarrassment skipping up her neck. She saw Brody looking at her with a mocking raised eyebrow and the skipping turned to a run and spread to her cheeks.

"That sounds interesting," he said. "I'll have to check it out."

Great. Just what she wanted. "We've filmed some serious segments, too," she said.

As if she needed to impress Brody Green? Okay, so she wanted to impress him. She was only human.

"Yeah, that one where Mom is talking about how to choose cabinets is really good," Hannah put in. "She's going to do one on how to stage a house, too."

"So you do more than sell houses," Brody concluded.

"I know something about decorating. And remodeling," Lucy added. *Now.*

Most of that she was learning as she went. And one thing she was learning first hand was that you never stayed on budget no matter the size of the remodel. Of course, everyone knew that. But now she *really* knew it.

The kids carried most of the conversation, and there was some joking about how hard Lucy and Hannah had slaved over their dinner—it took a lot of effort to make a selection at the grocery deli counter. Now that they'd laid down their swords, Brody seemed determined to be convivial, and the meal was a pleasant one.

Then Hannah and Declan announced that they'd be leaving. Sabrina Jones was hosting a party on the beach. So, bye parents.

Their departure left a ripple of unease in their wake. She and Brody had already had their peace accord, and they'd enjoyed the equivalent of a state dinner with the kids. It had all been lovely and polite and comfortable. But now they'd been left to their own devices and that feeling of comfort was starting its vanishing act. It was as if everything Lucy had felt earlier had been an illusion. She wasn't comfortable. Brody Green was still her business rival. They had nothing but ambition in common, no past and certainly no future. This was awkward. The scattered pieces she'd thought were coming together started running in all directions, crying, *What's going on here? What do we do?*

"Tell me what all you're going to do on the house," Brody said, answering the question. They were going to talk about her remodel.

Okay, she could do that. She talked about her plans for the kitchen, showed him the new flooring for the house, which was sitting piled in the living room. They talked paint and lighting fixtures, and she was pleasantly surprised to find they got along like two old friends.

"I see you took that wall out," he said, pointing.

"I did. It opened up the whole house."

"Good idea. The place is going to look great when it's done," he said. "Make sure you get the blue exterior paint dark enough so the mold doesn't show, because you'll get it down here."

"That's what Seth Waters told me," she said.

"He would know."

"He's going to do my exterior and interior painting."

Brody nodded. "He'll do a good job. You could flip this place and make a nice profit."

The more of her she was pouring into the place, the more in love she was falling with it. "That was my plan B for if things didn't work out here," she admitted, then studied him. "Are they?"

"So far neither of us is starving," he said. "I just sold a house on Beach Circle and you probably saw the listing for the new build on Dolphin."

"I did, and I think I have a client in Seattle interested in buying it for a vacation home. So maybe we really can manage to coexist in the same town," she said, half teasing.

"It's a free country," Brody said. "You have as much right to open a business as anyone."

It was about time he realized that.

"You definitely got the better location," he added.

Did she detect some resentment in his voice? "You snooze you lose." He could have grabbed that space if he'd wanted. "I don't like to lose," she added.

Evan had left her feeling like a big loser. She was never going there again. In any facet of her life.

"Me, either," Brody said, "but, hopefully, we can both be winners."

"I like the sound of that," Lucy said.

It had been the perfect thing for him to say. Brody Green was shedding his jerk persona bit by bit. It was like the Disney version of *Beauty and the Beast* where, in the end, with a sparkle of magic, the beast turned into a noble prince.

There weren't enough noble princes to go around. Those Disney princesses had taken them all. Still, Lucy was finding herself liking this man—more than she should have, considering what she'd been through with Evan. And considering the rocky start she and Brody had made.

They refreshed their wine and returned to the deck to enjoy the warm summer evening. Dusk began to cloak the sky, and lights in the homes across the canal winked on. Houses and fir trees slowly became silhouettes.

"I love this time of night," Lucy said.

"Me, too," he agreed, and they sat in surprisingly companionable silence and let the light fade around them until the stars put in their appearance and the last of the day's warmth disappeared.

She shivered and he set aside his empty glass. "I should take off."

Take off what?

Lucy told her hormones to behave.

"Thanks for having Dec and me," he said.

"I'm glad you came," she said, and meant it. What an interesting turn of events.

Events didn't turn any further. He started for the sliding glass door and she followed, then followed him through the house to the front door where he thanked her again. Was he looking at her lips? She could have sworn he was looking at her lips.

Oh, no. Not a good idea. She took a tiny step back.

He did, too. "Let me know if your client likes the house. The seller's going to entertain all offers come Tuesday."

"So, a bidding war."

He nodded. "It's looking that way. Good night, Lucy."

"It was at that," she said softly as he turned and started for his car.

* * *

It was unnerving how close Brody had come to giving in to temptation and grabbing Lucy Holmes and kissing her. So what if she was beautiful and clever? She was also the human equivalent of an electric eel. If he got close, he knew he was bound to get zapped.

He drove home and streamed the sci-fi classic *Alien* in an effort to scrub the image of those kissable lips of hers from his mind.

It didn't work. The woman had gotten under his skin from the moment he met her and now she was creeping toward his heart. No way could he allow that to happen. He was not going to get heart-deep in a relationship ever again.

Except when he went to bed and closed his eyes, there was Lucy Holmes, smiling at him.

"You can control this," he told himself. "Keep things professional. No more cozy dinners. No more getting within a ten-mile radius of those lips."

He craved them though, craved every inch of her, and could envision dragging her off to his bed. He could also see them waking up together in the morning and drinking coffee on his deck, watching the sunrise.

Yeah, he needed that like he needed to be in a higher tax bracket, like he needed high cholesterol. Like he needed a never-ending headache. Which was exactly what the woman had been since the day she hit Moonlight Harbor. How the heck was he going to stay away from her?

The new cabinets arrived on Tuesday, and Hannah was, of course, recording it all, making sure Lucy was front and center to comment.

"So far, so good," Lucy said to the camera. "But I know that if something can go wrong, it will. I'm taking a deep breath and staying zen. If you're in the middle of a house remodel, I recommend you do the same. Things always get resolved eventually."

"Uh, I'm glad you said that," Carl said as he unwrapped a cabinet.

Lucy un-zened. "What's the problem?"

"There's been a delay on the countertops."

Lucy had hoped to have a house-warming party to celebrate the end of her renovations at the beginning of August. She saw that drifting away with the tide. "How long of a delay?"

"Ten days."

Grrr. But okay, she could go with the flow, especially since her daughter was still filming a segment for their YouTube channel, using Declan as her lighting expert and videographer while she directed.

Lucy shrugged and smiled for all her new friends out there in Media Land. "All I can say is I'm glad we're not flipping this house and we're not in a time crunch."

"That is so boring, Mom," said Hannah the Director. "Can't you get a little mad?"

Lucy frowned at her. "What do you want me to do, throw a tantrum?"

"Something like that."

"No way am I going to do that. Who would trust a realtor who throws a tantrum?"

"Then I guess this would be a safe time to let you know I forgot to tell you that Mrs. Robinson called three days ago about that beach house and Dream Homes just sold it yesterday."

Lucy could feel her eyes expanding, probably to the size of dinner plates. "What?" she gasped.

Hannah grinned and said, "Cut. Just kidding."

"That was not a cute stunt," Lucy said, pointing a finger at her.

"Sorry," Hannah said. It didn't sound convincing.

"I've gotta get going," Declan said and scrammed.

Ten minutes later, Lucy sent a properly chastised Hannah off to open the office, then sat out on the deck to make a few calls before selecting furniture and decor she needed to stage a house she'd just listed. She and her daughter would have to have yet another serious talk about this whole social-influencer thing. She was glad Hannah was becoming so business-minded, working hard, both at the office and on building what she kept referring to as their brand, but she was going to have to stop hopping over the boundaries Lucy set. Making a fool of her mother was off the table. If Hannah wanted more drama, she was welcome to be the one providing it.

A text from her daughter came in. Still luv me?

Of course, she did.

Yes, but no more making a fool of your mother. Got it? Otherwise, you lose your funding.

K.

"You'd better have it or you're going to get it," Lucy muttered.

She drove by the beach house Brody had recently listed. Yes, this one would work for Mrs. Robinson.

She arranged a time to show it late that afternoon, then decided to reward herself with a swing by Beans and Books. There she ran into Jenna Waters, who was getting an iced coffee.

"Seth tells me you're making progress on the house," Jenna said.

"We are. I can hardly wait to see how it looks once the floors are in."

"Same here."

"I'm running into a couple of delays but I still hope to have a party to show off the finished place sometime next month. Seth's going to start painting the living room later this week and he assures me it won't take long to paint the outside."

"He'll do a good job for you," Jenna assured her.

"I know he will. Meanwhile, my daughter already has me entertaining."

"Oh?"

"We had Brody and his son over."

"Sounds like fun."

"It was interesting. We wound up picnicking on the deck."

"So, looks like those peace negotiations are going well," Jenna said.

"I don't think either of us will have to leave town," Lucy said. "And I'm glad about that. I love it here."

"It's a great town filled with a lot of great people. Including Brody," Jenna added.

Lucy cocked her head. "Do tell."

"Okay, is my matchmaking that obvious?" Jenna asked with a laugh.

"A little."

"What can I say? I'd like to see him happy. Sometimes I feel a little guilty that I broke things off."

"It had to be hard," Lucy said diplomatically.

"In the end it wasn't, because even though Seth and I had our challenges, I knew he was my soul mate. When it's right, you know. I loved Brody, I really did. But I realized I loved Seth even more. You can try and rationalize those feelings away, make what you think is a smart decision, but in the end, the heart wants what the heart wants."

Jenna was right, and that was unnerving. *Don't start wanting things that aren't good for you,* Lucy cautioned her heart.

Nineteen

Nine hundred followers on Instagram now! Hannah was pumped. Every post on the *Always Beachin'* website was getting comments, and the last reel she'd put up on their YouTube channel had gotten five-hundred thumbs-up. They were on their way.

She'd just posted pictures of the sand dollars she'd collected, dried and then painted with inspirational words such as *love*, *relax*, *hope* and *dream*. They'd turned out great and she'd gone to the beach to take pictures of them, artistically arranging them in the sand. She was already getting a ton of comments on them.

"That is adorable," Mom approved when Hannah showed her as they sat on the deck, enjoying croissants. "And you haven't gone over budget."

"You were right. Everything doesn't have to be about what people can buy," Hannah said.

"Showing people that they can do what we can do," Lucy said, quoting part of her speech back to her.

"Wait 'til you see what I'm going to do with those cute little blue jelly jars Mr. Sullivan was getting rid of," Hannah said.

"What are you going to do?" Mom asked.

"I'm thinking of making them into candles...with some shells embedded in the top, those cute tiny ones."

"Very clever," Mom approved. "You're doing a fabulous job, Hannah Honey Bear."

"*We're* doing a fabulous job," Hannah corrected her. "People really love us. They love you. At the rate we're growing, it won't be long before we have companies asking us to spotlight their products."

"That would be fun," Mom said.

"Maybe some of the local businesses will want to help decorate the house," Hannah continued. "How awesome would that be!"

Mom smiled at her. "It would be awesome."

"I'm glad you get that, because I want to look into hiring a videographer to film some segments when you start pulling things together. To take things up a notch, make everything more polished and professional." There, she'd done a good job of slipping that in, right after pointing out that she was budgeting wisely and growing the business.

"And is that in the budget?" Mom asked suspiciously.

"I might go over a little. But, honest, Mom, it won't be long before I start hearing from casting agents, offering to collaborate on a campaign."

"A campaign," Mom repeated.

"For a company's products."

"Darling, I don't want to burst your bubble, but it might take a while before you reach that point."

It looked like Mom was about to drag out the wet blanket. "I'll get there. You have to find a way to stand out. I think I'm doing that. We've got that mother-daughter vibe going, plus I'm doing things on my own. I've got all kinds of ideas for future posts and reels and blogs—even for fall and winter. And don't worry," she hastily added, "I won't let it interfere with school."

She pulled out her iPad, where she'd been keeping track of both expenses and their growing numbers of followers, as well as planning future posts and showed the documents to her mother.

Mom studied them, nodded slowly. "I'm impressed." She smiled at Hannah. "You've really put the work in here."

"I'm loving doing this and I really want to succeed. I think I've discovered my passion."

Mom was silent a moment, contemplating. It was a very long moment.

At last she said, "I'm proud of your dedication, and I'm impressed with how hard you've been working this summer. The website looks great and you've done an excellent job of greeting walk-ins and clients. That kind of hard work should be rewarded."

"So, it's okay?" Hannah asked eagerly. "Can we put a little extra money in the budget?"

"Go for it," Mom said. "A woman should always follow her dreams."

"Yes!" Hannah crowed. "Hiring a pro is going to take us to the next level."

"Your mom is so lit," Declan said approvingly when Hannah shared the news with him as they paddled their way down the canal. "And forward thinking. My dad could learn a few things from her. You know he doesn't even have an Insta account."

"Right now women own social media," Hannah said. "Too bad our parents aren't working together. They could do all kinds of stuff." She thought a moment. "You know, we could take advantage of the fact that they're not, film them competing for houses."

Declan's brows pulled together. "How would you show that?"

"I don't know," Hannah admitted. "Maybe we could shoot some shots of each of us standing by the for-sale sign in front of a house our parent is selling. Make it like a contest where people have to vote. Who'll sell their house first? Who's going to be the best in Moonlight Harbor?"

He grinned. "That could be cool. But maybe let's not tell 'em. If your mom beat out my dad, I think he'd be pissed to have the whole world see it."

"Good point," she said. "Let's go take pictures as soon as we're done here. Looks like it's gonna cloud up a little and the light should be perfect."

The light cooperated and they both got pictures of each other mugging for the camera. Declan convinced his dad to pose in front of his Beach Dreams Realty office and Hannah got a similar shot of Mom.

She posted them side by side, along with the pictures of the houses. *Who'll sell their beach house first?* she captioned it. *Do you love Lucy or are you betting on the competition? #AlwaysBeachin' #bestbeachhomes #beach-houses #DreamHomesRealty.* Ha! That should get Mom some business.

"What the heck?" Taylor said, turning her phone so Brody could see.

He walked over to her desk, took it and checked out the Instagram post. And swore. Lucy Holmes was at it again.

"I'll be back," he said, and headed for his convertible. He had no problem with some friendly competition, but putting her company name in a hashtag and not his wasn't friendly.

Both she and Hannah were at their desks when he strode into the office. Lucy smiled at him, but he armored up.

"If you have an offer on one of my listings, you can simply call, you know," she said teasingly.

"Just thought maybe I'd come in and cast my vote," he said, not quite so teasingly. "No mention of who the competition is. I guess you must have run out of hashtags."

"I have no idea what you're talking about," Lucy said, slowly shaking her head.

Right. "It's a clever idea. It would have been nice to be asked whether I wanted to be part of it."

"What on earth?" she said, looking confused.

"My broker found it on Instagram." He turned his phone so she could see.

"Instagram." Lucy's eyes narrowed and she turned to her daughter. "Hannah, what's this about?"

Hannah's cheeks acquired an instant sunburn. "Umm. Promotion? Declan and I thought it would be cool."

"Declan. He was in on this?" Brody asked. Betrayed by his own flesh and blood.

"I'm sorry, Mr. Green. It never occurred to me to give you a hashtag," Hannah said, her face turning even more red. "I was just trying to promote our brand, and you don't have an Insta."

He could feel his own cheeks starting to sizzle. Now he looked like a first-class jerk. He was a first-class jerk with a knee-jerk reaction.

"Well, it is a good idea," he said, trying to rescue the moment. "Clever advertising, Hannah," he added. "I should hire you away from your mom."

Hannah beamed, and Lucy managed a tentative smile and said, "Hannah will fix this in her future posts."

"How about we just leave me out of this particular campaign?" Brody suggested.

Maybe it was small of him, maybe it made him look like a poor sport, but he didn't like being blindsided. He felt a little like a fighter being put in the ring with the proverbial one hand tied behind his back.

I can beat you with one hand tied behind my back. Ha ha. Except he hadn't been put in the ring face-to-face with his competition. He'd been sneaked up on and clunked on the head.

Still, it wasn't Lucy's fault and, really, he couldn't fault her daughter, either. She'd just been trying to help her mom. And it had been a clever idea.

"Of course," Lucy said. To her daughter she said, "Next post needs to read *we're calling it a draw.*"

Her daughter made a face. "That is so lame."

"So is pulling a stunt like this without consulting me," Lucy said firmly.

"Fine," Hannah muttered.

Watching this mother-daughter exchange, Brody suddenly felt mildly guilty. For no logical reason. What did he have to feel guilty about here?

"How about we walk next door and mend fences over ice-cream sundaes?" he suggested.

"Good idea," Hannah said, smiling at him and avoiding looking at her mother.

As they ate, Hannah talked about her dreams of becoming a social media influencer and how she and Declan had hopes of being able to travel someday at some lucky sponsor's expense.

"Obviously, you take after your mother," Brody said. Lucy looked wary and he quickly added, "You're creative and ambitious."

"There's nothing wrong with that," Lucy was quick to say, with a challenging tilt of the lips.

"No, there's not," he agreed, and smiled back.

Hannah was also sweet and just as charming as her mother. She'd charmed Declan.

And damn, Lucy was continuing to charm Brody.

Okay, was it Hannah's imagination or were Mom and Mr. Green kind of flirting? He was smiling at Mom as they talked, and at one point he said something teasing and she actually gave his arm a playful swat. But Mom was a toucher, so it probably wasn't anything.

Or maybe it was.

They went to the tennis courts on Saturday morning to get in a quick mother-daughter set before going to work, Declan tagging along to film, and there was Mr. Green on the court next to theirs, playing doubles with three other men.

Mom was checking him out and trying to pretend not to. He waved and called hello and she waved back and... blushed. Mom never blushed.

She never hit the ball that hard when she and Hannah were playing, either. Trying to impress Mr. Green? Okay, this was interesting.

It was also potentially...not good.

Later that day, after Declan was done working at the pool and they were paddleboarding, she brought up the subject of parental romance. "You know how I was thinking our parents hated each other?"

"Yeah."

"I think they've gone the other way. They're acting like they've got the hot itchies for each other."

He blinked in surprise. "No."

"Yes, seriously. They were all flirty yesterday at Good Times, joking back and forth and grinning at each other like a couple of Cheshire cats. Then this morning, when we were on the tennis courts, Mom was, like, showing off for your dad."

"Whoa, really?"

"Really."

He gave a couple of thoughtful paddles, moving away from a pair of ducks swimming nearby. "Does that seem kind of weird to you?"

"Yeah, kinda. I mean, what if they fall in love?"

"Then I guess everybody will be happy," Declan said.

"Unless it doesn't work out and they break up. Then it will be…"

"Okay," he said before she could bring up *Romeo and Juliet* again. "Our parents are gonna do whatever they're gonna do. We can't let what's going on with them mess us up. Anyway, nothing's gonna happen. Dad won't get serious about anyone, not after breaking up with Jenna Jones. Uh, Waters."

Then he shouldn't have taken them out for ice cream, and he shouldn't have been flirting. "Well, he better not hurt Mom."

"Hey, what about him?" Declan said hotly. "Your mom only got shit on once. It's happened to Dad twice."

"They probably better just stay friends," Hannah decided. "Poor Mom," she added wistfully. "I hate to see her all alone. It's not right that she should be while my dad…" She found herself unable to finish the sentence.

They paddled in silence for a while until Declan finally said, "I'm sorry your dad was such a tool."

"Me, too. I can't forgive him. He broke Mom's heart. Plus, Pandora's only six years older than me. It's creepy."

Declan said nothing to that. What could he say?

"I wish he'd lose her and get back together with Mom," Hannah said.

"I used to hope that for my dad, too," Declan said. "It never happens. You may as well get used to your dad's new woman."

"I refuse to," Hannah said vehemently. "Anyway, maybe Daddy will get tired of her."

"Not if she's hot," said Declan.

Hannah frowned. "Men are so fickle."

"Hey, not all of them," he protested. He shot a look her direction, "You do know I've got the feels for you big-time, right? I don't want what we've got to end when summer's over."

His words sent her heart soaring. "Me, either," she said.

"So, you're not gonna dump me for some U-Dub jock when we get back to Seattle this fall?" he asked.

"Why would I want another dumb jock?" she teased, then gave him a poke with her paddle, tipping him into the canal. Oh, yes, life was good.

Later, they were crashed on the patio, drinking pop and checking their various feeds on their phones when she got her first taste of the dark side of putting yourself out there—a negative comment on her Insta post. *You on a paddleboard. Big deal. What makes you so special?*

Actually, other than the fact that she had a happy life, nothing. But she wasn't a loser, either, though, and she was working hard at this, so it hurt. She swore under her breath.

Declan looked up from his phone. "What?"

She turned hers so he could read the comment. She wanted to hunt that bitch down and slap her.

He frowned. "Well, now you know you're getting successful. You got your first troll."

"It's just so…mean," she said.

"You can't let the haters get to you," he told her.

"I'd like to see this little be-atch stay up on a paddle-board," she said hotly.

Declan chuckled.

"What?" Hannah demanded.

"You've got a great mom, you're livin' at the beach, having a good life. So what do you care about what someone who doesn't even know you thinks?"

"Because it's mean. I never did anything to her."

"Except maybe have the life she wants. Maybe she's jealous."

Hannah chewed on that for a moment. "Maybe it looks like I'm showing off. Maybe this person thinks I don't have a right to. I mean, we all post the good stuff on social media."

"Your parents just got divorced. Your life's not perfect. Nobody's is. What you're doing isn't about having a perfect life. It's about getting out there and making the best one you can, and making other people want to do the same, right? Isn't that what influencers do?"

She took a thoughtful drink of her Pepsi. "Yeah, but maybe I need to be a little more real. I keep telling Mom she needs to be." Inspiration struck. "Here. Take my phone."

"I know what that means," he said.

"It means I'm gonna get real."

She did. She leaned back in her chair, crossed her legs and began to talk.

"You know, it's easy to post the good stuff happening in our lives. We all do. And, I'll admit, there's a lot of good stuff happening in mine. Like my amazing boyfriend, Declan." She acknowledged him with a smile and he smiled back from behind the phone. "And the fact that

I get to live at the beach with my mom. But I'm here only with my mom because my parents split this year. Talk about a shock. I always thought they were solid, always thought we were a perfect family. Then, suddenly, we weren't. It's been hard. And if you think getting to paddleboard can make up for that, then you are just not thinking. But, hey, my mom is my inspiration. She's working on starting over and making a great new life for herself, and so am I. So I hope next time you see a post from me, you'll think, wow, look at that new thing she's discovered. Look at the life she's making for herself. Maybe I can do that, too."

She stopped talking, ending with a slightly teary smile. Ha! She'd moved herself to tears.

"That was pretty damn amazing," Declan said after he'd stopped filming.

"It was real. I hope people will connect with it."

"Pretty cool what you said about your mom."

"I meant every word." If she could become half the woman her mom was, Hannah knew she'd really have made it.

It was a big day when the delayed countertops arrived and, of course, Hannah had Eric the videographer on hand to record the moment. She brought him back again once the floors were in place.

"Hey, everybody," she said to their growing collection of viewers, "we've got floors! The house is really coming together, isn't it? And wait 'til you see how pretty Mom fixes it up." After they'd finished filming, she said to Lucy, "Now, I'm going to contact Beachcomber and see if they'd like some of their products featured on our website. It's good to work with local businesses," she added, sounding like the pro she was becoming.

The next day an excited Hannah brought Lucy into the home decor shop to meet with the shop owner and select final house-staging touches she'd like to show and then keep. Lucy was delighted to find a large wooden sand dollar painted a delicate seafoam green to hang on the entryway wall. She also selected a white clamshell vase that would make a great coffee table accent as well as a rustic spliced wood clock for the kitchen. It felt a little like Christmas and Lucy began to see why her daughter was getting so hooked on becoming an influencer.

"This is only the beginning," she told Lucy as they left with their treasures. "Before I'm done, we'll be doing things with Wayfair and Pottery Barn. Maybe someday we'll have our own line of home decor stuff."

Thinking big. Good for Hannah. "You're a natural-born entrepreneur, darling," Lucy said, and kissed her daughter's cheek.

"I just want to be as successful as you, Mom. You're my hero."

You're my hero. Three little words. Put them together and they were priceless.

They were also undeserved. Lucy had failed to keep her marriage together. That surely wasn't something to emulate.

"Maybe you need to aim a little higher for your heroes," she suggested.

"I don't think so. Don't worry, I'll make you proud."

"You already have," Lucy assured her. She was, indeed, proud to see how quickly and how much her daughter was maturing, coming into her own as a woman.

As the days slipped by, Hannah's creativity continued to bloom. Once the kitchen was finally set up (and pictures taken to feature both the clock and some other items Hannah had procured, including a vintage light blue Streamline kitchen timer), it was time for *Always Beachin'* to branch out into lifestyle content.

Still sticking with the beach theme, Hannah created a recipe for an ice-cream octopus, using Lucy as her assistant. Once more she had her professional videographer on hand and lights set up.

"Now, we need to make the trailer," she said to Lucy, and pulled Octopus Number Two from the freezer. "We'll stand in front of the eating bar, cheek to cheek." She tipped the plate sightly. "How's this?" she asked Eric.

"Tip it a little more," he instructed, and she complied. "Okay, good to go."

"Just ring in with our tag line when I'm done talking," Hannah instructed Lucy, and then they were filming.

"Guess what we've been up to," Hannah said. "We've been making ice-cream octopuses."

"That's octopi," Lucy added, failing to follow instructions.

"Whatever you want to call it," Hannah said with an eye roll, "you'll want to make one. So be sure to visit us here where…"

"We're always beachin'," they both said together.

After the camera was off, Lucy apologized for correcting Hannah. "That was tacky of me. We should shoot it again."

"No. We need to be a little bitchy once in a while," Hannah said.

Once in a while came for Lucy when Hannah was off at Beans and Books, drinking frappés and posting content on her various social media platforms and the call came. As always, when she saw Evan's number show up on her phone screen, she felt a mix of nausea and irritation.

"What is it, Evan?" she snapped.

"Hello to you, too," he said.

The fact that he sounded so offended irritated her even more. "What do you want?"

"I want you to put in a good word for me with Hannah," he said, coming right to the point. "Even though things, uh, didn't work out for us," he began.

Didn't work out. "There's a polite way of putting it."

"We should be able to parent together."

Other than each kicking in for tuition, there wasn't much co-parenting needed at this point and Lucy said as much. "I'm not sure what you need from me," she finished.

"Hannah's still not speaking to me and it's killing me."

"I bet it is," Lucy said. She didn't even want to try to imagine how it felt to be estranged from your child. "But how is that my problem?"

"I'd think you'd want her to have a good relationship with her father," Evan said stiffly.

Did she? She should, of course, because that was the right attitude to have. But she realized that, in some ways, it suited her perfectly fine that her daughter had turned her back on her father. Hannah was all hers and she didn't have to share.

"I think she's having a hard time understanding that even though you and I broke up, I still love her and I always will," he said.

Why was that? How was it that people could stay constant in their love for their children but not each other?

She sighed. The breakup of a marriage was like a virus that spread the misery from the couple breaking up to those around them. There was no quick cure.

"You have to give her time, Evan."

"It's been months," he protested.

Only months. So much had happened since. Their breakup felt like years ago.

And yet the wound it inflicted sometimes felt as raw as if it had just happened.

"I can't make her forgive you, Evan."

"But she'll listen to you," he insisted.

The little angel on her shoulder reminded Lucy that in spite of what Evan had done to her, he was still a good father, and he didn't deserve to lose his daughter. "I'll try," she said.

"Thanks, Luc," he said, his voice gentle.

She remembered that gentleness, how lovely it used to sound when they were having a tender moment or making up after an argument. She could feel the tears collecting to mourn and ended the call without bothering to say goodbye. That was something they'd said months ago and there was no need to keep saying it.

That night Declan and his dad were having some male bonding at the bowling alley, so it was just Lucy and Hannah, propped against pillows on Lucy's bed, streaming *Love It Or List It*.

"They should list it," Hannah said as they watched the TV couple retreat to another room to discuss their options.

"I think they've fallen in love with that house all over again. They'll never let it go," Lucy predicted.

It turned out she was right. The couple did love their house.

"How'd you know they'd keep the house?" Hannah asked.

Lucy shrugged. "Intuition, I guess. Sometimes it's good to give an old place a second chance. Sometimes it's good to give people a second chance, too." There. Perfect transition into the subject of Daddy.

She could feel Hannah stiffen next to her.

"Your father misses you," she said, laying a hand on Hannah's arm.

"Well, I don't miss him. And how do you know?"

"He told me."

Hannah turned an eager face to her. "Daddy called you? Is he breaking up with Pandora?"

The hope in her daughter's voice sliced across Lucy's heart.

"Honey, you're not hoping your father and I will get back together, are you?"

That would never happen. How could Lucy ever trust him again after what he'd done?

"Would you take him back?" Hannah asked. Of course, what child didn't dream of their parents getting back together, of that perfect movie ending?

Lucy shook her head. "We've both moved on. Which is why you have my blessing to forgive him."

"Why should I?" Hannah demanded with a scowl. "He doesn't deserve it."

"Most of us, sooner or later, do something that doesn't deserve forgiveness, but we need it all the same."

Listen to her, all noble and big-hearted. Had she forgiven Evan?

Her daughter posed the same question.

Probably not completely, but encouraging Hannah to do so was a step in the right direction. So close enough.

"Yes, I have."

"I'll think about it," Hannah said.

"I hope you will. Life's too short to hold a grudge."

You couldn't move forward with a ball and chain holding you back. Anyway, when you let go of grudges, it freed you up for new adventures. Like moving to a new town, meeting new people.

Brody Green strolled into Lucy's mind. She turned him around and marched him right back out. Not that kind of new people. Life was too short to hold grudges, but it was also too short to keep getting hurt.

The first Saturday in August, after his morning tennis match, Brody stopped by the new home of Paulina Waters with a housewarming present. Brody and Jenna and the rest of Jenna's family were busy moving her in, Seth and his brother-in-law and Sabrina's boyfriend doing the heavy lifting and the women unpacking boxes. Baby Edie was toddling everywhere. She would have been Brody's niece if he and Jenna had married.

He shoved aside the thought and handed over his gift to Paulina.

"You already took us to dinner," she protested as she took the lavender, a popular deer-proof plant. "This is so kind."

"You've got to have a present when you move into a house," he told her. "It's good luck."

"You are a very nice man," Paulina informed him.

"Yes, he is," put in Jenna, who'd stopped unpacking dishes to come say hello. "And he's not too shabby as a real estate broker, either," she added.

"Mom, where do you want this?" Seth called as he and his brother-in-law came through with a sofa.

That pulled Paulina out of the conversation, and then it was just Brody and Jenna standing there. Conversation between them had once been easy. Not anymore. What was there to say when you were no longer a couple?

He was about to say the one thing he felt comfortable with—goodbye—when she asked, "Speaking of real estate, how are things going with Lucy Holmes?"

I'm falling for her. I wish she'd leave town. Look how screwed up you left me.

"Okay," he said.

"She's awfully nice."

"Is it my imagination or are you trying to push us together?"

Jenna looked at him, all wide-eyed and innocent. "Pushing? No."

"Good."

"But you do have a lot in common."

"Just because we sell houses, doesn't mean we're a match made in heaven."

"Then again, maybe it does."

He shook his head at her, gave her a smile, then wished Paulina all the best in her new digs and got out of there. Jenna needed to stop trying to bring his heart back to life after having pulverized it. It wasn't helping.

In fact, Jenna thinking he needed her help only made him feel like more of a love loser. He could have a woman if he wanted one. He just didn't happen to want one. Not even Lucy Holmes.

Okay, that was a lie. He did want Lucy Holmes. She'd irritated the snot out of him when he first met her but the irritation had worn off, changing to intrigue.

Which was worse. He didn't want to be intrigued. That was what happened with Jenna and history was not going to repeat itself.

And that was why he kept thinking about Lucy all day.

Okay, enough already. He needed ice cream.

And it was purely coincidence that Good Times Ice Cream Parlor was right next to Lucy's office. Purely coincidence that he happened to park where he'd have to walk past her office. She was in there, all by herself, which meant her daughter and his son were off doing something together.

Aliens took over his body and marched him right on in. "Hi," the aliens said. "Is it quitting time yet?"

She looked up and rewarded him with a smile and the aliens kept him talking. "I was thinking of getting some ice cream. Thought you might like to join me."

"I do like ice cream," she said.

And I do like you. Heaven help him.

Ice cream turned into drinks at Sandy's where they talked real estate and then did some tennis smack-talking, which wound up with them setting a date to play the next afternoon. Drinks dragged on so long they simply had to get dinner. The aliens stayed in charge, and after dinner they wound up sitting on a log at the beach, sharing a blanket.

It was shocking how right it all felt. For the first time since his breakup, Brody realized he was actually enjoying watching the sun set over the water, turning it gold.

"Never thought I'd be able to sit here and enjoy a sunset again," he said.

"Why is that?" Lucy asked.

"Memories. Good ones, but painful." The first time he'd kissed Jenna, they'd been at the beach. "Jenna may have mentioned to you that we were engaged."

"Yes, she did. I'm sorry it didn't work out."

He shrugged. "I guess if it were meant to be, it would have. It still sucks."

"I get that. It's no fun being rejected. But it's also no fun never getting to enjoy a sunset. I refuse to let losing my marriage take away the rest of my life from me."

"Good point." He couldn't help admiring this woman for her determination to move on and do it well.

"You've probably got a lot of sunsets left to enjoy," Lucy said. "Sunrises, too."

"I do at that."

"That's not to negate your feelings though." She sighed, stared out at the water. "It's been hard to put myself back together after my divorce."

"Not so unusual," Brody pointed out.

"No, and it's not unusual for a man to take up with another woman. But when she's a baby real estate broker in your own office..." She shook her head. "That tore me apart so thoroughly I wasn't sure if I'd ever find all the pieces. I caught the two of them together. In the shower."

So that was what had happened. "Shit," was all Brody could think to say.

"At a condo I was showing."

It sounded like a bad movie. "I don't even know what to say to that."

"I did. I said *we're through*. We'd been together since college, built the business together."

It explained Lucy's antagonistic attitude toward him at the beginning. "A lot to lose," he said.

"More like throw away, which was what he did." She bit her lip, stared out at the waves.

"Good for you for letting it all go."

"Not much choice there, but I think, actually, it was good. It was hard to see at the time, but we'd been growing apart for years. So what happened with your marriage?"

"No midlife crisis, no cheating, just a slow unraveling. She wanted the moon and I couldn't give it to her. She eventually found someone with deeper pockets. I got over it."

"How long did it take?"

"About a million years. It was hard to get back on my feet, both emotionally and financially. Divorce isn't exactly the way to build wealth."

"I'm sorry," Lucy said softly, and laid a hand on his arm.

"Hey, don't be. I don't want to be with someone who doesn't want to be with me one hundred percent," Brody said.

"Well, then, here's to one hundred percent," she said, finding her smile. "Let's make a pact. We both hold out for that."

"To one hundred percent," he agreed.

But if Lucy was waiting for him to give her that hundred, she'd be waiting a lifetime because he was done putting his heart on the line.

Twenty

"I don't know where the summer's going," Lucy said to Bonnie as they sat on Lucy's deck, enjoying a late afternoon glass of wine.

"Good places, hopefully," Bonnie said, and waved to a couple kayaking past on the canal.

"Oh, yes," Lucy said. "The house is turning out great." The kitchen was done, the interior walls painted and the floor laid. Seth was about to start painting the exterior and the furniture Lucy had picked out would be arriving in a week.

"It is. I love how you opened the place up, and your kitchen is gorgeous. It looks so beachy. By the way, I read the post on the website comparing decorating a house to seasoning a dish. It was great."

"Hannah did all the work. I just fed her some ideas."

"You two make a great team," Bonnie said.

"Like you and your daughter," Lucy told her. "Pretty fun to be in a band with both your mom and your kid."

"While it lasts. I wish I could keep her safe with me forever, but she's getting itchy to move on." Bonnie didn't look happy about the prospect.

"Will you be looking for a new mermaid?" Lucy asked.

"Who knows? Want to audition?"

"Oh, no. When I sing, dogs howl. People would pay me to shut up."

Bonnie chuckled. "We all have our strengths. Obviously, making things beautiful is one of yours. That and selling houses. I'm seeing quite a few For Sale by Dream Homes Realty signs around town."

"The business is going well," Lucy said. "Hannah's been a great help. I don't know what I'm going to do when she goes back to school. I hope I can find someone to work in the office part-time."

"Part-time? What would the job entail?" Bonnie asked.

Lucy looked at her in surprise. "You'd be interested?"

"I might. Musicians are always looking for extra cash. I can type and I'm fairly internet savvy."

It had never occurred to Lucy to see if her neighbor might be interested in a job. With her long auburn hair, the collection of small gold hoops on her ears and that treble clef tattoo on her arm, she seemed too exotic to be confined in an office space. Did she own anything beyond denim skirts and cowgirl boots? So far that was all Lucy had seen her in. Except for this particular day, Bonnie was in torn jeans, a tie-dyed T-shirt and flip-flops. Her toenails were painted blue.

As if reading Lucy's mind she said, "I have a couple of dresses to my name," which made Lucy laugh.

"And I've got a pretty good work ethic. I need to do something more than sit around and write songs that I end up hating."

"That is so fabulous that you write songs." Sometimes, talking to Bonnie, Lucy felt downright boring.

"That was really more part of another life. So, what do

you think? I could provide references from about a million years ago but I don't think any of my old bosses are even around anymore."

"Will your mother vouch for you?" Lucy teased.

Bonnie half chuckled. "She'd do her best to talk you out of hiring me."

There was an unexpected answer. Lucy blinked in surprise.

"Mom really wanted me to stick it out in Nashville, use my gift. She was sure I was going to become a star, make up for her not making it. It's a long story."

And one that Bonnie obviously didn't want to share.

"What do you think about giving it a try for a week and seeing if it works?" Bonnie suggested. "If we decide we'd rather share a street than an office, we can go back to just being neighbors. And you can feel free to be totally honest," she added.

"That sounds good to me," Lucy said.

A rather unique way to hire someone, but she had a good feeling about Bonnie. So far she'd been a considerate neighbor, keeping the noise down when the band practiced, inviting Lucy over for coffee once in a while, sharing brownies when she got the urge to bake some from a mix. She seemed easygoing. She was certainly fine with the salary Lucy offered and happy to hold down the office from midmornings to early afternoons four days a week.

"Perfect hours," she said. "Gives me time to sleep in in the morning and lets me get off early enough to pack up band equipment if we get a gig outside of town."

"It's got to be fun playing in a band," Lucy said. If only she could sing. Or play an instrument.

Bonnie nodded. "For the most part, it is. Sometimes

though, I want to jump off the stage and start dancing with everyone."

"Have you ever done that?"

"A few times, when I was young and wild. I did a lot of things when I was young and wild," Bonnie said with a shake of her head. She took a sip of wine. "There's a lot to be said for being older and wiser."

"Yes, there is," Lucy agreed.

"Not that I am," Bonnie added. "Well, older." She drank the last of her wine and stood. "I better get back home. Mom's coming over for dinner and bringing her new boyfriend for me to check out. I need to throw together my shrimp salad."

Lucy had only talked to Bonnie's mother once since the night of the street dance on the third of July, but the woman had left an impression. She was sixty-something going on timeless. According to Bonnie, she'd already gone through two husbands. Bonnie claimed her mother's motto was So Many Men, So Little Time.

"When it comes to love, she's the eternal optimist," Bonnie once said.

Maybe Lucy was turning into a bit of an optimist herself. The further along August slid, the more time she seemed to be spending with Brody and the happier she felt about her future. So far they were managing to both do business in Moonlight Harbor without stepping on each other's toes, and their earlier antagonism was gone. They'd eased into friendship and were skirting around the edges of something more. When they weren't kayaking on the canal or enjoying clam chowder on the beach, they were playing tennis with the kids or watching the sun set either from her deck or the deck of Brody's beach house.

It was those sunset times with just the two of them when

she was most aware of that something more lying between them like a live wire they were both afraid to touch. It seemed like she spent more and more time checking out his biceps and the strong line of his chin, and she was often sure she felt his gaze on her when she wasn't looking.

But they were perfectly happy just as they were. Keeping things platonic was the wise thing to do. Older and wiser, right?

Wisdom was overrated.

Anyway, there was more to life than love. Than sex.

Life in Moonlight Harbor was as close to perfect as a woman could get. Her business was doing well. She was having fun selling houses and working with her daughter. Hannah was happily growing their online presence and was showing a flair for staging houses. They were both busy with the Green men but were still logging plenty of mother–daughter time.

Lucy was enjoying her developing friendships as well. Jenna Jones was positive and supportive, and Lucy looked forward to the Friday night gatherings at her house with so many of the other women who ran businesses in town. It sometimes felt as if all of Moonlight Harbor had opened its arms and taken her in.

"It's funny," she told her sister as they chatted on the phone a couple of days before Lucy's house party, "even though I've been here a short time, I feel like the friendships I'm making are more real than ones I've had for ten years."

"I'm glad it's working out for you," Darla said. "Although sometimes I wish you'd moved somewhere closer."

"It's not that far," Lucy said. "And, you know, I could find you a cute little bungalow here if you want a summer house."

"Why would I want that when I can come and stay with you for free?" Darla joked.

"Good point. And you guys are going to spend the night after the party, right?"

"Oh, yeah. Orren already has his fishing pole packed. He's determined to catch a fish in the canal. I swear, you'll never get rid of us until he does. No, I take that back. If he does catch one, we'll be down here constantly."

Lucy chuckled. "Works for me." She loved to see her new home filling up with happiness.

She also loved all the positive comments she got when she held her party and her new friends came to check out the finished house and help her celebrate. She'd settled on a dark blue with white trim for the exterior, and the paint job coupled with removing the front lawn and replacing it with rock and driftwood had made the place look like a whole new house. Hannah had done a photo shoot of the finished product, taking plenty of pictures of both the outside and the inside.

She also had her trusty videographer on hand to record the first moments of the party, catching early arrivals—Brody and Declan, naturally—as they came in, followed by Bonnie, who was born to be on camera. Lucy was happy that for the occasion she looked as good as her house.

"So we're done here, Mom," Hannah said for the benefit of the camera as she and Lucy stood next to the kitchen bar, everyone standing ready to toast them with glasses of champagne. "What's next for us?"

"I'm sure we'll have more houses to stage and sell, and more opportunities for beachin'," Lucy said, following the script they'd come up with.

"That's my mom," Hannah ad-libbed. "Isn't she amazing?"

The words made tears pool at the corners of Lucy's eyes,

but she held it together, smiled and kissed her daughter's cheek as their friends cheered and raised their glasses in salute.

"That was a sweet thing to say," she said once the camera was off.

"And true," Hannah said. "When I grow up, I want to be just like you."

Minus the divorce, Lucy thought.

In some ways she was almost grateful to Evan. Not for humiliating and hurting her, of course, but for freeing her. She hadn't realized how very mediocre their life together had become in spite of its fancy trimmings. Here at the beach, every morning felt filled with promise and every sunset was special.

Now she was filling her new house on Sand Dollar Lane with special memories. She smiled as she looked around at her guests enjoying the appetizers Annie had created for her. Ellis West and his wife, Melody, stood chatting with Kiki Strom and her husband over by the punch bowl. Orren, Mr. Sullivan from next door and Cynthia Redmond's husband were out on the back deck, probably talking fishing. Darla had hit it off with Tyrella Lamb, and was yakking up a storm with her and her fiancé. Bonnie was visiting with Jenna's sister, Celeste, and obviously enjoying holding her youngest, a boy. Seth and Celeste's husband were parked on the new sofa, looking handsome and casual in jeans and shirts rolled up to the elbow.

And there came Brody to refresh her glass. Lucy's heart gave a happy squeeze at the sight of him.

"I can't get over what you've done with it," said Jenna, who was standing next to her and checking out the before and after slideshow on the computer Hannah had set up on the quartz-topped eating bar.

"I'm happy with it," Lucy said. "And happy here."

Jenna smiled at Brody. "A lot of great people here."

"Yes, there are," Lucy said, grinning at him.

The finished house looked great. The woman who'd done it looked irresistible in her white skirt and turquoise blouse and wedge sandals. Simple jewelry, hair down. Understated elegance.

Except there was nothing understated about Lucy herself. Boy, had Brody been wrong in his initial assessment of her. She was ambitious, yes, and competitive, but certainly not the witchy woman he'd first thought she was.

Well, maybe she was a little witchy because it sure felt like she was casting a spell on him. Not that he was going to let her though. They'd keep things light, have fun together, be pals. Enjoy some beachside romance, maybe. But that was it. That was the way it needed to stay.

She smiled her hundred-watt Lucy smile at him and he returned it as he came to stand next to her.

"Honestly, you two could do toothpaste commercials," Jenna teased, then made herself scarce to go join her husband.

"That was subtle," Lucy said.

"As always," he said. "This place really did turn out great."

"Yes, it did," Lucy said, pleased with herself.

"I sure wasn't happy when you beat me out, but I must say it went to the right person. You showed it way more love than I would have."

"It feels like a home ought to feel," she said.

"That's because you made it a home."

"I'm going to make a lot of happy memories here," Lucy predicted.

"I believe you are. For a lot of people," he added, nodding to where their kids stood in the kitchen. Hannah was leaning against the counter, a bottle of pop in her hand, and Declan was leaning against her.

"Do you think it's serious?" Lucy asked.

"It sure looks that way. I know Dec is."

"So is Hannah. It's sweet and lovely, and terrifying. They're so young,"

"Yeah, they are. But they're both good kids. Let's hope they're smarter than we were when we were their age."

"Is anyone smart at that age?" Lucy mused.

When it came to love, was anyone smart at any age?

A person could be, Brody told himself when he finally drove home from Lucy's house. Once the guests and the food were gone—and it was just the two of them on her back deck, sipping the wine he'd brought and eating the box of chocolates he'd given her as a housewarming present— it seemed all his mind had wanted to focus on was coming up with suave and clever ways to get them back inside and really warm up her new house.

He'd resisted, partly because they all felt lame, but also because it was simply too soon. Lucy hadn't even been divorced a year. She was vulnerable and no way did he want to take advantage of her.

If he had any brains at all, he'd start cooling down their relationship. They'd been spending too much time together, getting way too chummy, like some old married couple.

Marriage. It was still one of the most popular words in the English language. It was especially popular with women. Men, maybe not so much. They often blundered their way into that happy estate only to find themselves back on the street, missing half their possessions and half their hearts. He'd been there, done that. He didn't need to do it again. With anyone. No matter how tempting she was.

Some part of him was not listening, obviously. He dreamed about Lucy that night. He'd walked out onto the deck of his very own beach house and found he suddenly had a hot tub there, and it wasn't empty. It was filled with pink bubbles and in the middle of those bubbles, with her bare shoulders showing, sat Lucy.

"Come on in, the water's fine," she said, and beckoned him with a finger tipped with pink nail polish.

"Nooooo!" He woke up before he had a chance to strip down and get in that tub.

He took a deep breath and let it out, then went in search of coffee and his laptop so he could read the morning news. There was more to life than hot tubs and hot women.

Somewhere. In some distant universe.

He frowned. He was definitely going to cool things before it was too late.

So the next week when Lucy called to see if he was interested in checking out the new blockbuster playing at Beach Cinema, he declined, claiming too much work. And when the kids wanted to play doubles, he suddenly realized he'd pulled a muscle in his back. On the weekend he went to Seattle to visit his parents, he took Lucy's call on his Bluetooth as he was on the road.

"Your son's coming over for burgers tonight. I thought you might like to join him," she said.

"Sorry, I can't. I forgot to tell Dec. I'm on my way to Seattle for the weekend."

There was a moment's silence on her end of the call, and he began to squirm. It was followed by, "Oh." He could hear the disappointment in her voice. Her next words left him simultaneously relieved and miserable. "I guess we're cooling things."

He felt like a rat.

But there was no need to feel like a rat. He was saving her, both of them, from grief down the road. They were damaged, and this thing between them was bound to end in an emotional shipwreck.

"We can't be rushing into something," he said. "It's too soon for you."

"And what about you?" she asked.

Yeah, what about him? "And it's too late for me."

There was another uncomfortable silence.

"Lucy?" he prompted.

"What if it's not too late?" she asked softly. Then, before he could speak, she said, "Never mind. I didn't mean to push." She gave a mirthless chuckle. "You know me. I don't like to lose."

"It's a win to be rid of me," he said. "Better for our working relationship, anyway."

"Yes, I know all about that," she said, her voice suddenly bitter. "All right, Brody. Have a nice time in Seattle."

He would.

And he'd be miserable. Doing the right thing was overrated.

Twenty-One

After dinner Mom vanished inside the house and left the deck to Hannah and Declan.

She'd barely been gone before Hannah asked, "Now what's going on with our parents? They haven't done anything together in ages and Mom's not talking," she added. As if he hadn't noticed. As if anyone with eyes couldn't see.

Declan shrugged, finished off the pop in his can. "I dunno. It's weird. One minute, every time I turned around he was off doing stuff with your mom. Now, when he's not working, he's just hanging around the house, watching the sports channel."

Hannah sighed. "I knew it was a bad idea for them to start hanging out. Mom was so happy. I think it's pretty crappy of your dad to start ditching her."

Declan looked at her in surprise. "Huh? How do you know Dad's doing that?"

"Every time she asks him to do something, he can't. Like tonight."

"He was going to see my grandparents."

"Yeah, right. Pretty soon he'll be ghosting her."

"Well, maybe he's worried she'll hurt him."

"Well, he's hurting her," Hannah snapped.

Declan looked like a man who was on the verge of making an important scientific discovery. "Wait a minute," he said slowly. "Do you see what's happening?"

"What," she said, biting off the word.

"We're about to let what's going on with our parents mess with what's going on with us."

He was right. "Truth," she said.

"We weren't gonna do that. Remember?"

"You're right." She felt badly that her mom was unhappy again, but she knew Mom wouldn't want her to be unhappy, too. And she sure would be if she lost Declan.

"We're gonna have to let them figure out their own lives. Too bad for them if they don't want to be together, but they'll have to deal with us being us. You can't let other people steal your good thing."

"Absolutely," she agreed, and kissed him to prove she meant it.

Later that night she had a serious woman-to-woman talk with her mother.

"Of course, you can't let what's going on with us affect you and Declan," Mom said after Hannah had finished her speech. "I wouldn't expect you to. Brody and I are only friends. That's all. And Declan is a wonderful young man."

"I really think he's the one," Hannah warned.

"If he is, he looks like an excellent choice. But, honey, take your time. Be sure that who you're with now is who you want to be with for a lifetime."

"I know, Mom," Hannah assured her. *Duh.*

She didn't add that Mom had probably been sure she'd wanted to be with Daddy for a lifetime when they first got together. When it came to love, it was so easy to mess up. But she and Declan weren't going to. Just because their parents hadn't gotten it right, didn't mean she and Dec had to follow in their footsteps.

If only Daddy hadn't done what he'd done. If only he'd come to his senses and dump Pandora. If only...

"Do you still love Daddy at all?" Hannah asked.

Her mother gave a thoughtful sigh. "I love the man he was when we were first together. I love the memory of him. I'm afraid what he did didn't make him very loveable."

"But you've forgiven him, right?"

"Yes. I told you I had. Have you yet?"

Hannah shrugged. "I'm working on it," she lied.

But, really, the only way she'd be able to forgive her father was if he got rid of Pandora and made things right with Mom. He'd taken a wrecking ball to their family. He couldn't expect his daughter to stand in the ruins with a big smile and her arms outstretched.

At least Mom was moving on.

Or had been until Mr. Green dumped her. Why any man would want to dump her mother was a mystery to Hannah. It was so unfair. So wrong. And soon she'd be leaving, too, going back to school, and Mom would be in this house all alone.

"I'll come down every weekend," she promised.

Mom blinked in surprise. "That came out of nowhere."

"I just don't want you to be alone."

Mom smiled at that. "I won't be. I've made lots of good friends down here."

"Yeah, all women," Hannah sneered.

"There's nothing wrong with women," Mom said with a chuckle.

"Anyway, we need to do stuff for the website and Insta."

"Don't want to lose our followers," Mom teased.

Her mother complimented her a lot, praised her plenty,

but sometimes that praise felt kind of patronizing. It was as if Hannah was a little girl, trying to bake her first batch of cookies.

She wasn't a little girl anymore though. She was a woman. She had a year of college behind her now and she was starting a business. In case Mom hadn't noticed, Hannah had been reading books, studying how to do this influencer thing, reaching out and making connections. She was getting good at it. Someday, she'd be as successful as her mother. Maybe even more successful.

"You're going to end up getting clients from this," Hannah informed her. "Just wait and see."

"I'm sure I will," Mom said in her indulgent-mom tone of voice.

"I'm going to be someone," Hannah insisted. *And I'm not going to screw up my love life.*

She wisely kept that last thought to herself. *Poor Mom.*

The last of summer vanished. Lucy hosted a barbecue at her house the Saturday of Labor Day weekend. All her neighbors attended as well as her new friends from the chamber of commerce. Brody Green was conspicuous by his absence. It looked like they were downgrading their relationship from friends to business acquaintances.

"No Brody," Jenna observed.

"He had plans," Lucy said. Probably. Somewhere else. With someone else? The thought put an ache in her heart.

So stupid to fall for a new man when she'd been barely done with the old one, but that was what she'd done. Falling hurt.

Jenna got the underlying message. "He's gun shy. He'll come around."

"Well, maybe I won't be interested in seeing him when he does," Lucy said lightly. Ha! What a liar she was.

Come the September chamber of commerce meeting, she plunked herself right down next to him at the table. "Is this seat taken?"

He gave her half a smile. "Now it is."

"How've you been?" she asked.

"Busy."

"I haven't seen any new listings."

"Yeah, but you've seen sales. I'm doing okay."

Okay enough to never take her calls when she had a client interested in one of his houses. She'd been forced to deal with Taylor Marsh, who was always frostily polite. As if Lucy was somehow the villain in all this. She was back to being Maleficent.

She laid a hand on his forearm and felt the muscles tense. She said it anyway. "I miss you."

He looked around as if fearing someone had heard her. She'd made it awkward for him. Stupid to be so honest. Men said they liked women to be honest, but really, they didn't, not when it was something they didn't want to hear.

"How about we talk later?" he suggested.

"How about you come over to the house for a glass of wine?" she suggested. He hesitated and she held her breath.

Then he nodded. "Sure. Five?"

"Five works for me," she said, and removed her hand before he could.

He put on his mover-and-shaker smile, placed his lunch order with their server, and then started talking to Kiki, who was on his other side.

Lucy got the message loud and clear. He was going to humor her and stop by, but it would be an obligatory visit.

That was what he thought. She missed him, missed

spending time with him. Darn it all, she wasn't going to let go of what they were building without a fight.

She put on her fighting clothes that afternoon—capris and a cropped top, a silver ankle bracelet and sandals. And a good spritz of perfume. She kept her hair down because she knew he'd like that, and she applied eyeliner, plenty of mascara and a coral lipstick. Okay, she was ready.

On seeing the flash of admiration in his eye when he walked in the door, she felt well-armed and her confidence boosted. "Thanks for coming," she said.

"I shouldn't have. Lucy, I'm really not in a place to be starting anything."

"We're just having a glass of wine," she said. "I'm not asking you to put me in the will."

He made a face. "I know where that can lead."

"Putting me in the will?" she teased.

"Having a glass of wine with you," he said, and followed her into the kitchen.

"Don't you miss hanging out together, even a little bit?"

"Of course, I do," he said irritably.

She handed him the bottle and corkscrew. "Then let's hang out."

And hang out they did. They took advantage of the warm late afternoon, probably one of the last they'd have, and sat on the deck.

"It would be nice to go kayaking one last time before the cold weather sets in," she said.

"Good idea," he said, and that was that.

Stupid him. Before he knew it, he was back to hanging out with Lucy, having lunch together, dinners at each other's places, stopping by to say hi when she was working an open house on a property, hanging out with the kids when they came down on weekends. She'd met his daughter Mariah, and Mariah had given Lucy an enthusiastic thumbs-up, saying, "She's perfect for you."

So now they were a pair. Everywhere but the bedroom, and he was sure getting tired of that.

So was Lucy. "You know, this lipstick doesn't have to stay on," she said one evening when they were on her couch, watching the ending credits to a rom-com.

"Don't be tempting me," he joked. Then, to make sure that was the end of the conversation, he stood and started for the door. "I better get going. Got an open house tomorrow."

"And you have to get to bed early for that, I know," she taunted, trailing after him.

"I do," he insisted.

She caught his arm, preventing a quick escape, then sidled up to him and slipped an arm around his neck. Looked up at him with those big eyes of hers.

"Well, then, how about a kiss for luck tomorrow?" she said softly.

A man always needed luck on his side. One kiss.

Shit. He knew he shouldn't have done that. Lucy's lips were as soft and fabulous as he'd always imagined they'd be. He was willing to bet the rest of her was equally fabulous.

He gently disengaged her arms and smiled at her. "Okay, I feel lucky now."

And he could have gotten lucky. He swore all the way home and raced for the shower. He hated cold showers.

He took a lot of them during October. Lucy always could find a reason why he needed a kiss for luck. And sometimes she needed a little luck, too, come to think of it. This was ridiculous. She wanted him. He wanted her. Why was he holding back?

He knew why. He could not, would not, take this thing any further.

Who was he kidding? They were neck-deep in quicksand and sinking farther by the moment.

When he picked her up to take her to the chamber of commerce Halloween party at Kiki's house, he knew they were bound to go under. She wore that great black dress he'd seen her in before, the one with a neck scooped low enough to tease him with a hint of cleavage. She was also wearing black nylons and black heels with little bows on them. She had a black velvet collar around her neck and a headband with black cat ears on her head. He was dressed in his usual devil costume but he wanted to howl like a tomcat.

"You look incredible," he said.

"So do you, you handsome devil," she replied, coming up to him and running a hand up his chest.

Her husband had to be a fool. Only a fool would leave a woman like this.

"You ready?" he asked, but he wasn't thinking about the party.

"I am," she said, and grabbed her coat.

As usual Jenna and Courtney had plenty of fun and games planned, including a silly game they'd dubbed Trick or Treat, which involved Tootsie Rolls and silly pranks. Brody was more than happy to play pass the orange this time, and made it worth his while when he had to take that orange from Lucy's chin. The scent of her perfume went to his head like a double shot of whiskey.

He visited with everyone, played every game, complimented Annie on her spooky punch bowl setup and the

Halloween-themed treats she'd concocted. Then announced he needed to get Lucy home.

"I bet you do," said Ellis with a smirk.

Lucy blushed, but the smile she gave Brody told him she was more than ready to leave.

He wasn't about to rush her back to the house and turn Neanderthal though. Brody knew the importance of romance. They detoured by way of the beach, to enjoy the sight of dark waters under a waning crescent moon.

"Did you have fun tonight?" he asked, turning and putting an arm across her seat.

"I did," she said. "Know what my favorite part of the evening was?"

"Tell me."

"Playing pass the orange."

"Yeah? Funny. That was my favorite part, too. Come here, you," he said, and tugged her close for a kiss.

"I think we need to go back to my place," she whispered.

"Me, too," he agreed, and about broke the sound barrier taking them there.

She lost her coat. He took off his devil cape with a flourish. She grabbed him by his red necktie and led him to the couch. Brody never wore neckties anymore, but he was sure having fun wearing this one. Once on the couch though, he whipped it off.

She took his face between her hands and pulled him down, kissing him as they went. A kiss for luck. Yep, getting lucky tonight.

Going under the quicksand. What were they thinking?

He pulled back. "You should have come as a witch, you little spell-caster."

"That's me," she said lightly, and kissed him again.

Oh, man. He felt light-headed, like he'd just stepped off a cliff.

"This is not a good idea, Luc." They had to stop this nonsense right now.

Her brows furrowed. "Please don't call me that. It's what Evan used to call me."

Brody sat back up, pulled her up, too. "We've got way too much baggage to be doing this."

She bit her lip.

"It's not smart and it's not kind. I'm done with the whole getting-serious thing and I don't want to hurt you."

It took a moment for her to answer. The moment was filled with regret. He half wished he'd kept his big mouth shut, taken what she was offering. But that would have been wrong. He had to be honest.

She nodded knowingly. "Friends forever, is that it? No strings attached."

"Something like that. Strings can choke you. We both know that."

She nodded. Sighed. "Yes, they can. I don't want to get hurt again."

"Me, either. I'm done with wedding bells and gold bands and long-term commitment. If that's what you're looking for…"

"I didn't say I was."

"What are you looking for, Luc, er, Lucy?"

"To not get hurt."

"As long as we're both on the same page, I think we can both dodge that bullet," he said.

No commitment, just pals. Pals for life, who would share experiences and fun times, but who wouldn't argue over money, who wouldn't hire lawyers and come after each other. Even if things slid a little sideways, they'd still be friends. No pressure, no demands.

But would she really be content with that? They could stop right then—horrible thought!—walk away from the edge of the cliff, pull themselves out of the quicksand. Say no to any kind of entanglement. Go back to being business buddies.

"I don't want either of us to get hurt," he added.

"So, no strings," she said.

"Are you sure that's enough? If not, say the word."

She moved closer. "Meow," she purred, and kissed him.

Twenty-Two

Life was good. No, life was wonderful. Lucy was crazy in love.

Maybe *crazy* was the right word. As Brody had pointed out once, it hadn't been that long since her divorce. Her judgment was about as clear as a Seattle sky in November. And he came with his own set of baggage. Surely, a sane woman wouldn't gamble so with her heart. Surely, a sane woman would back away from a relationship that guaranteed no stability.

But what relationship did? None. She'd learned that the hard way. You took vows before God and man and you signed papers. Then someone broke those vows and, again, you signed papers. This was no bigger gamble. She could live with the status quo.

She reminded herself of that when her mind drifted toward visions of bridal bouquets and honeymoons. Brody had already given her flowers—a lovely fall bouquet that Hannah had taken a picture of for Instagram. As for honeymoons, they were only trips with sex. She and Brody were a couple but they were going about it the smart way, keeping their finances, their futures and their hearts intact.

Deep down, where she was careful not to look, she still wanted to be married, still believed that marriage was a good thing, that it didn't always have to end in broken hearts and broken families. Still, she knew the statistics. The odds for success didn't exactly skyrocket for the second time around. Why take that chance and ruin a good thing?

"You two are pretty glued together these days," Bonnie observed after Lucy came back to the office from a long lunch with Brody.

"He is becoming a habit," Lucy said. Bonnie just nodded, and Lucy sensed that she wanted to say something. "What?" she prompted.

"Nothing."

"You don't like Brody?"

"Everyone likes Brody," said Bonnie.

"For sure. What's not to like?"

"Nothing. A lot of women here have liked him."

That didn't quite sound like a compliment. "Including you?"

"For about two minutes. He was too much of a player. But he wasn't ready to settle down back then," Bonnie hurried on. "So don't mind me. I'm just looking through my own dirty filter and seeing the worst in people. After all, he was ready to marry Jenna Jones." She shook her head. "Funny, she almost married Brody and then my band wound up playing at her wedding to Seth. Sometimes it's like musical chairs down here."

Except in musical chairs someone always wound up without a chair.

That wasn't going to happen to Lucy though. She'd already played that game.

Still, she wished Bonnie hadn't planted the image in her

brain. Who was she kidding? Keeping things light with Brody was a concept her heart wasn't truly grasping. If what they had going fell apart, she'd be devastated, even if there were no legal papers to sign.

Brody is not Evan, she reminded herself as they sat at their favorite window table in The Porthole, sharing a lunch-break meal with Jenna. Her husband was missing, and Lucy suspected he hadn't been told about it. Jenna continued to play Cupid every chance she got, obviously determined to cement the relationship between her old love and her new friend.

"You know, you two should join forces," she suggested as they finished their coffee. "You're both really good at what you do. If you teamed up, you could take over all of Gray's County."

Complicating a relationship by going into business together was guaranteed disaster.

"Hmm," Brody said thoughtfully.

"Not a good idea," Lucy said. "I've been there and lived through that."

"Not every man's a shit, Lucy," he said.

"I don't have a working shit-o-meter, so it's hard to tell."

"Even with me?" he asked.

"I can vouch for him," Jenna said.

This man had a reputation for helping people, bailing out businesses. He was not Evan.

"Not you," Lucy conceded. "But my father always says the one ship that won't float is a partnership. I'm beginning to think he was right."

"Your father hasn't met me," Brody said with a grin.

No, he hadn't yet. What would her father think of Brody Green?

Lucy knew what she thought. When it came to men, Brody was prime real estate.

Except she would never take full possession. He'd put barbed wire around his heart and had no intention of committing to anything beyond what he already had. They'd both agreed to that. But if they were going to play it safe, they needed to play it safe in all areas of their lives.

"We have separate houses and our own lives," she pointed out after Jenna had left to get back to the motel office. "I think it's wise to keep those same fences up when it comes to business as well. Fewer complications."

He took a thoughtful drink of his coffee, then nodded and said, "Yeah, you're right. Sometimes I think it would be great to expand, but you really need a team for that."

Chip and Joanna Gaines are a team, both in business and in life.

Lucy pushed away the thought. Successful couples were the exception, not the rule. She and Evan had proved that.

"I should have kept my big mouth shut at lunch," Jenna said to Lucy when the women gathered at her house Friday night. "Sorry about that."

"I can see how you'd think it was a good idea," Lucy told her. "But business complicates things."

Jenna nodded. "When it comes to men and women, everything complicates things. Still, I'm glad to see you and Brody enjoying each other so much. You're perfect for each other."

But not perfect enough to risk everything. Still… "We are happy," Lucy said.

Seth had passed through the dining room before going off to play pool at The Drunken Sailor, giving Jenna a kiss before he left. It may have been quick, just like the look they exchanged, but it was rooted in a solid love, and it made Lucy downright jealous.

She'd had that with Evan when they were first married. Or at least something very like it. They'd enjoyed their times of passion and they'd also had their little jokes and shared looks. Even when things weren't going perfectly between them she'd felt secure. After all, every marriage experienced tremors. That didn't mean it wasn't solid. Talk about false security.

How many tremors had there been that she hadn't even noticed? How had they gone from solid to the big quake where everything fell apart?

Perhaps they'd never been as solid as she'd thought. Perhaps there had always been a deep fault line running through their relationship.

Was that the case with every relationship? Could the big quake happen at any time to anyone? Or when she had these thoughts, was it simply a case of divorce PTSD? Maybe Brody had been right when he'd told her it was too soon for her to be getting serious with anyone.

Too late. She liked what she was building with him too much to think about a possible fault line.

Between school, working on becoming an influencer and hanging out with Declan in between their classes, fall raced by for Hannah. November was half over when her father texted her, asking to meet for coffee.

She read it and rolled her eyes. He was still trying to act like he'd done nothing wrong.

Kind of busy, she texted back.

It's only coffee, he reminded her. Can't you spare a little time for your old man?

How about asking her if she wanted to?

Who's paying for your tuition.

Now he was blackmailing her! She frowned at her phone screen. She was still so bitter, so offended on her mother's behalf. But she was also letting the man she was mad at help pay her college tuition. Which kind of made her a hypocrite.

It *was* only coffee. Okay, she texted back.

They met at a Starbucks in the U District, and even though she was angry at him and determined not to speak to him, her heart squeezed at the sight of him. This was the man who'd taught her how to swim and how to water ski, who'd taken her to the Space Needle for her sixteenth birthday. This was the man who had always been part of her life—maybe not the biggest part, but still there…until he'd chosen another woman over her mother and ended life as she knew it. Her heart began hardening once more.

As she joined him at a tall table, she saw he'd gotten her a pumpkin latte, her favorite. He didn't make an effort to hug her, just slid it across to her. "You're a treat for a father's eyes, Honey Bear."

She got right to the point. "Why'd you want to see me?"

"Because I miss you."

Actually, she missed him, too. But not this version of him. She missed the Dad she'd had before Pandora came along. This version looked the same on the outside, but he wasn't the same inside. This version was a stranger who only said the right words. She found it suddenly hard to speak. All she could do was stare at the drink in front of her.

"I know I blew it," he said, "and I want you to know that I'm sorry."

Okay, now those sounded like the right words, and they gave her hope. "Does that mean you're breaking up with Pandora?"

His brows pulled together and he shook his head. "No. I love her."

"That's so sick," Hannah said in disgust.

"You can't help who you love," Daddy said in his own defense.

"You loved Mom once."

"I still care for your mother. I just…"

"Just what?" Hannah demanded.

Now it was his turn to stare at his coffee cup. "It's hard to put it in words you'll understand."

"I bet it is," she said, disgusted.

"I still care for your mom. Back when all this first happened… I would have been willing to work things out, but your mother didn't want to."

Now he was blaming Mom? Hannah glared at him, opened her mouth to tell him what she thought of that.

He beat her to the punch. "I don't blame her."

What a miserable mess. Thinking about it made Hannah feel sick.

She pushed away her drink. "Why'd you do it?"

"I wanted more. I guess your mom and I had fallen into a rut, let what we had grow stale. Then I met Pandora and… she's really a wonderful woman."

Hannah glared at him. "And Mom isn't?"

"Of course, she is. I regret what happened. I want you to know that." It was probably as close as he was going to come to admitting he'd done something wrong.

"If you regret it so much, you should be asking Mom to take you back," Hannah informed him.

"Your mother and I have both moved on, built separate

lives. But we both want you in them. I never meant for you to be hurt. I miss my girl," he added.

Magic words, hard to resist.

"I'm sorry you got hurt in all this."

More magic words, drawing Hannah back to him. Maybe it was time to forgive her father. After all, if Mom could, so could she.

She wanted to. She wanted to be back in the boat on the lake in the summer sunshine, next to her dad, him grinning at her or her skiing behind the boat as he towed her. She wanted those special moments like when they'd all gone out to dinner and he'd ask, "What looks good to you, Honey Bear?" She wanted to recapture a portion of her happy past, at least. And she wanted a future. She wanted him to walk her down the aisle someday.

"I want to see you, want to spend time together."

"I'm spending Thanksgiving with Mom," she cautioned. 'Cause even though she was forgiving him, that didn't mean she wanted to spend Thanksgiving with Pandora. She didn't have to forgive him that much.

Thanksgiving was a success. Lucy's siblings and their families came down to spend the day at the beach, and Darla and Orren spent the night. Hannah stayed for the weekend and come Saturday mother and daughter did a holiday feast encore with Brody's family.

Earlier in the week she'd sold a dog of a house she'd listed and there had been much real estate smack talking.

"Yeah, well, the year's not over yet," Brody had said.

True. December would bring the Seaside with Santa festival, and she knew he was determined to best her during that after the success of her bounce house on the Fourth. Well, she had a few things up her sleeve. Wait until he saw the float she had Bruno, one of Seth's friends, building for her. Ha!

Of course, it was a good-natured competition now that they'd learned Moonlight Harbor was, indeed, big enough for the both of them. But she still wanted to outdo him with her parade float. And wasn't he going to be surprised? Hehe.

Twenty-Three

"Mom, you and Daddy are paying a lot of money for me to live in the sorority house," Hannah said during a phone chat.

Where was she going with this? Lucy was pretty sure she knew and she didn't like it.

"We don't mind," she said. "You're making lifelong friends there."

It was more than Lucy had had a chance to do when she was in college. Both money and time had been too scarce to even think about splurging on a sorority, and she'd often driven past those fancy houses on Greek Row and felt more than a little envious of the girls living in them. Hannah had no idea how lucky she was.

"Yeah, right. Friends that steal your boyfriend."

"What is this really about?" Lucy asked. There was no point in beating around the bush.

"I was just thinking that it would save a lot of money if Declan and I moved in together."

"And what got you thinking that?" As if she couldn't guess.

"We were just talking about it."

"Well, you just un-talk about it," Lucy said sternly. "You two haven't been together long enough to take such a big step."

"It's been almost six months," Hannah protested.

Almost was stretching it.

Time to try another tack. "Look, I can't tell you what to do, but I can advise you. Wait a while and be sure. It's easy when you're in the throes of new love to not see anything but what you want to see. You've heard the expression love is blind, right? Well, it's true. And when you can't see clearly, you walk into walls and fall into ditches and get hurt."

"Declan would never hurt me," Hannah protested.

"He certainly wouldn't plan to."

"He loves me."

"Then if he loves you, he'll wait. Give this some time, darling. It hasn't been that long since your last breakup."

Listen to her, the pot giving the kettle advice. She was such a hypocrite.

"Thanks a lot, Mom," Hannah said, her voice surly.

"I'm just trying to protect you. I want you to seriously consider what I'm telling you. There's no need to rush. Promise me you'll at least think about what I'm saying. Please."

"All right. I'll think about it."

Lucy could tell by the tone of her daughter's voice that there was very little conviction in her promise. "While you're thinking, remember how awful it was when Daddy and I got divorced."

"That's why we should move in together, to be sure it's going to work," Hannah argued.

"It's no guarantee you won't be hurt. Have you forgotten how hurt you were last spring?"

"No," Hannah said irritably.

"It hurts to break up with someone you're dating, but once you've moved in together, invested time and energy into turning a house into a home, shared a bedroom, that unhappiness triples."

There was a long silence on her daughter's end of the call.

Lucy pushed home her point. "You've seen how long it takes to remodel a house. It's really no different with building a relationship. Time and care give you a better chance of building something lasting."

Oh, listen to her. Wasn't she the expert on relationships all of a sudden?

"Okay, I'll think about it," Hannah said grudgingly.

"That's all I ask. I love you."

"I love you, too."

Not quite so much at the moment, obviously.

Brody was at Lucy's place, enjoying homemade turkey potpie, when she brought up the subject of their kids.

"Did you know they're talking about moving in together?" she asked. She didn't sound particularly happy about it.

"You had to know that was coming," he said.

She nodded, shoved a bit of crust around her plate. "Of course, they're crazy about each other. And Declan is sweet with her. But they're so young," she added, her voice threaded with worry.

"They're old enough to do what they want," he said.

She frowned. "You can't think this is a good idea. They haven't been together that long."

"Neither have we," he pointed out. Although he felt so comfortable with Lucy, it was as if he'd known her forever.

"But we're older. They're…vulnerable."

As if he and Lucy weren't. "If it's any consolation, I tried to talk Dec out of rushing into anything. At least they're not talking about getting married."

"Moving in together is almost as big of a commitment, and if they break up, they can get just as hurt," she insisted. "I've asked Hannah to wait."

"I gave Dec the same advice."

"Good. Maybe they'll listen. I don't want them to make a mistake."

"Like we each did?"

She nodded. "I was so sure Evan was the only man I'd ever love. I thought we'd be together our whole lives, that we'd end up celebrating our golden anniversary. I thought I knew him so well."

"Maybe you did at first. Maybe he changed."

"People do. We're not the same person at forty that we are at twenty."

"Thank God for that," Brody quipped. "You know, a lot of us grow together instead of apart." It hadn't happened for him but he hoped it would be the case with his son and whomever he finally ended up with. "I can see why Declan wants to be with Hannah. She's like her mom. She's got a lot going for her."

That brought a smile from Lucy, but it was joined with a sigh. "They shouldn't rush into this."

"It's not like they're eloping," he reminded her.

"Oh, Lord. Don't put that idea in their heads. My daughter needs to finish college."

"I get that. I'm sure she will, no matter what they do."

"It's not that I don't like Declan," Lucy hurried to say. "I think he's great."

"So's Hannah. She's exactly the kind of girl I'd want to see my son end up with."

"But I don't want her hurt like…" She didn't have to finish the sentence. He knew where she was going.

"There are no guarantees when it comes to love. You and I both know that. We all have to take a gamble sooner or later."

The kids, he clarified to himself later as he drove home. Not him. A man reached a point when he needed to stay away from the tables.

But what if, while he was staying away from the tables, Lucy found someone who was willing to take a bet on her and propose marriage? How long would she be happy with the status quo? He sure didn't like the idea of losing her.

What was he going to do about it?

"I think we should wait to move in together," Hannah said to Declan as they sat in his car at Dick's Drive-In, eating hamburgers.

He frowned. "Has your mom been talking to you?"

No way was she going to admit to him that she'd talked with Mom. This was a decision that was theirs to make, not their parents'. But what her mother had said made a lot of sense. Why go to all the trouble to find a place and pack up your stuff and move in with somebody, only to find out a few months later it had been a bad idea?

Instead of giving him a straight answer, she prevaricated. "Why do you think that?"

"'Cause when we first talked about this, I thought you were all in."

"So I thought some more," she said.

And the more she'd thought, the more she decided maybe her mother was right. When it came down to it, she wasn't that wild about the living situation Declan had proposed. He wanted her to move into the big old house he shared with two of his buddies. It was dumpy and none of the guys were very good at keeping it clean. Would that change once she moved in? Probably only if she did the cleaning. Or turned into the resident nag. Declan claimed he did his part, but that wasn't saying much as there were always shirts draped over chairs and shoes scattered every which way in the entryway, as well as dirty dishes in the sink, which was gross. Half the time when she was over there visiting, she and Declan wound up doing them all after they'd eaten. It was an affordable arrangement but it didn't sound like a very romantic way to launch their life together.

Sometimes she really hated to admit when her mother was right, but this time she had to.

He nodded reluctantly when she shared her thoughts. "You're right. We need to save our money and make a plan."

He looked so sad. "Hey, I'm not saying a total no. Just no for now," she said.

"I get it. I guess I want to make sure we're really together."

"You dummy," she said, and threw a French fry at him. "Of course, we're together. How else can I build an internet empire?"

He pointed a teasing finger at her. "So, you're using me."

"You bet. And I intend to use you for the rest of my life."

"Sounds good to me," he said. "So let's start workin' on that plan."

After she got back to her room at the sorority house, she texted her mom. You win. We're waiting.

That's a win for both of you, Mom texted back. Better to be sure than sorry.

Hannah couldn't help wondering as she tossed aside her phone if Grandma had said something like that to Mom. She had to have been sure when she married Daddy. And look how long they'd been together. It didn't make sense that after all those years they'd break up.

They should be together and there was only one reason they weren't. Pandora needed to go. How could she make that happen?

Lucy got a surprise text from Evan.

Talk to your daughter.

Oh, good grief, now what?

She's sending me weird texts.

Lucy abandoned the texting and called him. "What on earth is going on?"

"I can't talk right now. Pandora just came in. I'll call you later," he said.

Oh, goody. She'd be all anticipation.

He did call later that day. "Hannah is not respecting Pandora," he informed Lucy.

"Gee, what a coincidence. I don't, either," she said lightly.

"Not funny. Have you been poisoning her against Pandora?"

What? "Evan, give me a break. I am way too busy to bother sabotaging your lust life."

"Well, tell her to stop. I'm tired of hearing how much

older I am than Pandora and how old she'll be when I'm eighty. Hannah's got me in a wheelchair and Pandora off clubbing with other men."

It was hard for Lucy not to laugh. It was a distinct possibility.

"She insists Pandora only wants me for my money."

"Money is nice," Lucy said.

"I'm serious, Luc. What prompted this?"

"I have no idea, honestly."

"Well, talk to her," he commanded.

"Evan, this is your problem. You talk to her."

"Thanks a lot," he snapped and ended the call, leaving Lucy laughing. The life of a philanderer obviously wasn't an easy one.

But she did decide to have a talk with her daughter. "Darling, you can't be harassing your father."

"I'm not," Hannah insisted. "I'm just trying to open his eyes."

"Remember what I said. Love is blind." So was infatuation.

"Love, right," Hannah scoffed.

"Take a lesson from Daddy. He's a great example of why people shouldn't rush into things," Lucy said, then went to get ready to go over to Brody's house.

Yep, no rushing on her part.

Twenty-Four

The Seaside with Santa festival was right around the corner and the town began to transform. Businesses went all out decorating, hoping to win the contest for the business best-dressed for the holidays. Bonnie and Lucy decorated the Dream Homes office—it had been great having her as an employee and a friend—and Hannah came down to celebrate, taking pictures of the life-sized plush Santa they'd seated in an old-fashioned rocking chair. At his feet sat a dollhouse with a big red bow on it. Lucy had purchased a gingerbread house from Sunbaked and that sat on the reception desk.

"As you can see," Lucy said to the camera, "we at Dream Homes Realty are ready for the holidays and hoping to win the competition here in Moonlight Harbor for the best-dressed business. I hope you'll come down and join us for the Seaside with Santa festival. Stop by and say hi, and let's talk about *your* dream home." She added the date of the festival and that was a wrap.

"That was great, Mom," Hannah said.

"You're a natural," added Bonnie.

She had to admit, she was starting to enjoy all the fun

little reels they were making. Surprisingly, they were paying off, not only with bringing in potential home buyers. A furniture store in nearby Aberdeen was letting her use their merchandise at no cost when staging houses, as long as she tagged them in the photos.

She was also able to help some of her new friends at the beach as well. Courtney Greer was thrilled to see the orders that came in for her beach line after Hannah did some shots of herself and Lucy wearing some of her designs, and the Driftwood Inn was booked solid for the festival.

Lucy couldn't take full credit for that though. Some of Jenna's guests were return customers who had fallen in love with both the classic motel and its friendly owner.

"I just hope the weather cooperates," Jenna fretted when she and her sister, Celeste, and Lucy all went to lunch together.

"She's still scarred from our first Seaside with Santa festival," Celeste explained. "So am I," she added. "I about froze my mermaid tail off on that float."

The sisters went on to regale Lucy with tales of the great storm and the power outage that had come along with it.

"We wound up with half the motel guests staying in our house. I almost had a nervous breakdown," Jenna finished.

"It all worked out in the end though," Celeste reminded her sister. "Brody and Courtney and Tyrella took in the ones Jenna couldn't house."

Saint Brody again. He was a good man to have around in an emergency. He was a good man to have around, period.

"We actually made some good friends from that adventure, including Taylor Marsh," Jenna said.

Lucy wasn't sure if Taylor would ever want to be her good friend. From Taylor's polite but cool reception of her whenever she stopped by the Beach Dreams office, it was plain she wished Lucy would have found some other town to settle in. But, oh, well. Lucy had her hands full pleasing her clients. She couldn't worry about pleasing the competition.

She thought of Brody and half smiled. Their competition had lost its angry edge.

Ooh, he was going to be irritated when he saw her float in the parade though.

It far surpassed his, as she knew it would. Seth's buddy and his crew had created a miniature housing development for her, with an arch over it all that read Dream Homes Realty. It outdid Brody's one-house special. She felt immensely pleased with herself on the day of the parade as it floated in wobbly majesty down Harbor Boulevard, carrying her and Hannah, the float's sparkly blue fringe caressing the asphalt.

But, as she watched the reaction of the crowd of parade goers, she realized he'd had a trick up his sleeve as well. What on earth was he throwing out to them? From where she was, three floats back, it looked like some kind of coupons. Rather silly, if you asked Lucy. What if it had rained? His coupons would have melted.

The weather had almost cooperated, bringing winter-blue skies. But a nippy breeze kept her teeth chattering in spite of the red faux fur trimmed wool coat and gloves she was wearing. She and Hannah were both waving and throwing out wrapped saltwater taffy (a much better idea), while Declan tagged alongside, snapping pictures, and Hannah's faithful videographer recorded the event.

"I can't feel my feet," Hannah called to Lucy as she threw out more candy to the crowd, making the children scramble.

"The price of fame," she called back, and blew her daughter a kiss.

They weren't hugely famous yet but the number of Hannah's online followers continued to increase and the number of subscribers to their YouTube channel was starting to get impressive. Lucy was proud of how her daughter was managing all of it while keeping up with school. While she didn't have a 4.0 grade point average, she was still doing well with a 3.5, and Lucy had no intention of riding her to do better. Her daughter was getting quite a business education running her online empire. Hannah Holmes was going places.

It looked like she was going to take Declan right along with her. He would be graduating with a business degree and could be a big help to her if they partnered up.

Partnering up. In the end that hadn't worked for Lucy and Evan. Was her daughter doomed to follow in her footsteps?

She shoved away the thought. Of course, she was being paranoid. Declan showed no signs of selfishness or insecurity. They'd actually taken their parents' advice and were taking their time, letting their relationship grow. They'd be fine.

And what about Lucy and Brody? Would they be fine as well? So far, so good. But it was easy for things to be good when there was no real commitment. It was also safer.

She had to keep reminding herself of that because lately her heart was becoming increasingly forgetful of the deal they'd made. No strings.

Three floats ahead the crowd was screaming as more bits of paper flew through the air from Brody's float, people rushing from the sidelines to scoop them up before the next float could run them over. Okay, what was he throwing to people?

Lucy stepped to the edge of the float and leaned out to see. One of the little papers drifted her direction, as if it were looking for her. Oh, yes. Here it came. She reached out to grab it.

She lost her balance and pitched forward with a screech, her thoughts tumbling faster than her body. *Face-plant, new teeth needed. Put out your hands! No, don't do that! You'll break your wrists. Better broken wrists than broken teeth. Where's a parachute when you need one?*

Instead of falling to the pavement, she fell into the arms of a big man in his thirties with a beard. Carl. He was wearing jeans, a jacket and a hunting cap, and had a red face.

"Uh, hi, Lucy," he said.

"Whoa, look what you caught," said one of his friends, who was standing nearby.

Meanwhile, Hannah's videographer was happily recording the whole event. They would have to do a serious segment to balance this latest Lucy moment.

"I don't suppose you could get me back home, could you?" she asked, pointing to her float, which was lumbering on without her.

"I sure can," he said.

In a few long strides, he'd reached the float and set her back on it. She blew him a kiss and the crowd cheered. Someone called, "We love Lucy!" And it was all recorded for the internet.

Lucy knew exactly what Hannah was going to say even before she said, "People are going to love it."

At least she hadn't landed on her face and she still had all her teeth. A girl should always look on the bright side.

The bright side dulled a little when she sneaked a peek at

what was written on the little piece of paper in her gloved hand. *That stinker!*

She wasn't holding a coupon. She was holding play money featuring Brody's smiling face. It was a Brody Buck and promised some lucky winner a chance at an all-expense paid vacation in Cancun. On the back was the usual legalese and room to write in name and contact information. All people had to do was come by Beach Dreams Realty and drop their Brody Buck in a big piggy bank. And, of course, check out the great homes available in Moonlight Harbor. Very clever.

She showed Hannah after they'd finished the parade route and were off the float. "How about a reel of you checking out the competition?" Hannah suggested.

"No. That didn't go over so well last time you pulled that stunt. Anyway, he's getting enough mileage out of this without any help from us. And that's hardly on brand," she pointed out, using one of Hannah's favorite new terms.

Hannah nodded thoughtfully. "Good point."

Bruno, who'd been their driver, left to deliver the Lucy housing development float to a special storage company where most of the Moonlight Harbor businesses kept their floats and Hannah and Declan went off to check out the various food booths on the pier, leaving Lucy on her own to text Brody.

You stinker! she texted him.

You got a Brody buck? he texted back. Beats a bounce house. This was punctuated with a smile emoji.

It sure did. Brody Green was a very clever man.

Later, as they enjoyed hot buttered rum in front of her fireplace, he brought up the idea Jenna had of them teaming up.

Lucy shook her head. "I've been down that road and it didn't work out."

"I understand, but I think we could draw up a contract in such a way as to be beneficial to both of us," he said.

"With a great big escape clause?"

He nodded. "I'm not out to swallow your company. I'm just thinking we might be able to combine forces and be even better together than we are separately."

Better together. She liked the sound of that. What would it be like to team up with Brody Green...both in business and in life?

Really, neither idea was good. They both had too much baggage, and after two love disappointments, his appeared to be even heavier than hers. Still, there was her stupid heart, picturing the two of them building a life together in Moonlight Harbor, not the no-strings-attached one they were living, but something lasting.

But how could you ever know if something was going to last? She stared into her mug, seeing once more that awful moment when she'd caught Evan with Pandora.

Actually, her baggage was pretty darned heavy, too.

It was a moot point, anyway. Brody didn't want to risk getting hurt again. She shouldn't, either.

Yet, she was. She could slap a "romance light" label on what they had but, in truth, it was becoming much more for her. And mixing love and business was sure to produce a dangerous drink.

"Hey, if you don't like the idea, no worries. I just keep thinking how good we could be together."

They already were. So why mess it up?

"But I'm not going to push you," he said.

"After what happened with Evan, it's hard to trust anyone."

"I hear you. You've moved on so fast and done so much since you hit town, I tend to forget that it hasn't been that long since your whole business was destroyed in your divorce. The wounds haven't finished healing. Anyway, it was a thought. I like to dream big."

So did she, but she didn't want a dream to turn into a nightmare.

"Anyway, we're good just as we are. Two separate businesses working well together." He drained the last of his drink and gave her shoulders a little squeeze. "Ah, this is the life, isn't it?"

"Yes, it is," she agreed, even though she could, like him, dream big, and she could see so much more for them than what they had.

Something is better than nothing, she told herself.

After he'd gone home, she sat, staring at the dying fire and had a different conversation with herself. Was the something she had with Brody enough? She wanted the man but she also wanted a sense of security.

Brody had been up front letting her know he couldn't give her that. But then, could anyone really give her a sense of security after everything she'd been through?

Twenty-Five

With money to spend before the end of the year, the Moonlight Harbor Chamber of Commerce decided to take over Sandy's restaurant for their annual Christmas party. The restaurant hadn't won the best-dressed business contest—that had gone to Courtney Greer's Beach Babes Boutique—but it had received a good many votes. The artificial tree in the reception area had been decked out with blue-and-white lights and all manner of beach-themed ornaments. As diners were shown to their tables, they passed a large sculpted lobster, bearing a serving tray and sporting a Santa hat. The windows had all been festooned with red garlands and every table held a miniature poinsettia.

Chamber members and their families mingled back and forth, and after dining on seafood fettuccini, garlic toast and Caesar salad, enjoyed a dessert buffet. After dinner many of the celebrants hung out at their various tables, chatting, while others made their way to the bar, where The Mermaids were offering a mix of dance music.

Jenna had told Lucy that Brody would never dance, but he'd been more than happy to prove her wrong, showing off some impressive moves on the floor, turning and spinning Lucy like a pro.

"You could be on *Dancing With the Stars*," Tyrella informed him.

He'd never been a fan of the show but it was one of his daughter's favorites, so he decided to take Tyrella's comparison as a compliment, especially since he didn't have anywhere near the moves her fiancé, Darrell Banks, did.

"Nothing wrong with dancing with your woman," Darrell said when Brody expressed surprise at seeing a pastor out on the floor. "And David danced before the Lord. Not like that, I admit," he added. "But when the woman you're gonna marry wants to dance, you dance."

Jenna and Seth passed them on their way to get more drinks. She cocked an eyebrow at Brody. "Since when do you dance?"

"Since I don't have to stand in a line and only look at a woman," he shot back. "Line dancing," he said to Lucy as if that explained the exchange.

Seth half smiled at that and put an arm around Jenna, leading her away.

"I don't get it," Lucy said.

"She was always wanting me to line dance with her at The Drunken Sailor on Sunday nights. I passed on the offer. What's the point of dancing if you can't hold a woman?"

"And you do such a good job of it," Lucy said.

Back at her place, they settled in for a nightcap and he thought how funny it was that he'd become so comfortable and content around a woman he'd had no use for only a few months earlier. He'd thought she was a bitch, and that habit she had of always touching people had really irritated him. It had seemed so fake.

But it wasn't. It was all part of who Lucy Holmes was, and it sure didn't irritate him anymore, especially when he was the one getting touched. She was good company, and he liked the idea of them spending a lot of time together for the rest of their lives. The way things were going with their kids, it looked like they would be.

Soon they were talking about family plans for the holidays. He didn't have to hint around much for Lucy to invite him over for the afternoon of Christmas Day. "I'll be back from my family's gathering by four and Hannah will be coming down. I suspect we'll be hauling down more leftovers than we can possibly eat. If your kids are coming down, they're welcome to join us."

"Sounds like a plan. I think I'll have some leftovers of my own to contribute."

"Christmas potluck," she said happily.

Fa-la-la. Lucy Holmes knew how to make the holidays bright.

It was a different holiday. Hannah spent Christmas Eve with her father.

Of course, it was a good thing that she'd forgiven him because what had happened between him and Lucy had had nothing to do with her. Except it had affected her and she'd complained to Lucy how weird Christmas was going to be without the three of them together.

"It doesn't feel right," she'd said. "And I hate seeing Daddy with Pandora." That much was obvious from her earlier texting campaign.

Lucy got that. It should have been Evan and her and their daughter seated by the tree, opening presents on Christmas morning. In another lifetime they'd have all gone to his parents' house the night before. In another lifetime they'd have all been gathering at Darla's place with her family later on Christmas Day.

Now they were fractured, and maybe some of that was Lucy's fault. She'd as much as handed him over to the other woman, not even putting up a fight.

Putting up a fight for a cheater, for a man who'd valued his own cheap thrills more than his marriage? Where was the wisdom in that? Maybe, if when he'd first been caught, his remorse had been genuine, if he'd had the sense to try to win her back, it could have been a different story. The fact that he hadn't fought for her told her where his heart truly was. And now they all were where they were.

The strangeness of the whole thing would soon become familiar. Weird would fade to normal. Meanwhile, they'd find new ways to celebrate the joys of Christmas.

One of the new ways involved Lucy going up to her sister's house the day before Christmas Eve to party with Darla and her brother, Jeremy, their families and her parents while Hannah spent time with her dad.

"You look great, sis," Jeremy said, hugging her.

"I feel great," she said.

Well, she would once her daughter was with them.

Hannah's absence poked a huge hole in Lucy's enjoyment of the evening. The family gathering didn't seem right until she arrived in the morning to open presents and enjoy the breakfast buffet that Darla, their mother, Donna, and Lucy had put together.

Hannah had Declan in tow and Donna gave him her stamp of approval. "He's a lovely boy," she told Lucy as they put away the leftovers.

"His dad's not bad, either," said Darla, looking in Lucy's direction with a smirk.

"It's not serious," Lucy said, and concentrated on wrapping the ham slices Darla had insisted she take home in foil. At least, not for him.

"Friendship can grow into something more," Donna said. "That's how it worked with your father and me."

"That's how it started with Evan and me," Lucy said with a frown. "Maybe we should have just stayed friends."

Her mother pointed a serving spoon she was about to load in the dishwasher at Lucy. "You jumped into things too quickly with Evan."

"Oh, now you tell me," Lucy retorted.

"I could see he wasn't right for you," Donna continued. The same Evan her father had golfed with in Palm Springs. The same Evan her mother had always baked cookies for whenever they'd come to visit. That Evan?

"You seemed to think he was pretty wonderful the whole time we were together."

"So I had vision problems for a while," Donna said, and went back to loading the dishwasher. "But I knew at the start he wasn't enough for you. He wasn't as smart."

He'd been smart enough to hide an affair from his wife.

"You never said anything the whole time we were dating," Lucy reminded her mother.

"What would have been the point? You were in love. Anyway, you wouldn't have listened. The young never listen to the old."

"Sometimes they do," Lucy said, thinking of how her daughter had actually taken her advice.

Hannah chose that moment to come into the kitchen, carrying the bowl with the last of the fruit salad. "Who does what?" she asked.

"I think your mother was about to brag on you," Darla guessed.

"Only a little," Lucy said. "Hannah's being wise and making smart life decisions."

"You need to decide to keep that young man," said Donna. "Did you see how he pulled the chair out for me at dinner?" she asked her daughters. "Very thoughtful."

"Yes, he is," Hannah agreed. She set down the bowl and slung an arm around Lucy's shoulders. "We're taking our time, thanks to someone's advice, but I know he's the one. And don't worry, Mom. We won't end up like you and Daddy," Hannah assured her as if reading her mind. "Declan's not like Daddy at all. He would never cheat on me, and he wouldn't be so stupid as to pick someone like Pandora," she said in disgust. "She actually asked me if I wanted to call her Mom," Hannah finished with an eye roll.

Mom! Anger shot through Lucy faster than lightning. "She what?"

"Don't worry. I told her she was an idiot. Which is no lie. All she can talk about is clothes and her diet. She's quit working. Now she just shops for stuff for the house and plays games on her phone."

Evan had picked a leech. It was hard not to feel a tiny bit…gleeful. Philandering men who wanted to recapture their youth should be careful what they wished for.

"She really thought it would be so easy to sell houses," Hannah finished in disgust.

"There's no easy way to success," Lucy said.

"I sure found that out," Hannah said.

Yes, she had. "And you're doing so great," Darla said to her. "We're all proud of you."

"Well-deserved success," Lucy said. "She's working hard for every new plateau she reaches."

Hannah beamed. "Adulting, Mom. I am never going to be a Pandora," she added in disgust.

"I should hope not," said her grandmother. "You have too much going for you."

"Speaking of going, we should get on the road if we're going to beat Declan's dad and Mariah to the house," Lucy said.

Declan's dad. Rather a formal way to describe Brody, but also the safest way. Her sister knew she'd fallen hard for him and her mom suspected it, but if she admitted it to them, she was sure she'd jinx the whole thing.

They got going, Declan and Hannah following Lucy in his car, and arrived at the house on Sand Dollar Lane with half an hour to spare before Brody and Mariah showed up, both bearing food to contribute to the feast. By the time they were all ready to eat, the table was crowded with goodies, everything from sliced ham and turkey, leftover dressing and layered salad to dinner rolls and red velvet cupcakes. Lucy topped it off with eggnog punch.

As the guys were playing Wii bowling, Mariah joined Hannah and Lucy in the kitchen, where they were filling a platter with the last of the Christmas cookies Lucy had baked earlier in the week.

"Thanks for having us over," Mariah said to Lucy.

"I'm happy you could come."

"I love coming here," Mariah said. She focused on helping transfer some brownies from a tin to the platter. "And I love seeing Dad so happy. I haven't seen him this way in a long time. I'm glad you guys are together."

Sort of, Lucy thought. "We're enjoying each other's company," she said, staying vague. Kind of like their relationship.

Except they were together. So what if they weren't locked in legally? It was safer that way.

If only she weren't getting tired of being safe.

* * *

The kids all went back to Seattle to ring in the New Year, and Lucy and Brody did some celebrating of their own. He had her over to his place for dinner, grilling steaks and lobster, and she made chocolate lava cake for their dessert.

They spent the next day together at her house, camped on the sofa, watching football. Well, him watching football. Her half watching and working on a listicle she'd promised Hannah for the website: *Six ways to make your house irresistible to buyers*. In between plays, Brody would check it out and offer comments and suggestions. It all felt so comfortable, as if they'd been together for years rather than months. She wondered if he felt it, too.

She decided not to ask.

It was late in the day when he finally went home and, after all that togetherness, she needed…more. Lucy wasn't wired for solitude and the house felt empty.

She called Bonnie. "I'm about to make some good old-fashioned mac and cheese. Care to join me?"

"Sure," Bonnie said, and was over ten minutes later, bringing a big box of chocolates to share.

"Whoa, where'd you get those?"

"Glen Olsen. He came to the Elks last night to watch the band and brought them for me."

One of Bonnie's groupie wannabes. Glen had fifteen years on her and had the build of a jellyfish. Bonnie kept him at arm's length but claimed it had nothing to do with his looks or their age difference.

"You gotta feel the love, soul-deep," she liked to say. "Otherwise it's a waste of everybody's time. Anyway, if I want romance, I can stream a movie or live vicariously through you."

Which she was ready to do, after she'd settled in at the kitchen bar with a glass of eggnog and was watching Lucy work. "How was your New Year's Eve?"

"Brody made dinner—steak and lobster."

"Here's to being with a man who cooks," Bonnie said, raising her glass to Lucy. "It sure looks like you've settled him down."

Had she? She wasn't so sure.

They were finishing their mac and cheese when Hannah texted Lucy. Pandora left Daddy!!!!

Lucy blinked at the screen, sure she had to have misread. Nope, there it was. Well, well.

"Good news, I hope?" Bonnie prompted.

"Not for Evan."

Lucy still didn't know a lot about Bonnie's past, but Bonnie had learned the whole sorry tale of Lucy's failed marriage. "The home-wrecker dumped him," she guessed.

It was wrong to take pleasure in someone else's misery. Lucy smiled. "Yep."

"What goes around comes around. That's what my mama always says."

"It's hard to feel sorry for him," Lucy said.

"Good, because you shouldn't."

"He wrecked our marriage for nothing."

"That's the problem with nothing. It seems like something at the time," said Bonnie.

I think he's sorry for what he did to you, came the next text. Lucy gave a snort and read it to Bonnie.

I feel kind of bad for him.

Bonnie read that one and rolled her eyes. "Gack."

"Well, he is her father," Lucy said, and texted back, I

know. But he'll be ok. "He'll have a new girlfriend by Valentine's Day," she predicted. He'd have to. His ego couldn't take the rejection.

"Interesting how your New Year is beginning," Bonnie said. "Think he'll come crawling back?"

Lucy shook her head. "No. That would be too humiliating. Anyway, now he's acquired a taste for youth."

Bonnie wrinkled her nose. "A taste for youth? You make him sound like a vampire. Young blood," she said, wriggling her fingers.

"Maybe, in a way, he is. A psychic vampire. He sure tried to suck the life out of me."

Bonnie cocked her head. "There's got to be a song in there somewhere."

Lucy chuckled. "I can see the music video now—a cowboy running around in jeans, a Stetson and a big black cape."

"The only thing big on you is your cape," Bonnie cracked and they both laughed.

Funny how unlaughable Lucy's life had looked all those months ago. She was living proof that you could turn your back on the bad stuff and bring good things into your life.

Later that night she lay in bed, thinking about Evan and the life they'd had together. It hadn't been all bad. They'd had plenty of good times, shared both laughter and tears. Where along the way had they lost that love they'd shared when they were young and starting their business, starting a family? She still didn't know. She supposed she never would.

Brody lay in bed thinking of Lucy. He thought about Lucy a lot lately. She had come to mean more to him than he ever imagined she would. He loved her creativity, her laugh, her dimples.

But did he love her? As much as he'd loved Jenna?

How could he compare? What he had with Lucy was different than what he'd had with Jenna. In some ways it felt more solid. Even after they'd gotten engaged, he'd always felt like Jenna was holding back.

Lucy, on the other hand, had jumped into their relationship—even with all its caveats—with both feet. Was it worth taking a third try at something permanent? Did he dare put himself out there?

He was still asking himself that the next day.

"Kind of sucks that your dad got dumped," Declan said as he and Hannah walked down a snowy Seattle street toward Starbucks for eggnog lattes.

"He should never have been with her," Hannah said. "Maybe now he'll come to his senses and go back to Mom."

Declan gave her a funny look. "You'd want him to?"

"If he's really sorry. They should be together."

"In case you hadn't noticed, your mom and my dad are together."

"I don't think that's really serious," Hannah said.

"You got to be kidding. They're together all the time. Dad's really into her."

Hannah wasn't sure what to say to that. She liked Declan's dad a lot. But Mom and Dad had been a couple for decades. It only seemed right that they get their heads glued back on straight and get back together. The three of them were a family. They needed to be together again, doing things as a family, celebrating holidays in the same house.

"I know they've been hanging out," she said. But that

was because Daddy was with someone else. What choice did Mom have?

"If you think that's all they've been doing, you are blind. If she dumps Dad, it'll kill him."

Declan sounded almost angry. Hmm. As angry when she'd voiced the same concern about his dad dumping Mom.

"But my parents aren't like yours. They were together almost their whole life."

"You know, it's interesting how quick you are to want them back together after how pissed you were at him," Declan pointed out. "Your dad was a shit, but now you want him to go back to your mom and mess up her life, a good life that she's having with my dad. Isn't that a little bit selfish?"

"It's not," Hannah insisted. "I want what's best for her."

"Or do you want this fantasy you're building up in your mind about you all living happily together."

She scowled at him. "That's rude."

"Maybe. But is it true?"

She clamped her lips shut.

"Look, I'm not trying to be a shit. I just think you should let your parents work out their own lives. Okay? Then whatever happens, happens."

It took her a long time to say, "Okay," but she finally did. Of course, that didn't mean she couldn't share Mom's address with her father.

By the time January had eased into February, Brody knew he wanted to take what he had with Lucy to the next level. If he didn't, he was liable to lose her, and he couldn't stand the idea of not having her in his life.

"Don't make any plans for Valentine's Day," he told her. "I'm taking you someplace special."

"Someplace special. That sounds intriguing," she said. "How about giving me a hint?"

"No hints. It'll be a surprise."

"How should I dress?"

In as little as possible. "I love you in that black dress," he said.

"So, someplace fancy."

"Only the best for you. Which is why you're with me," he cracked.

"I do have excellent taste," she said.

Oh, yeah. It looked like the third try really was the charm. He ended their call and went to Cindy's Candies where he bought the biggest box of chocolates he could find.

"Gee, I wonder who that might be for," Cynthia Redmond teased.

"My mother," he joked.

At the flower shop he did order some flowers for his mom. Then he ordered a corsage for Lucy. It would look great on that delicate little wrist of hers.

Now he was set. He'd reserved a window table in the elegant restaurant at the Ocean Crest Hotel. He'd ply her with champagne, give her the chocolates and ask her if she'd like to up the ante and make what they had something more permanent.

Lucy had just gotten home from the office when a text came in from Hannah. Stay home 2nite.

On Valentine's Day? What on earth was her daughter thinking?

I have plans, she texted back.

???

Honestly, did her daughter expect her to sit at home on Valentine's Day? Hadn't Hannah been paying attention to what had been developing between Brody and her?

Possibly not, she realized. They avoided PDA in front of the kids, kept everything casual and light. When it came right down to it, she realized she hadn't shared with her daughter much of what was going on with her. Partly because when she was with Hannah, their conversation was all about Hannah's latest project for them or about what was going on in her life, either with school or with Declan. That was part of it, but Lucy realized another part had to do with her preferring not to say anything.

How did one go about doing that? *I'm falling in love with the man I claimed to hate... Surprise! Your mother has rushed into a relationship and is now in heart-deep with someone and she's not sure where that's going. She's doing exactly what she told you not to do.*

No wonder she hadn't said anything about how serious she'd gotten.

I'm going out to dinner with Brody. There. Valentine's dinner with Brody ought to say something and say it loud and clear.

A surprise is coming, came the next text.

Whatever it was, it would most likely get delivered before she left. How sweet of her girl to think of her.

OK. Will keep my eyes peeled. And if this mysterious surprise didn't arrive in time, it could sit on the porch until she got home.

This received a thumbs up and a Luv U.

Luv U 2. That old "to the moon and back" saying didn't even come close. It was more like to the moon and beyond.

Have fun with D, she added.

No need to tell Hannah that. She would. It looked like what they had was definitely going to turn into something permanent, and that would be more than fine with Lucy.

Meanwhile, it was great to see her daughter happy and moving forward with her life. She'd survived her parents' divorce and now was thriving.

That which doesn't kill me makes me stronger. Maybe Nietzsche had something there. Both she and Hannah had come through that messy ordeal a little stronger, Lucy was sure of it. And they were both making a good life for themselves.

She brewed herself a cup of her favorite chocolate-mint tea and relaxed with an episode of *House Hunters*. Then it was time to start getting ready for her evening out. She began by indulging in a bubble bath, after which she slathered on her favorite lotion, Hempz Sugar Lemon Squares. Brody had given it to her for Christmas and she was addicted to the fragrance. Of course, that addiction was nothing compared to what she felt for the man himself.

As she put on her makeup, she wondered when this surprise her daughter was sending would arrive. The mail had already come, and it was past the hour when FedEx and UPS usually showed up at her door. Brody would be arriving soon. She hoped whatever it was that it would get to her before she had to leave as her curiosity was growing by the minute.

She was in her sexy black dress that Brody loved seeing her in, ready to go, when the doorbell rang.

The surprise would have to wait.

She opened the door with a smile and started to purr, "Happy Valentine's…" The rest of the sentence died on her lips.

Twenty-Six

"Evan?" Lucy had to be hallucinating. Or dreaming. Or… something.

She blinked, hoping he wouldn't be there when she opened her eyes. It didn't work. He still was, dressed in slacks, a jacket and gray sweater and holding a bouquet of pink roses.

"You look amazing, Luc," he said, handing them to her and giving her the smile that had so charmed her when they were young.

It wasn't nearly as charming as Brody's.

And the pink roses. He'd given them to her every Valentine's Day since they'd been married. Even when they were first starting their business and broke, he'd always found the money for those roses. Her heart did a sick flop and then lay there right in the middle of Memory Lane.

Get up, Stupid, she told it. That was a different Evan and a different time.

"What are you doing here?" she demanded.

"I came to see you. Aren't you going to invite me in?"

No.

Polite-woman disease won out and she stepped aside.

"How did you find me?" she asked.

Stupid question. Hannah, of course. Evan was, obviously, the surprise she'd wanted Lucy to stick around for. Every child's dream, that Mom and Dad would get back together.

She wished Brody had already come and that they were on their way out to dinner.

He strolled into the living room, looked around, gave an approving nod. "Hannah. Did she tell you? I've been following what you two were doing online. I'm one of your YouTube subscribers. Pretty damned clever of you, Luc."

"It was Hannah's idea."

"She's smart. She takes after her mom."

Lucy frowned at him. All this flattery he was spewing was spoiling her appetite.

"You still haven't told me what you want." she said.

"You."

Now that he had no one. "Well, I don't want you."

"I blew it. I'll be the first to admit that. But we had something good. We could have it again."

Yes, they'd had something good and she'd been content enough with it. But what she had with Brody was something great.

"Let's sit down."

"I'm sorry, but I don't have time. I'm going out. You need to leave."

"Just like that? I came all this way. Can't you change your plans?"

The arrogance of the man! "No."

The doorbell rang. Brody. How was this going to look to him? It was all Lucy could do not to stuff Evan in the coat closet.

She pointed a finger at him. "You are just leaving."

He frowned, then went to the sofa and settled in, crossing his legs and stretching an arm across the back of it like he belonged there, like he was expecting her to join him.

Lucy glared at him. "I mean it, Evan."

She grabbed her coat and opened the door. Again. Take two. This time the man she wanted to see was standing there.

"Hey there," he said, his voice a caress.

She practically pushed him back onto the porch. "Let's go. I'm starving."

"Aren't you going to introduce me, Luc?" Evan called. He left the couch and strolled up behind her, smiling. "Hi, I'm Evan Anderson," he said to Brody, and stuck out his hand.

Brody juggled the giant box of chocolates and the plastic container with the corsage he was holding, and shook it, frowning as he did so.

"I didn't know you had company," he said to Lucy as he gave her the gifts. His usual thousand-watt smile was barely up to fifty.

"I wanted to surprise Luc," Evan said.

"You did," she said, and scowled at him. She put Brody's gifts on the hall table. Next to the pink roses.

"It seemed like the perfect time for a reconciliation," Evan said, and laid a hand on Lucy's shoulder.

She shrugged it off. "Well, I'm afraid it's not."

Brody was already backing away. "You two probably need to talk."

"No, we don't," Lucy said.

"Yes, we do," said Evan.

"I'll talk to you later," Brody said to Lucy.

"Brody, don't go," she pleaded.

Too late. He was already gone. Taking all his twice-burned baggage and hauling it down her front walk.

She started after him, but Evan caught her arm. "Lucy, come on. Give us a chance. It's only been a year. You can't have fallen for someone else that fast."

Yes, she could have. "You've got to be kidding! You fell for someone when we were still together."

"It was a mistake. Come on, come sit down. Let's see if we can talk this out."

She shook off his hand and ran for Brody's car. It was too late. He was already driving off. She marched back to the porch, wishing the glare she was directing at her ex was hot enough to burn him to cinders.

"You shit," she snarled. "You awful, selfish, conceited shit."

He held up both hands. "Whoa, take it easy, Luc."

She snatched the pink roses from the hall table and whacked him with them, sending leaves and petals flying. Oh, that felt good.

In fact, it felt so good she did it again. And again.

"Ouch! Hey, those things have thorns," he protested, holding up his hands.

"Get. Out," she growled.

"This is a mistake. We should be together. Luc! You're not even being rational."

Like he'd been when he'd stripped off and got dirty in the shower with their employee.

"Get out!" she screeched.

Now he was glaring. "Okay, fine. If that's how you want it. Hannah's going to be heartbroken and that's on you."

"No, that's on you, you unfaithful dog." She gave him a shove, propelling him out the door, slammed it after him and locked it. Then she dug her cell phone out of her purse and called Brody.

It went straight to his voice mail. "Hey there, you reached Brody Green of Beach Dreams Realty. Leave me a message and I'll get back to you ASAP."

"Please call me," she said, sounding teary and pathetic. Probably because she was. "Evan showed up out of the blue. He's gone. For good," she added.

She ended the call, then settled on the couch, phone in hand, and waited.

And waited.

Half an hour passed. Then another.

She cleaned up the mess of rose petals in the entry-way, then she put on her jammie bottoms and a sweatshirt, poured herself a glass of wine, donned the corsage and opened the chocolates.

And cried.

Lucy's ex had finally wised up and realized what he'd lost. Good for him. Good for them. They should try to repair their broken marriage. In the long run it would be best for their whole family.

Except the tool didn't deserve her. He was bound to hurt her again.

Brody listened to her phone message. For the seventh time so far, but who was counting? As before, his fingers hovered over the phone screen, itching to call her back. The dinner reservation was lost but the night was still young. He could go back over there, drag her away to his place. She wanted to be with him.

But if she didn't patch things up with the tool, she'd probably live to regret it.

And if he let the tool have her, he'd regret it.

Unbelievable. Here he was again, losing out to another man, and this time was even worse than the first.

He frowned. Competing with another man over a woman? Uh, no. Been there, done that. He refused to go down that road again. He was glad he hadn't opened his big mouth and said the *M* word. Let Lucy have her ex back and rebuild her life. It was fine with him.

Who was he kidding?

He shut off his phone and went in search of a beer and a bag of chips. It was time for some Netflix binging. Lots of Bourne and Bond and Jack Reacher—all good reminders that heroes walked alone.

Except he wasn't a hero.

Hannah and Declan were spending the big night in at his place. He'd shooed his roommates away and cleaned the house. The two of them had made dinner together—fettucini Alfredo with French bread and tossed salad, and she'd succeeded at her first attempt at cheesecake, Declan's favorite. He'd bought her a single white rose and she'd saved up and bought a vinyl collector's edition album from his favorite band. With both his roommates out, they'd been free to have at it on the sagging living room sofa. By nine o'clock they were streaming the latest Marvel movie and she couldn't stand the suspense anymore.

"I've got to call Mom," she said.

"If she's with your dad, she probably doesn't want to be bothered," Declan said. "And if she's not with your dad, I'm betting she's with mine and she still doesn't want to be bothered."

"I need to know what's going on," Hannah said, reaching for her phone.

Declan shrugged. "I still think you should have kept out of the middle of things but…"

"But I couldn't. Wouldn't you want your mom and dad to get together?"

"Are you kidding? All they did was fight."

"Well, mine didn't."

He shrugged. "Nope. He just screwed around on her."

The harsh words hurt. But they were true. Why was she risking possible hurt for Mom by trying to push her and Daddy back together? The fantasy Declan had talked about, of course. But what if it could become reality? What if Daddy was really, truly sorry? Then shouldn't they get back together?

She called Mom.

The first words out of her mother's mouth were, "Hannah, what were you thinking?"

Uh-oh. "What do you mean?"

"You know perfectly well what I mean."

She hadn't heard her mother so angry since she'd stayed out an hour past curfew when she was sixteen. "Daddy wanted to see you."

"Did you give him the idea that I wanted to see him?"

Okay, so maybe she had. A little. "Um."

"What did you say?"

Hannah could feel Declan watching her and her cheeks starting to do a slow burn. "I just said I didn't think you were with anyone."

"How could you think that?"

"I didn't know things were serious with you and Mr. Green."

She was lying to her mom and herself. They'd never showed any PDA, but anyone with eyeballs could have seen there was something between them by the way they looked at each other, not to mention how much they hung out together.

At one point she'd thought it was great that Mom was spending so much time with Declan's dad. But getting back together with Daddy and rebuilding what they'd once had—that had to trump starting new with someone else. And Daddy was so miserable. And sorry that he'd blown it with Mom.

"You never said anything," Hannah added in her own defense.

Mom's words came out like ice chips. "That's because it's none of your business."

Hannah did some ice-chipping of her own. "It is, too, my business. If I'm about to get a stepfather, don't you think I should know?"

"I didn't say that," Mom said, a tiny bit less snappish.

"Well, am I?"

"I doubt it now. Daddy was here when Brody showed up to take me to dinner."

Hannah wasn't quite sure how to respond, so she settled for, "Oh."

"I know you were trying to help," Mom said, her voice softening, "and I know you'd love it if things could go back to the way they were, but they can't. Your father made a wrong choice, and while I've forgiven him, I have no intention of taking him back. He and I will always be there for you, but he and I cannot be together. It would be a mistake. Can you understand that?"

Stupid her. Of course, she did. She'd understood a lot more clearly when her parents first split. Somewhere along the way she'd regressed to a twelve-year-old, believing in happy endings and fairy tales. Next she'd be believing in the tooth fairy.

"It would be like me asking you to dump Declan and take back the boyfriend who cheated on you," Mom said.

That made things crystal clear. Steps backward never took a woman anywhere. Still, Hannah wanted to cry—for what her father had thrown away, for what they'd never get back.

She nodded. As if Mom could see her. Duh. But it was all she could do because her throat was closing up and her vocal cords refused to work.

"I'm afraid you're going to have to let me find my own way, just as I'm letting you find yours," Mom added. "I want you to be happy and I know you want the same for me."

"I do," Hannah managed. Of course, she did. She wanted both her parents to be happy, but especially Mom. Daddy was miserable now, but Mom had for sure suffered the most. And maybe it was time for Daddy to do some suffering of his own. Maybe it would be good for him.

"Then that's settled. Now, I'm sure you and Declan are doing something together. Go back to enjoying your first Valentine's Day. I love you," she added.

"I love you, too," Hannah said, and ended the call. She tossed the phone back on the coffee table and swiped at the tears starting down her cheeks. "They're not getting back together."

She'd had such hopes. Stupid hopes.

"You're still a family, whether your parents get back together or not," Declan pointed out. "And remember how pissed you were when he cheated on her? How do you know he won't do that again? Do you really want your mom to take that gamble?"

"No," she said. "I was in la-la land. And Daddy was, too,

if he thought she'd take him back." Although she'd been the one who bought him the ticket to la-la land.

"Sometimes you can't go back," Declan said. "The only way is forward."

"Truth," she said. But what if she'd made it so her mom couldn't go forward?

Her lower lip began to tremble and she felt the sting of tears in her eyes.

"What?" he prompted.

"I think I've just ruined things for your dad and my mom," she said, and began to cry.

"Hey, now," he said gently, pulling her close. "You were just trying to—"

She cut him off. "Don't say help. I wasn't helping. I was being selfish and stupid."

"Maybe a little. But I'd probably have done the same if I were you."

"Your dad will never trust my mom enough to get together now and it's all my fault," she said miserably. Here she'd wanted Mom to be happy and she'd come in with a giant pair of scissors and sliced that happiness to pieces.

"You don't know that," Declan said. "If they really want to be together, they'll find a way."

"There's got to be something I can do," she said.

"Yeah, there is. Stay out of it."

Easy for him to say. He wasn't the one who had messed up two people's lives.

"Okay, who shot the moon out of the sky?" Bonnie said when Lucy dragged herself into the office the next day looking like she belonged in a Tim Burton movie.

Lucy tried to play dumb. "What do you mean?"

"You look like you had a date with a vampire last night," Bonnie said.

Lucy sighed and plopped down at her desk. "I had a visit from a psychic vampire."

"Yow. You are living out a country song," Bonnie said after Lucy had told her about Evan's ill-timed visit. "What are you going to do?"

"There's not much I can do. Brody's not returning my calls. He just jumped on his conclusions and rode away," she added with a frown.

"Now there's a great line for a song if ever I heard one," Bonnie said.

"You can have it with my blessing."

Lucy opened her laptop, ready to get to work. She hadn't expected to find a love life when she came to Moonlight Harbor and it looked like she still hadn't. No, take that back. She'd found a great one. She'd simply managed to lose it.

She'd been miserable after what happened with Evan, but this was a different kind of misery. That breakup had been a painful shock and a blow to her ego. This one had been torpedoed by outside forces and it brought a whole other kind of misery, one that came from hope denied. It felt like being bedridden with some awful disease when on the other side of the door the cure lay just out of reach.

She typed in her password, then stared at the screen. She'd put a new picture up as a screen saver. It was a selfie she'd taken with Brody at Christmas. There they were, both in red sweaters, him with a goofy Santa hat on his head. Both looking as if all was well with their world.

It had been until Evan had come to town like a steamroller and squashed what they'd been building. She was going to have to change that screen saver.

Or change her life.

It was as if Bonnie had seen where her thoughts were headed. "So, do you want to let him go, just like that, without a fight?"

"No," Lucy said firmly. She hadn't fought for Evan. He didn't deserve it. Brody was another matter.

"Well, then?" Bonnie prompted.

Lucy tapped her fingers on the desktop. *Come on, think.*

"You need a movie moment," Bonnie said.

"A movie moment?"

"Yeah, you know. A grand gesture, a big finish where the other person has no choice but to give you the happy ending you deserve."

"A movie moment," Lucy repeated again, staring at Bonnie, seated over at Hannah's desk.

"Are you sure?"

She wasn't sure of anything except that she didn't want to lose Brody. She tapped her fingers some more, thought some more.

And then it came to her.

Twenty-Seven

The day had been a bust and·Brody had gotten nothing done. He'd been crabby at the office and, after accusing him of male PMS, both Taylor and Missy insisted he go home and eat some chocolate. Ha ha.

But he did leave. In his present state of mind, he was no good to anyone. He picked up some clam chowder at Ellis West's Seafood Shack, then took it to the beach and sat in his car, watching the gulls coast over the water.

Not a bad thing to be a seagull. They didn't have a care in the world. They just rode the wind. No entanglements, no emotions to mess with their heads.

He and Lucy had sat on this very beach, eating clam chowder, watching the gulls and looking at the water. He scowled, put the last of his unfinished chowder back in the paper bag and left.

He stopped by Beachside Grocery, passed the chocolate and went straight for the beer and chips. Then he grabbed a frozen pizza and went home.

That evening he settled in with his man food and more guy movies, starting with *The Great Escape*. Prisoners of war. Yes! Not a woman in sight. When that ended he streamed *The Magnificent Seven*, not the remake but the classic his dad had introduced him to when he was a kid with Yul Brynner and Steve McQueen and Charles Bronson and James Coburn, all the old kings of cool. Yeah, no women needed there.

Oh, except for the kid who fell for the cute Mexican girl. He abandoned that movie and moved on to *Saving Private Ryan*. He was just getting into it when his doorbell rang. Whoever it was, sorry but he wasn't home. He ignored it.

It rang again. And then again. Insistently. As he went downstairs to the front entry, he could hear voices singing. It was hardly the right time of year for caroling.

The doorbell rang one more time and Brody yanked the door open, ready to punch whoever was pestering him. Yep, male PMS.

There stood Moonlight Harbor's favorite band, The Mermaids, all bundled up and singing an acapella version of "Better Together." In front of them stood Lucy, holding the very big box of chocolates Brody had given her.

Before he could say anything, she slipped past the door. She waved goodbye to The Mermaids, who waved back and kept singing.

She shut the door and held out the box of chocolates. "I don't want to eat these by myself."

"You had someone to help you eat them," Brody pointed out.

"I don't want him. He's ancient history. I prefer to live in the present and look to the future. Anyway, why would I settle for second best when the best is right here in Moonlight Harbor?"

The best, huh? His ego took a bow.

Still, he hesitated, determined to be noble. "Lucy, if

there's any chance you can patch things up with your ex, I don't want to stand in your way."

"With that cheater? Seriously? That's what you'd want for me?" She didn't give him a chance to answer. "We're done for good, and the only thing I don't want you standing in the way of is us. I want to take a second chance on love, Brody, and I want to do it with you." She smiled that adorable Lucy smile at him and jiggled the box of chocolates. "Come on, help me out here."

To heck with the chocolates and never mind Private Ryan. Brody needed to save himself. He pulled Lucy to him and kissed her, and it was like coming home.

He was whistling when he walked into the office the next day. "Looks like the chocolate did the trick," Missy joked.

"Yeah, it did," he said.

That night he went over to Lucy's for dinner. She made pot roast and he brought the wine and the box of chocolates. After dinner the chocolates went ignored again. It felt good to be back with her, like a sailboat about to capsize had been righted.

The rest of the week was busy with work and spending time with Lucy and it flew by. So did the next month and the month after that, and before he knew it, it was spring. Then Memorial Day and all the kids were coming down to hang out at the beach.

And at Lucy's place, where they ate sandwiches on the back deck and kayaked and paddleboarded on the canal. And hung out with their friends. But they also hung out with him and Lucy a lot. It all felt so right. So much like family should feel. So...permanent.

He began to circle back around to the thought of making what he had with Lucy permanent. Did he dare? The Valentine's Day disaster had stabbed his heart all over again and sometimes he wondered if he was as healed as he thought he was.

The Fourth of July drew near, and with the Fourth came all the usual festivities as well as the usual invitation to Jenna's beach party. The same beach party that had signaled the beginning of the end of her and him. Last year he'd refused the invitation.

This year he accepted it and invited Lucy to come with him. This year he, once again, had a ring ready. This year he knew the woman he was going to give it to would wholeheartedly accept it.

They walked across the sand dunes to where the action was happening, hand in hand, her carrying a little basket with cookies nestled under a red-checked cloth and him with a grocery bag filled with various brands of chips. Behind them came their kids, bearing soda pop, beer and a giant watermelon.

"About time you got here," Jenna greeted him, and hugged Lucy.

"We knew the party wouldn't really start until we were here," he joked.

"Oh, yeah? I heard that," said Jenna's sister, who was giving her toddler a can of orange pop from a cooler propped against a log.

"We haven't missed 'Girls Just Want to Have Fun,' have we?" he asked her.

"No. We were waiting for you," Celeste replied.

He grinned. "Like I said."

Nora and her husband were already there, as was Tyrella Lamb and her man.

Waters was on hand to put a possessive arm around Jenna, and Brody wasn't even remotely jealous. He realized there was no longer any residual heartache when he looked at the two of them together. That almost felt like a miracle. Maybe, in a way, it was.

"Haven't seen you in a while," Jenna's scruffy old hotel handyman, Pete Long, said to him as he put two hot dogs on a fork to roast for Lucy and himself. "Now I see why. She's a looker."

"Yeah, she is," Brody said, smiling at Lucy, who was drinking pop and chatting with Nora.

She was a lot more than that though. She was everything he'd always dreamed of, everything he'd ever want.

The kids ate, played Frisbee and hung around for some singing around the campfire, then faded along with the light. Celeste and her husband took their sleepy little ones home and then it was a small group, gathered around the fire, talking about their lives.

Darkness finally took over and the thousands of visitors to Moonlight Harbor who'd been camped along the beach all day began setting off their fireworks. Bursts of light and color displayed against a black sky and the light of bonfires glowed up and down the beach.

"It's magical," Lucy said to Brody. "I feel like I'm at Disneyland or something."

So did he, but now he was anxious to start the ride he'd been anticipating all day. He had the champagne on ice at his place and the ring already sitting at the bottom of one of the glasses. Bring on the strings!

"How about the two of us go to my place and watch the rest of the show and make some fireworks of our own?" he suggested.

"I think that sounds like an excellent idea," she said, and the smile she gave him lit him up inside like a sparkler.

Back at the house, he had her favorite chocolate truffles from Cindy's Candies on a plate and the champagne ready. She nibbled on one and watched as he uncorked the champagne.

"Are we celebrating something?" she asked.

"Us," he said as he poured it. He picked up the glasses and handed her the one with the ring in it. "Be careful when you drink that," he said. "It's a very expensive drink."

"Like the Algonquin's $10,000 cocktail?" she teased.

"Maybe not quite that much," he admitted. But he had spent a pretty penny on the ring and he hoped she'd like it. "Check it out."

She lost her teasing expression and studied the glass. Then she gasped. Then she gave a little cry and threw her arms around him, spilling champagne all over them both.

"Really?" she asked. "Really? Really?"

"You okay with that?" he asked in return. "Are you willing to take a second chance on love?"

"With you? It'll be more like a sure thing," she said, and kissed him.

Brody and Lucy announced their engagement at the next Moonlight Harbor Chamber of Commerce meeting. The announcement was received with applause and many good wishes.

"Saw it coming from a mile away," Ellis West said as he shook Brody's hand.

"Me, too," said Jenna, and hugged them both. "I'm so happy for you guys. You finally found your soul mate," she said to him, beaming.

She was right. He had.

"You two going to combine your businesses and become real estate royalty?" Kiki asked.

"Well, we're for sure going to share office space," Lucy said. "We'll see how we do with that."

"And which house are you going to live in?" Ellis wanted to know. "That was a hard decision for Mel and me."

"The beach is nice," Brody said, "but the house on Sand Dollar Lane feels like home. Probably because Lucy's there," he finished, snuggling her up against him.

Happy Endings All 'Round

Labor Day weekend always brought a crowd of visitors to Moonlight Harbor. This particular weekend was no exception. Except there was one difference. Almost everyone staying at the Driftwood Inn had come to town for the wedding of Brody Green and Lucy Holmes.

It was supposed to be a small affair, but the small affair grew into a crowd and in the end, though Jenna had offered to host the wedding, she'd had to settle for the ceremony taking place on the beach behind her house with the reception being held at The Porthole restaurant.

The bride carried a bouquet of burnt orange and burgundy silk flowers and wore a cream-colored dress. Her daughter, who acted as her bridesmaid, wore a paprika-colored, calf-length chiffon gown. She also wore an engagement ring on her left hand.

Of course, there was a videographer on hand to capture the moment because Always Beachin' fans (whose number was continuing to swell) wanted to be part of Lucy's wedding.

Before moving on to the restaurant, the couple stopped

by the new offices of Beach Dream Homes Realty and posed for more pictures.

"How does it feel to be married and sharing an office?" Hannah asked them as the camera rolled.

"Great," Lucy said, smiling up at Brody. "I've found the perfect partner for business and life."

"Same here," he said, and kissed her.

Hannah turned to the camera, and her final words said it all, "Life is good at the beach, and when you're in love, it's great."

* * * * *

Acknowledgments

I have to give a few shout outs. Thank you Elizabeth Toedt, real estate broker extraordinaire, for taking time to make sure I got all those little real estate details right. Thank you to my ever-patient editor, April Osborn, for your insight and great input. And to my agent, Paige Wheeler. You are, and always will be, the best. Finally, thank you to the team at MIRA who work so hard to complete the process of turning a tale into a book. And to you, dear reader, for being willing to come along on the imaginary adventure.